WHITE HARVEST

A KINE

Grail Publishing House

A Kine / Grail Publishing House

Printed in the United States of America by Kindle Direct Publishing.

Publisher's Note: This is a work of fiction. Names, characters, places, and incidents are a product of the author's imagination. Any resemblance to actual people living or dead or to businesses, companies, events, institutions, or locales is completely coincidental. However, locales and public names have been used for atmospheric purposes and snippets from newspapers and websites are true and correct in several chapters—including named persons.

White Harvest / A Kine -- 1st ed.
ISBN – 9780473479954

Authors Note:

When I was ten I had my first unpleasant psychic experience. In adulthood I was comfortable with my mild abilities until I started having a bizarre lucid dream I could recall the next day. Like a TV series, the dream continued night after night.

I've woven various elements of my dream into this novel and the book's storyline is based upon it and my accompanying research.

As a side note, I should add that I've been living in a city that's witnessed several state-sponsored terror attacks. I wasn't going to cover these in this book, but overwhelmed by them, I changed my mind, so several chapters are dedicated to them. Snippets from newspapers and websites that appear are true and correct, including named persons.

Other books by A KINE
Series: Beyond the veil of propaganda
ELIXIR OF IMMORTALITY and the Whore of Babylon

Tomorrow the lilies will open to the sky; the budded rose will learn her destiny and service — another interval of rest, then the dawn. I charge you, O daughters of the Chakras, that you stir not up, nor awake my love, until he desires.

She is born of mortal men in the garden; her birth from the waters is as a second birth. A renewal in the mind of God. She will be carried in a shell—in an ark—a chariot of fire. To be seated at the end of days in her final place, beyond the partings of the veil

CONTENTS

CHAPTER ONE

The cell

Lilly groaned and held her head. It felt like a bottle of tequila had given it a good kicking. Wiping away thickened sleep-dust, she stared at an unknown concrete block wall only inches away. Frowning, she rolled over on a hard pillow and looked around. The tiny room had a wall constructed of iron bars.

A prison cell!

With her heart racing and her mind scrambling, Lilly tried to think of a crime she might've committed that could've resulted in her being tossed into a cell. Shaking her head, she dismissed the idea because she wasn't a criminal. Trying to control her breathing and calm herself, she recalled her last memory. She'd been in a little library café sipping coffee and chatting with a thoroughly pleasant man, and nothing had seemed amiss. She tried to remember leaving the café or anything since, but couldn't.

What's going on?

With her heart pounding, she snatched away the gray woolen blanket that covered her and sat up quickly—too quickly. A wave of wooziness swept over her as the room began to rotate. Flopping back on the pillow, she closed her eyes. Suddenly anxious, she rubbed her extended belly; little heels kicked out at her in response. Breathing a sigh of relief, she said, "Thank goodness you're all right!" Grateful that apart from feeling considerably unwell, she and her baby were okay.

As soon as her head stopped spinning, she sat up carefully, mindful of her tender head. After massaging her scalp and running her fingers through her long blond hair to soothe her throbbing head, she groaned and eased herself off the bed. Her belly's voluptuous size and her queasy stomach made her move cautiously. After getting down from the bed in a most ungainly fashion, she stumbled to the cell's bars—bra and panties her only attire. Peering through the bars, she couldn't see another cell, only a short corridor running in either direction. Gripping two of the door's bars with trembling hands, she yanked, but the door wouldn't budge.

"Is anybody there?" she cried. Her voice echoed eerily around the corridor. Straining her ears for a reply, she heard none. There was nothing but walls—cold, hard walls.

After turning her back to the bars, and leaning on them for support, she studied her dismal abode. The gray shoe-box cell was stark and crudely functional; her bed, a slab and mattress. A stainless-steel toilet glinted in the corner of the room, reflecting the light above. On the ceiling, an old-fashioned fluorescent light flickered and buzzed. Beside it, a camera watched her.

She shuddered and lowered her eyes as a chill ran down her spine. Her multi-colored sundress lay on the foot of the bed; it was the most cheerful thing in the room. After taking several unsteady steps towards it, Lilly fumbled with it and pulled it over her head. The light-weight dress floated down and around her. With tears welling in her eyes, she wrapped her arms around her bulging belly for comfort and warmth, then rubbed the goose-bumps on her bare arms.

Who undressed me? How did I get here?

Turning, she came face to face with a Chinese nurse. Wondering how she'd snuck up on her so quietly, Lilly looked at her feet; she was wearing rubber-soled nursing shoes. Returning her gaze to her face, the nurse's chilly demeanor unnerved her. Her hair was swept up into a severe bun and her slender arms were folded determinedly across her chest. Taken back by the ice in her eyes, Lilly said, "Oh!" startled. "Have I done something wrong? Have I committed a crime?"

The chill in the nurse's eyes dissipated. "No," she said, relaxing her stance. "There's been a large earthquake ... Don't you remember?" she added, almost casually.

Lilly blinked several times. "No."

"That's not surprising," the nurse said. "You were knocked out in the quake. Patients with head injuries often can't recall the incidents in which they're injured. Over time, you may or may not remember what happened."

Lilly stared blankly at the nurse. "Am I all right? Is my baby all right?"

"You've been assessed by a doctor. Your baby's fine and it seems you've only a mild head injury. There shouldn't be any long-term effects."

Scanning the concrete block walls in the corridor for telltale cracking, Lilly noticed a few hairline cracks in the mortar between the blocks. "I must've been unconscious for a while," she said, now staring at the nurse. She didn't know what the go was with her, but she didn't trust her, and found her presence unsettling.

"Do you remember your name?"

"Yes ... Lilly."

"I don't think there's anything to worry about ... Lilly," the nurse said somewhat reassuringly. "A doctor will be along shortly to check on you."

"But, I'm in prison. Why am I in prison?"

"Christchurch Hospital has partially collapsed. You're in an old abandoned prison that's been regularly maintained and supplied in case of such an emergency. Previous earthquake strengthening and this facility's distance from the quake's epicenter has allowed it to escape serious damage ... All non-acute patients have been transported here."

Lilly raised her brow in surprise.

"The government has everything under control," the nurse said calmly.

Lilly supposed plans were drawn up and actioned after the city's last big quake. She rubbed her temples. "Can I leave this cell?"

"Not for a while. We're keeping you isolated for your own good. People are getting sick here, and we don't want any harm to come to you or your baby."

"Aren't I sick already?" Lilly said, still rubbing her brow. "My head's a mess and I feel terrible."

"I'll bring you some painkillers and food shortly. Hopefully, you'll feel better after that."

Lilly shifted her weight, uneasy. Swaying, she clung to the cell's bars.

"Please don't panic," the nurse said in a tone that made Lilly think, for the first time, that she gave a damn.

"I should never have moved to Christchurch," she said, "this city is cursed with quakes! How big was this one?"

"It was a shallow 7.6, right under the city."

"7.6! Oh, my God ... Thank goodness my family doesn't live here. My children will be worried sick. Can I ring them?"

"Cell towers and power lines are down across the region ... they're on the ground," the nurse said with a hint of amusement. "Power won't be restored for some time." She rubbed her mouth and chin in an exaggerated fashion, as if she was trying to conceal her ill-placed humor.

Lilly was unwell and off her game, but she'd noticed. She stared at her.

"We were able to get a message to your husband," the nurse said, as if trying to break the tension. "He knows your whereabouts and medical condition, and your medical status will be updated to conscious and doing well, so he, and anybody else making inquiries after you, can be reassured of your good health and wellbeing."

Lilly thought her "good health" was stretching the truth at best and lying at worst, but, none-the-less, the tension in her shoulders eased slightly. "Thank you," she said, deciding she wasn't up to an argument. "Do you have my handbag?"

"Yes. We've placed people's personal belongings in a locked room for safekeeping."

Looking up at the fluorescent light that hung from two rusty chains in the corridor, Lilly said, "How come the power's on in here?"

"Prisons are like hospitals," the nurse said informatively, resuming her stern stance. "They have large backup generators. You're lucky to have been brought here. Please go back to your bed and wait for a doctor. I'll return with some food shortly."

Lilly stumbled to the bed. After clambering up onto it, she caught her breath before using her arms to aid her as she shuffled backwards towards the wall. When her bare skin touched the wall's cold surface, she jolted and shuddered. Breathing heavily, and with arms as frail as an old woman's, she weakly pulled the woolen blanket around her. After pushing the pillow between her and the wall, she rubbed her belly affectionately. "You're massive!" she whispered tenderly.

A clattering sound announced the nurse's timely return. After unlocking the cell door, she dragged in a rickety old trolley. "I have a couple of painkillers," she said, lifting a large glass of water and a tiny paper cup off the top of the trolley and handing them to Lilly.

Lilly picked out the tiny tablets from within the paper cup and gulped them down with a large swallow of water. "Thank you," she said, holding out the half-empty glass.

The nurse refused it with a determined shake of her head. "Drink it all," she said forcefully.

Lilly opened her mouth to rebuke her unpleasant demeanor, but rather than say anything, she thought about how difficult the nurse's job might be in the crisis. She sighed, drank the rest of the water, then offered the empty glass to the nurse.

The nurse took it, a hint of smug satisfaction on her face. "I can't bring you any food right now, but I have a milkshake for you," she said, handing it to Lilly. "It has everything in it you require."

Lilly barely glanced at the frothy pink shake, placing it unceremoniously down beside her. "Nurse, I was with a man named John in a library café before the quake, did he come here with me?"

"No. Is he a friend of yours…? A relative?"

Lilly shook her head. "I'd only just met him."

"If he wasn't injured, he probably left to check on his family."

Lilly nodded in agreement. "Of course," she said, sniffing back tears that caught her off guard. Her unwell state and current predicament was getting the better of her, and the nurse offered little comfort.

"Do you need anything else?"

Lilly rubbed the goose-bumps on her pale arms. "Could I please have another blanket?"

"There's a blanket shortage, but I can turn the heating up for you."

"Thank you," Lilly said absentmindedly, thinking of her family.

The nurse dragged the trolley into the corridor and pulled the door to. The lock clunked noisily into place as she turned the key.

Lilly shuddered. "Do I really need to be *locked* in?"

The nurse cleared her throat. "We need to keep track of who is where; operations need to be streamlined. It's only a temporary measure." Turning on her heel, she headed off down the corridor.

"Nurse!" Lilly cried out as isolation threatened to overwhelm her.

The nurse stopped walking and looked over her shoulder, a frosty look on her face.

"I'm from Auckland," Lilly blurted out. "I was only staying in Christchurch temporarily. Can I be placed on a flight?"

The nurse shook her head. "The runway's damaged and you're not allowed to fly in your condition, even in an emergency." She rounded the corner.

Lilly groaned. Sighing heavily, she looked down at the strawberry-colored milkshake. Eyeing it suspiciously, and thinking it was probably a horrid power-shake concoction, she raised it to her nose and gave it a good sniff, then pulled a face before taking a sip. It not only smelt odd: it tasted odd. She skewed her face and wanted to complain, but knew a complaint would be viewed poorly in the current circumstances, and, as intolerable as her situation was, things would probably get worse if she started whining. Deciding there was nothing wrong with the milkshake, other than odd flavoring, she gulped it down.

An attractive Indian woman with nicely styled black hair falling gently around her shoulders, appeared in front of her cell carrying a medical bag.

"Hello, my name is Chanda. I'm a doctor," she said, letting herself in. "Can you please lie down so I can feel your tummy?"

Lilly shuffled awkwardly across the bed. After placing the milkshake cup down on a rust-colored plastic stool by the head of the bed, she lay down. Pulling her dress up to expose her swollen belly, she stared at its voluminous size.

"Is your baby moving?" Chanda said, warming her hands by rubbing them together.

"Yes."

"That's good." After blowing on her hands to further warm them, Chanda felt for the baby's position. "Are you bleeding?"

Lilly frowned. "No ... well ... at least, I don't think so."

"Good. That's good."

Lilly looked at the ceiling while the doctor listened to her baby's heartbeat through an old-fashioned, tubular instrument. The ceiling was freshly painted and free of cracks. "I'm worried about my baby. Do you think my baby's okay?"

"We had a heart monitor on you earlier. Your baby's heart-trace was normal. If he's moving and you're not bleeding, there's nothing to worry about."

He? Lilly didn't know her baby was a "he" and she was secretly hoping for a girl. After pondering on the doctor's apparent slip of the tongue for a moment, she decided Chanda had employed a generic term and hadn't accidentally disclosed her baby's sex, or at least, she hoped she hadn't.

"We need to check your details ... Are you Lilly Reynolds?"

"Yes," Lilly said, struggling to sit up.

Chanda sat on the edge of the bed as if they were old friends and smiled sweetly. "I think you're all right," she said, shining a medical torch into Lilly's green eyes. "Tell me, Lilly, why were you living in Christchurch when you're heavily pregnant and your husband lives half the country away in Auckland?"

Lilly hated nosy professionals. She stared at the doctor.

Chanda reached out to gently rub her arm. "I'm only asking because you're likely to be here a while and you're about to give birth. It could happen any time ... We need to know your circumstances."

Lilly fought back tears.

"We're not going to judge or disclose anything," Chanda reassured.

Lilly shifted her shoulders, uneasy. "Matthew and I separated eighteen months ago. We're both professional people. He's a prominent lawyer and I'm a school principal; a headmistress of a Christian girls' school. We're members of the same church. Only our closest friends and family know we've separated—know Matthew is living with his secretary."

"I see," Chanda said compassionately. "Do you have any other children?"

"Yes, two. Josh and Megan. They're in their early twenties. They moved to London for study and job advancement a year or so ago." Lilly pressed her lips together. "Everything was going fine until I met a man online and—"

"You got pregnant? Where is this man now?"

"I don't know," Lilly said, shrugging her shoulders dismissively and looking down, her face colored. "I can't recall much of our date. I woke up alone in my bed ... I got rotten drunk and slept with him, I guess," She sighed. "I didn't think so at the time, but I must have. I thought I was going through the menopause, so when I started getting fat it didn't occur to me I might be pregnant. I blamed my ballooning size on middle-age spread and comfort eating. I was well into my second trimester when I found out I was pregnant. I took extended leave from my job, and Matthew helped me move to Christchurch ... He doesn't want anybody to know about the baby."

"And you intend to adopt your baby out and return to your previous life as if nothing happened?"

"That's right," Lilly said. "Even my children don't know I'm pregnant. I've made adoption arrangements, but to tell you the truth, I'm attached to my baby and every day I feel less and less sure of my decision." She rubbed her brow. "I don't know what to do."

"I see," Chanda said, "and now this terrible quake has happened and it's making a difficult time more difficult. We're aware of your adoption arrangements ... I was hoping you'd volunteer this information. If you wish to continue with your arrangements, we'll make sure everything goes as planned. Obviously, if you change your mind and choose to keep your baby, we'll help you as much as we can. The facilities here are adequate to give birth in, even if complications arise."

"Can't I return to my apartment? It could be weeks before I give birth."

Chanda shook her head. "Not only is your apartment wrecked, but the power, water, and sewer are all off. Not to mention that the roads are a mess— grid locked or damaged. We think you're better off here." She gently squeezed her hand. "I'm going to give you a sedative to help you relax and sleep."

"Will it hurt my baby?"

"Not at all," Chanda said, readying a syringe. "Lie down and roll over."

As if on autopilot, Lilly did as she asked.

"There ... all done," Chanda said cheerfully after administering the jab.

Lilly rubbed the injection site before rolling over and covering herself with the blanket. Chanda was already exiting the cell. She pulled the door to.

After turning the key, she smiled warmly and turned out the light. "I'll see you when you wake."

Lilly returned her smile, pleased the buzzing light was turned out. Relaxing, she closed her eyes.

CHAPTER TWO

The cave

Lilly moaned and gasped as a strong stomach cramp roused her from a near-unconscious state. Propped up on pillows, she was lying naked on a theatre bed. Squinting to shield her eyes from a bright surgical light, she looked around a state-of-the-art operating theater. There were two nurses in the room. The nurse she'd already met, and decided was Chinese, and a short, plump nurse who looked like she was from the Philippines.

Chanda was also in the room. She stood beside her dressed in a theater gown, her hair swept up into a bun. She gently squeezed her hand, "It's all right."

Lilly groaned as her sizable belly tightened once more. When the cramp eased and the pain subsided, she gasped, "I'm in labor!"

"Yes," Chanda said. "I've sedated you through the first stages of your labor but now I need you to push ... When your next contraction comes ... push!"

Lilly groaned as her belly tightened again, gripped once more by a merciless cramp. Grabbing hold of her thighs and drawing them up while leaning forward, she did as her body demanded; she pushed.

After several more contractions, Chanda said, "Now I need you to pant."

The Filipino nurse placed a sheet over her stomach and knees. Lilly panted and groaned as strong contractions eased her baby into the world. Moments later, the Filipino nurse scooped the baby up into the sheet that covered her knees and left the room, so she didn't get so much as a glimpse of her newborn.

Drugged and confused, Lilly cried out, "Why have you taken my baby away?"

"The nurse is going to clean him up and check him over for you," the Chinese nurse said tightly. "Don't worry, she'll bring him back in a few minutes wrapped in a nice blanket."

"I have a son?"

"Lie back and let the doctor examine you," the nurse said shortly.

Laying back on the pillows, Lilly groaned as Chanda prodded her nether regions, giving her what felt like a thorough examination. After making a satisfied sound, she indicated to the nurse that all was well, and left the room without so much as a parting word.

"I'm going to take you to your cell now," the nurse said as she roughly removed the drip from Lilly's hand. "The other nurse will bring your baby along in a few minutes."

Two large orderlies entered the room. One of them tossed a blanket roughly around Lilly's shoulders before hauling her off the bed and, not so gently, shoving her towards a waiting wheelchair. After stumbling and tripping over its footrests, she plonked down into it. The nurse grabbed its handles and started pushing it without even checking if her feet were clear. Fortunately, Lilly had pulled her feet up in time. She felt for the footrests with her toes, pushed them into place, then rested her feet upon them.

The nurse pushed her out of the theater and down a long, wide corridor that was both modern and oversized. The walls, and vaulted ceiling that towered above them, seemed to be made of shining white marble. Lilly couldn't believe what she was looking at. She'd been in government hospitals before. They were utilitarian places, nothing like this. She supposed a flash new wing had been built beside the old prison and they interconnected, but she couldn't think of a single reason why the new section would be so elaborate. It was as if no expense had been spared.

"How come I woke up in labor?" she said, her mind returning to her baby. "Is my baby all right?"

"He's fine!" the nurse snapped as they approached an enormous elevator. Lilly was stunned silent by its huge doors. Several times her height and wider than they were tall, they towered in front of her.

Shadowed by the orderlies, the nurse pushed Lilly into the elevator as its doors opened. Proportioned like an ample room, the group were almost swallowed up in the copious space. Looking about, Lilly wondered what kind of equipment it normally carried.

The two orderlies stood over her like henchmen as the elevator sped downwards. After grounding to a halt a considerable distance below, frigid air rushed in as its doors opened. Pulling the blanket up tight around her shoulders, Lilly peered out and into a massive cave in front of her. She shuddered and shivered. Staring into the pitch-black void was like staring into an abyss.

Before she had time to consider why they were there, the orderlies each grabbed hold of one of her arms and yanked her out of her wheelchair. Then, together, they pushed her into the cave. Lilly staggered, then fell onto the damp, hard-packed sand. An orderly stepped forward and whipped her blanket away before stepping back into the elevator as its doors began to close.

Lilly quickly got to her feet. "What are you doing!" she screamed as the huge doors clanged shut in front of her. Staring at them in near disbelief, she listened to the ascending elevator as it whizzed skywards. When it fell silent, she both felt and looked for a button to send it back to her. There was no button.

What the hell? There must be a button!

After searching for a non-existent button for some time, Lilly's attention shifted to her chilly surroundings. When her eyes adjusted to the dim light she was mesmerized by its subtle beauty. The dimly lit cave had an overwhelming glow of blue. Twinkling on the cave's ceiling like jewels were dainty, glimmering blue lights.

A large body of water surrounded the small beach she stood upon on two sides. Standing midway between the water on her right, and an undulating cave wall twenty feet away on her left, she stared at the water in front of her, not thirty feet away. There, in the distance, the beach curved as the left-hand wall met up with the water.

Lilly breathed out heavily to gauge how cold the air was. When she failed to see her breath plume in front of her, she realized the temperature was above freezing, and decided the bitter air was about 41 degrees Fahrenheit, or 5 degrees Celsius.

Almost forgetting how cold she was, she started walking towards the blue-green water in front of her. In her peripheral vision, she noticed something large on the beach. Blending in with the reddish-brown walls, not ten feet away on her left, was a large hairy humanoid sitting up like Buddha.

"Oh my God!" she screamed, turning and running back to the elevator. She frantically searched for a non-existent button once more. After failing to find one, yet again, she stumbled away from the wooly creature on unsteady legs. Confused, and her mind muddled, she ran clumsily. After putting the maximum distance between her and the beast without entering the water, she collapsed onto the sand.

The huge, wooly humanoid had only followed her with its eyes. "It's all right, I don't bite."

Lilly awkwardly got to her feet, the damp sand too cold to sit on. Shivering, she wrapped her arms around herself. "You talk?" she said, stunned, her words slurring together. "You speak English?"

"Yes," the large humanoid said, observing her closely while keeping its head low.

"What are you ... a Yeti?" Lilly had tried her best to speak clearly but, never-the-less, her words had run together.

"I'm a large wooly humanoid. Humans call us Sasquatch, Bigfoot, or Yeti ... but I prefer the term Bigfoot."

Lilly blinked several times. "You're real?"

The Bigfoot shrugged. "Apparently."

Eyeing the cold, dark walls of the cave and then the water, Lilly couldn't see a way out, apart from the elevator. Returning her attention to the Bigfoot, she said, "Why am I even talking to you? What's your intellect ... fifty ... less?"

"Well ... that was rude! Do you normally quiz people on their intellectual abilities before engaging in conversation?"

Lilly's eyes widened. She blinked several times. "Wow, that was quite the retort. You're not brain-dead?"

"I'm a humanoid. That ought to give you some indication of my intellect."

"I don't know about that," Lilly said dryly. "I've met plenty of dumb people."

"Do I appear to be keeping up my end of the conversation?"

"You do, yes ... Your apparent intellect is doing nothing to quell my fears." Lilly said, slurring her words. Frustrated by her diminished speech, she wondered if the creature considered her a bumbling, inept fool. She wanted to appear confident and be on high alert, but her senses were dull, tainted—off. "If you were stupid, then maybe I'd stand a chance," she said, deciding her vulnerability was just too obvious.

"I'm not your enemy. I have no intention of hurting you, quite the opposite, in fact."

The cold air biting into Lilly's flesh made her shiver. She jiggled about to keep warm. "I've just given birth and the people upstairs have taken my baby away and dumped me in here with you ... do you know why?"

"They said you were injured in a large earthquake ... right?

"Yes."

"No earthquake brought you here."

Lilly blinked several times. "What are you saying ... there was no earthquake?"

"Correct."

"They told me I was knocked out. There's a gap in my memory."

"Well, you're in remarkable shape for someone who's just suffered a major head injury. Do you have a lump on your head?"

Lilly felt her head. There was no lump and her skull wasn't even sore. Feeling stupid, she said, "No, but I felt terrible and I had an awful headache, and now I can't control my speech ... I'm slurring my words like a drunken idiot."

"That's hardly surprising. They drugged you and brought you here, and they've continued to drug you. And now you're cold and scared," the Bigfoot said with surprising tenderness. "You had a dehydration headache earlier ... Did they give you a large glass of water?"

"Yes." Lilly rubbed her brow. "I'm confused. I was in a prison cell ... wasn't I?"

"You were in a cell, but it wasn't part of some old abandoned prison near Christchurch. It was a stage set ... a carefully constructed prop."

Lilly frowned. "Is there an old prison near Christchurch?"

"There is, yes, but it's not near Christchurch, it's in Christchurch ... in Addington. It was converted into a hostel years ago."

"Holy shit!" Lilly said, jiggling about intensely to keep warm. "What's going on here? Who were those people?"

"Not friends of yours."

"I don't know what happened," Lilly said, shaking her head and shrugging, confused. "In my last memory, I was in a library café. I was sitting with a man named John. We'd only just met—"

"Did he stir sugar into your coffee?"

Frowning, she recalled the charming fashion in which John had pulled her coffee toward him and asked her how many sugars she took. "Yes."

"Old trick ... he spiked it."

Lilly looked down. Why had she been stupid enough to let a strange man sidle up to her? She knew why, he was good looking and charming and she was lonely in a strange city. She'd dropped her guard. She sighed, and then shrugged. She didn't have time for self-recriminations. Her focus had to remain on her baby and finding a way to get to him. "It's not right they've taken my baby away," she said, deflated. "Don't they have any compassion?"

"Logic is their thing."

"Logic?" she said, her body trembling from both emotional distress and cold. "How can it be logical to take my baby away?"

"The people upstairs think your baby will be better off with the parents they've found him."

Lilly's eyes nearly popped out of her head. "They've given him away...? They've sold him!" Feeling her loss most acutely, she stumbled and almost fell onto the cold sand. She felt like someone had ripped her guts out.

"I'm sorry. I really am, but you're going to have to pull yourself together. You need to survive. Your baby's needs are being met. You need to take care of you."

Finally comprehending how dire her predicament was, Lilly

gasped as her heart pounded. "I'm naked in a cold cave ... They've left me to die!" Frantic, she once again scanned the cave for an exit.

"There's no need to panic. I'll help you."

"You will? How? You know a way out?"

"There is no way out of this cave, other than the elevator, and it can't be opened from in here."

"Can't you open it?"

"No. They don't want *me* getting out."

"Isn't that a bit defeatist?" Lilly said. "If we work together, maybe we can prise it open."

"I gather you're acquainted with zoo cages? You do know they're designed to keep the animals in ... right?"

"I'm not an animal!" Lilly grumbled. She had been about to say *'you might be an animal but I'm not!'* but she'd thought better of it. She didn't know him. For all she knew, he had a hairpin trigger and flew into a rage at the slightest provocation. "What about the water," she said, relieved that even in a diminished mental state, she'd held her tongue. "Maybe there's an exit under the water?"

"The water's freezing. It would kill you in a matter of minutes."

"The water's freezing? Are you sure? The waters around New Zealand aren't bitterly cold in summer." Lilly was tempted to test the water's temperature with her toes, but being cold was bad enough. She certainly didn't want to be cold *and* wet.

"We're beneath an underground facility in Antarctica."

"Antarctica! Why would anyone bring me to Antarctica?"

"They have their reasons."

"Their reasons!" Lilly's breath caught in her throat. She fought for air, her eyes bulging. "Are you sure that's where we are?" she said, catching her breath. "It's cold in here, sure, but it's not minus fifty."

"This cave gets some warmth from the facility above."

"Not enough," Lilly grumbled. "How did I get here?"

"They transported you here while you were out to it."

"Did they hurt my baby? That can't have been good for him."

"He's fine," the Bigfoot said dismissively.

"Aren't governments the only ones in Antarctica? Oh, the American man I met at the library café, he could've been with the

United States Antarctic Program that's based in Christchurch ... It wasn't an accidental meeting?"

"Now you're beginning to glimpse the caliber of the people who've brought you here. They're not ordinary people, and this is no ordinary place."

Lilly tilted her head. Studying the Bigfoot, she said, "You're appearing more human by the minute ... Your skull's quite humanoid."

"I know."

Her jiggling about to keep warm, now resembled dancing. She folded her arms under her heavy breasts to support their weight. "Oh, I get it!" she said through chattering teeth. "They're disposing of me. They've thrown me in here to feed you."

"I'm not about to gobble you up."

"Play with me first, like a cat does a mouse?"

"No."

"What then...? Why did they dump me in here?"

The Bigfoot leaned his bulky body forward slightly. "To entertain them."

"To entertain them!" Lilly was aghast. "How?"

"They're watching you via hidden camera."

Lilly shook her head in stunned disbelief. "Well, I think that's beyond callous! They intend to watch me suffer and die ... *for entertainment?*"

"No, they intend to observe our interactions. Watch us become acquainted. See you accept my help—"

"Your help? What is this ... a sicko experiment?" Lilly's teeth were now chattering so hard she was almost incapable of speech. "Can you please cut to the chase and tell me how you'll be helping?"

"You need to come over here and share my body heat," the Bigfoot said as he opened his huge muscle-bound arms in an inviting gesture and beckoned Lilly forward with long, lean fingers. "Come."

She lowered her brow. Staring up at him from beneath it, she stomped her foot as if she were warning off a stray dog that'd ventured too close. "Not bloody likely!" she growled.

The Bigfoot dropped his arms. "Well, freeze to death then."

Lilly relaxed her stance. Sighing heavily, she rubbed her brow before turning on the spot like a bewildered child unsure what to do. Facing the Bigfoot once more, she said, "Are you sure you're not going to eat me?"

"Positive ... Come, Baby, before you get too cold," the Bigfood added tenderly.

Seeing no other option, and driven on by the biting cold, Lilly walked tentatively towards him. His ability to talk and reason giving her confidence. "If you're going to eat me, will you at least be humane about it?"

"I'm not going to eat you ... I promise."

Lilly thought that's exactly what someone would say if they *were* going to eat you. Nearing, she said, "You called me Baby?"

"A term of endearment," the Bigfoot said as he continued to beckon her on.

Lilly hesitated, nervous, before edging in front of him.

The Bigfoot slowly reached out his huge arms and gently picked her up. Placing her upon his chest, he gently wrapped his huge, muscle-bound arms around her. "There ... is that better?"

Lilly closed her eyes and snuggled in. "Yes, thank you." She ran her fingers through his fur. "Your hair's like a big wooly dog's coat. It's not coarse at all. It's lovely and soft."

"I aim to please," the Bigfoot said almost smuggly.

"You're like a big teddy bear, all warm and cuddly. Thank you."

"My pleasure, Baby." The Bigfoot leaned back against a large sandy mound. "I'm sorry I don't have a blanket to wrap you in," he said, positioning his face near hers.

"Why are you being so nice to me?" she said, her eyelids drooping.

"I want to be sweet to you ... care for you. Treat you like my baby."

"So, you're *really* not going to eat me?" Lilly said, requiring further reassurance.

"I don't have fangs and I don't eat meat."

Lilly gazed into the Bigfoot's large, intelligent, moss-green eyes. Holding his mouth slightly ajar, so she could see his teeth, he smiled.

Lilly reached up and gently touched his face. "I don't know why I thought you had fangs. That was silly of me."

"Not as silly as you think ... Humans associate large furry mammals with fangs."

Lilly shrugged. "I guess we do."

"Are you warming?"

"Yes, you're lovely and warm. Thank you ... What shall I call you?"

"Daddy."

Startled by his answer, like someone had splashed water on her face, Lilly pulled her head back sharply and stared at him. "Daddy...?" she said, suspiciously.

"That's right," the Bigfoot said innocently.

Lilly drew in a sharp breath, then blew it out noisily. "Right!"

An uneasy silence developed between them as her anxiety grew. "What are you really up to ... ah, Daddy?"

"My name is Ox. You can call me Ox if you prefer."

"Your name is Ox?"

"Yes. I'm a Bigfoot named Ox ... Relax."

Lilly's muscles were tense. Her fight-or-flight reflex acute. "I'm grateful for your help ... Ox ... I really am, but I'm too scared and upset to relax."

"I'm not going to hurt you ... I promise. Please try and relax."

"Your name suits you," she said. "I gather they named you Ox in light of your huge size?"

"That's right. Snuggle in and enjoy my warmth."

Tears welled in Lilly's eyes, then streamed down her face. "They stole my baby," she sobbed.

"It's all right ... you're safe with me," Ox soothed as he rubbed her back like a loving parent. "Relax. Let your body rest and sleep away those nasty drugs."

"Drugs?" Lilly said absentmindedly.

"Yes. You've just had a twilight birth. You'll probably forget giving birth."

Lilly had been wondering why she'd just stumbled over to a giant Bigfoot and let him pick her up. Now, in a small window of mental clarity, she knew why, she was off her face. "What's a twilight birth?"

"It's the name given to a birth where a selection of drugs is given in early labor to reduce pain. The drugs cause a mental haze. Such births were common in the middle of the twentieth century, but you weren't given the exact combination of drugs given back then. They gave you the date-rape drug among others ... You'll forget giving birth."

"I will...?" Lilly's eyes drooped closed. Wrought with emotion and exhausted, she was unable to concentrate any longer.

"Sleep, Baby," Ox said as he gently rocked her.

CHAPTER THREE

The beast

Lilly tried to bury her cold nose in her pillow, but it was strangely hairy. She sniffed and rubbed her nose. Something wasn't right, her bed was on an incline and it was an odd shape, and her pillow had a loud, slow heartbeat. And topping all of that off, the huge hairy things wrapped around her had started to cradle and gently rock her. She opened her eyes and looked up and into the eyes of an enormous beast. Screaming, she thrashed about to free herself, terrified.

The huge creature carefully placed her down on the ground in front of it. As soon as it let her go, she clumsily ran away. Glancing back over her shoulder in fear, she saw the creature hadn't moved. Relieved, she slowed her pace. When she reached the cave wall, she turned around. Leaning forward to catch her breath with her hands upon her hips, she looked back at a huge hominoid bewildered. *How did I get here and what is it?*

"It's all right," Ox said. "I was only keeping you warm."

Lilly's eyes widened, stunned not only was the beast speaking, it was speaking English. "What are you … a Yeti?"

Ox nodded and shrugged. "Bigfoot or Sasquatch, but I prefer the term Bigfoot."

Lilly cupped her belly. It had dropped and gone spongy and was noticeably lighter and smaller. "I can't feel my baby!" she shrieked.

"You gave birth to your son hours ago. The people upstairs drugged you and took him away."

"Oh, my God! Where is he?" Lilly said looking about frantically.

"Your son's being cared for above," Ox said, before patiently recapping their earlier conversation.

Lilly couldn't remember giving birth, but after Ox filled her in, she recalled splintered fragments of their previous conversation. Looking around, she saw a roll of toilet paper and a dug-out hole beside the cave wall—a crude toilet. A mound of sand was piled beside it. Lilly squatted down, shielding her private parts from Ox's gaze with her hands as she did so. "I'm gathering there's no ladies room?"

"You're gathering correctly."

After wiping herself with her left hand, Lilly looked around for a way to wash it. Beside her, dew pooled in a rocky crevice. She rinsed her hands in the cold water, then shook them dry.

"I think you only went for a pee," Ox said, "but if you do the other ... kick some sand over it."

"I've camped before," Lilly said, walking slowly towards him, unsure why she felt comfortable enough to do so. "Explain what the nasty people upstairs are doing again, my mind's all fuzzy."

"They've hidden cameras in this cave. The people upstairs want to watch us become acquainted ... You're trapped in an extreme, secret version of *Survivor*."

Lilly frowned, then blinked several times.

"They're studying Bigfoot behavior, and they want to see if we'll cooperate for our mutual benefit."

Lilly folded her arms. "That can't be right ... How can a naked woman help a Bigfoot? They must have rocks in their heads!"

"You know people like to observe animal and human interactions."

"Sure, but they don't usually stick naked women inside gorilla enclosures!" Lilly said, quickened her pace. The biting cold driving her on.

"I can't be compared to an ape," Ox said, offended. "Your survival depends upon me. We need to cooperate to save each other."

"Save each other?" Lilly said, standing in front of him. "I can't save you."

Ox reached out and tenderly stroked her head with his long fingers. "Let me pick you up and keep you warm."

Lilly shifted her weight, uneasy. Sighing, she reluctantly lifted her arms up like a toddler waiting to be picked up by daddy.

Ox picked her up and cradled her to his chest.

"I thought Bigfoot was the figment of overactive imaginations," she said, snuggling in.

Ox cradled her. "You've never heard of Gigantopithecus blacki?" he said as he rocked her in his arms again.

"No? Who or what is that?"

"A large humanoid," Ox said. "In 1935, paleontologist Ralph von Koenigswald came across an unusually large molar while searching through fossilized teeth in a Hong Kong drugstore. There, such teeth were called dragon's teeth, and they were sold for medicinal purposes. Koenigswald realized the tooth belonged to an unknown primate species. He named the species Gigantopithecus blacki. Further fossilized remains proved that Gigantopithecus blacki stood approximately 10 feet tall and weighed about 540 kilograms or 1,190 pounds."

Lilly raised her brow in surprise.

"In 1941, von Koenigswald unearthed a fragment of an enormous jawbone that contained three teeth in Java. These teeth were even more human like. He named the newly discovered species Meganthropus palaeojavanicus. Most paleoanthropologists believe Meganthropus was related to Homo erectus because evidence of tool use was found with skeletal remains. It's argued, Gigantopithecus and Meganthropus were giant hominids on the line leading to modern man. Anthropologist Grover Krantz believed them to be bipedal hominids because the back of their lower jaws spread wider than gorilla's jaws; suggesting they carried their heads vertically and were capable of erect, bipedal locomotion. Ivan Sanderson, another anthropologist, similarly concluded they were tool-making hominids."

"I've never heard a word of this," Lilly said.

"David Attenborough suggested on his television show *David Attenborough's Natural History Museum Alive* that Gigantopithecus blacki stood upright and had a human-like face. He also suggested, given the countless sightings over the years, that the species, or one related to it, might still be alive."

"Really ...? David Attenborough said that? Are you bigger than Gigantopithecus blacki was?"

"Yes."

"Do you use tools?"

"Do I look like I'm capable of making and using tools?"

"Absolutely."

Ox nodded. "Of course I am."

Lilly frowned. "Remains were found so long ago ... It's like there's been a conspiracy of silence."

"Indeed."

"What about bones—skeletal remains? How come I've never heard of anyone stumbling across your bones in the bush?"

"People assume the bones of wild animals persist long after their death, it isn't so. Bones only fossilize in the rarest of circumstances. In dense forests, the biomass will reabsorb an animal's carcass through weathering, decay, insects, and scavenging animals. The odds of the bones of a rare, elusive, forest-dwelling species being found in any recognizable form is remote, even more so, if you consider we bury our dead."

"You bury your dead?"

"Of course. Tell me, how often have you come across human remains?"

"Never."

"Would it be wise to assume humans don't exist because you've never stumbled across their bones?"

"No." Warm once more, and grateful for Ox's pleasant demeanor, Lilly sighed and wondered if meeting him wasn't a spot of luck. It was one thing she supposed to find a friendly horse or dog, but another to find a large humanoid she could communicate with. She figured that had to be lucky. All she needed to do now was get him to open the elevator.

Ox covered her body as much as he could with his large arms and fur without touching her inappropriately manner. "Are you all right, Baby?" he said sweetly.

"Yes, thank you, Daddy," Lilly said, hatching a plan. "It's terrible what they've done to you ... locked you up in this nasty cave."

Ox rubbed her back. "I'm more concerned with your well-being, I'm built for rough terrain."

"Daddy ... I need to see my baby. I need to hold him in my arms and love him. Can you help me get out of here ... please?"

Ox sighed. "The men upstairs are familiar with my abilities. They've chosen this enclosure for a reason."

"What about the elevator?"

"I explained to you when you first arrived that it can't be opened from in here."

"Can't you pull it open?"

Ox got up and walked to the elevator with Lilly. "Look at it," he said. "You can't even slide a piece of paper between its doors ... they can't be forced open."

Lilly stared at the massive steel doors. They looked like something you'd expect to find at Fort Knox. The job required an explosive. *Even MacGyver couldn't escape from this cave.* "How about we get them to come down here and we'll give them the jump?"

"You've been watching too many movies. They never come down here alone, and the elevator is monitored and alarmed. Not to mention that its controls can be remotely overridden."

Lilly slumped and pouted. Tears trickled down her face, then streamed down. Overcome with grief, she wailed and her body shook.

Ox returned to his sandy mount. After sitting down, he tenderly rubbed her back.

Lilly's tears slowed, then stopped. Wiping her eyes, she said, "I never saw my son ... did I?"

"No," Ox said, shaking his head. "You never saw him."

Lilly covered her eyes with her hands and bit her lip. "I want to die."

"Don't be silly," Ox said, continuing to rub her back. "You'll get over it."

"No, I won't!" Lilly snapped as more tears spilled. "He's my baby. I know I never planned him, but he's my baby! I want him ... I love him."

"Maternal instinct is a powerful thing. Your hormones will settle."

"I can't bear the pain!"

"It will ease," Ox said, cradling her slumped body. "Be kind to yourself. Let it pass. You'll be all right, love, truly you will."

Lilly's bottom lip quivered. "I've never been suicidal before, but now I am. I'm too miserable to carry on ... This stupid game or observation, or whatever it is ... is pointless. We can't survive in this barren cave, so what's the point in trying? We might as well give up and die. They should've done the decent thing and given us a pistol."

"I'll keep you warm," Ox pledged. "You'll be all right."

Lilly groaned and looked around. "What about food?"

"Worry about that later."

"Later? I'm hungry now!"

Ox pressed his lips together. "Hmm."

"Will they bring us some food? Leave it outside the elevator?"

"No."

"No? What do you mean ... no?"

"I mean, no ... We have to survive on our own."

Lilly looked at the water, it was glistening in the low light. "Will you fish for us?"

"There isn't any fishing equipment."

"Would you normally use fishing equipment? Does Bigfoot cast a line?"

"If I were to try and catch a fish, I would use a line, yes, but clearly, there's nothing here to make a line with."

"I hate *Survivor!*" Lilly grumbled. "It's never been a favorite show of mine. Besides, I can't see how we can save each other. Especially if you're not going to fish for us. What else is there to eat around here...? I don't suppose you eat sand?"

"No, I don't eat sand ... There's food in this cave, and plenty of it."

"Where?" Lilly grumped. "I don't see any food. Is it hidden?"

"Yes."

"Do we have to dig around in the sand to find hidden parcels of food?"

"There are no hidden parcels of food."

Ignoring Ox's claim of no hidden food, Lilly continued to scan the cave walls.

Ox exhaled loudly. "Do you really want to do this now?"

"Do what now? Look for food? Of course, I'm hungry."

Ox looked down at Lilly's breasts. "Your breasts look swollen and sore ... Are they sore, Baby?"

Lilly looked at her breasts. "Yes, they're sore. I'm trying not to think about them."

"I can relieve your suffering," Ox said as his head darted forward. He masterfully latched his big mouth onto one of Lilly's nipples and began to suckle.

"Get off!" Lilly screamed, slapping him around the head. "Good God! What the hell do you think you're doing?"

"We're down here without supplies. I need to feed from you."

"What do you suppose I am ... a cow?"

Ox ignored Lilly's protest as he reattached himself to her breast and fed ravenously from her while clasping her hands firmly in one of his above her head, so she couldn't hit him.

Lilly glared at him. "So ... they did toss me in here to feed you!"

Continuing to ignore Lilly's indignant protests, Ox licked and groped her breasts as he suckled. Lilly was both sickened and furious. She tried to pull away, but Ox had a firm hold of her. She pushed his big head with her own, but it wouldn't budge.

Music flooded into the cave: "Sugar, Sugar," by the Archies. "Sugar, oh honey, honey, you are my candy girl ..."

Lilly glared at the ceiling, to where she thought a camera might be. "How dare you bastards degrade me like this for your own entertainment! When I get out of here, I'm going to tell the authorities!"

When Ox finished feeding from her, he sat up and tapped her nose gently with one of his surprisingly slender fingers. Lilly thought his fingers ought to look like oversized bananas, but they didn't.

"You can feed from me now," he said.

"Eww!" Lilly said, screwing up her nose. "I don't even want to imagine what you might mean by that!"

"Are you hungry?"

"I am, yes!" Lilly said, giving Ox the filthiest of looks. "But there are some things I simply will not drink!"

Ox laughed. "You think you can be choosy?"

Lilly folded her arms and glared at him. "I'd rather die!"

Ox parroted her words, mimicking her stuck-up tone perfectly, he mocked, "There are some things I simply will not drink ... I'd rather die!"

Lilly snorted, then stuck her nose in the air.

"Drop the attitude!" Ox boomed.

Lilly trembled as a wave of fear swept over her. Groaning, she wondered if finding a large male humanoid wasn't so fortuitous after all. *Typical.*

"I've got news for you little Miss Uppity Britches who doesn't happen to have any britches on," Ox said. "There's nothing you won't do or eat."

"There is too!" Lilly screeched.

"Okay," Ox said as he placed her down on the ground. "Thank you for the nice meal. It'll sustain me for a while." He lay on his side facing her and closed his eyes.

Lilly folded her arms in a huff and stared at his closed eyes. She retained her indignant position till the cold air biting into her angry flesh weakened her resolve. After deciding keeping warm was more important than dignity, she sniffed back tears and wrapped her arms around herself, before jiggling about to warm up.

Ox opened an eye and peeked at her.

"What have I done to deserve this?" she wailed.

"Stop making a fuss and let me feed you."

"How exactly?" Lilly demanded, her arms folded again. "Dare I even ask?"

"I have a breast," Ox said, sitting up. He exposed a naked, saggy breast hidden under a fold of skin beneath his ribs.

Lilly stared at the exposed breast. It wasn't covered in fur, and it seemed anatomically incorrect. "You've got to be shitting me! I'm not drinking from that!"

"Well ... that was rude! I offered to feed you and you threw my kind gesture back in my face."

"Ah, um ..." Lilly felt ashamed. She'd always been an animal lover.

She had the deepest respect for all of God's creatures, no matter how odd. She relaxed her arms. Looking at her feet, she muttered, "Sorry," as if she were talking to her toes. When she looked up, Ox's breast was nowhere to be seen. His well-developed pecs were obvious, but his breast had disappeared. Curiosity got the better of her. "Where did your saggy tit go?"

"Why? You've changed your mind? You want to drink from me after all?"

Lilly shook her head. "No. I'm just curious. Was it under your rib cage? It was naked like my skin, I'm sure of it. Where did it go?"

"If you agree to drink from it, I'll show you."

Lilly stuck her nose in the air. "No. I won't drink from you. It's not right. The bastards' upstairs need to come down here and give me some real food. I have rights! They can't treat me this way."

"My breast will save your life," Ox said gently. "Try it ... it tastes good."

Lilly stood firm, her arms folded determinedly.

"Are you hungry, Baby?" Ox said as he looked back and forth between her face and the place where his breast had appeared.

Lilly relaxed her stance. "I'm famished, but—"

"It's not a butt, it's a breast, and it's the only food in this cave."

Lilly hesitated. She wondered if she should hold out—force the hand of the people upstairs. But what if they really didn't care? How long would she stand there starving and cold before they'd relent and feed her? She had a sinking feeling they never would. Instead, she thought they'd set a timer and take bets on how long it would be before she either relented and drank from the offered breast, or collapsed. Then they'd pay whoever took the correct bet. She exhaled loudly and moved forward.

Ox remained still. He waited till she was cuddling into him, then he exposed his breast and cradled her to him. "Good girl," he said. "Are you ready to drink?"

Lilly shrugged, and tears welled in her eyes. "I suppose. Nobody cares about me," she wailed. "The bastards upstairs have left me to die!"

"I care," Ox cooed.

"You want something! You want to continue drinking from me."

"I do, yes, but I'm offering a fair exchange."

Lilly reluctantly latched onto Ox's waiting nipple. She gave it a few sucks then pulled away. "It doesn't want to give me anything," she said sourly.

"Yes, it does. You've forgotten the right action. It's not a straw. Put your tongue under my nipple and squeeze a little as you suck."

Lilly tried again. This time milk gushed into her mouth. She gulped it down as fast as she could, but some still spilled from the corners of her mouth.

"There you go, you greedy wee thing," Ox said. "It tastes good, doesn't it?"

Nearly choking on the milk, Lilly coughed and splattered. When the flow finally stopped, she looked up, embarrassed. "I wasn't being greedy. It gushes out."

"I was only teasing. Drink up. I enjoy the sensation. You'll learn to master it ... get it to flow at a rate you can cope with."

Lilly reattached herself. This time she didn't suck so strongly and the reduced flow was easier to cope with. After drinking for a while, she raised her head. "It does taste good."

"I'm pleased you like it. Enjoy."

Cuddling into Ox, Lilly closed her eyes and drank. It wasn't long before her belly was pleasantly full. "Thank you," she said, sitting up. "I'm sorry I was so grumpy and rude. It's not every day that someone offers you their breast, and it's a strange breast at that."

"I understand."

Thinking about the cameras and the creeps upstairs, Lilly's cheeks reddened. She wondered what they were saying about her. She exhaled loudly. *Who cares what they think.*

Seeming to sense her distress, Ox stroked her back.

"Ox, why do you have a breast in such an odd place? And surely if you have a breast, and you make milk, you're a female?"

"I'm a male ... Human males can also produce breast milk, and like me, they can suckle an infant."

"No, they can't ... can they?"

"There have been many incidents of it, even in modern times.

Other male animals also lactate. Male goats are famous for it."

"They are?" Lilly frowned. What a strange day she was having. "It's odd that you can talk."

"Why?"

"No other primate can. It's physically impossible for them to do so, so how come you can?"

"I'm not an ape, remember," Ox said curtly. "I'm a humanoid, only bigger than you and covered in hair."

"Sorry ... I'm not sure why I'm having trouble grasping that."

"It's the fur ... Your mind will adjust."

Maybe it is the fur?

CHAPTER FOUR

Down the rabbit hole

Tucked up in a frog-legged position against Ox's belly, Lilly woke with an uncomfortably full bladder. She got down and made her way to the hole by the cave wall. Looking back, she couldn't help but be amazed at how quickly she'd adjusted to living with Ox. She'd only been in the cave a matter of days, and yet she was already at ease with a giant Bigfoot. She looked down at her belly. "Something's wrong! My stomach's swelling. My womb's filling with pus! I'm dying!"

"Always with the drama," Ox said without an inkling of sympathy and a touch of amusement.

Lilly glared at him. "How can you be so heartless?"

"You're not dying."

"My womb didn't go down as much as it should have, and now it's swelling. It's getting bigger and firmer! I don't know if my placenta came out ... You'd better tell the bastards upstairs I need medical attention."

"They won't care. It'll only make for more entertainment, but I can help."

"You? How?" Lilly looked around. "I don't see any medical supplies?"

"I don't need any," Ox said. "I'll suck it out of you."

"Suck it out of me!"

Ox briefly poked his tongue out. "With my long, hollow tongue, I'll suck it out of you."

Lilly shook her hands dry, then walked towards him. Placing her damp hands on her hips, she said, "Poke your tongue out again."

Ox did as she asked.

She edged closer. Eyeing his tongue suspiciously, she said, "You have a long, narrow ... *hollow* ... tongue?"

"I do ... yes," Ox said.

"You've been lying to me!" Lilly growled. "You're not human!"

"I never said I was! I said I was a humanoid."

"Well, that's hardly the same thing."

"Lie down and let me help you!" Ox boomed.

Terrified, Lilly dropped to the ground like a petulant child regretting her rude behavior. "You're not going to hurt me ... are you?" she whimpered, laying on the cold sand.

"No, Baby, I'm not going to hurt you ... You'll be fine ... Now open your legs."

Lilly opened her legs a little before thinking better of it. She went to sit up.

Ox grabbed her legs, and with one sharp upward motion, he made her go splat, flat on her back. Then he opened her limp legs. "Stop making a fuss and let me help you."

Lilly gasped for breath. "I'm scared. Agh!"

"Relax," Ox said as he set to work. He licked her clitoris several times with his tongue before probing her vagina with it, then he returned his attention to her clitoris; this time he gave it more attention. After pleasing her clitoris for a longer period, he once again probed her vagina. When he returned his tongue's attention to her clitoris, Lilly's breathing had deepened and her head had rolled back. When he reinserted his probing tongue into her vagina, she started moaning and moving her hips—keeping time with him. Ox prodded her rapidly, then rammed his tongue deep inside of her and began sucking powerfully. Strong orgasmic waves swept over Lilly. When they passed, Ox stopped sucking and withdrew his tongue.

When Lilly's breathing returned to normal, she sat up, eyes to the ground and cheeks aflame. "I'm sorry. I didn't mean to have an orgasm ... I ... I couldn't help it."

"No problem. It made my job easier ... Does your stomach feel better?"

Keeping her head low, Lilly felt her belly, its size had reduced. "I think so."

Ox stroked her head. "Don't be embarrassed. You're fine." He picked her up and cradled her to him.

"Did you deliberately stimulate my clitoris to make me orgasm?"

"Yes, it facilitated the emptying of your womb."

Lilly glared at him. "You're a disgusting pig! The men upstairs will come down here and shoot you where you stand."

Ox laughed. "They'll do nothing of the sort. I'm the one they value, you're yesterday's trash. They couldn't give two shits about you."

Ox's words bit into Lilly like vampire's teeth. She looked down.

"But I care about you," Ox said sweetly as he rubbed her back.

"Do you?" Lilly said in a childish voice; her bottom lip quivering.

"Of course, Baby ... Daddy wants to take care of you."

"I'm sorry I was rude. I ... I was embarrassed."

"Why?"

"An animal pleased me ... I've committed bestiality ... I'm disgusting!"

"Hey! Easy on with the beast comments," Ox said as he ran tender fingers through Lilly's blonde hair. "Don't you think you're overreacting?"

"No ... bestiality is a terrible crime. One can never be overly dramatic about such a thing ... Soon I'll be locked up in one of those cells above for real," she said, but as soon as she uttered the words, she knew they were silly.

"You're being ridiculous," Ox said. "That's about as silly as thinking video footage of us is about to go viral on YouTube."

"Oh my God! I hadn't thought of that ... If this is a game, then maybe we're being filmed and footage will appear on some sick, reality show."

"We won't."

"Imagine if people saw me having intimate relations with a beast ... the shame!"

Ox cleared his throat. "You didn't commit bestiality because I'm not a beast! And I pleasured you ... remember? Your beast comments are really starting to piss me off."

Lilly frowned. "Piss you off? You talk like that?"

"I do, yes."

Lilly's chin sunk. "But I had an orgasm."

"That's what happens when an expert licks your clitoris."

Lilly rolled her eyes. *Men ... they're all the same!* "We're not even the same species. I must be really sick. My shame knows no bounds."

Lilly heard and felt Ox draw in a breath of exasperation. She clung to him as a wave of fear swept over her. "I'm sorry I called you a beast," she said quickly. "I'll try not to do it again."

Ox sighed. "Don't you think you're overreacting ... making a big deal out of nothing? I gave you a little pleasure, where's the harm?"

Lilly placed her head in her hands and shook it. "I've fallen down the rabbit hole."

"I'm pretty sure I'm not a rabbit."

"It's a saying."

"I know."

Lilly wondered what Ox did or didn't know. He seemed to know a lot.

Music flooded into the cave: "White Rabbit," by Jefferson Airplane.

Lilly looked up. "They're playing us music again. What do you think they're thinking?"

"Yong's laughing his arse off."

"Yong?"

"Yes, the creepy little Chinese man upstairs who spies on us is laughing."

Lilly listened to the song's words. When she heard the words, *if you go chasing rabbits*, she knew Yong had indeed been listening, and the song choice was deliberate. "He's laughing because you gave me an orgasm?"

"No, he's laughing because you're making such a fuss about it."

Lilly scowled. "How can sucking pus out of someone be funny?" She glared up at the ceiling, to where she imagined a camera might be, and growled, "You should be ashamed of yourself! Why don't you come down here and check on my well-being instead of laughing at me?"

"I told you ... the men upstairs couldn't give two shits about your well-being, and Yong especially doesn't care."

"Arseholes! You better spit that pus out before it makes you sick."

"I'll be fine," Ox said. "I have a strong constitution."

Tears welled in Lilly's eyes. She wiped them away and sniffled.

"It's all right," Ox soothed. "You're all right."

"I'm not all right! I need medical attention and it's being denied," Lilly said, her voice cracking with emotion. "I've never been deprived of medical attention before. I lived in a caring society where my basic needs were met. Even if I'd gone to prison, I could've expected medical care."

"Daddy's taking care of you."

"You're not taking care of me!" Lilly snapped. "My baby's placenta is rotting inside of me! It needs to be removed."

Ox stroked her head. "Baby, you don't have a fever. Trust that your body will sort this out ... You don't want somebody to stick their hand up there and scrape it off ... do you?"

Lilly considered this for a moment. "Well, that would be preferable to becoming desperately ill and dying."

"Sweetheart, you're not dying. I'll sort this problem out for you."

"Doesn't it disgust you to be so intimately involved with my private parts, you being another species and all? Doesn't that cross a boundary for you?"

"No."

Holy shit!

"Besides, you and most other humans are part Neanderthal. You're not a pure species. Humans are made up of differing percentages of other humanoid species. To be offended is to deny your own existence. Humans like a bit of variety ... that's who you are."

Lilly folded her arms indignantly. "It's *not* who I am!"

"Your DNA says differently."

Lilly felt like she'd fallen off the edge of the map, arrived in Wonderland, or some other crazy place nobody ever wanted to visit. Her face was wrought with emotion and wet with tears. Ox licked her face.

Lilly whacked his tongue away. "What do you think you're doing!"

"Washing you. Daddy wants to wash you."

"No!"

Ox ignored Lilly's protest. He licked her back, flicking his tongue up under her armpits every now and then.

Lilly found the sensation most pleasing. It bothered her more than the licking. "Stop it. Yuck!"

"You need a bath … You've been here a while and you're getting all stinky."

"I'll go and wash myself in the water."

"The water's too cold. You'll get pneumonia. Washing you comes naturally to me. It's what I do. Let me wash you." Without waiting for an invitation, Ox resumed his licking.

Lilly closed her eyes. The idea of being washed by Ox's tongue was highly objectionable, but it felt good. She couldn't remember the last time her personal needs were attended to in such a caring way. Even so, being washed by a Bigfoot's tongue was gross, and it certainly wasn't her idea of clean.

Ox's tongue traveled downwards. It flicked up between her legs.

Lilly squealed. "Stop it! You don't need to lick me there."

"You've just given birth. You're all stinky … covered in dry and fresh blood. You need a bath."

"Didn't you just wash me down there?"

"I didn't do a good enough job. You've still got lots of dried blood on the tops of your inner thighs."

"Ox … that's yucky. I can't expect you to clean me with your tongue. I need a shower and the bastards upstairs aren't letting me have one. They haven't even supplied me with sanitary pads," Lilly said, her voice shill. "How can they be so mean?"

"You really are a spoilt princess, aren't you?" Ox said, cradling her. "It's all right. I'll take care of you. Daddy will wash you and attend to your needs."

Emotionally overwrought, Lilly flopped against him. When Ox resumed his licking, she ordered her body not to respond to his tongue's attention.

"There you go, Baby," Ox said as he finished. "You're all fresh and clean."

"That was sweet, Daddy," Lilly husked. *Bloody hell, his tongue's pure magic.* "I can't remember the last time anyone did anything as sweet as that for me."

"It was my pleasure, Baby."

Licking his fur clean of dry and fresh blood, Ox groomed himself.

Lilly sighed. "I'm not a spoilt princess."

"There's no point in denying it," Ox said, his voice bouncing off the cave walls. "You're a spoilt brat, all right."

Startled, Lilly trembled and clung to him like a scolded child clinging to daddy.

Cradling her to his breast, Ox cooed, "Feed from me."

Lilly latched on to his nipple and closed her eyes. Tucked up in her big scary daddy's arms, and warmed by his body, she felt strangely secure.

Ox rubbed her back. "There, there ..."

◆ ◆ ◆

Lilly groaned and opened her eyes. The shaggy fur on Ox's protective arms wasn't covering all of her, and her exposed bits were chilled to the bone. Her muscles were shivering so hard they ached. When she breathed out, her breath plumed in front of her. "It's really cold in here," she said, noticing the cave walls had a glimmer of ice on them.

"The bastards upstairs have turned the heating down. They're upping the ante ... making life more difficult for us."

Lilly was snuggled into Ox so tightly, it was as if she was trying to get inside of him. "Arseholes!"

"I could make you more comfortable," Ox said, cradling her.

"You could? How?"

"You asked me why I have a breast under my rib cage, in a fold of skin ... it's there because I have a pouch. That's how we keep our infants warm, how we protect them from the cold. Would you like to slip into my pouch? It's nice and warm in there."

"You have a pouch?" Lilly said through chattering teeth. "How can that be? Humans aren't marsupials."

"Marsupials range from small four-footed moles to two-legged kangaroos. The koala bear and the wombat are both marsupials. There was even a marsupial wolf. It's extinct now, but there was. Mammals and marsupials occupy the same ecological niche."

Lilly blinked several times. "Really? Do Bigfoot males carry their young because they're larger than female Bigfoots?"

"Yes. Would you like to slip into my pouch?"

Lilly's lips were turning blue, and the white-knuckled grip she had on Ox was making her arms ache. "It's tempting," she said desperate to escape the cold.

Careful to keep Lilly's legs in their current frog-leg position, up by her sides, Ox placed a hand under her bottom as he propelled her forward onto his chest. He then let his pouch hang open a little while placing his hands on Lilly's hips. Slowly, he pushed her downwards.

When Lilly's toes entered his pouch, the sensation of slipping into another's body made her gasp. She shrieked and clambered back up onto his chest. Ox stopped her forward momentum by grasping her hips firmly, then he started pushing her back down and into his pouch.

"No!" Lilly screeched. "I don't want to go in there! It's all silky and weird ... It's the inside of your body!"

In one sudden, smooth motion, Ox pushed Lilly down and into his pouch. Then he locked her inside with the muscles that encircled the top of his pouch. The muscles formed a loose, yet strong ring around Lilly's neck. Still squatting in a frog-leg position, Lilly braced herself and using all of her lower body strength, she tried to torpedo her way through Ox's ring of muscles, but her efforts were in vain. Ox was Goliath in comparison to her. Compared to him, she was smaller than a two-year-old child.

"Let me out!"

"Shh. Relax," Ox said. "There's no point in struggling. You can't get out until I let you out ... Now settle down."

Tears welled in Lilly's eyes. She wanted to wipe them away, but she couldn't get a hand out to do so. "I can't even wipe my eyes!" she sobbed.

"If I relax my muscles, will you quit trying to get out?"

Lilly was beat. She sighed and shrugged her unhappy agreement. The wall of solid muscles around her neck relaxed and then draped loosely upon her shoulders. She pushed a hand past them and wiped her eyes.

"I'm not trying to hurt you," Ox said. "Quite the opposite, I'm saving you."

Lilly's body was still shuddering from her sobs.

"Relax, Baby," Ox soothed.

Lilly closed her eyes. The relaxed pouch was as soft and pliable as a luxurious bedspread, and the reprieve from the cold was heavenly. Nestling her face into Ox's warm fur, she slumped and sighed and melted into him.

"Comfy, Baby?"

"Yes. Thank you."

Lilly couldn't think of any muscles she had that were quite like Ox's pouch muscles. Muscles that could tighten like a vice, or relax completely, except perhaps her vagina muscles and that was overselling them. She touched the pouch's silky interior. It was as soft as the finest chamois leather she'd ever felt. Ox briefly opened his pouch so she could look at its pinky-red interior.

Lilly shuddered as cold air rushed in. When Ox closed his pouch again, she buried her face in his warm fur, thankful for the hair on her head. After a few minutes consideration, she said, "There's something odd about your pouch."

"What would that be?"

"I have a protruding belly and your stomach seems to have a concave pocket for it to slip into. Isn't that odd?"

"Not at all. Bigfoot babies have protruding bellies. Our pouches are designed to accommodate them."

"Of course," Lilly said, wondering why she hadn't thought of that.

"You're not sitting properly. Let me adjust you," Ox said as he slid his hands into his pouch and grabbed hold of her legs. After he pulled them up, her feet slipped into little pockets that seemed to be designed for the job. Then Ox pushed her buttocks down to the bottom of his pouch, so she sat deep in his pelvis.

"There, that's better," he said. "I can lean forward with you in this position if I open my legs … Are you comfortable?"

"Yes, it's almost like being in a swing chair. Thank you."

"Relax, little one… enjoy."

Lilly sighed. "I'm so weak and pathetic compared to you. I'd be dead if it wasn't for you … This cave is so nasty!"

"Nasty? I think it's beautiful."

Lilly looked around. The tiny lights above were twinkling like diamonds and they seemed even more beautiful than usual. Dew glistened on the cave walls. Where it had turned to ice, it shimmered and sparkled in the low light. The water was an intense shade of blue with a hint of green, and the sand, rustic gold. "I guess you're right. This cave seemed like death a minute ago, but now I see it's quite beautiful."

Ox rubbed Lilly's back through his pouch wall.

She sighed. "Your pouch is silky and warm. It's very cozy in here … Thank you for letting me rest in you."

"My pleasure, Baby."

"You're so magnanimous. I … I'm a little bitch."

Ox kissed the top of her head. "There, there, little one. Everything is all right. Daddy's taking care of you."

Lilly closed her eyes, but only for a moment. Squirming about, she said, "Drat. I need to go to the toilet."

"Let me do that for you," Ox said all too eagerly.

"What do you mean … do that for me? Let me down. I'll go against the cave wall."

"I don't want you to get cold. I have a probe that can remove your waste."

"What…? No!"

Lilly struggled to get out of Ox's pouch, but her current position made escape even more impossible than before. Ox had her trapped. "I'm such an idiot!" she despaired. "Only a complete moron would get into the pouch of another!"

"Calm down and let me help you."

"You tricked me! Your pouch is a prison!"

"I'm helping you."

Lilly breathed deeply to try and calm herself. She sighed. Surely her mind was running away with her. *I must have misunderstood.* "What exactly do you mean by ... probe?"

"What do you think I mean?"

Lilly chuckled. "Well, for a moment there, I thought you were talking about having a snake-like probe that you were going to shove up my arse." She laughed at the absurdity of the idea.

Ox's brow rose. "You think that's funny?"

"You won't get the joke," Lilly said. "Supposedly, alien abductees claim they've been probed up the arse. Anal probes are often joked about in movies, they're part of pop culture."

"Really?"

"Yes ... sorry for freaking out. So, what did you mean?"

"That."

A crease shot across Lilly's brow. "That? What do you mean ... that?"

"You described it and I'm confirming it, that's what I meant."

Lilly's jaw dropped. *Surely he's joking?*

"How do you think we care for our babies in a cold environment? We take care of their needs."

Lilly blinked several times. "Kangaroos don't do that! I'm sure of it."

"No, they don't. They stick their long tongues in their pouches and lick up the mess ... Do you want to crap all over yourself?"

"I'm not your baby! I'm an adult woman, and I can go to the toilet by myself."

"You *are* my baby."

"I can deal with a bit of cold."

Ox cleared his throat. "No! You'll let me attend to you."

"No, I won't! Bloody hell, MEN! You're all such overbearing wankers. Listen, I'm not your infant. I appreciate your kind gesture and all, but I'm perfectly capable of going wee-wee and poo-poo by myself."

"You're not grasping what I'm saying. I'm saying ... I'm NOT letting you down."

Tears burned at the back of Lilly's eyes. "Bastard!"

"If you don't let me feed from you, I can't continue to care for you."

Lilly frowned. "You drink piss?"

"Yes."

Shocked, Lilly's eyes whizzed left and right. "But, I'm not your infant," she said. "I think you're getting all confused."

"I'm not the one who's getting confused."

"I need to go for a shit!"

"I know."

"You eat shit? You gobble it up with your probe? You're teasing ... Tell me you're teasing!"

"I'm not teasing," Ox said. "Lots of animals eat shit. There's nothing wrong with it."

"Ah ... yes, there is!"

"My probe won't hurt you. I'll be gentle ... I promise."

"Yeah, right! I've heard that before. No. I'm saying NO!"

"Protest noted. Now hold still and relax or I'll hurt you."

"No, No, NO!" Lilly screamed, feeling a silky snake-like probe slither up from the base of the pouch and position itself directly under her anus. Ox had her locked into the perfect position.

"Relax. Breathe ... I'm going to do this either way, so you'd better relax."

Lilly glared up at Ox. His face showed nothing but grim determination.

"Breathe, Baby ... Relax."

Lilly closed her eyes and willed her body to relax. When the tension in her anal sphincter eased, Ox's probe slithered up effortlessly. Lilly pulled a face as it entered. The head of Ox's probe was about the same size as a modest human penis, but its tip was considerably more pointy and flexible.

"There, I'm in ... all done," Ox said. "Now that didn't hurt, did it?"

Lilly couldn't believe how strong Ox's probe was. It felt like a twisting viper when it entered her. "Get it out of me!"

"No. You'll get used to it."

"Get it out!" Lilly screamed.

"Calm down! It's hardly as if it's the first time you've had a probe up your arse."

"It is too!"

"Pfft. You've had plenty of anal sex ... no doubt you enjoy it very much."

"How dare you speak to me like that!" Lilly said in her most hoity-toity voice.

"You can drop the indignation. You were no anal virgin. My probe slid up there effortlessly ... That's a well-traveled path."

"It is not!"

Ox gave Lilly a knowing look.

"Get it out," Lilly demanded, "or I'm going to sic my lawyer onto you!"

"Pfft ... for what? Poking you up the arse? You'll do no such thing. I bet you haven't been telling all in sundry that your husband poked you up the arse on a regular basis for years."

Lilly looked down. "He made me do it."

"Yeah, right ... That's what they all say."

"My husband likes anal," Lilly muttered. "He used to get me drunk and have his way with me. I'm sure he spiked my wine with vodka. Even after we separated, he still tried to have his way with me ... He'd sneak around to our house with bottles of wine."

Ox smirked. "Well, you can't blame a man for trying."

"Shut up!"

Ox laughed. "Relax. No one is judging you ... certainly not me."

"Please take it out."

"My probe mimics the shape of your bowel ... it's designed for its job. It squeezes down to almost nothing at your anus's entrance and expands inside of you," Ox explained in doctorly fashion. "I'm sure it isn't causing you any pain. You probably can hardly feel it ... Forget about it."

"I most certainly can feel it! It's not meant to be in there ... It's uncomfortable," Lilly said, exaggerating her level of discomfort. "Take it out."

"No," Ox said. "You'll have to get used to it, and while you're at it, you might as well get used to my catheter as well."

"Your what?"

Lilly felt a second, smaller, probe enter her urethra. This *was* something new. She'd never had a catheter inserted before.

"Agh."

"That didn't hurt. I've done nothing more invasive than a doctor would if he inserted a catheter into your bladder."

"I'll be the judge of that!" Lilly growled. "Bastard!"

"Calm down."

"Shut the hell up! I'd rather freeze to death than tolerate this."

"Don't be silly," Ox said. "Now drink from me and be quiet."

CHAPTER FIVE

You're a parasite

Lilly glared at Ox. If looks could kill, he'd be dead.

"Baby, I can't help who I am or how I'm made, any more than you can."

Feeling guilty and ashamed of her behavior, Lilly looked down. She sighed. *Don't be so pathetic. Surely, you're not going to be so easily manipulated?*

As if he'd sensed her resolve, Ox said, "Baby, I've been so hungry my stomach aches, and all the while I've had to watch you dump my food in that sandy pit by the wall. Well, no more ... the people upstairs threw you in here to feed me, and I have no intentions of starving."

Lilly looked up. "So, I was right!" she said triumphantly. "They did throw me in here to feed you."

"Yes, you were right ... happy?"

"No ... Why would they do such a thing? It's a terrible thing to do! What's happening down here, I couldn't have imagined in my wildest nightmares."

"Would you prefer I starve to death?"

Lilly buried her face in Ox's fur. *He's guilt-tripping me!* "Look, I appreciate you keeping me warm and feeding me, and I'm grateful ... I really am. But look at it from my point of view. I was busy minding my own business when suddenly I was thrown into a cave with a giant Bigfoot, and now he's probing me up the arse."

"I guess you're down on your luck," Ox said dryly.

"Thanks!"

"You could see it as a blessing."

"A blessing? You know, when I knelt down to pray it never occurred to me to say, 'Dear God, please toss me into a cave with a Bigfoot and have him probe me up the arse.' Maybe it's just me … but it never occurred to me."

"I feel blessed," Ox said. "You're a blessing to me."

Oh man, he's really pulling a number on me. "Ox, my world has been turned upside down. I've lost my baby, my home, and my family. I've been cast out of my very society. Worse than that … they've turned on me. Can you imagine how that feels?"

"You need to start living in the here and now. I need you, and I want to take care of you … I'll love you in a way no ordinary man ever could."

Oh, he's good. "Look, Ox, I appreciate you keeping me alive, and I guess you can't help who you are … I'm not upset with you … I'm angry with the creeps upstairs."

"They care for me. They've provided for me."

Lilly groaned. *Of course, that's how he sees it.* "You said my poop is food for you? So, you're like a dung beetle—a scarab beetle?"

"Sort of," Ox said. "I don't like your body when it's full of toxins and dead meat. That's why they gave you a cleansing drink, and why I let you poop against the cave wall."

"Are you talking about that odd-tasting milkshake?"

"It was made with my breast milk."

"So, that's why they never gave me any food?"

"My milk is food … it's liquid food. Breast milk has the goodness of the body in it. It's like dissolving your body and feeding it to another."

"Did drinking your milk make me more attractive to you? Sheep will reject another's lamb, but if they've fed it, they'll accept it."

"The men upstairs made you highly desirable to me … yes."

"Their generosity abounds!" Lilly said sarcastically.

"I could smell you the moment you arrived in this cave; even if you'd been placed amongst a group of people, I still could've picked you out."

"Gee," Lilly said, "How comforting."

"Your life was in my hands. Had I not desired you intensely, you'd be dead."

"The bastards upstairs fed me to you ... Don't try and turn it around and make out their saints and you're some kind of superhero! You're not. You're a parasite!"

"So are you."

"I'm *not* a parasite."

"Really?" Ox said. "And just how are you surviving right now? I'm keeping you warm and feeding you. How long do you think you'd survive without my help?"

"I shouldn't need your help! I shouldn't be here ... I understand what's going on ... You're the pet of the creeps upstairs, and they've thrown me in here to feed you. That's why I'm stuck in your pouch with a probe up my arse!"

"You'll get used to it."

"I don't want to get used to it! More to the point, I shouldn't have to."

"Our symbiotic relationship is mutually beneficial ... We're maintaining each other."

"Your body's inside of mine!" Lilly growled. "And it's not like your probes are sterile hospital tubes!"

"I see ... So, you think I'm dirty ... full of disease? A filthy animal?"

"You might be!"

"Listen, Miss Uppity Britches, I'm clean. I'm not riddled with diseases and my probes aren't crude medical tubes."

"Your body's inside of mine! I can feel you ... It's an intimacy I'm not desiring!"

"Nobody gives a shit what you desire!"

"Stop that!" Lilly snarled. "Stop making out that I'm nothing ... that I don't matter."

"Your only value is to feed me. That's it ... Other than that, you're garbage."

"What a terrible thing to say!"

"Why?" Ox said. "Does the truth hurt?"

"Yes, it hurts. But whose opinion is that? You're only talking about the creeps upstairs."

"It seems it was your husband's opinion as well."

"That was a cheap shot," Lilly said, blinking rapidly to hide the tears filling her eyes. "It was just plain mean."

"So, you're the only one who's allowed to be rude and disrespectful? If you stop being so obnoxious, then so will I."

Lilly sniffed back her tears and rubbed her eyes. "Look, on an intellectual level, I can understand why you're doing what you're doing … I can even understand why the creeps upstairs have done what they've done … I don't want to be nasty—"

"Then don't."

Yeah, it's that simple. Lilly wondered if she could pull Ox's probes out with her hands. She tried to reach them but Ox was onto her before she'd even got her hands near. He clamped his pouch tight around her.

"My hands are stuck!"

"If you take them away from your bum, I'll relax my pouch. There's no point in trying to pull my probes out anyway, they're stronger than you. Your wee hands aren't up to the job," Ox said, releasing his pouch's grip.

Lilly groaned. Returning her hands to their previous position, she decided to try and shut out all thoughts of his probes—if that was at all possible. Changing the subject, she said, "Do you usually speak English or even human?"

"My primary language isn't English, but there's no such thing as human language."

"Of course there is."

"Do you understand French or Arabic?"

"No, but I could learn to."

"The same goes for any language spoken by a Bigfoot."

"How many languages can you speak?"

"Quite a few."

Lilly shrugged. "Well, I guess that makes me stupid. I can only speak English."

"That's all you need to speak because I'm looking after you … Daddy is taking care of you."

Lilly rolled her eyes.

"Drink from me and rest. You've had a big few days. Your wee body is tired," Ox said as he freed her feet from their holders.

Lilly curled up in his pouch and suckled on his nipple. She didn't want to admit it, but she was comfortable. When Ox lay down and relaxed his pouch, it was like she was lying in a comfy bed, able to toss and turn in her usual manner. She closed her eyes.

Ox stroked her head lovingly.

Lilly opened an eye and peeked up at him. "Are you an alien?"

"What makes you ask?"

"You have a probe up my arse. Earthly creatures don't feed in such a manner. Marsupials on this planet, don't have probes they insert into the arses of other creatures."

"There are millions of different forms of life on this planet, many unique. Is a platypus an alien because it lays eggs, has a duck's bill, and a beaver's tail?"

"I can't imagine a platypus flying around in a flying saucer, therefore, they're not aliens."

"I can imagine humans flying around in flying saucers, so does that mean they *are* aliens?"

Lilly shrugged.

Ox raised his brow. "There's something you've not considered."

"What?"

"My body is designed to encapsulate yours, feed it and feed off it. If I'm an alien, what are you?"

Lilly scoffed. "You probably feed off lots of creatures."

"No, I don't ... I feed off your kind exclusively."

"There could be any number of humanoids in the universe."

"Of course," Ox said. "I'm a predator who flies from planet to planet in my spaceship looking for humanoids to stuff into my pouch to feed off."

"So I was right?"

"No. I was being sarcastic."

"Many a truth is said in jest."

"My tastes are quite refined."

Lilly caught a cough in her throat. "You ... refined. Now that is funny."

"I am refined ... You, on the other hand, are a selfish, judgemental little bitch. Would you like to get out of my pouch?"

Lilly didn't want to get out of his pouch. She was tired, really tired. Exhaustion had swept over her like a wave. "No, I'm sorry. You're right ... I'm a rude bitch. I'll try to refrain from being rude in the future." She snuggled down. Ox's pouch muscles cradled her body, and within minutes she was asleep.

CHAPTER SIX

It's freezing

Lilly rubbed her cold nose. Shivering, she snuggled down in the pouch. "Bloody hell, it's freezing in here!"

Ox closed his pouch over the top of her head. "The temperature has dropped considerably, yes. I could open the top of my pouch just enough for you to peer out through my fur, then you could see me and keep warm."

"That sounds good, thanks."

After doing as he suggested, Ox rubbed Lilly's back through his pouch wall. "Are you snug, Baby?"

Peering up at him through a curtain of thick fur, Lilly could hardly see Ox. "Yes, thank you," she said while searching for his nipple. "You're a female Bigfoot. You have a pouch and a nipple ... Why don't you want me to know you're a girl?"

"I'd tell you if I was a girl. I'm not a female. I'm a male ... A pouch isn't an exclusively *female thing*. Male seahorses have pouches, so do male sungrebe birds."

"Really? There are male birds that have pouches?"

"Yes, they have two actually, one under each wing."

"Well, I'm still not convinced you're a male."

Ox cleared his throat. "Do you want me to flop it out?"

"What?" *Shit, how big would that thing be?* "No, it's fine. I don't need to see it. I believe you."

"Are you sure? You seem to be requiring *absolute* proof."

"I'm not, it's fine," Lilly stuttered. "I believe you." *Idiot, why did you question him?*

Ox coughed. "But how can you be sure if you haven't seen it ... touched it? Don't you want to see it in action? Get some scientific proof?"

"I'm not a scientist. A man's word is good enough for me."

"But, clearly, it isn't. I told you I was a male and you accused me of lying."

"I was wrong, I apologize." Rebuking herself internally, Lilly hit herself on the forehead. "Sometimes I'm an idiot and I say stupid things."

"Really? You know, I wouldn't mind if you ran your lovely little fingers all over it and gave it a taste test. You know ... to be sure."

Oh, crap! Lilly sank down further in the pouch.

Ox tucked his head inside his pouch. He nestled his face against hers. "Tell me, Baby, are you trying to hide from me ... in me? I'm just curious."

Lilly was astounded by his flexibility. "I'm feeling sleepy. I have a headache."

Ox kissed the top of her head as he withdrew his head from his pouch. Then he rippled his pouch muscles over her body in a gentle, rhythmic wave to comfort her.

Lilly closed her eyes and tried to shut him out, but it was impossible when he was making his presence so acutely felt.

"It's all right, Baby," he said. "Just remember, I was made to go with you. I'm not going to hurt you ... Does a bee hurt a flower?"

Oh, God! So, he does want me to give his cock a workout.

"You're safe in my pouch, it's specially designed for you. My ribs and pelvis bones form a roll cage around you. I'll never crush you or hurt you in any way ... You can rest easy in me."

Lilly breathed a sigh of relief. *He's letting the subject drop. Thank God.* Ox's probe suckled on Lilly's bowel wall. She could feel it up under her ribs. "Your probe is deep inside of me! How did it get up there?"

"My probe isn't a crude piece of human technology like a colonoscopy probe that grabs hold of your bowel and tries to straighten it as it moves forward. Rather, my probe excretes a lubricating substance that aids its movement, along with enzymes that relax your bowel and prevent it from cramping. The probe's natural smooth motion combines both the snake's and snail's methods of momentum. Stretching forward, it attaches suckers before pulling itself up behind, then it stretches out once more. In reverse, it moves more like a snake. Riding your bowel's waves, it effortlessly exits your bowel ... It can easily move both up and down your large intestine."

Lilly pulled a face. "Creepy."

"My probe likes to be deep inside of you. It's not hurting you ... is it?"

"No, it's kind of stroking and suckling on my bowel ... It feels weird, but it's not painful."

"Comforting, I hope? Suckling on your bowel gives me pleasure."

Lilly was suddenly angry, not because of an overwhelming emotional response, but because she felt she should be. "I shouldn't have to tolerate this! Do the people upstairs know what you're doing to me? Are they okay with it?"

"They're acutely aware of what I'm doing, and yes, they're okay with it."

"I feel so betrayed!"

"Why can't you admit you're enjoying my probe...? You like it when it suckles on you, just like I enjoy it when you suckle on my breast."

Lilly snorted and glared up at Ox through a curtain of his fur.

He ran a tender finger through her hair. "Baby, you were made to enjoy being with me."

"I highly doubt that! I think your kind developed a predatory adaption ... Aren't you stealing food from my very belly!"

"Are you referring to the food I give you?"

"Ah ... yes."

"Your body has almost no interest in what reaches your large intestine. You do extract vitamins and fluids from your bowel, but after I've processed what I extract, I excrete your requirements back into your bowel, along with beneficial substances from my own body."

Lilly groaned. Ox always had an answer and the answer was

usually creepy. She covered her ears.

"Do you believe in God?"

"Yes," Lilly said after wondering if she should ignore him and pretend she hadn't heard him.

"Tell me about your God."

Lilly sighed. Ox's distraction tactic was lame at best. "God is a spirit in the sky," she said authoritatively. "Mary bore his son Jesus. He died on a cross to save believers. Jesus is now like God. He'll return someday to save humanity and pass judgment on sinners."

Ox laughed a loud, raucous laugh. "Does that make sense to you?"

Lilly's face fell. "Yes. Why?"

"Who are the sinners?"

"Non-believers."

"So, if someone doesn't believe that crazy story, they're a sinner?"

"Yes," Lilly said, "and it's not a crazy story!"

"What about all the people who believe in other gods?"

"They'll die because only Jesus saves."

"Really?"

"Yes."

"Baby, what you've just described is a religion. Religion is a control system ... a means of controlling the masses. There may be some truth to it, but religion isn't *the truth*."

"How would you know!"

"You mean because I'm a dumb, stupid animal?"

Lilly glared up at him.

"I see ... so you do think I'm a dumb, stupid animal. Would you rather I changed the subject, seeing as you're getting all bent out of shape over my reaction to your silly belief?"

Lilly glared at him and folded her arms. "What shall we discuss? How much you're enjoying having your nasty probe up my arse? How much entertainment I'm providing for the evil pricks upstairs?"

"You're a miserable wee thing, aren't you?"

"Yes, I am! Thank you very much! That tends to happen when arseholes steal your baby and then let some beast probe you up the arse."

"Well, if you weren't such a snotty bitch, maybe things would've turned out better."

"Shut up!"

Ox smacked Lilly's arse through his pouch wall. The impact made his probe jolt inside of her. Lilly caught her breath. *Good God.* She buried her face. Ox hadn't hurt her. His smack was very restrained, but it had frightened her.

"Nearly all situations have a silver lining," Ox said. "Maybe you should look for yours."

Lilly snorted. "What would the silver lining be in this case?"

"You're not dead."

"Right! Well, I think if there's nothing to be grateful for apart from *not being dead*, then life's pretty crappy!"

"I'm looking after you. I care for you."

"You're not looking after me! You're looking after you! You've imprisoned me in your stupid pouch so you can feed off me continuously with your nasty probe!"

"You're beginning to taste bad. You're leaving a sour taste in my probe. I'm going to spit you out."

Lilly frowned as her eyes widened. "What?"

Ox opened his pouch and unceremoniously dumped her out onto the cold ground.

Lilly got to her feet. Shivering intensely, she crouched down and wrapped her arms around her knees. Unable to help it, she burst into tears.

"Beg."

"What?"

"I said ... beg!" Ox said. "You're not getting back into my pouch until you do. When you tell me you want to be with me, and you're absolutely desperate to have my big, juicy probe up your arse, I'll let you back in my pouch."

"But, Daddy, I'll die!"

"That's right ... you will. Now beg!"

Lilly folded her arms, indignant. "You'll go hungry. You need me!"

"If I reject you they'll bring me another. There are billions of women on Earth."

"Oh. Okay ... well, I guess I'd be better off dead, anyway. I'll die with my values intact and make my way to Jesus."

Ox snorted as he got to his feet. Lilly was stunned by his enormous size. He must have been at least 14 feet tall. She'd always been a bit short, but now she felt like a midget—even smaller. Ox walked away and sat down. His back turned.

The elevator dinged. Lilly turned to see its huge doors opening. A small Chinese man was standing in front of the two Indian henchmen she'd already met. This time, however, they weren't dressed as orderlies. They towered over the little man who made a beeline for her.

Lilly was excited to see him. Covering her womanly bits as best she could, she stood up to greet him. She knew he'd already seen her naked body, but she still felt the need to cover herself. The Chinese man's face contorted with anger as he walked determinedly towards her carrying a wrecking bar in his clenched fist.

Fear swept over Lilly and she backed away. "Daddy, please help me!" she cried, retreating from the little man.

Ox didn't move. He remained seated: his back turned. The man made no sound as he moved towards Lilly. She ran and hid behind Ox. Clinging to him, she peered around his side, her eyes wide with terror.

The man waved the wrecking bar at her. "Listen, bitch. I want nothing more than to smash your silly head in with this wrecking bar and have these men drag your sorry arse off to a garbage heap full of rats and yesterday's trash. Then they'll toss your bitch arse into a furnace and be rid of you!"

Lilly could hardly believe the words that were coming out of his mouth. She stared at him, her mouth ajar.

"You either beg Ox to take you back and let him do whatever he wants to you, or I'll come back down here and beat you to death ... and I'll enjoy it!" With that, he turned and strode back to the elevator. He banged his fist on a button and was gone.

Lilly was aghast. She gulped and stepped back from Ox. Looking up at his face and then down at her feet, alternately, she said, "I'm sorry. I really am. May I please get back in your pouch?"

"Do you think that's going to cut it?" Ox said without even looking at her.

"I'm going to die soon," Lilly whimpered. "My stomach is much larger than it should be. The infection in my womb is out of control. You haven't managed to clear it. I know you tried and I'm grateful, I really am. I'm not blaming you, but I'm dying. Can I please die in your pouch?"

Ox scoffed. "What about not compromising your values and finding your way to Jesus?"

"Jesus forgives ... he'll understand."

"Really?" Ox said sarcastically. "Well, I'm not satisfied. I need a demonstration of your love."

Freezing and desperate, Lilly thought for a moment. Unable to think of anything else, she said, "Would you like it if I serenaded you?"

Ox's face softened. "Yes, I think I would like that."

Lilly had never serenaded anybody before, and her voice wasn't particularly good. She looked up at the ceiling. "Could you please play, 'Where did our love go' by the Supremes?"

Waiting for the opening beats, time seemed to stand still. When the song flooded into the cave, she sighed a sigh of relief, then sang along with the words, surprised she remembered them.

"Very nice," Ox said when the song ended. "But let's get something straight. I'm not interested in your nerdy sense of morality or your stupid feminist crap! And I couldn't give two shits about the Geneva Convention. You were given to me ... Do you understand? You belong to me!"

Lilly eyed her toes. "Yes, Daddy. I understand."

"And I don't want your Jesus coming between us. You must renounce your former faith and worship me."

Looking up, Lilly blinked several times. "What?"

"Where is your Jesus savior now? Is he here saving you from the men upstairs, or am I? Am I not your savior? Am I not taking care of you? Now renounce your former faith and declare me your god."

Lilly stared at him. *Is he serious?* "You're my new god and I will worship no other," she said without hesitation. *Good God. I've denied my Jesus!*

"Say it with conviction," Ox said. "I think you were only saying that."

"You're my new and wonderful god. I will worship no other ... and I'm sorry for being rude."

Ox reached down and picked her up. He tapped and dusted the sand off her feet with a few masterful strokes. Then rubbed her feet against the fur of one of his legs to be sure all the sand was gone. "Haven't you forgotten something?"

Without missing a beat, Lilly said, "I'm absolutely desperate to have your big juicy probe up my arse."

"Course you are!" Ox said as he pushed her back into his pouch.

Lilly was too relieved to be out of the cold to make a retort.

CHAPTER SEVEN

Worship

Lilly's buttocks had barely touched the bottom of the pouch when Ox's probe whizzed back up inside of her. She gasped, then sighed. "Your pouch is lovely and warm," she said, snuggling in and feeling strangely comforted by his probe. She shook her head. *I can't believe I denied my Jesus.*

"Good girl?"

Lilly hugged Ox from inside his pouch. "I'm sorry I was a bad girl, Daddy."

Ox sighed. "You don't have much faith in that Jesus of yours, do you?"

Lilly shrugged.

"You're not still worshipping him in your head ... are you?"

Yes. "Wow, you can't expect me to quit my religion just like that?"

"I most certainly can and do."

"How can you presume it to be so easy? My religion is about the afterlife. It's about going to heaven."

"It's about threats," Ox said. "Worship Jesus or die. I gave you the same threat and you jumped ship."

"What about the afterlife?"

"What about it?"

"Well, what's going to happen to my soul when I die?"

"You'll be dead."

"See! You can't offer me heaven, so you're not a god." Lilly regretted her outburst almost immediately. *Shut up!*

"Tell me about this heaven of yours. What happens there?"

Phew, he let it pass. "You can't marry because you serve God and live as a spirit," Lilly said, remembering a passage in the Bible.

"It sounds like crap! You'd be better off dead."

"But that's not the other option," Lilly protested. "The other option is being tortured in the presence of the Lamb and punished for being a non-believer. If you haven't dedicated your life to Jesus, then Satan owns your soul and you'll be punished in hell. You'll burn for all eternity."

Ox scoffed. "Do you believe that? Silly girl. It's brainwashing crap designed to control the masses. Forget that garbage. Worship your new god who carries you around, feeds you, and loves you."

Lilly shrugged. "Okay, God."

"Call me daddy, I'd prefer that. But don't forget ... I AM your God and you'll worship no other."

"Okay." Bloody hell, he's crazy!

"Now, drink from me."

Lilly latched onto his nipple as Ox's probe latched onto her bowel wall and resumed its suckling; the sensation had a soothing effect on her. Her muscles relaxed and she felt drunk. She moaned.

Ox ran tender fingers through her hair. "Good girl."

"Daddy, it feels like you have a large hook in me. Your probe is forming a hook shape in my belly."

"That's the shape of your large bowel. It runs up your left-hand side, then under your ribs before going half-way down your right-hand side."

Lilly felt her belly. "My womb is huge: it's full of pus." Her chin drooped. "I'm dying."

"You're not dying! Your placenta didn't come away because it wasn't meant to. It was designed to grow into an organ that looks and acts like a set of lungs, and it's done just that. However, unlike your lungs, it doesn't breathe air, rather, it fills with liquid drawn from your body. It's milking your body of goodness to feed me."

"What?" *Holy fuck!* "How can that be? Placentas are designed to come away ... they all do."

"Not the one in you. It was specially engineered."

Lilly stared at Ox through a curtain of his fur, her mouth ajar.

"That's why you drink so much," he said. "Why you're always thirsty."

"I am not!"

"Baby, my nipple is constantly in your mouth. You're always drinking ... haven't you noticed?"

Lilly frowned. She hadn't thought about it.

"I'm going to drain your womb. You need to be emptied ... you're getting frantic."

"I'll get cold. I haven't warmed up enough yet."

"You won't get cold because I have a probe for the job."

"You have?"

Ox removed the little probe from inside Lilly's urethra and used it to suckle on her clitoris. She moaned. She tried not to, but couldn't help it.

Lilly's moaning deepened. Oh, my God that feels amazing.

"Enjoy, Baby," Ox whispered as he stroked her head tenderly. "I'm going to pleasure you in ways you could never have imagined."

Lilly was tempted to say, "Promises, promises," but she lost her chain of thought. A probe much like Ox's anal probe, only a bit smaller, shot up her vagina. It burst into her womb, into the strange placenta. Lilly gasped, expecting pain, but the action wasn't painful, quite the opposite; it was highly pleasurable. She climaxed more intensely than she'd ever done before. *Oh, my God, that was unbelievable!*

"Your cervix isn't closed," Ox said as if he'd read her mind and was answering an unasked question of hers. "The placenta is keeping it ajar with a valve. A valve that pleasures you when it's forced open and prodded."

"I don't understand," Lilly husked, still breathless. "How come I can feel the placenta? Isn't it a foreign body, in my body?"

"It's now part of you. It's integrated itself by growing into the wall of your womb and linking with your nervous system. That's why you can feel it."

Lilly's eyes nearly popped out of her head. "Why hasn't my body rejected it? Attacked it ... protected me from invasion?"

"Because the placenta's far too clever for that," Ox said. "It bypassed your defenses by making your body think it was you. Its blood type is the same as yours, and its tissue cloned yours after you gave birth to your baby. Your body won't reject it ... not now ... not ever."

"What are you saying? It's grown into my actual womb? It's not simply attached to the surface; it can't be scraped off?"

"After you gave birth, drugs that make your womb contract strongly could have forced it out, but they won't work now because it's anchored itself with tentacle-like hooks and grown into your womb. You and the placenta are now one. You've gained a new organ."

"Thanks for the heads-up!" Lilly said bitterly.

"You *should* be thanking me."

"What the hell for? It's not something to be grateful for ... it's a scene straight out of a horror movie!"

Ox laid back and closed his eyes. "Don't make me mad."

Lilly exhaled loudly and rubbed her face. *Shut up!* She scolded herself before feeling her belly. It felt smaller, lighter.

Ox positioned his face beside hers, his eyes soft and filled with love. He tenderly stroked her head. "I'm sorry I was horrid to you. I was hanging out for that."

Lilly didn't know what to say or do. Should I accept his apology and stroke his head in return? Sighing, she did so.

"I make you orgasm intensely to empty your womb and get what I need."

Lilly frowned. "The product collected by the placenta is more than food to you?"

"Much more. It's like wine ... we call it wine. It affects my entire body ... makes me feel relaxed, calm ... tender."

"Thank God! You were scaring me."

"Yes, thank me," Ox said. "You were referring to me ... weren't you?"

"What?" Lilly's brain scrambled. *Oh, I said, thank God.* "Daddy, 'thank God' is a saying. It means thank goodness. You say it when you're relieved. It isn't worship."

"When you say it in the future ... you will mean me, and it *will be* worship."

Lilly blinked several times. Is he serious? Surely he's having me on? "Okay." Whatever!

"Good."

Lilly continued to rub her belly. "Daddy, surely I don't have a specially engineered placenta inside of me? I mean ... how can that be?"

"You can feel it ... can't you?"

"Yes, but science hasn't advanced that far. Man can't engineer placentas. Hell, man hasn't even found a way to grow new teeth."

"How exactly did you get pregnant?"

"A bad night out. I went out with a creep. Later, I discovered I was pregnant. I was too far along to do anything about it. I don't even know the full name of my baby's father. It's embarrassing. I was undecided about keeping my baby because of my career and social standing. Not to mention, I'm in my early fifties and I've already raised a family."

"So, it's not a big deal they stole your baby?"

"Of course it's a big deal!" Lilly snapped, offended.

"The baby was implanted. It wasn't that creep's baby. The baby is normal, but its placenta isn't."

Lilly frowned. "Are you saying that horrid man's connected to the people above? That he drugged me and had me implanted?" She shook her head in disbelief. "Are you serious?"

"Yes," Ox said. "The placenta was designed to feed me. The baby is a waste product."

"What a disgusting thing to say!"

"None-the-less, he is being cared for."

"How do you know? They've probably killed him. Either that, or he's part of some sicko science experiment."

"He's not ... babies are worth money. He'll be fine."

"Oh, of course, I forgot ... it's only me that's garbage!" Lilly spat out. "How stupid of me!"

"Not to me, Baby," Ox said, rubbing her back. "You're not garbage to me."

Lilly groaned. "This placenta ... organ. Will it come out in time?"

"No. It will keep on keeping on."

Lilly rubbed her brow. "Daddy, how can you be adapted to feeding from my kind, from a placenta in a human female's womb if this placenta was genetically engineered and a normal placenta would be expelled after a woman gives birth?"

Ox rubbed his nose.

"And … how can a placenta change itself so radically? How did it suddenly become a lung-type structure?"

"Part of it didn't change at all. A placenta's main function is to collect nutrients from the body. The parts of the placenta that were no longer required dissolved. When a caterpillar transforms into a butterfly, it dissolves itself into a soup and uses its dissolved tissue to rapidly grow tiny, immature adult structures to transform itself. The placenta did the same thing, except it rapidly grew tiny, immature lung-type structures as its tissue cloned yours. Your new placenta-organ milks your body of goodness and produces special enzymes and proteins."

"Well, that's very ingenious, but isn't that light years ahead of man's bio-engineering technical abilities?"

"His known abilities … yes."

"Okay … Say I accept that man has developed something as clever as this," Lilly said, still feeling her swollen belly. "It still doesn't explain how you've adapted to feeding from it. How can you be adapted to feeding from a biologically engineered placenta … it doesn't make sense."

"It does," Ox said. "You just don't have all the information … yet."

Lilly's eyes narrowed. "What aren't you telling me?"

"All in good time … Relax. Let me love you. Let me take care of you."

"You don't love me! You need me!"

"Love is need … It's the very embodiment of the word. Examine anyone's claim of love. What they're really saying is, 'Such and such fulfills my needs.'"

"What about the love one has for their child?" Lilly said. "Isn't that pure love?"

"There's no such thing as 'pure love,' rather, needs and

hormonally induced desires. Children fulfill emotional needs in their parents. The hormone oxytocin helps a mother bond with her newborn baby. A woman produces copious amounts of it when she gives birth. It also stimulates milk production. It's called the love drug because it's also released during orgasm."

"Do you want me to love you ... need you?"

"You already do. I'm meeting your needs and getting you to release significant amounts of oxytocin. Not to mention that your system was flooded with it from giving birth when we first met ... You have feelings for me."

Lilly wondered if oxytocin did, indeed, explain her behavior—her strange acceptance of a huge Bigfoot. Had it aided him? "You're pretty sure of yourself there, Ox."

"Absolutely. You're totally dependent on me. I'm your food, your warmth, and your bed. All you need do is put my nipple in your mouth, and I'm your everything. Be patient with yourself. Let your mind adjust."

She groaned.

"I'm growing on you, aren't I?"

"You're not growing on me!" Lilly snapped, unable to help it. "I'm entombed in you!"

"Always with the drama," Ox said nonchalantly. "You're not entombed in me. I'm keeping you warm. Did you know ... womb and tomb used to mean the same thing?"

"No. I didn't know, and who gives a shit!"

Ox cleared his throat. "You will love me and worship me as your god. You say these words now, but you'll come to mean them."

Lilly scoffed. "You're not even a member of my species. It's hardly as if I'm going to fall head over heels in love with you!"

"You don't realize what you're up against," Ox said. "You called me a parasite before ... if you replace that word with another, you'll get a handle on your predicament."

"Predator! Is that the right word?"

"Yes, and what do all predators have in common?"

"Specialist ways of hunting their prey?"

"There you go ... and you're my prey. My kind has been hunting your kind for the longest time. I'm designed for the job."

"You didn't hunt me!"

"No, I didn't … My kind are smarter than that. We get your kind to just give us women."

Lilly rolled her eyes. "Look … the dummies upstairs only gave me to you to see what would happen. Humans are curious like that."

"Really?"

"Yes. Really!" Big stupid Bigfoot.

"So, that's why it's a long-established practice, then?"

Lilly frowned. "No, it's not … is it?"

"Get some sleep, Baby."

CHAPTER EIGHT

The beat of a different drum

Life in the pouch was becoming routine for Lilly, when she woke, Ox relaxed his pouch and lowered his head to greet her. Day after day she poked her nose out to test the air, and day after day she tucked back down, the air freezing. Today, however, was different, there was no chill in the air.

"It's not nippy in here," she said. "What a relief!"

"How are you feeling? Are you starting to adapt ... feel comfortable with me?"

"I've surrendered if that's what you're asking? You've broken me in like a horse!"

"Well, that was sour."

Lilly shrugged her shoulders. It was true enough, she did as she was told and to make matters worse, as bitter as she felt about it, she was finding it harder and harder to suppress her growing feelings for Ox.

"I haven't broken you in like a horse," he said. "I've shown you a different way of being ... a new life."

"Oh, flower it up all you like! You said you own me. Said I belong to you and I'll do as I'm told, and I do."

"What's wrong with being in love with someone and wanting to please them?"

"I'm *not* in love! You and I are different. We march to the beat of a different drum."

"Do we indeed?"

"Yes," Lilly said as music flooded into the cave. 'Different Drum,' by Linda Ronstadt had begun to play. Lilly shook her head in stunned disbelief. *How could anybody search out a song title that quickly?* She sang along with the words because it was, after all, one of her favorite songs and she hadn't heard it in a while.

"Very nice," Ox said as the song ended. "But the feeling isn't mutual. Besides, I don't know why you're even bothered. You've only changed handlers ... moved from one set of owners to another. You know every citizen is an asset of the nation they reside in?"

"That's as maybe, but they weren't sticking a snake-like probe up my arse now, were they?"

"Are you still banging on about that? You like my probe."

"I'm used to it is all."

Ox gave Lilly a knowing look. "You've been sacrificed. All of humanity learns about sacrifice."

"Nonsense! I know nothing of it."

"Yes, you do. War teaches nations to accept the sacrificial offerings of the few to save the many. If you lose a war, chances are you'll also lose your freedoms and basic rights, and you'll likely be dominated and controlled by others. The Bible teaches you sacrifice is required. Sacrifice is man's most fundamental lesson."

"You're saying ... offering up sacrifices to preserve the greater good, is humanity's core lesson?"

"Yes," Ox said. "There's always been a need for it, and there always will be. Instruction on it is given to all of humanity. Your oldest religious texts instruct, sacrifice is not only important, it is essential. Consider what is written in the book of the Hindus, in the Sathapatha Brahmana:

> *It is through sacrifice that man reaches heaven.*

> *By means of sacrifice, not only men, but gods acquire immortality.*"

"I'm not a Hindu," Lilly said dryly.

"Your religion also requires sacrifice. Christ was sacrificed for the greater good ... was he not?"

Lilly shrugged. "What do you think people will say when they find out their leaders have been handing over women to your kind? Do you think they'll just say, 'Righty-ho?'"

"They accept men going to war and dying to preserve their way of life."

Lilly frowned. "Are our leaders really in the habit of handing women over to your kind...? That can't be right."

"Of course it's right."

"Listen ... if they're keeping it a secret, they know people won't accept it."

"It's only a secret for now," Ox said. "But that will change."

"When will it change?"

"Soon." Ox ran a tender finger down Lilly's back. "I could make life more bearable for you."

"How?"

"Close your eyes and let your mind go blank. It'll help if I close my pouch."

Ox drew Lilly back down into his pouch with a ripple of his muscles like she was on a conveyor belt with some added suction, then he closed his pouch.

Lilly groaned, finding Ox's prowess over her body most disturbing. After taking a few deep breaths, she closed her eyes. Visions of the cave flickered in her mind's eye. *What am I seeing ... a memory of the cave?*

"No," Ox said, his voice popping into her head as if it were a thought of her own. "I'm opening up a channel between us. My probe is like a placenta, it latches onto your system and links us together. I exchange carbon dioxide for oxygen for you. When you're asleep and my pouch is sealed, you almost stop breathing. A casual observer would be forgiven for thinking you were dead."

"Now you're really freaking me out!" Lilly said internally. "You're talking to me in my head? I stop breathing when I sleep? We can communicate telepathically?"

"Yes ... The big stupid Bigfoot has been reading your mind."

What the fuck?

"You swear a lot."

Lilly groaned. "For years I tried to be a better person. I tried to fit into upper society, but now who cares? Do you care?"

"No."

Lilly sighed. "Constantly trying to keep up appearances and be the person other people thought I should be was draining." The cave came into sharper focus for Lilly as the image stabilized.

Ox looked around so she could see the cave from his perspective. "When our nervous systems are linked via the probe, your brain is constantly communicating with mine. I'm teaching you how to use my eyes. When you've mastered this skill you won't feel so imprisoned. If your mind tells me via the natural impulse you use to control your own eyes, to look left I'll usually do so. I'll always have master control, but unless I need to override you, I'll let you see what you want to see; thus my eyes will become your eyes."

"Your vision is sharper than mine in this low light."

"My eyes are better than yours in many ways."

"Really?"

"I can see clearly underwater, something you can't manage without goggles."

Lilly stared at the large expanse of blue-green water in front of them. "It's a shame the water's too cold for you to give me a demonstration."

Ox walked to the water's edge. "With you inside of me keeping me warm, I can go into the water."

Lilly's heart pounded. "Will I be all right?"

"You'll be fine, my pouch is designed to keep water out and insulate you from the cold."

"Isn't the water freezing?"

"No."

"But you said—"

Ox waded into the water and dove under. Lilly was immediately mesmerized by the diversity of life in the water.

"It's incredible under here, Daddy. I'm amazed how much better you can see in this dark water than I can—I'd be blind as a bat."

"I know."

"We've been sleeping beside another world ... a beautiful world."

"I'm pleased you like it because I enjoy swimming."

"The variety of life in this water is astounding. You're amazing, Daddy. I see why the people upstairs want to study and save your kind. How long can you remain underwater?"

"About five minutes."

"I love it down here?" Lilly said. "This world has never been open to me before. Well ... not without a heavy oxygen tank, at least." She spotted a spiny lobster. "Hey, look ... a crayfish!"

The crayfish scurried away on long scaly orange legs before disappearing under a rock.

"So, it was."

"Stick your hand under that rock and grab it."

"No, I'm not going to ... *grab it.*"

"Why not?" Lilly said. "Crayfish taste good."

"Do you want to eat it raw?"

"Daddy—"

"Yes?"

"You've been telling fibs!"

"Have I?"

"That was a crayfish," Lilly said, "and look, another. We're not in Antarctica. We're in New Zealand. Crayfish don't live in Antarctica."

"Do they not? Well ... there's no fooling you."

"Are we on the West coast, aren't we? There are glow-worms in here. I should have realized."

"We're on the West Coast of New Zealand. I can't tell you exactly where we are, but we're near Fox Glacier."

"Are we in Fiordland?"

Continuing on with his underwater safari, Ox didn't answer.

"Why did you lie to me and tell me we were in Antarctica? Did you want me to feel vulnerable and cling to you?"

"Yes."

"That was naughty, Daddy."

"I didn't want you to hurt yourself in some half-baked escape attempt."

"And you think I won't try to escape now?"

"You're not going anywhere and you know it."

Lilly groaned. "So, this water isn't freezing?"

"No, it's refreshing. I like to swim. I often swim when you're asleep." Ox headed for the shore. After wading out of the water, he shook his fur.

Lilly was too happy to be mad. She was still in her homeland and her adventure under the water had made her heart sing. "Daddy, you're blessed with an amazing body."

"So are you. I want nothing more than to share my body with you."

Lilly felt relaxed and content. Tired, she suckled on Ox's nipple and closed her eyes.

"Sweetie, can you suck my nipple in a little further ... draw it down your throat?"

Lilly frowned. "What?"

"A human nipple goes down a baby's throat past its gag reflex, and babies don't gag. You won't either."

"You're scaring me."

"Don't be alarmed," Ox soothed. "Try it."

Lilly drew in his nipple a little further than usual. It immediately animated and shot down her throat. Shocked, she panicked. She hadn't gagged but his tube was right down her throat. She tried to talk but was unable. She tried to pull away but Ox's pouch held her firm.

"Relax," Ox said. "You're getting an anti-gag agent from me. My nipple tube is narrow and designed for its job. It will sit comfortably down your throat and feed you while you're asleep without interrupting your breathing. When I have my nipple tube down your throat and my anal probe up your arse, I'm breathing for you, so there's no need to panic. This will all feel normal soon enough. Your body is adapting to being with me. When you wake, I'll remove my nipple tube. In the meantime, you can talk to me in your head."

Tears welled in Lilly's eyes. "It's scaring me!"

"You're okay, Baby. I'm feeding you. You need a lot of food. Relax. Get some sleep."

Lilly inhaled a few deep breaths. Ox was right, she could breathe easily. After her pulse settled and the familiar wave of exhaustion flooded over her, she closed her eyes. Ox's nipple tube was strangely comforting and intimate. *Am I losing my mind?*

CHAPTER NINE

The Savannah Theory

Lilly yawned and wiped away sleep dust from her eyes. Ox's pouch was open and relaxed, and the air warm. "What a relief," she said, stretching out.

"They're giving us a reprieve from the cold," Ox said as he propelled Lilly forward and upwards with his pouch muscles; her upper body emerging for the first time in weeks. She wrapped her arms wide around him and sighed. Ox lay upon a huge oak bed covered in a multi-skinned fur, his head propped up on an enormous pillow. Beside the bed was an Ox-sized armless wooden chair. It was also made of oak.

"It's lovely to see you, Baby," he said as he ran tender fingers down her spine. "Do you like our bedroom?"

"Did the men upstairs bring the furniture down?"

"Yes, they've decided to treat us."

"How generous," Lilly said with the barest hint of sarcasm. "It's cozier in here with a bed. It was a nice gift."

"My thoughts exactly."

Lilly studied the fur on the bed. "Wow, it's a nice fur."

"Nothing but the best for you, my love."

"Isn't it for you. I sleep inside of you."

"You're designed to live in a Bigfoot."

Lilly groaned. "Surely, I'm not *designed* to?"

"Has it ever occurred to you how odd it is that you're a mammal and yet you have no adaptation to keep your heat in, like a fur coat? When it's a primary requirement for all other mammals? Don't you think it's more than a little odd that people have to wear clothes?"

"We came from Africa. When we moved out of the forests and onto the savannah, we ditched our fur coats because they were too hot."

"The Savannah Theory is nonsense. It's been disproved and officially dumped."

Lilly frowned. "Really? Nobody told me."

"Why would humans ditch their fur coat when no other animal has ever felt the need to do so...? In the nineties, paleontologists' looked at the microfauna and herbivores that lived at the same time, and in the same place as early hominids, and they weren't savannah species. They also analyzed the fossilized pollen found with early humans, and it wasn't savannah vegetation. Your ancestors were running around in the forest long before the savannah ecosystem even existed. They lived beside monkeys covered in fur in the bush."

Lilly's brow rose. "Maybe, I should have been reading *Time* magazine or *National Geographic?*"

"You're designed to live in me: you're my little lamp within. Once you grasp this, much of what you thought to be true and correct will be brought into question."

Lilly frowned. "I'm designed to let my heat out?"

"A typical human sitting in a room of average temperature generates around 100 watts of heat, it flows into the surrounding air. Energy, as heat, flows from a higher temperature to a lower temperature; the greater the differential, the faster the flow. My body doesn't need to generate much heat because you're warming me."

"But when I was cold, I climbed into you and your pouch was warm."

"I can warm my own body, or I can economize by using yours."

"Surely, if I'm warm and in a warm environment, I'm not releasing any heat? And if that's true, how do I warm you?"

"My body draws heat away from you. If it didn't, you'd overheat. I release any excess heat into the environment. I, like you, can sweat."

"Do you suffer when it's hot?"

"Bigfoots aren't desert dwellers. We live in temperate environments, preferring mountainous regions. If we do get hot, we cool down by letting our pouches hang open, or by taking a dip."

"So, you're not only feeding off me, you're also stealing my heat!"

"We're a duet ... We pool our resources. You give me energy in the form of heat and food, and in return, I keep you warm and feed you."

Lilly blinked several times. "I can't believe the quote by Morpheus in the *Matrix* movie is actually true! The human body generates bioelectricity and BTU's of heat and combined with a form of fusion, the machines had found all the energy they would ever need.'"

"Except we're not machines, of course. Did you notice they never explained the fusion? They just threw that out there. However, if you looked closely at the beetle machine that released Neo from his matrix pod, you could see a human pod encapsulated in its belly."

"You're talking about perpetual energy? Surely, there's a leak in the circuit that needs to be replenished?"

"Do you think any woman could hop into my pouch and fulfill your role?"

Lilly's eyes narrowed. *Is he changing the subject?* She shrugged her shoulders. "I guess?"

"Wrong."

"Really?"

"What did I tell you about the placenta?" Ox quizzed.

"That its tissue assimilated with mine and it has the same blood type as me ... Are Bigfoots like humans, they have different blood types?"

"No, we all have the same blood type ... your blood type."

"The genetically engineered placenta inside of me still doesn't make sense to me ... You're not telling me something."

Ox ran tender fingers through Lilly's hair. "You're so cute."

Lilly exhaled loudly. "Why can't I read your mind like you can mine? Why can I only hear the thoughts you project?"

"You don't have a protective barrier like I do. I need to know what you're thinking."

"So you can control me?"

"No, so I can take better care of you. Humans are very secretive, often not articulating their concerns. I need to know where your head's at."

"I think you're the secretive one!"

Sitting up, Ox grasped hold of Lilly. Rippling his pouch muscles upwards, he pushed and lifted her out of his pouch in one easy motion. "It's warm enough in here for me to give you a proper wash," he said as he laid her between his legs on the bed without extracting his anal probe. His luscious tongue started licking her all over while his probe suckled on her bowel within to relax her.

When Ox wanted Lilly to sleep, she tired quickly and fell asleep within minutes. To achieve this, Lilly thought he secreted a drug into her bowel. As her breathing deepened, she wondered if he was currently secreting a different drug—an aphrodisiac.

After carefully changing position, so he was kneeling on the bed behind her, Ox extracted his urethra probe from within Lilly's bladder and began suckling on her clitoris with it while seductively licking behind an ear.

She moaned and rolled her head back. Oh god, I'm ashamed of how I'm responding.

"Relax, Baby," Ox said telepathically. "Let yourself go."

Lilly's breathing deepened as Ox started rhythmically moving his anal probe back and forth in her anus while simultaneously making it fatter and fatter. Then, when she was about to climax, he removed his anal probe and inserted his penis. Her anus pulsated rhythmically on his manly member as she came. Omitting a deep, primal groan while gripping her hips gently, but firmly, Ox climaxed with her. After a few moments, he withdrew his penis and reinserted his probe.

Lilly slapped a hand over her eyes. She tried not to think, but it was impossible. She was exposed. Yong had probably seen it all. *I wish the floor would gobble me up!*

After changing position, so he was once again sitting on the bed with Lilly between his legs, Ox scooped her up. He sat her upon his chest as he lay back against the pillow. After drawing the tops of her feet into his mouth, he suckled upon her toes. Lilly quivered as the last shudders of her orgasm were reignited. With a satisfied smile on his face, Ox pushed her bum down and into his pouch. With the aid of a strong downward ripple of his muscles, she slid effortlessly into place.

Her cheeks blazed. Ashamed, she had no words.

"It's all right, Baby," Ox said. "Relax, nobody is judging you. Yong's seen it all countless times before. You're one of many women down here ... Your behavior is perfectly normal."

Finding her tongue, Lilly said, "Really? I'm so ashamed."

"You hurt my feelings when you say things like that. I understand it's your conditioning, but it's hurtful."

"Sorry."

"It's all right, love."

Ox's pouch was chewing on Lilly: like a big mouth delighting on a morsel of food, it moved her about before positioning her more firmly in place.

Powerless to do anything about it, like a child being swept along by a powerful tide, a deep rage ignited in her. "You know, Ox, it's rude to go straight for anal," she fumed.

"I wasn't trying to impregnate you. I was feeding you. Your body absorbs liquid food in your bowel, not in your vagina."

Lilly groaned. "When you first offered to feed me from your body, I thought you wanted me to drink your sperm. I was relieved to be wrong, but now I see I was right ... that *was* your intention all along!"

Ox ran tender fingers through her hair. "It's okay to give me pleasure ... When you love someone, it's normal."

"Having a beast's cock up your arse is not normal!"

"Baby, if you're having a moment of personal conflict, and you're struggling to cope with it, don't project your inner chastising onto me. You knew I was prepping you for my penis. Don't pretend you didn't, and don't deny how deeply satisfying you found my big cock."

"It was all kinds of wrong! You had no right to do that! I'm surprised you didn't split me in two. You're absolutely *huge* in comparison to me."

"I told you I was made to go with you. My cock isn't much bigger than the average human male's penis."

"That's no excuse! You still shouldn't have done it. It was

despicable! The grossest thing I could ever imagine!"

"When are you going to get it into your head, you no longer exist! You're part of my body, and I'm recycling myself through you— including the goodness in my sperm. They've deleted you from the book of life ... put a line through your name!"

"Wow, that was cold!" Lilly said fighting back tears. "What a hideous thing to say!"

Ox sighed. "You hurt my feelings! I gave you my loving attention and you threw it back in my face."

Lilly groaned and buried her face in his fur. "Oh God, I've become a Bigfoot's whore ... the shame!"

"No, you haven't," Ox snapped. "You're not getting paid."

"Oh, yeah, thanks ... you're right. I'm not getting paid. I'm a victim of people smuggling!"

"Calm down. Everything's all right. Daddy didn't hurt you. He gave you a much needed feed ... You'll feel better in the morning."

"Stop talking about yourself in the third person, and don't patronize me! You stuck your cock up my arse to please you! It wasn't for my benefit, it was for yours!"

"Your moral indignation is falling on deaf ears. You wanted it and you enjoyed it ... a lot."

Lilly looked down. "I couldn't help it."

"I enjoyed it too, Baby," Ox said sweetly. "I like feeding you, and as it so happens, I especially like feeding you with my big cock."

"*As it so happens!*" Lilly parroted sarcastically.

"Stop focusing on the negative and look toward the positive."

"What positive! That I'm not *actually* dead? Or is it that you love me and you want to take care of me?"

"Both. You could choose to see yourself as lucky and special."

"Ha. Doubt it. I'm too old and cynical to indulge in that kind of fantasy!" Lilly buried her face. How had it come to this? When she first entered the cave, she thought Ox was a big stupid lug despite his obvious ability to converse. Now she realized he was smart and he'd pulled a number on her. Slowly, but surely he'd encroached upon her personal space to such an extent, he now felt comfortable sticking his big cock up her arse and not apologizing.

Lilly wondered if this made her stupid, or had she been in a losing position from the beginning, the result inevitable? She felt her swollen belly. She could feel the placenta from inside and out. It was a foreign body within that she was fast adjusting to.

Currently, she looked and felt about five months pregnant. When Ox probed her womb it contracted in size and afterwards she hardly looked pregnant at all. She thought about the strange organ within that filled and emptied like a lung. After drawing in a long liquid breath, it waited for its master to draw food out of it.

Was he her master? Lilly decided he was. He controlled her completely, even reading her thoughts. Was he reading them now? Did he know the placenta felt full and its building pressure was strangely pleasurable? Was it playing tricks on her mind, making her enjoy its expansion? Did her body perceive a child within? When she ran her hands over her belly, she enjoyed the feel of its smooth, swollen contour.

Ox kissed the top of her head. "How about I wait a while before I empty you? I'll let you enjoy that building pressure a bit longer."

So, he is reading my mind. Lilly exhaled loudly. "It is strangely pleasurable. Aren't you hungry?"

"I can wait," Ox said as he lifted and pushed Lilly out of his pouch in a smooth motion. He turned her around on his knee. "I love your belly. The sight of you stroking it would please me so," he said, running tender fingers over it.

"I bet it would!" Lilly said sourly.

"Don't be like that. The placenta pleases us both. It's only right we should enjoy it."

Ox rubbed a big hand over Lilly's belly. She closed her eyes and leaned back. The building pressure and his gentle rubbing was highly pleasurable. She moaned. It was hard to resent something that delighted her senses so. Almost by instinct, she pushed her belly out into his hand, to both enjoy his touch more and to give her womb room to expand.

"Good girl," Ox cooed as he rubbed her belly more firmly to heighten her pleasure.

CHAPTER TEN

Conspiracy theorist

Lilly briefly opened her eyes in response to Ox rubbing her back through his pouch's outer wall.

"How are you feeling?" he asked telepathically.

"I'm still sleepy, Daddy."

"There's no need to wake. We can communicate in your dreamy state."

"Really?"

"Yes, we're doing it now … Relax, Baby."

"I love you, Daddy," Lilly murmured contentedly.

"I know, sweetie. I love you too."

The thud of Ox's footsteps, and the associated motion that pulsed through his body as he walked rocked Lilly, and it heightened the pleasure her swollen womb was currently giving her. She sighed. "Daddy, I don't like the external world anymore, everyone is so judgemental. It's such a horrid, harsh place … so tiring."

"You can rest in me, in my room. Shut that nasty old world out."

"I do feel safe in you."

"Good, that's how you're meant to feel … Did you understand your society, Baby?"

"I didn't think about it much till I came here. At first, I really missed it, but now I'm not so sure."

"You missed the benefits of membership, like being able to ring the emergency services for help, but now you're thinking more critically about it?"

"Yes. I always felt pressure at work. The Ministry of Education was so demanding, and at home, Matthew and my kids thought my life should revolve around them. And the TV and church told me what I should think and believe."

Ox nodded. "That's right, because society is more than a safety net—it's a control system."

"I didn't get that till my life crashed and burned. I tried to live by the rules ... I did. I wanted to be a valuable member of society. I was a member of my church, a teacher, a headmistress, and a good wife and loving mother. Correction: apparently, I wasn't a good wife or mother. Supposedly, I neglected my wifely duties, and Matthew thought I competed with him. He thought I hungered for external praise when I should've been happy with the love he and the kids provided."

"Do you wish you'd played it differently?"

"I don't know," Lilly shrugged. "All I know is ... the longer I'm away from society, the longer I want to be away. I was rude to you yesterday because I had society's rules playing in my ears like a broken record. I was imagining what people would say and think if they knew what I'd done. I could see their judgemental eyes and hear their scorn."

"I know."

Lilly shook her head as if she was trying to shake off society's influence. "Daddy, you make me feel safe. You didn't hurt me, and you're right, you did pleasure me. I shouldn't care what people would think and say if they knew what I've done ... how they'd look down on me. They'd expect me to claw my way out of here and run back to them with tales of woe, and speak ill of the big, bad monster that lives in the basement of a government facility."

"That would earn you a bullet."

Lilly nodded. "I know because society is controlled by governments who lie and run secret programs."

"Indeed it is ... Do you know how the control system works ... how it's held in place? Why people don't buck the system and make it crash?"

Lilly blinked several times. "No?"

"What happens if you start to see society itself as villainous? View the government as an enemy?"

"You're labeled a crazy conspiracy theorist, or a loon. You might even be locked up if you're too vocal."

"The first line of attack would come from your family and friends," Ox said. "They've been conditioned from birth to believe the worst thing that one can be is crazy. Not accepting society's rules makes you a reject.

People turn their backs on non-conforming members of society, even if they're family. Humans are essentially herd animals: they follow the herd and can't bear to be separated—separation is like death to them. They'd rather turn their backs on rogue members of their own family than be rejected themselves. People hunger for the rewards they get from playing by the rules. Acceptance and respect is an addictive drug to them ... just like it was to you."

"Yes, it was," Lilly said. "If my womb was cut out of me and I returned home, I could never discuss what's happened here. Not even with my closest friends because they'd be disgusted. If they didn't openly say cruel things to my face, they'd sure as hell say them behind my back. They may hang around initially to get all the gory details, then, odds are, they'd mock me and reject me ... They'd think I'd lost my mind."

"And if you went to the media with your story they wouldn't run it. Similarly, if you told the police, they'd roll their eyes and call a doctor who'd likely admit you to a nuthouse."

"Well, I don't want to run back to them anyway! I don't think any of them cared about me ... not really ... not even my kids."

"Put them out of your mind."

Lilly couldn't see where Ox was going because he had his eyes switched off to her. She thought he was doing a quick lap around the beach, but he'd been walking for too long now. "Where are we?" she said. "Are we still in the cave?"

"No," Ox said. "I'm getting some exercise and sunlight."

"You can leave the cave!"

"I can, yes. I like to walk in the bush."

"You're outside?" Lilly said, excited. "Let me see!"

Ox opened the ocular channel between them so she could see the native bush surrounding them.

Observing the bush from Ox's perspective, from his great height, Lilly saw dramatic glacial peaks, sparkling waterfalls, and a forest filled with tree ferns and orchids. She was sure they were in Fiordland's national park, within the 1.2 million hectares of majestic uninhabited wilderness at the bottom of the South Island. A World Heritage site filled with lakes. Lilly had always wanted to visit the area. She'd dreamed of glimpsing the rare, prehistoric-looking bird called a kakapo—a large, flightless, green parrot.

The sound of a branch snapping under one of Ox's huge feet made Lilly realize she wasn't only using his eyes, she was also using his ears. Not far off, she could hear the squawking of a kea: a noisy green parrot native to New Zealand.

"Open your pouch," she said. "Let me poke my head out."

"I realize you're excited, Baby, but I can't open my pouch ... not even a little. Besides, seeing with my eyes is virtually the same as seeing with yours."

"Are you worried I'll run off?"

"No, I have a firm hold of you. I'm concerned there may be a remote hunter about, even though it's not likely because we have surveillance cameras sprinkled throughout this bush. Even so, I can't take that gamble. A deerstalker might have slipped through with a mobile phone—camera at the ready. If a hunter got a photo of me, that would be bad, but you and me ... disastrous."

"Wouldn't it be worse if he shot you?"

Ox "ticked" his tongue. "That goes without saying."

"I want to feel the breeze on my face."

"Have you forgotten that sand flies and mosquitos down here are as big as sparrows?"

"Oh, that's right," Lilly said, knowing Ox was exaggerating. The bugs weren't literally the size of small birds, but they *were* plentiful and huge. "On second thoughts, I think I prefer to view the bush with your eyes. It's probably cold out there anyway."

"Good, because walking with you in my arms, or facing forward in my pouch, is more difficult for me. I'm designed to carry you facing inwards."

Lilly frowned. "I'm a burden?"

"Not at all. I can sprint with you on board, but not when you're in your current, relaxed position because you're altering my center of gravity ... it makes running more difficult."

"Can you run as fast as a human?"

"I could outrun any human. I run much faster."

"Really? You seem so bulky."

"Don't be fooled," Ox said. "Running may not be my usual speed, but if need be, I can cover a lot of ground quickly. When I do, I clamp my pouch muscles shut and pull my baby up under my ribs. This is both uncomfortable and distressing for a baby, so I send it off to sleep."

"You do?"

"It's a natural Bigfoot reflex. The moment I clamp my pouch shut, I involuntarily release a large dose of a knockout drug via my main probe—my anal probe. This renders a baby unconscious in seconds and allows me to concentrate on getting to safety ... My body naturally protects and takes care of a baby, even when I'm distracted."

"So, you wouldn't ditch me to save your own skin."

"No. Never. I wouldn't intentionally fight with a baby on board, but it's better to do so than put it down and leave it exposed."

"Well, that's comforting I suppose. Are you likely to get into a fight?"

"No, and a fight between a human and me is not a fight at all. I can easily kill a man with a single blow."

Lilly frowned. "I thought you were a prisoner locked up in a pen."

"I need exercise like any humanoid. I have access to a large unfenced outdoor area."

"So, we are in Fiordland ... in Milford Sound?"

"Yes. We're miles off the beaten track."

"I've reconsidered," Lilly said. "I'd like to get some sun on my skin. Get some vitamin D."

"I'm your sun. I'm supplying you with vitamin D."

"None-the-less, it would be nice to feel the sun on my skin. It's a lovely day, Daddy."

"I'm sorry, Baby, but I can't risk it."

Lilly gasped. "What about your footprints!"

"It's okay. I wear special boots to disguise them. The souls have a mixture of shapes on them to break up the outline of my footprint, and the grounds hard at the moment."

"What do your boots look like?"

"Furry ugg boots. I pull them on. The fur on the outside is a synthetic version of my own fur. When I have them on, you can hardly tell." Ox looked down at his feet so Lilly could see his boots.

"I don't suppose anybody would suspect that," she said. "I think people who believe in Bigfoot, think he's stupid because he's covered in fur. They overlook the fact that you're a humanoid species and write you off as a creature. Then there's the rest of the population who think you're a myth, or the imaginings of fools."

"That's because media programming has been very effective in brainwashing people's minds. In the television series *Harry and the Hendersons*, Harry was a Bigfoot found in an American forest; his head was ape shaped and he had limited intelligence. Thus, people have been programmed to believe if Bigfoot does exist, he's likely slow and stupid ... People watch television programs without considering they're being brainwashed. They think the idiot box provides them with news and mindless entertainment, but that isn't its primary purpose. The foremost objective of the broadcasting corporations is to project a daily brainwashing syllabus into the homes and minds of the masses. The public education system has a similar objective: preschools, schools, and universities are government-controlled brainwashing facilities."

"I was a teacher," Lilly said. "So, how is it I didn't know this?"

"You weren't supposed to notice ... People are trained from birth to turn a blind eye, and conditioned to fear labels like 'paranoid' or 'schizophrenic.' The masses turn a blind eye to government agendas beyond the next budget because the hordes don't want to be labeled crazy or delusional ... Nothing is true unless it's announced on the six o'clock news."

"That's overstating it," Lilly said. "A lot of people believe in aliens and government conspiracies. They're the subject of many a film."

"Those films always have an element of the ridiculous about

them. In general, they don't encourage belief, but rather, disbelief. They also spread disinformation. If people do buy into the theory, their eyes are diverted from what's really going on. For example, people are busy looking for little gray aliens flying around in spaceships, when no such creature exists. The real action is going on under their feet. The cattle's minds are also deliberately swamped with work, family obligations, religion, consumerism, video games, music, television, and movies."

"Cattle? Is that what they call us?"

"That or sheep ... Your enemy is strong."

Unable to concentrate any longer, Lilly shrugged as her focus shifted to their glorious surroundings. "It's a good thing you're not an abominable snowman. You'd stand out like a sore toe in this environment."

"You're the one who needs to be white."

"Me? Why?"

"Pale skin like yours: skin so pale it almost glows in the dark, is thinner than other skin types and it expels more heat. It also has lower light requirements which allows you to receive sufficient vitamin D when you're living in my pouch ... You're perfectly adapted to living in another."

"But you're not letting me see the sun at all," Lilly grizzled.

"The lighting in the cave is specially designed to give you what you need, and, as I said, your requirements are minimal. When you're with me, they're practically non-existent."

"Are you saying you only feed off Caucasians?"

"Yes," Ox said. "The other races have nothing to fear from us. Our culinary tastes are very refined. We also require rhesus negative blood, which, although reasonably common among white people, is rare to non-existent in the other races."

"You prey on Caucasians? Wow, that's some news!"

"Hence, why our existence's a secret."

"The whole world would love to know about Bigfoot. It's wrong to keep a fellow humanoid a secret, especially one as wonderful as you."

"I think you're going a bit fuzzy in the head there, Baby.

Caucasians would be horrified, not delighted."

"Is that why all the workers at the facility are either Asian or Indian?"

"It's helpful if the people working with you don't identify too closely."

"Daddy! I was beginning to feel comfortable with you, but now you're upsetting me!"

"Try to stay focused on the positive. There are many positives to your situation."

"Like what!"

"I can't tell you right now, but there are."

Ox retraced his steps to the cave. As he neared its entrance, he switched off the channel between them.

CHAPTER ELEVEN

Lilly's eyes grow heavy

Back in the confines of the warm cave once more, Ox sat down on his enormous oak chair. After propelling Lilly up and out of his pouch, he gently set her down on his knee, her back to his stomach. He placed a big hand on her swollen abdomen. Giving it a firm rub, he said, "Your belly's gorgeous, Baby."

Lilly sighed and moaned. "I don't know about that. I look like I'm about five months pregnant, but I really like it when you rub my tummy. It feels nice, Daddy."

"Bellies like yours are the most wondrous thing in the universe. I want to pleasure you by rubbing it and stroking it. I want to admire it and hold it in my hands."

"That's nice."

Ox leaned over Lilly to gently kiss her abdomen. "I want to kiss it and rub precious oils into it, and onto your delicious breasts." He reached down and picked up a jar of oil. After pouring a little onto Lilly's belly, he rubbed it in with his long fingers.

"That feels nice," Lilly said. "Where did you get the oil from?"

"A man from upstairs came down while you were sleeping. He left it here for you as a special treat."

"Really? I don't trust the men upstairs," Lilly said, but she let Ox continue to rub oil in. "How come it's so warm in here? It's positively balmy … Only a few days ago, the air was bone-chillingly cold."

"You've been a good girl, so the people upstairs have turned up the heating. If you continue to be agreeable, the heating will stay on."

Lilly groaned. "The creeps upstairs will stop at nothing to get their own way."

Every few minutes, Ox poured more oil onto Lilly's belly and rubbed it in. Her eyes grew heavy and her contented moaning deepened till it more closely resembled a cat's purr, then she fell asleep.

◆ ◆ ◆

Minutes later, the elevator dinged and opened. Two young Arab men dressed in long linen shorts stepped out. They made their way to Ox dragging a stretcher laden with equipment behind them.

"It's good to see you, Cat," Ox said quietly to one of the pair.

"How's it going?" Cat replied in an equally subdued tone.

"Good. She's a delight."

"So, I see … This is Kumea, my new trainee." Cat said gesturing to his companion.

"Nice to meet you," Ox said.

"Right," Cat said. "Let's get on with it … time's a ticking."

"You'll be careful with her," Ox said, quietly.

Cat grinned. "Of course. I'm always careful with the merchandise."

Ox placed Lilly's lightly unconscious body onto the stretcher and stepped away.

Cat looked her over. "Nice wee bunny you have here. She's got lovely breasts … nice and full."

Ox beamed like a proud father.

Kumea sucked on one of Lilly's nipples to harden it and draw it out, then he applied a little milking cup to it. After doing the same to the other nipple, he turned on a milking machine under the stretcher. Milk squirted out of Lilly's breasts in little bursts and flowed down clear tubes into a glass urn below. Standing on either side of Lilly, the men each raised one of her knees so her heels touched her bottom, then let her knees fall gently outwards. They positioned her in the pose a woman assumes when having her genitals examined by a doctor.

Cat thoroughly examined Lilly's vagina and then her anus. "I see you've been careful with her," he said. "She's in good shape."

"Of course," Ox said, almost offended, "but it's not all my doing. Her husband primed her for me. He did a good job."

"Well, that's a bonus," Cat said. "She likes anal?"

"Yes. She doesn't want to admit it, but she does."

"I watched on the monitor. She took your big cock first time without a grizzle ... What a champ."

Ox shrugged. "I was careful to prepare her properly ... she was fully open. I didn't hurt her, but none-the-less, she complained bitterly afterwards."

"You've masterful technique, no doubt about it ... I was impressed."

"I'm guessing her husband is well hung, much like yourself."

"Don't be modest," Cat said, pointing a playful finger at Ox. "You're the man!"

A smile touched upon the corners of Ox's mouth.

"I thought it would take longer for you to deliver your load," Cat said, tipping an imaginary hat. "You've surprised us all. Training this one is going to be a breeze. Pity they don't all have such obliging, well-hung husbands."

"She's got her hang-ups, and she can be quite gnarly."

"Nothing a bit of growling at won't fix," Cat said confidently, but quietly. "I'm going to enjoy training her."

"I like her," Ox said. "She's got spirit, but not too much."

Cat pulled a long tube out from under the stretcher. It had a special attachment on its end that looked like a thin penis. He pushed it into Lilly's vagina. When tiny cameras embedded in its head showed him he'd positioned it correctly on a handheld monitor, he turned on a pump. Clear liquid flowed from Lilly's vagina in bursts and drained into a second glass urn under the stretcher.

"Look at that," Cat said as he stimulated her clitoris. "Her wine is fair gushing out. She's got good-flow for this early in the piece ... plenty of wine."

"You're pleased with her?" Ox said, his voice brimming with pride.

"I am, yes."

When Lilly's milk stopped flowing, and the last drips of her wine had drained from her womb, Cat turned off the pumps and removed the uterine probe while Kumea detached the milking cups. Cat placed a cap on the narrow-necked glass urns, sealing them shut, then packed up the equipment.

"That didn't take long," Ox said.

Cat grinned. "I don't muck about. I'll return every sixteen hours ... We'll do eight-hour alternate shifts. You feed from her next time. Make sure you delay your feed till her belly's so full it's almost hurting her."

"I know how this works," Ox said. "We'll gradually draw out the time between her milking sessions. Slowly, but surely, we'll make her womb expand to hold more wine."

"That's right," Cat said. "Probe her hard ... make sure you pig out."

Ox smiled. "I don't need any encouragement."

"Good," Cat said. "Continue to make sure she's out of it for me by rubbing in plenty of oil. I want her mind and body to be accustomed to the pumps before I attempt this when she's awake."

"Of course," Ox said as he stepped forward and inserted his main probe. He carefully picked Lilly up and raised her to his shoulder like a precious infant.

Cat and Kumea dragged the stretcher to the elevator leaving wheel tracks in the firm sand as they went.

Ox followed them to the elevator, disturbing the sand as he went, so their tracks were no longer visible. Then he carried Lilly to his chair. Cradling her sleeping body, he whispered, "Even though I know you still think I'm a beast, I love you."

Returning her to his pouch, he positioned her head beside his breast and rubbed her cheek against his nipple. Lilly opened her mouth and drew his nipple in as if by instinct and began to feed. "Good, Baby," Ox cooed as he placed her limp arms on either side of him like she was hugging him, and tenderly stroked one of her arms. "You have beautiful little arms. You're a lovely baby."

♦ ♦ ♦

Upstairs, Cat and Kumea stepped out of the elevator into a luxurious Persian-styled room with a domed ceiling. Warm candlelight glistened from silver filigree lanterns set into niches in the white plastered walls, and large Persian rugs hung on the walls. There was a bench and cupboards on the left, but on the right, a large, luxurious pool with sculptured seats built into its sides adorned the room.

The pair left the stretcher standing awkwardly beside the pool and hopped in. Cat looked at the large screen in front of the pool, it was displaying the scene below. "Love is … a woman and her Bigfoot."

"Yeah, that's sweet," Kumea said.

"It doesn't get much sweeter, but no matter how much of a bitch you may think a baby is, never hurt her. Her Bigfoot's likely to turn on you in a flash and tear you limb from limb."

"I'm sure you're right."

"I most certainly am," Cat said. "This is a dangerous occupation if you're stupid. The boys upstairs will throw your dismembered body into an incinerator without even blinking." Cat reached for one of two glasses standing ready on a tray beside the pool. "Wine?"

CHAPTER TWELVE

No need for guilt

Lilly snuggled into Ox, her head on his shoulder. "I'm so cumbersome!" she said. "I have to turn side-on when you hold me like this because my belly's getting so big, is that normal?"

"Yes." Ox lovingly stroked her swollen white belly with the back of one hand. "Your belly's positively gorgeous, I'm hoping it will swell a bit more yet. You're enjoying its swelling aren't you?"

Lilly sighed, unsure how she felt about it. "But it's burdensome. When I was heavily pregnant, I waddled like a duck and looked like a beached whale."

"I'm sure you're exaggerating ... You don't need to worry about that anyway. I'm your high horse. I carry you."

"What's with this daily oil routine of yours? Why does it send me off to sleep, and why do I wake to find my womb drained? What are you doing to me when I'm asleep?"

Ox's hand was down by his side, by the bottle of oil. He returned his hand to Lilly's belly without picking it up and kissed her brow. "You're all right, love."

Lilly seriously doubted she was all right. Technically she was well, she supposed if that's what he meant. But how could she be all right if she lived in the belly of another and had a foreign organ in her womb? She decided she was definitely *not* all right.

Looking around the cave with a sour pout on her face, she noticed the cave was pristine—the roll of toilet paper gone and the hole covered over. That meant Ox wasn't digging holes to bury his poo. Maybe, he was going in the water, or maybe their symbiotic relationship was so perfect, he wasn't going at all which meant he was feeding her whatever he wasn't using. Lilly shuddered at the thought.

When she first entered the cave, she'd thought her survival was nigh on impossible, and yet here she was, weeks later, alive. She looked at her arms, they weren't skinny. They weren't fat either, but she clearly wasn't losing weight. She should be pleased, happy to be alive, but she wasn't, she was bitter.

Ox stroked her head. "You're all right, Baby."

Lilly groaned. The bastard's reading my thoughts again.

Ox lay her on the bed. He put his head between her legs and licked her clitoris. The pleasing rhythm of his flicking tongue made her forget what she was thinking and he was in her in no time at all. The rocking of her full womb was almost as satisfying as the sex. They came together, then Ox withdrew.

Lilly dreamily opened her eyes, but the sour pout on her face quickly returned. "Oh, God, somebody save me. All I do is sleep, feed, and get fucked by you."

"Ah ... the wonders of life," Ox said. "Don't tell anybody, they'll be jealous."

"Ox! This is not how life is meant to be!"

"Why not? You've never had it so good; no cooking or cleaning. Why are you complaining?"

"What about books ... learning?"

"You've done plenty of that already. There's nothing like a bit of life experience."

"What about my friends and family?"

"Stuff them! You're busy with your new life. You don't have time for their shit."

"Really," Lilly said. "You think I should just forget them?"

"Well, it's not up to you, is it? So, there's no need for guilt."

"Stop it! There should be more to my life than pleasing you."

"Why...? What if I thought like that? What if I said, 'Why am I bothering to take care of her? There should be more to my life than caring for her!' How would that make you feel?"

Lilly groaned. "Not good, I suppose, but that's because I'm

dependent upon you."

"Didn't you willingly become dependent on your husband? Wasn't that something you not only desired but embraced?"

Lilly frowned. "No ... well, maybe." She thought about her mother's plot to land her a wealthy man. She'd brought her lovely dresses and driven her to Matthew's church in an affluent neighborhood every Sunday when she was just eighteen. The plan had worked brilliantly. When Lilly first met Matthew, she wasn't a Christian. When they dated, she attended church with him but behind the scenes, with her mother's encouragement, she was his saucy minx. But when they finally married, she was a Christian and a devout one at that.

Her growing faith put a strain on their relationship. It increasingly causing her to view Matthew as a pseudo-Christian—a fake. After deciding he was a sexual deviant and a bit of a bully in the final years of their marriage, Lilly took on multiple obligations to distance herself from him. "You're right, I suppose, but it sure didn't turn out the way I thought it would."

Ox cleared his throat. "Do you think, maybe, it was you who changed? When you met Matthew, you weren't religious, and you had your heart set on marrying him—"

Lilly groaned. "Okay ... yes, it was me who changed, but there's only so much butt licking a girl can do. After the kids came along and my position was secure, I didn't feel the need to be so obliging, and Matthew's ways and tastes clashed with my growing faith. He kept getting me drunk on a bottle of wine or two and coercing me into yet another round of ... what he liked to call normal sex ... I felt dirty."

"No doubt feminism contributed to your great unhappiness," Ox said. "Women are all confused these days and men have never had it so good. Now women are expected to wash, cook, clean, attend to the kids, *and* hold down a job. Feminism is the cause of infinite misery."

Lilly shrugged. In a moment of clarity, she said, "I don't understand why Europeans are so silly ... Is progress a spiraling divorce rate?"

"Europeans? Tell me, Baby, who do you think is running your lands?"

Lilly frowned. "Aren't we?"

"No. Two thousand years ago, Romans ruled the world and they set up control systems that continue to this day ... You're not a Roman."

"I'm not? I thought the Romans were Caucasians?"

"Romans were renowned for the shape of their noses. A Roman nose is an aquiline nose—a nose that has a prominent bridge that is curved or slightly bent—hook-shaped. The word 'aquiline' comes from the Latin word *aquilinus*, 'eagle-like.' It's an allusion to the curved beak of an eagle. The people most commonly associated with this look are Mediterraneans from Turkey or Iran. Rome may have been surrounded by Greeks to the south and Etruscans to the north, but it was a city of migrants. The Romans were Middle Eastern refugees from the Trojan War.

"I'm not sure why you would honor them at any rate because they were a morally bankrupt people who stole their spoken language from the Etruscans, their written language from the Phoenicians, and their cultural heritage from the Greeks. Their only claim to fame was their blood sports and their ability to commit genocide on a grand scale—raping and pillaging their way across the known world. Your racial type is Germanic or Nordic.

Lilly frowned. Of course, she'd heard of Roman noses but she'd never considered the implication.

"The average height of a soldier in the Roman legions was five feet three inches, or 160cm. They thought Scandinavians were giants. The dispersion of the Nordic genes throughout the European gene pool has increased the average height in the West. The Romans commented on how white your people were in their letters; ergo, they were racially different.

"Your people, whom the Romans rudely called barbarians, were blamed for the fall of the Roman Empire, but they weren't responsible for it. The Roman Empire never fell ... it changed. A Germanic tribe called the Vandals sacked Rome in 455 A.D. They live on in infamy because their name, 'vandal' came to mean someone who willfully or ignorantly destroys, damages or defaces property belonging either to another or to the public."

"Right," Lilly said. "And it's not like the Romans didn't destroy plenty of property themselves."

"Indeed. When you went to school, Latin was still taught even though it had been a dead language for ages. You were told the Romans were mighty and clever, and the Roman Empire was praised and celebrated even though its culture was merely a copy and paste of Greek culture. In contrast, your own people's history was ignored, and they were called barbarians and vandals because they managed to defeat the mighty Roman Empire on several occasions. This one-eyed view was instilled in you because the descendants of the Roman Empire, or those who've pledged allegiance to them, are still in power today and winners write the history books."

"Why are their statues white, then?"

"They were Semite interlopers. The original inhabitants of the area were Greek and white. This accounts for the statues, busts, and the general population remaining white for some time after the founding of Rome. The violent male thugs who founded Rome abducted and raped neighboring women to help infiltrate themselves into their newly acquired land. The resulting war only ended when the abducted women threw themselves and their children between the armies of their fathers and their husbands."

"Really? I didn't know they were Jews."

"Semites are not all Jews. Semites speak or spoke a Semitic language and are Arabs and Jews ... racially they're the same people."

"So, you're saying a bunch of Semites invaded Italy and founded Rome?"

"You don't have to invade a country to be an interloper. You can infiltrate its political sphere and slowly attune it to your wants and needs. But, yes, I'm saying the founders of Rome invaded Italy, bred into the local population and spoke their tongue. Evidence of who they were can be glimpsed when you consider the Romans never fought the Arabs. Rather, they happily came under their rule and their most dominant feature—the shape of their nose—became the identifying Roman facial feature. Adding to this, Jewish political power rose within the Roman Empire in the third century A.D."

"But surely setting up some lasting political system doesn't equate to controlling foreign lands. When the Romans left Britain their influence ended ... didn't it?"

"No, it got stronger."

Lilly frowned. Ox's statement made no sense to her, but she did wonder about the choice of an eagle as a symbol for the United States. Was it a nod to the Roman Empire whose legions carried an eagle standard into battle, or was it a nod to the Roman people themselves? "I thought I lived in a democracy and we voted for everything?"

"Hardly," Ox said. "I'm sure you've heard President Kennedy's speech about Secret Societies and watched a recording of him saying they shouldn't be tolerated. You know he was assassinated shortly after he gave that speech?"

"Yes."

"Well, do you think, maybe, he was telling the masses he wasn't the leader of the free world?"

"That was the inference."

"Who do you suppose is really running the world?"

Lilly shrugged. "The Freemasons?"

"You're partly correct ... The world's power structure was established long ago. Now a multi-armed octopus, its dominance and influence has grown over time. The Freemasons, the Secret Society called Skulls and Bones, and the Catholic Church are three arms of the monster. The oppressive beast has other arms besides, and layers and tiers."

Lilly groaned. "Matthew's a Mason, he said it was important for his job, but I don't get it ... how can they be controlling the world?"

"Have you ever wondered why the high judges of the land are high Masons and the chief of police is a grandmaster? Wondered why the presidents of the US have almost all been members of Skulls and Bones?"

"I didn't know that—"

"I guess the world just isn't what you thought it was?"

Lilly's belly was so full it was beginning to ache, but she was still enjoying its swelling. She rubbed her hands over it.

Ox cleared his throat. "Tell me, Baby, what's your favorite song of devotion? If you could sing a song to your god, what song would you choose?"

Lilly looked at Ox suspiciously. *Why is he asking? Has he changed his mind? Is he going to let me worship my god?* Lilly thought for a moment. "George Harrison's 'My Sweet Lord.' It wasn't written for my god because it ends with Krishna worship, but I really like the first three minutes ... I sing it to my Lord."

"Do you indeed?" Ox said, setting her down upon her feet. "Would you like to sing it now?" Almost as soon as he clicked his fingers, the opening beats flooded into the cave.

Lilly placed a hand on her heart, closed her eyes, and began to sing, "I really want to see you ... be with you ..."

Ox stood patiently by, respecting her devoted stance. When the song finished, he picked her up. "Very nice ... Thank you."

Lilly groaned. Is there no end to his arrogance!

Ox sat down. After placing her on his knee, he reached down for a bottle of oil conveniently placed beside his chair and began to pour it onto her belly. "You get more beautiful every day," he said. "Look at your gorgeous swollen belly ... Daddy adores you."

CHAPTER THIRTEEN

Good observation

Cat leaned into one of the sculptured seats set into the side of the pool. Although the exquisite room surrounding him had a definite Persian flavor, in many ways it resembled a Roman bathhouse. He grabbed a remote and flicked on the screen in front of him. Ox was center stage, lying on his bed cradling Lilly in his arms.

"Are you looking forward to talking to her?" Kumea said.

Cat groaned. "No. The first meeting usually doesn't go well."

"Are you going to give her a massage?"

"Of course. For the next few days, I'll pamper her and make her feel special: wash her hair, cut her hair, massage her body and trim her nails."

"Groom her in more ways than one?"

"Good observation, Kumea. Yes, I'm going to groom her in more ways than one."

"I wonder how she'll respond when you go down there."

Cat shrugged. "I've got to admit I'm nervous."

"You are?"

"Yeah, a bit."

After twirling his wine glass nervously between his thumb and forefinger and placing it behind him, Cat got up. "Okay, I'm going," he said as he stepped out of the pool. He dried himself off, then dressed in standard western men's clothes. "I hate these bloody clothes," he grumbled as he headed for the elevator.

"Good luck," Kumea called after him.

A young Arab male

Startled by the ding of the elevator, Lilly stared at it nervously as a young Arab male entered the cave. "What does he want?" she said defensively, remembering the last time a man had stepped out of the elevator—his merciless words were etched into her mind.

"He wants to meet you and be your friend."

Lilly snuggled into Ox for protection. "Really?"

Cat crossed the cave quickly and extended a hand. "Hi, Baby, my name's Cat."

Lilly regarded his hand but she didn't extend hers. "Lilly," she said shortly, her eyes wide. She stared at him, caught off guard by his good looks. Besides his handsome brown eyes, he had an aquiline nose—not a feature she would normally find attractive—but the mild version he had of it, along with his warm Mediterranean skin tone and nicely balanced features, created an overall image that was most pleasing to the eye.

"I hope you don't mind if I call you Baby," he said.

"I most certainly do," Lilly said in her hoity-toity voice. "You're younger than me ... a lot younger."

"This is not your usual place. I mean no disrespect. I've come down here to groom you—"

"Ah, no!" Lilly said, glaring at him. "You can't just come down here and decide to groom me!"

Cat let his hand drop. He blinked several times then looked to Ox for support.

Ox smiled sweetly. "Baby, your hair and nails need to be trimmed—"

"And I'd like to give you a soothing massage," Cat added quickly. "I have a massage table on wheels in the elevator."

Lilly couldn't see it. The fact that it was hiding out of view made her suspicious. She narrowed her eyes.

"It's fine, Baby," Ox said. "He only wants to groom you ... spoil you a little. He's an excellent masseur."

"I'm not in the habit of letting strangers see and touch my naked body!" Lilly growled.

"Cat's a doctor," Ox said. "It'll be fine. He's a most respectful man."

Lilly frowned. Cat didn't look a day over eighteen. *Doctor? Did he start medical school when he was five?* Lilly's last massage was a distant memory. Even so, she thought she should reject the offer, but instead, she nodded her agreement.

"I have a nice warm towel to drape over you," Cat said obviously relieved. "It'll make you feel secure and cozy."

Lilly continued to eye him suspiciously. "When will I graduate from this silly game? Haven't I humbled myself enough already?"

"Oh," Cat said, momentarily thrown off balance by her forthrightness. "This isn't a game. I thought you would have realized by now ... You know your placenta isn't going to come away?"

"I'm aware," Lilly said shortly. "I guess I was hoping someone would tell me I was dreaming or having a delusional episode, or something."

"I'm afraid not," Cat said. "But it's not all bad ... is it? You love Ox?"

"Pfft. I don't know about that," Lilly said, in an act of defiance while still clinging to Ox. "Who knows what I think? I can't trust my thoughts or feelings. Ox has messed with my hormones and emotions ... He's done all kinds of shit to me!"

"Well, you need a massage, then. It'll help you relax."

Lilly rolled her eyes.

Cat acted like he didn't notice, instead, he went to fetch the stretcher. No hint of its usual purpose was evident—the milking equipment removed. As soon as Cat had moved it into position and secured it in place, Ox sat Lilly upon it. Cat draped a heated towel loosely around her. Then he removed a section at the top of the stretcher while Ox lay her down upon it and positioned the towel appropriately while supporting her head.

Cat then held her head above a large bowl of water set into the head of the stretcher while he carefully and proficiently washed her hair with his other hand. Lilly hadn't had her hair washed in this manner since she was a child. When Cat finished, he slid the removed section carefully into place and gently laid her head upon its padded surface. After giving her head an exquisite massage, he carefully dried her hair with a towel.

"I wonder if you aren't too good at that," Lilly said.

Cat looked bewildered. "Whatever do you mean?"

Lilly shrugged. "Nothing."

Cat trimmed her nails and gave her a pedicure before rubbing scented oil into her skin and giving her body a luxurious massage. "I need to cut your hair so it won't get tangled in your pouch and hurt you."

Lilly's hair had been getting pulled in her pouch. "Okay," she said reluctantly.

Cat lowered the stretcher and helped Lilly sit up in the towel before he masterfully cut her hair.

Lilly could tell he was cutting her hair short, but when she reached up and felt how short, she was shocked. "Good grief, you've cut all my hair off."

"You were getting it caught in your pouch. I've done you a kindness."

Ox leaned down and picked Lilly up as Cat took his leave. Beating a hasty retreat to the elevator, Cat dragged the stretcher behind him.

Lilly looked up at Ox as the elevator doors closed. "What was that all about?"

"The men upstairs think you've done well and you deserve a bit of spoiling," Ox said as he carried her back to their bed.

CHAPTER FIFTEEN

Chemically addicted

Cat regarded Lilly's sleeping body on the stretcher. After positioning her legs correctly for a genital examination and assuring himself she was sound asleep, he reached under the stretcher and picked up an object that looked like an oversized turkey baster while Kumea lowered the head of the stretcher so Lilly's head was considerably lower than her buttocks.

"What's in that ... sperm?" Ox said quietly. "Yours? Are you planning on casting a spell?"

"Yes," Cat said in an equally hushed tone. "I'm hoping to make her chemically addicted to me. Well, that's the plan anyway at least. Hopefully, then she'll be willing."

Ox laughed a muted laugh. "Do you really think sticking your sperm up her arse is going to make her fall hopelessly in love with you?"

"It might," Cat said defensively.

"Why don't you just stick your cock in her?"

"I don't want to get into her when she's unconscious," Cat said as he inserted the long, flexible turkey baster into Lilly's arse and pumped in a milky substance.

"Why not? Not much fun? You actually have a few scruples?"

Cat glared at Ox. "What's with the attitude? I'm being kind."

"Really? So, poking your sperm up her arse and hoping she'll become chemically addicted to you ... is kind?"

"It might help. I want things to go smoothly. Anything that might aid in that outcome is worth a try. I'm also going to rub my precum into her nasal tissue, so she'll breathe me in."

Ox snorted. "Because that's not dodgy at all."

"It's scientifically proven to be effective."

"No doubt the pheromones in your sperm and pre-cum will have a profound effect on her. I just think it's a sneaky, chicken shit thing to do."

Cat sighed. "I don't want her to get upset and reject me."

"None of you bastards helped me," Ox said, the volume in his voice rising. "You didn't stick my sperm up her arse. I had to go it alone without the voodoo tricks."

Cat played with himself for a few moments before he smeared some pre-cum into Lilly's nasal passages. Then he tenderly stroked her head. "Surely, you're not pissed about that?" he said in a hushed whisper. "It's not as if we didn't blow freezing air into the cave to help you out, or anything! You didn't require any further assistance."

Kumea attended to the milking while Ox and Cat continued to argue in barely contained whispers.

"Imagine if she woke now," Ox said, "and discovered what you two are up to. She'd have a mental. I half wish she'd wake … Do you think if I kicked the stretcher, she'd wake?"

"Shut up, Ox, and back off!" Cat growled in a raised whisper. "You can be such a jerk. I'm trying to be kind to her."

Ox snorted before stepping back. "You'd better hurry, she doesn't stay under long."

Cat and Kumea were as quick as they could be, then Cat motioned to Ox to come and pick Lilly up. Afterwards, Cat and Kumea packed up and scurried off to the elevator like frightened mice.

Cat fumed in the elevator. "I'm not going to let that prick get away with that!"

Kumea frowned. "Doesn't he have feelings for her?"

"Course he does!" Cat snapped. "He was having a go at me … I told you a Bigfoot could be aggressively protective of his baby. If you don't wise up you'll end up dead."

"But he told you to just get into her—"

"Yeah, like I was going to fall for that!"

As soon as the elevator opened, Cat stormed out and headed to a small screen to begin searching through music titles. Finding a suitable file, he cut to one minute into the song and hit play. Music flooded into the cave below. 'I'm a creep, I'm a weirdo.'

Ox recognized Radiohead's song 'Creep' immediately. He glared at a camera and exaggeratedly rolled his eyes with a rude wobble of his head.

♦ ♦ ♦

Cat didn't let Ox mess with his head. Pressing on, he was back in the cave within hours.

Lilly glanced at him from under heavy lids. She was in her pouch, Ox's nipple in her mouth and only moments away from closing her eyes.

Cat climbed the stairs at the foot of the bed. After walking across the bed to where Ox sat, he reached up and gently stroked her head. "How are you feeling, Baby?"

Lilly didn't recoil from his touch. Instead, she closed her eyes as he tenderly ran his fingers through her hair.

"It's nice to see you so relaxed," Cat said as he looked up at Ox, triumphant. Not wanting to push his luck, and fearing Ox might swat him away like he would a blow-fly, he removed his hand. He turned and quickly made his way back down the stairs, then beat a hasty retreat to the elevator, his face aglow.

♦ ♦ ♦

Cat hopped out of the pool and grabbed a decanter of wine and two glasses before hopping back in. He was nervous, but he hoped it didn't show. "Want a wine?"

Kumea nodded.

"She's been asleep for hours now. When she wakes, I'm going down there to milk her."

"What?" Kumea said. "When she's conscious! Do you think that's wise?"

"I can't delay any longer. Her womb's grown and she's tolerating me."

"Is she ready for that … when she's awake?"

"Course not!" Cat snapped. "But time's ticking, I need to press on." He gulped his wine down before rolling the wineglass's stem nervously between two fingers while eyeing the screen. Below, Ox was opening his pouch. He propelled Lilly up and out onto his chest. Cat got out of the pool, dried himself and started dressing.

"Do you want me to come down there with you?" Kumea asked hesitantly.

"No. Watch the screen, I'll let you know if I need assistance."

Cat tied his shoelaces, stood up, grabbed the stretcher with one hand and then dragged it to the elevator. "Right. Well … off I go."

"Good luck."

CHAPTER SIXTEEN

The test

Cat dragged the stretcher into the cave, locked it into position, and then strode confidently over to Ox and Lilly. "Good morning," he said boldly, feigning confidence.

Lilly blinked several times. It had only been a day or two since she was last groomed.

"I won't be grooming you today, Baby, or giving you a massage," Cat said. "I need to test your wine and milk."

Lilly frowned. "Why?"

"We need to check the quality and quantity of your wine and milk ... Ox needs to be fed properly."

Lilly groaned. The men upstairs were spending plenty of money on their secret project, and testing her wine and milk seemed like just the sort of thing they'd do. She didn't want to agree, but she was hesitant to refuse. What would happen if she did refuse? Would they start blowing freezing air into the cave again? "That sounds invasive," she said nervously.

"It's not a big deal. I'll guide you through the process ... It won't hurt."

Lilly looked up at Ox. He was nonchalant about the whole affair. Taking her cue from his relaxed demeanor, she said, "Okay. I guess."

Ox carried her to the stretcher and laid her upon it as usual while Cat stood by holding two miniature milking cups attached to a clear hose.

"First, I'll attach these little milking cups to your nipples and milk your breasts," he said. "That should give us an indication of how much milk you're making. We'll test it to assess its quality."

"Surely, those milking cups will hurt?" Lilly said, alarmed. "I've never seen milking cups like those before. Are they designed for a human?"

"My equipment is state-of-the-art," Cat said. "It won't hurt. Here, I'll show you." He gently pulled on one of Lilly's nipples to make it erect, then attached a little milking cup to it before doing the same to the other and setting the pump in motion. After a few moments, milk squirted out of Lilly's breasts in short bursts.

"There, that didn't hurt now, did it?" he said.

Lilly frowned. Her breasts were tolerating the machine and the sensation seemed vaguely familiar.

"Now I need to drain your womb," Cat said. "If I do this while the breast pump is working it will aid the process," he said, grabbing the wine probe. "This is simple enough. Get into the same position you would if a doctor was about to examine your genitals: pull your heels up to your bottom and drop your knees."

Lilly did as he asked with a scowl on her face.

Cat ignored her scathing look. Continuing unabashed, he said, "The head of the probe is like a man's penis. When I insert it, I want you to greet it; welcome it in by lifting your hips and wiggling about a bit. When I push it through your cervix valve, give some resistance so I can secure it into place."

Lilly did as he asked. Isn't this an odd way for a doctor to talk?

Cat slid the probe easily into place. "Good, Baby."

The probe prodded and sucked till it made Lilly's womb cramp. She expected pain but experienced none. She supposed, just as a woman's womb contracts violently during orgasm, and it's not painful, that this was no different.

The pump stopped prodding and sucked intensely when her womb cramped but only a small amount of fluid was sucked out, then it started prodding and sucking again. The intensity of the suction and the insistent prodding increased, making her womb cramp again and again till a rhythm developed and her wine gushed out in bursts.

"Can you feel your womb contracting and squeezing the wine

out?" Cat said. "The probe works with the natural rhythm of your womb. It encourages the placenta to contract and then it keeps pace with your womb's rhythm. Embrace the probe—enjoy it. It'll pleasure you like Ox does. The more you relax and work with the probe, the more pleasure you'll get."

Lilly glared at Cat, but she said nothing, deciding instead to get the invasive procedure over and done with. She closed her eyes and relaxed. Cat reached between her legs and stroked her clitoris. Her eyes flew open. She was about to complain bitterly but Cat's touch was heavenly. She closed her eyes again and moaned as her breathing deepened.

"Good, Baby," Cat cooed. "That's very good. Being milked should be a pleasurable experience, whether I do it or Ox does. I'll attach a special clitoris clip, it'll help you enjoy the pump."

Cat attached something small and soft to Lilly's clitoris. It latched on and began to suck; its tiny flicking tongue licking as it sucked. Lilly raised her hips and her head rolled back—the sensation intensely pleasurable. The milking machine found another gear: it prodded and sucked even harder. Nearing climax, Lilly's womb contracted strongly, the probe keeping perfect time.

As she climaxed, the probe kept pace with every shudder that pulsated through her body. When her womb stopped contracting, she slumped and sighed. But less than a minute later, the clitoris clip resumed its licking, and the probe sucked and prodded her womb back into action. Lilly groaned, but it wasn't long before she was enjoying another climax. Then, even though fully drained of her wine, the clitoris clip started licking yet again, and the probe sucked even harder. When the pump finally stopped prodding and sucking, and the clitoris clip fell off, Lilly was exhausted, but pleasantly so.

Cat picked up the clip and withdrew the probe. "Well done, Baby. You did well," he said as he ran his hands over her belly. "You're nice and empty. The probe sucks your womb hard even when you're empty."

"Why?" Lilly husked as her pulse settled.

"The machine is telling your body to make more wine."

"I thought you were testing my wine!" Lilly growled, her mind once again sharp.

"Ox is a large Bigfoot. I need to encourage you to make more wine," Cat said. "You don't want Ox to go hungry now, do you? There's nothing to worry about … a little encouragement from the wine machine is all that's required."

Lilly frowned. "Haven't you just deprived Ox of his feed?"

"The little I take now will be more than made up for in increased production."

Lilly glared at Cat, but he didn't notice because he was retrieving something from under the stretcher.

Cat produced a large turkey baster filled with a cloudy substance. "Milking your womb has drawn liquid out of your body," he said. "I need to put some back in."

"Why?" Lilly said, suspiciously. "Daddy feeds me."

"Ox needs the liquid I'm about to put into your body. I've taken some of his feed, so I need to give him something in return."

Lilly blinked several times. "Surely, you're not about to insert that?"

"I am," Cat said. "Roll over onto your left side and pull your knees up."

Lilly huffed out a breath before reluctantly doing as he asked. Cat dropped the head of the stretcher so her body was on a sharp lean— her legs elevated. Then he inserted the turkey baster up her arse and pumped its contents into her.

"What is that liquid?"

"Food for Ox … We call it 'Ox special.'" Cat said glibly before removing the turkey baster. Then he tucked all the equipment back under the stretcher and drew the curtain. "I need to come back down here tomorrow and milk you again … and every day after that."

Lilly rolled over and stared at him, her mouth ajar.

Ox stepped forward. He quickly inserted his main probe and carefully picked her up and cuddled her. "Good, Baby," he said. "Daddy's proud of you."

As Ox carried Lilly back to the bed, she glared over his shoulder at Cat. Diverting his eyes to the stretcher, Cat grabbed the end with one hand and quickly dragged it to the elevator. After pressing a button, he looked back and gave Lilly a polite nod before disappearing.

"Good God!" she said, still staring at the closed elevator doors. "He milked me like a cow, and he wants to keep doing it!"

"There, there," Ox said as he gently patted her back. "It's okay, he just needed to test your milk and wine."

"Didn't you hear what he said?" Lilly exploded. "He said he's going to come down here and do that every day!"

"I thought you'd be excited ... maybe even a little grateful."

"What the Fuck! What he did was a travesty ... He milked me like a cow!"

"Oh, come on ... You enjoyed yourself."

"That's ... that's not the point!" Lilly blushed. "He treated me like a cow!"

"And you can never be treated like a cow?"

"Exactly!" Lilly said, pleased he'd finally heard her. "A cow is an animal, whereas I'm a person!"

"Do you look down on cows, even though their sustenance sustained your children?"

"No," Lilly said, taken aback. "I don't look down on cows. I like cows, but *I'm* not a cow!"

"You have a problem with producing milk for others?"

"Too right I do," Lilly said in her hoity-toity voice.

"I see ... How dare anybody expect you to share your milk?"

Lilly frowned. "I share it with you. I don't mind if you drink it, and I breastfed my children. That's normal ... but being milked to feed others is not right!"

The elevator dinged. Lilly's eyes zoomed to its doors, glaring at Cat as he re-entered the cave. If looks could kill, he'd be dead.

"I assume you realize we're trying to save the Bigfoot?" he said quickly.

Lilly was about to yell at him but his words stopped her. She gave him the filthiest look while impatiently waiting for him to finish saying, whatever it was he was trying to say.

"Mankind is working hard to save the Bigfoot from extinction, but as you know, they have specialized culinary requirements. That's why this program is kept under wraps … you understand?"

Lilly snorted and folded her arms.

"The situation is dire."

Lilly's face softened, but only marginally.

"I need to milk your womb so we can feed the juvenile Bigfoots we have housed at this facility. We also require your breast milk to feed your own baby."

"My baby is here!" Lilly said, excited.

"Yes, and he needs his mother's milk."

"Well, bring him down here! I'll feed him."

"I can't do that."

Lilly's face dropped. "Well, feed him your bloody selves then, you bastards!"

Turning her head away, she buried her face in Ox's fur.

"It wouldn't be right to bring him down here and let you nurse him," Cat said. "You'd bond with him, and then I'd only have to take him away again … It's better for you if you don't see him."

Lilly was no longer listening. Sobbing, she was lost in her misery.

"I don't want to cause you any further distress," Cat said earnestly. "We're taking good care of your baby."

Lilly glared at him. "Fuck off!"

"I'll be back in the morning," Cat said, walking briskly to the elevator. "I hope you'll be feeling better by then."

CHAPTER SEVENTEEN

Quality food and vitamins

The memory of what happened flooded back before Lilly even opened her eyes. She groaned.

Ox lay on his back his head propped up on a pillow. He opened his pouch and propelled her forwards and upwards until she lay on top of him, half in and half out of his pouch. He ran tender fingers down her back. "Are you all right, Baby?"

Lilly rubbed her brow. "I suppose ... I thought I was going to see my baby." She sighed. "I should've known better!"

"Seeing him would've only caused you pain. Your baby's fine. He just needs his mother's milk."

"Why do you tolerate those pricks?"

"Do I have a choice? Besides, they care for me."

"Lucky you!" Lilly said bitterly.

"Cat's a nice guy. He's only an employee. He didn't take your baby away, and he's not stopping you from seeing him."

Lilly shrugged. She huffed out a breath.

"Cat's job is a difficult one. He must come down here and milk you, if he doesn't he'll get in trouble. He can't refuse to do his job. If he does, there'll be serious consequences for him."

Lilly sighed heavily. "Okay. I get what you're saying. I'll try to be nice to Cat ... Is that what you want?"

"It is, yes. The best way to cope with being milked is to relax and go with the flow. Then it'll be over and done with quickly and painlessly, and you'll enjoy yourself like you did yesterday."

"That was embarrassing!"

"Cat and I enjoyed watching your pleasure. It was a beautiful thing ... Don't be so uptight."

"It caught me off guard," Lilly said coyly. "I'm not used to making a public spectacle of myself."

"No one was watching ... well, almost no one. Yong sees it all the time, he probably didn't even notice."

"Really? I thought you said the people upstairs like to amuse themselves with what goes on down here?"

"I did say that," Ox said. "But that was then ... now you know this isn't a game. Yong's the only one who watches and who cares what he thinks?"

"Daddy—?"

"Yes?"

"What did Cat stick up my arse?"

"Quality food and vitamins. Don't concern yourself ... Cat won't hurt you."

"Are you sure?"

"Positive."

CHAPTER EIGHTEEN

Let's get serious

Cat walked into the cave, stretcher in tow. After locking it in place, he smiled at Ox and Lilly. Ox got up and carried Lilly to the waiting stretcher and laid her upon it.

She folded her arms and stared at Cat. "Are you really going to milk me *every day?*"

"There's no need to stress, Baby," Cat said. "It doesn't hurt ... How about I give you a soothing massage first? It will help you relax."

Lilly sighed heavily as Cat carefully poured oil onto her skin and rubbed it in. She closed her eyes and her breathing deepened.

"Good, Baby," Cat cooed. "You've probably noticed this oil has a relaxant in it." He gently kissed her brow as he ran tender fingers through her hair. "I hope you'll enjoy your time with me."

Lilly groaned.

"You're my baby," Cat cooed. "A deep and loving relationship should develop between us. I don't want to be your taskmaster. If you let me, I'll be nice to you ... real nice."

Lilly sighed heavily. "You shouldn't come down here and milk me like a cow ... it's not right!"

"Soon enough," Cat said as he seductively rubbed oil into Lilly's breasts. "You'll look forward to my visits and be addicted to the milking machine. When you see me, you'll become sexually aroused, wet, before I even touch you."

Lilly coughed. "Wow, it's not like you fancy yourself or anything."

"Not at all," Cat said earnestly.

"Why not?" Lilly said, surprised by his sudden show of humility. "You're hot ... smoking hot. You've got to be the best-looking Arab

I've ever seen. The sight of you dressed in sultan attire, riding a fine Arab charger, would make me wet."

Cat put his hand between Lilly's legs and quickly inserted two fingers into her vagina. She gasped at the suddenness of his actions. She was wet—very wet.

"It seems I don't require the attire or the horse."

Lilly's cheeks flamed. "I'm sorry. I don't know what came over me."

"Don't apologize. I'm flattered!"

Lilly slapped a hand over her eyes. While it was true, Cat did have the body of a man, he also had the face of an eighteen-year-old boy. She scolded herself. *What the hell is wrong with you? Bloody hell, the next thing you know you'll be a kiddie fiddler!*

"You're an attractive woman, Lilly," Cat said. "You have beautiful green eyes and your skin's the color of goats' milk. Nobody had to twist my arm to get me to come down here and be with you."

"Well, that's as maybe, but my attraction to you is despicable!" Lilly said, surprised Cat had found her white skin so attractive. She'd grown up in the *Coppertone*, 'brown is beautiful' era when women laid in the sun for hours. That time had long passed. These days she restricted her sun exposure. "You're only a lad," she said. "I apologize for my disgusting cougar outburst."

"It wasn't disgusting, and I'm older than you think."

Lilly studied Cat's face. His youthful eyes reflected a maturity that belied them like he was an old soul or something.

"The training I need to give you requires that we be intimate ... very intimate. Hopefully, we'll both enjoy it."

Training? Lilly scoffed. "I think you're being disingenuous. I'm old and fat with wrinkles aplenty. I'm sure you chopped the dye out of my hair. My graying roots are hardly attractive!" She sighed. "Why are you interested in me? I mean ... let's get serious."

"Let's get serious?"

Cat planted his mouth firmly on hers. Forcing her lips apart, he inserted his tongue. Once again, he pushed a hand between her legs and quickly reinserted a couple of fingers into her vagina. Lilly gasped and tried to pull away, but he'd have none of it. He stimulated her clitoris with the pad on his thumb while roughly inserting his little finger into her arse.

Lilly shoved him away. "Holy shit you're fast! Fuck!"

"Don't worry about me desiring you, Baby. You're a good-looking woman, and you're not fat. Now ... let's get on with your milking."

Lilly blinked several times. "Is being 'hot' a job requirement of yours?"

"It is ... yes."

Lilly groaned. "The bastards upstairs don't play fair. Your good looks are distracting me from being all morally outraged and pissed off."

Cat leaned over and sucked one of Lilly's nipples erect before attaching a little milking-cup to it. Lilly drew in a sharp breath as an intense rush of blood flooded to her genitals. More blood rushed as Cat sucked on her other nipple.

"Nice?" Cat said as he set the breast-pump in motion. "Let me know if the nipple cups are uncomfortable in any way, and I'll adjust them. Nothing about this process is meant to be painful. Now, let's get you flowing," he said as he reached for the wine probe. "Pull your heels up to your bottom and drop your knees ... You know the drill ... I shouldn't have to ask. When you see me reach for the probe, get into position."

Lilly did as Cat said. Why am I letting him manipulate me?

"I'm going to part the lovely petals of your rose and insert the probe."

When the probe was settled in place, and it was prodding and sucking Lilly's womb into action, Cat dipped a finger into some lubricant before stimulating her clitoris. Lilly moaned as her body flushed.

Cat leaned over and kissed her. After a few minutes in her willing mouth, he broke contact. "Good, Baby, now let's get your wine flowing," he said as he placed an arm behind her shoulders and kissed her again while continuing to stimulate her clitoris with a talented finger. Lilly's body curled forward, embracing the probe, her body was quick to climax.

"Good, Baby."

Strong climax waves were encouraged by continued stimulation. As soon as one orgasm faded, Cat's finger and the pump made another take hold. Lilly's climax seemed to go on and on. When the rhythmic waves finally ended, Cat removed his arm. Lilly flopped back onto the padded stretcher, exhausted.

"Very good," Cat said. "Your body is embracing the probe nicely." He removed the milking cups and the probe before feeling her belly and breasts. "Your belly feels nice and tight, and your breasts are lovely and soft ... they've given up all their milk."

Lilly closed her eyes. "You called my vagina a rose? I've never heard it called that before," she husked, still breathless.

Cat rubbed her spent vagina gently. "Really? The Bible calls it your flowers:

> *Leviticus 15:24 And if any man lies with her at all, and her flowers be upon him ..."*

CHAPTER NINETEEN

Productive cow

Lilly's belly had expanded rapidly over the past few weeks, and she'd been plagued by an almost endless fatigue.

"Daddy, my belly keeps getting bigger and bigger, and yet the concave pocket in your belly still accommodates it … supports it."

Ox rubbed Lilly's back. "Of course, Baby, because you belong in me."

"Your internal pocket envelops my belly, and your pouch is shaped in such a way, it gives my head a comfy spot to rest, feed and sleep."

"I aim to please."

"That's nice," Lilly said, "but surely, I don't need to make this much milk and wine, especially as you're not feeding from me anymore. I thought I was making milk and wine for you, but you've stopped feeding from me. As soon as I wake, Cat drains me of my goodness—"

"I am feeding from you. I insert my wine probe into your vagina while you're sleeping, and I have suckers that latch onto your breasts and draw off what I need so you can sleep longer."

Lilly frowned. "Then who am I making all this extra wine and milk for?"

"Your infant and baby Bigfoots. What they don't drink, the men upstairs do."

"What!" Lilly stormed. "My milk is being poured into the coffee of the pricks upstairs!"

"Yes, and into cookie dough, pasta, and anything else one makes with milk."

Lilly could almost feel steam coming out of her ears. "They're stressing my body to flavor their cookie dough and put milk in their coffee! That's disgusting!"

"You, and the many other women like you down here, are nothing more than merchandise to the men upstairs … productive cows."

"Merchandise! Cows!"

"Yes."

Lilly blinked rapidly to fend off tears, but it was no use. She rubbed her eyes. "They're milking me mercilessly … sapping my energy to put milk in their coffee! It's beyond disgusting. I'm sleeping my life away!"

"Women do tire and feel mentally drained during the growth phase of their placenta. You'll feel better soon. How about we delay your milking. I'll take you under the water?"

A swim did sound appealing, but Lilly was tired of being cooped up. "How about I get out of your pouch and walk around the cave?"

"Wouldn't you prefer a trip underwater? The cave is boring compared."

"Daddy!"

"Yes?"

"Why don't you want me to get out of your pouch?"

"You need to save what little energy you have for your milking. Besides, I like to feel connected to you … enjoy the feel of your lovely body in mine."

"I'm imprisoned in your stupid pouch!"

"I let you out," Ox protested.

"Apart from when I lie on top of you, the only time you let me out is when you dump me on the stretcher to collect food for you."

"I'm looking after you."

"Let me out!"

Ox nestled his face gently against Lilly's. "You're fragile."

"I am not!"

"Yes, you are."

"Let me out!"

Ox begrudgingly pushed and lifted Lilly out of his pouch. He set her down gently upon her feet. She wobbled on unsteady legs. Ox held the tops of her arms to steady her.

"Let go!"

Ox reluctantly let go, but he stood by.

"I'll forget how to walk if you keep me cooped up in your bloody pouch."

"No, you won't."

Lilly placed her hands on her hips and tilted her body backwards to balance out her weight. Her belly was almost as large as when she'd first arrived at the facility heavily pregnant, and her breasts were bigger than ever before. Ox shadowed her as she took a few unsteady steps.

"Leave me alone!"

Ox obediently stood still and watched her walk.

"I can hardly walk," Lilly grumbled. "My breasts are huge and my belly is swollen and heavy. Look how hideously unattractive I am ... I'm a freak!"

Ox took a step towards her. "You're not a freak. You're beautiful ... absolutely gorgeous."

"Stop lying!"

"You're too fragile and vulnerable to be out of my pouch. Let me put you back."

"Why? Am I going to be attacked?"

"No, of course not. Please, Baby, it's not good for you to walk."

Lilly gave Ox a frosty look. "Why isn't it?"

"Your wee back might get strained. I don't want you to hurt yourself."

"My back might get strained! Whose fault is that? You and Cat are selfish pricks. Look what you've done to me. You're the beast and his evil conspirator ... wankers!"

Music flooded into the cave. The sweet harmony of the Four Tops' song 'Reach out I'll be there' filled the cave.

Lilly glared up at the ceiling of the cave and groaned. "Typical. Of course, now is obviously the perfect time for a sweet love song." She rolled her eyes.

Ox held out his arms to her.

Lilly groaned and lifted up her arms so he could pick her up.

After scooping her up, Ox clutched her to him. "I'm looking after you. You don't need to walk because I walk for you. My legs are your legs." He pushed Lilly back into his pouch.

"I don't want you to be my steed—my high horse—I want to use my own legs. You're imprisoning me … I'm a slave!"

"You used to drive around in a car and fly in airplanes. You didn't think they imprisoned you?"

"No, they aided me."

"I'm aiding you, too."

Lilly's belly was so full it ached. Tears welled in her eyes.

The elevator dinged and opened. Cat walked briskly over to Ox who'd sat down on the cave floor so he could be eye-level with Lilly.

"You're all right, Baby," Cat said.

"I want my freedom!" Lilly cried. "I need to be free!"

"Free? Whatever for? You'd be lonely. Freedom isn't worth anything. Lonely people are free. Why would you choose that when you can be happy with Ox?"

"Ox has me all fucked in the head … I'm suffering from Stockholm syndrome."

"Never," Cat said. "You love Ox. That's why you've bonded with him, and he loves you."

"How would you know!"

"I'm a trained psychologist … I'm also a psychiatrist."

Lilly blinked several times. "You really are up your own arse! I thought maybe it was a summer thing, but now I see it's not … When did you start your training … when you were three?"

"I told you, I'm older than I look." Cat gently rubbed one of Lilly's arms.

Lilly found the gesture both insincere and patronizing. "Clearly, there's no level of shameful behavior the people at this facility aren't prepared to stoop to. Even considering all the crimes perpetrated against humanity, throughout the entire history of the world, an all-time low has been reached here!"

"You need to be milked," Cat said. "You're getting frantic. When I've relieved you of that nasty ache in your belly, you'll feel better."

Lilly spat at Cat.

Cat wiped the spit off his face before hurrying to retrieve the stretcher from the elevator.

CHAPTER TWENTY

A sickle

Cat helped Lilly roll onto her side after he finished milking her, after inserting the turkey-baster, he hopped up onto the stretcher behind her. Leaning upon an elbow, he rested his head on one hand and massaged her back with his other. "How's your back, Baby? Are you sore?"

"My back's fine!" Lilly snapped.

Making excellent use of the pad of his thumb, Cat continued to massage her back. "Baby, do you know how your colon works?"

"My large intestine? A little. It's shaped like a big hook ... like a sickle. Ox's probe forms that shape inside of me. He's the grim reaper! He drugs me with his fucking probe!"

Cat cleared his throat. "Important absorption occurs in the colon. Digestive enzymes, water, and minerals are reclaimed there. Microorganisms—healthy gastrointestinal inhabitants—complete the digestion of many foods within the large intestine. Humans also absorb free amino acids and short-chain fatty acids there."

"I knew water was absorbed in the colon."

"Liquid food administered anally doesn't meet with the acids of the stomach. Therefore, precious elements can be absorbed unharmed there."

"Is that why you stick food up my arse to feed Ox?"

"Yes," Cat said, "but mostly that food is for you. Ox just pushes it up so you can make better use of it."

"He does?"

Cat's hand drifted lower and lower.

"Do you have a girlfriend, Cat?"

"No. I'm not allowed a girlfriend or wife. I'm married to my job."

"How sad," Lilly said.

"No, it isn't … I like my life the way it is. You'll adapt to your new life. In many ways, you'll find it better."

"You think?"

"Sure," Cat said. "How much time did your family spend with you?"

"Not much, they all left."

"See? We're a better family already."

"Nonsense! The bastards upstairs stole my baby!"

"It doesn't pay to dwell on negative things," Cat said as he lay down fully on his side and tucked an arm under Lilly, so he could push it between her legs and stimulate her clitoris with a finger. He dipped a finger of his other hand into her vagina to moisten it before seductively circling her anus with it. "I'd like to feed you, Baby."

Lilly closed her eyes. She didn't want to let Cat take advantage of her, but the finger stimulating her clitoris was extremely talented. Her breathing deepened as Cat worked her anus open with one and then two fingers. When the battle in her head ceased, she moaned and wiggled her hips to greet his fingers and encourage him to push them in deeper. He inserted another finger, then repeatedly and firmly pushed them into her. Lilly gave his fingers some resistance and moaned.

Cat eased off her clitoris so she didn't cum too quickly, then he slid his fingers out and waited for her to nestle her buttocks into him and moan an invitation. "Good, Baby," he cooed when she did so. He eased his ample penis into her arse, then smacked himself into her. Lilly inhaled a sharp breath and moaned a satisfied moan. Quickly responding to the urgency in Cat's body, she pushed her buttocks firmly into him so he could pound her hard while she repeatedly gripped his member with her well-trained anal-sphincter, to heighten both of their pleasure. He groaned and grabbed hold of one of her thighs as he drove himself into her.

"You've a lovely arse, Baby," he husked, breathless as he stimulated her clitoris so she'd climax with him. After they came together, he said. "Your anus is very receptive and willing … that was very enjoyable."

Lilly blushed. *Why doesn't he just shut up?* She looked away—right into Ox's eyes. *Oh, God.* She slapped a hand over her face. *Shit!*

Ox stepped forward and picked her up. He walked slowly back to his bed with her. Lilly hung her head in shame as Cat dragged the stretcher from the cave.

Ox rubbed her back. "What's wrong?"

"I let Cat ... you know. I'm confused. I love you ... I do."

"It's normal for a baby to bond with her trainer and feel human love for him. It won't compromise our relationship."

"It won't? You're not upset?"

"No." Ox shook his head. "Why would I be?"

"I let Cat ... I'm starting to have feelings for Cat."

"That's good."

"You're not bothered? Really?"

"Do you wish you were with him now?"

"No. I want to be with you."

"Excellent!" Ox said. "That's exactly how you're meant to feel. Your love for me shouldn't interfere with your love for your master, or vice versa."

Lilly's brow furrowed. "My master?"

"Of course. Whatever Cat desires, you should do quickly and without hesitation."

Lilly's eyes widened. She coughed and then sighed. "I was worried you'd think I was a filthy whore."

"I would never think such a thing," Ox said. "I like whores."

Lilly glared at him.

Ox ignored her scolding look. "I hate parting with you, giving you to Cat, but it heightens our reconnection ... makes it special."

"And you want the food he puts up my arse?"

"Yes, and now that Cat is prepping you for me ... lubing you up ... things will be even better."

Lilly's mouth fell ajar. "That's the most disgusting thing I've ever heard."

"Well, you haven't heard much, then, have you?" Ox said as he carried her to their bed. "Now, let's have you on your hands and knees so Daddy can feed that hungry arse of yours some more."

CHAPTER TWENTY-ONE

You've become one

Lilly looked at the elevator, eager to hear its familiar ding. Her feelings for Cat had grown over the previous weeks. Their little chats and intimate moments meaning more and more to her every day. When the elevator finally dinged and Cat arrived, she sighed and looked lovingly into his eyes as Ox laid her upon the stretcher in front of him and backed away.

"You've bonded nicely with Ox," Cat said, "become one."

Lilly didn't want to talk about her relationship with Ox. "One?" she said dismissively.

"Yes. You and Ox have become one creature. You can be separated, but only briefly. You're like two strong magnets that snap together. You belong in Ox … you're part of his body."

"I am?" Lilly shuddered. "Don't freak me out."

"There's no need to be freaked out. There's nothing he wouldn't do for you."

"Shouldn't I be bothered by that statement?"

"No. It's a positive thing."

"What if another woman was placed in this cave? He might throw me over and put her in his pouch instead."

Cat shook his head. "He wouldn't do that."

"Why not?"

"He's put too much effort into bonding with you."

Lilly shrugged. "I guess."

"I can assure you, he's happy," Cat said. "He's not going to reject you."

"He's faithful?"

"Yes."

Lilly relaxed. "Thank God. I'd hate to think he'd cast me aside."

"Oh, you really do love him."

"I guess … You scared me."

"I could tell … You know you can never go back to your old life … to your old world."

"I know. How do you perceive love, Cat?"

"I believe almost any woman could be my wife and be good at it. Love is tolerance and acceptance. Most of all, love is commitment. You decide to be a good wife or husband, and you commit to it every day. When two people are committed to each other … there will be love."

"You think it's that simple?"

"I know it is … When you were assigned to me, I made a mental commitment to come down here, and not only train you, but be kind to you and love you."

"Really?"

"Yes."

Lilly frowned. "Even though you didn't know me?"

"I didn't need to know you. Love is like a garden, it flourishes when you attend to it, and withers and dies when you neglect it."

"That's beautiful, Cat. I didn't take you for the sensitive type … That was profound."

Cat gave Lilly a little kiss on the cheek and wrapped his arms around her.

Lilly warmly returned his embrace. "Okay. I'll commit to being a good baby and loving you."

"Thank you."

Lilly frowned at her words. "Did I just say that?"

"You did, yes … Did you mean it?"

"I did. I think … yes."

"Good, Baby," Cat said. "I'm grateful, but there was nothing profound in my words. Children need love … they crave it and naturally reciprocate it. If a child is naughty, a parent will be cross, and the child will likely feel the sting of parental rejection. Desperate for the return of their parent's love, children seek their re-approval by being both affectionate and good. Love isn't a mystery ... it's life's first lesson."

"You value love?"

"Of course," Cat said. "The outer world is a corrupt place where people put conditions on love. Women make ridiculous statements like, 'He must value my mind, have a big bank balance and drive a nice car.' And a man's love is often conditional upon a woman's looks, but likewise, it can be influenced by how much she earns or owns."

Lilly nodded. "You're right."

"Down here, we're back to basics. You own nothing, and your hair is cropped short. There's no makeup for you to put on, and we don't want you to put any on."

Lilly watched Cat as he reached for the milking cups.

"I'm not going to be intimate with you when I milk you from now on. Your womb is accustomed to the womb probe and it'll empty without any encouragement from me. I'll be intimate with you after I milk you from now on."

Lilly felt a little sting of rejection. It eased when Cat seductively sucked on one of her nipples to make it erect before attaching a milking cup. After doing the same to her other nipple, he set the milking machine in action and inserted the wine probe. It emptied Lilly's placenta proficiently without any clitoral stimulation. The milking, while still pleasurable, was almost devoid of any sexual arousal and physical exertion.

After inserting the special food for Ox, Cat rubbed the firm mound of Lilly's placenta in her belly. It was now the size of a four or five-month pregnancy when empty. "Your beautiful placenta is fully developed, and its powerful, well-developed muscles are attuned to your womb's natural rhythm ... the two now working in perfect harmony."

CHAPTER TWENTY-TWO

A tall man approaches

Ox gave Cat a nod before scooping Lilly up in his arms and carrying her to their bed. Lilly stared longingly after him, nervous and downhearted as he grabbed the stretcher and dragged it to the elevator, and left.

She sighed. "Why did Cat leave so abruptly without indulging in our usual intimate interlude, and without so much as a parting word? Have I done something wrong? Have I upset him?"

"No, Baby. There's to be a change in your routine today, that's all."

"Why didn't Cat say anything about it?"

"There's no need to be concerned," Ox said as he ran a couple of tender fingers through Lilly's hair before rubbing her back. "You'll get your feed."

Lilly frowned. Nestled into his breast, she pondered. *Am I concerned about getting my feed?*

The elevator dinged and opened. Lilly thought Cat had returned, but the approaching footsteps were heavier. She stopped drinking and looked around. A tall man covered in white fur with silver tips neared. He was as tall as Ox but not quite as solid, and his head was similarly elongated.

"Hello, Wolf," Ox greeted. "It's good to see you."

"Wolf?" Lilly said, strangely excited by the sight of a new humanoid. "Are you called that because your fur looks like a wolf's winter coat?"

Wolf nodded. "It's lovely to meet you, Baby."

"You're kind of like Ox?"

"I am, yes."

Wolf sat down on the large oak chair facing Lilly. He tilted his head slightly to one side to study her. The intensity of his stare made her uneasy. His penetrating gaze seemed to bore right into her. "Have you ever studied bees?" he said at last.

Lilly frowned. "Bees?" Why's he talking about bees?

"Yes," Wolf said. "You know a beehive has different types of bees, and they have different roles."

"I know a queen bee is fed a special jelly to make her a queen, and I know a hive has worker bees and drone bees."

"My kind," Wolf said, "Ox's kind and humans form a kind of hive."

"We do?" Lilly frowned. "Aren't beehives made up of just one species of bee? Cat and I are the same species, but you and Ox are different."

"My kind and your kind are also family ... we're related."

"I know I'm related to Ox and we have a genetic connection. Are you saying all humanoids are related and they have an interconnected social system that functions like a hive?"

Wolf reached out and gently ran a finger down one of Lilly's arms. "No, I'm saying you and me are related."

Wolf's touch was so electrifying, blood rushed to Lilly's genitals and her pulse quickened. Shocked, she recoiled.

"You feel the connection, Baby?"

Lilly's breathing deepened. A little moan escaped her lips. She blushed, embarrassed her body had given away her attraction with such a wanton display of lust.

"It's lovely to hear you moan, Baby," Wolf whispered as he leaned in.

Lilly was most uncomfortable. All kinds of alarm bells were going off in her head. She gripped Ox and buried her face in his fur, but he'd have none of it. He handed her to Wolf. He immediately cradled her in a loving embrace. Lilly stiffened and tried to push herself away.

"Your desire for me is normal, Baby," Wolf said as he ran a seductive finger down her spine.

Lilly's eyes widened. The strange man's touch was so sensual, she quivered.

"Relax," Wolf murmured. "I'm as attracted to you as you are to me." He nuzzled his face into hers, then licked her behind an ear. This was something Ox had previously done, but he'd stopped doing it.

Almost against her will, Lilly turned her face towards Wolf's. He held her chin gently, but firmly, in one hand and tenderly kissed her lips. Lilly tilted her head back and opened her mouth wide like a baby bird eager to be fed. The strangeness of her action bewildered her. Wolf's tongue entered her mouth: it shot down her throat like a dart, delivered something to her, and then withdrew. She gasped for breath as he lay her panting head upon his shoulder and rubbed her back.

Lilly's mind spun as her breathing settled. Shocked by what had just happened, and stunned by the complete absence of an urge to vomit, she blinked rapidly. *What just happened?*

"It's okay, Baby," Wolf said. "I gave you a needed feed. Your body craves the food I deliver, and my body yearns to give it to you."

Lilly's eyes whizzed left, then right. "A feed! Is that what you call it when you spit down someone's throat?"

"The food I deliver, along with special enzymes, is made and stored in a pocket in my throat. My specialized tongue facilitates its delivery."

Lilly was out of her depth. She wanted to get back in Ox's pouch. "I don't want you to do that ever again ... It was disgusting! Who the hell are you, anyway?"

Wolf rubbed her back. "Relax, sweetie."

Lilly tried, unsuccessfully, to push herself away again. "What do you want?" she growled.

"To be with you," Wolf said as he tenderly kissed her forehead. "It should be apparent by now that our species interconnect. We'll indulge, indeed, delight in a symbiotic relationship."

"We will not!" Lilly scowled. "I love Ox."

"Do you?"

"Yes!"

"Once upon a time, you thought he was a creep ... a beast no less."

"Ox is my everything."

"Well ... that's quite the statement considering you haven't known him long."

"What's that got to do with anything?"

Wolf smiled. "Soon enough you might be saying the same thing about me."

"I won't! I love Ox."

"Don't you also love Cat? Enjoy his affections?"

"Yeah, well, two lovers is quite enough."

"Why stop at two?"

"I'm not a whore! I get it on with Cat because he's my master ... I have to."

Wolf gave Lilly a knowing look. "Is that why you moan and encourage him?"

"You've been spying? That's low! You should crawl back under the rock you just crawled out from."

"Why?" Wolf said. "Don't you want me to pleasure you?"

"Certainly not!"

"Yes, you do. You're all flushed."

Lilly could feel the heat in her cheeks. She'd blushed. "That's no way to speak to a lady."

"Of course not," Wolf said. "I'd never dream of speaking to a *lady* like that."

Lilly glared at him. "You're positively hateful. Did you come down here to call me a whore?"

"No. I came down here to fuck a whore."

Pressing her lips together, Lilly's lips thinned. "Well ... you're never getting with me now!"

Wolf's brow rose. "So, you've already been considering it?"

Lilly's face reddened. "No!"

Wolf ran a sensual finger down her spine. "Are you sure about that, sweetie?"

"Quite sure!" Lilly's senses were on fire. If only she could get away from him.

Wolf rubbed his nose seductively against hers. "Why are you protesting? You know you want me. I want you too, so what's the problem?"

"What's the problem? You called me a whore!"

"When I call Ox a Bigfoot, he doesn't get all bent out of shape about it."

"Are you saying ... I am a whore ... so I shouldn't get upset about being called a whore because I am one?"

"That's it in a nutshell."

"I'm not a whore!"

"Oh, come on ..." Wolf said. "I've been watching you."

Lilly's cheeks blazed. "They make me do it."

"You said they were your lovers, and now you're saying they make you do it?"

"They drug me. I can't help it. I'm not a whore ... I love Ox and Cat."

"I'm loveable too," Wolf said. "You can love me too."

"I already have two lovers. That's quite enough ... Thank you very much!"

"Why?" Wolf said.

The question caught Lilly off guard. She fumbled for an answer. "I don't want to upset Ox."

Wolf looked at Ox. "You don't mind, do you?"

"No," Ox said casually. "I don't mind."

"What the hell is wrong with you people!" Lilly screeched.

"Ox and I are not people," Wolf clarified.

"Ox, can't you at least pretend to care?" Lilly challenged. "I love you, and you're busy passing me around."

Ox reached over and tenderly ran a finger down one of her hot cheeks. "Baby, what's mine is Wolf's. I want to please him."

Lilly shook her head in stunned disbelief. "How many other humanoid friends do you have that you want to please?"

"Just Wolf."

"And you're telling me this now?"

"I thought if I told you sooner it would hinder our bonding."

"You think? I trusted you ... I gave you my heart."

Ox shrugged. "I want to please Wolf."

Lilly lowered her head. "I've fallen down the rabbit hole. Surely, my rescuer will come?"

"Well, my wee bunny," Wolf quipped. "It seems you've found your way home."

Lilly was sure his words contained an implied insult somewhere. "Are you calling me a whore again? Are you comparing me to a Playboy bunny?"

Wolf ignored her question. "The White Rabbit is a guide … He leads his bunnies to the hole in the tree."

Lilly rolled her eyes. "What a load of nonsense! No white rabbit led me anywhere."

"Oh, but he did," Wolf said, "but we'll leave that story for another day. For now, I just want to be with my wee bunny."

"I'm not your wee bunny!"

"Would you prefer I call you my lamb? How about my kid goat?"

"Shut up! I don't want you to call me your lamb, your kid goat, or your bunny."

"You're teasing me," Wolf said. "Are you trying to get my sacks to fill with more juice, so I'll give you a bigger feed? It's working … just so you know."

"Eww!" Lilly screamed, trying to shove him away. "Get away from me!"

"Do you know why you can never be a boring lady?" Wolf said.

"Ladies are not boring!" Lilly declared in her most hoity-toity voice. "They're respected."

"Pfft," Wolf scoffed. "Why would anyone bother with a lady? I've no time for such creatures." He licked one of his fingers, then pushed his hand between Lilly's legs and used it to stimulate her clitoris. Lilly tried to push his hand away, but he was too strong for her. After he'd continued to stimulate her clitoris in a most pleasing way for a few moments, she moaned and relaxed.

"This is why you can never be a boring lady," Wolf said. "Ladies have this removed in childhood, so in adulthood, they're free of its influence."

Her pulse quickening, Lilly was no longer listening to his words. When Wolf put his head between her legs to lick her clitoris, her arms relaxed and her legs went astray. After Wolf dipped his little finger into her vagina, he seductively circled her anus with it before working it in while his tongue was busy performing a magic trick on her clitoris. She moaned as he repeatedly pushed it in. Soon enough, it's full length and breadth was within her. It was slim for his great size, but it felt like a modest-sized penis to her. She moaned with delight as its base repeatedly butted her anus.

"I'm wearing your ring," Wolf whispered in her ear before scooping her up in his other arm and laying her on the bed beside Ox on her back, his finger still inserted. He removed it to fold her knees back to her sides and enter her. Plunging his huge member, repeatedly, and deeply into her arse while gripping her hips and pulling her to him. He came quickly, then withdrew. Sitting back on the chair, he draped her limp legs over one of his arms.

"We don't want you to leak your food out," he said. "That will never do ... I want you to hang onto your lovely meal."

Lilly slapped a hand over her eyes, wishing the floor would gobble her up. *Who is this prick?*

"You got me so excited, I couldn't last," Wolf said. "Never mind, I'll be ready to go again in a minute."

Lilly breathed heavily. Wolf had stimulated her, but not enough to make her come. She wouldn't admit it, but she was hugely disappointed when he withdrew so quickly. Her urge to climax was overwhelming. She pushed a hand between her legs and started stimulating herself.

Wolf snatched her hand away. Holding it firmly in his, he said, "We'll have none of that! You'll wait for me to finish you off."

Lilly squealed in frustration.

"Let that tension die down a bit," Wolf commanded. "I don't want you to come until I've finished feeding you, then I'll let you have your release."

Lilly moaned and eagerly lifted her hips when Wolf once again pushed a hand between her legs to stimulate her clitoris once more.

"Good Baby," he husked in her ear as he laid her on the bed again and entered her for a second time. "You're a very good baby."

Lilly tried to shut out his words. Caught in the throes of passion, she decided to postpone her shame till later. She wasn't sure if he was bigger than Ox, or if he was just more energetic. Either way, he stretched her wide and when he pulled her hips up hard to meet him, the impact was almost too much. Although still relatively quick, he took longer to come this time, but Lilly was pleased when he withdrew even though she hadn't come because her arse wasn't used to his passion and it was beginning to ache.

After he withdrew, he raised her hips to his mouth and delighted her clitoris with his tongue. Moaning, she climaxed with a gush of fluid. Wolf licked it up as if it was the finest thing he'd ever tasted while continuing to lick her clitoris. When her body finally stopped shuddering, and the last of her orgasmic waves faded, he stopped licking. "That was lovely, Baby."

Lilly's hand was back over her eyes. "I'm so ashamed."

"Don't be silly," Wolf said. "You can no more change who you are than a leopard can change its spots. Don't be embarrassed."

"How did you get past Cat?"

"He let me come down here."

"Who'd ever know what the truth is?" Lilly grumbled. "You're all such consummate liars."

Wolf tenderly kissed her brow. "All you need know is, we have your best interests at heart."

Lilly scoffed. "I highly doubt that! It's far more likely you have *your* best interests at heart."

Wolf smiled a sly smile. "You'll be delighted when you find out how magnanimous we are."

"Pfft. I seriously doubt that!"

"You're such a delight," Wolf said. "I think I love you already."

"Well, it's not reciprocated. I think you're loathsome!"

Wolf kissed her brow again before tenderly stroking her head. "My wee bunny."

"Shut the hell up with that crap! Stop belittling me."

"I'd never dream of doing such a thing."

"I've had enough of your shit," Lilly growled. "I want to be with Ox."

Handing her back to Ox, Wolf gave her a parting kiss on the brow. "Till we meet again, my sweet," he said as he swept out of the cave.

Lilly groaned. *Will the humiliation ever end?* Wolf hadn't been in the cave that long, and yet he'd entered her twice. And he'd done more than just get into her, he'd made a meal of her. Now that her passion had faded, Lilly could really feel her arse, and it wasn't aching, it was throbbing. She gave her head a little shake. *Shit,* she scolded herself. *You're not only a whore, you're a bloody idiot!*

"Was that nice, Baby?" Ox said.

"Shut up! Let me get back in my pouch and close the bloody lid, will you? I'm not in the mood for chit-chat!"

Lilly noticed Ox didn't suckle on her bowel for some time. Instead, he let her body absorb the meal Wolf had given her.

CHAPTER TWENTY-THREE

Have I been drugged?

Lilly felt dreamy and relaxed. She rubbed the sleep-dust from her eyes and changed position before snuggling back down again. Ox acknowledged her awakened state by rubbing her back through his pouch wall.

"I'm sleepy," she protested. "I want to keep on sleeping."

"You're enjoying being drugged?"

"What?" Lilly blinked rapidly, trying to focus. "Have I been drugged? I mean ... more than usual?"

"Yes. Wolf's fingertips were coated in a drug ... he transferred it to your skin, and the food he spat down your throat was loaded with another drug—a sexual stimulant."

"Oh, for shit's sake!" Lilly exploded, "and there I was thinking I really *am* a disgusting whore!"

"Why do you think such things...? Who's judging you? Who are you trying to impress?"

Lilly shrugged. "Old habits die hard, I suppose."

"You didn't realize you were being drugged?"

"No, yes ... I don't know. I should've guessed, I suppose? I got so crazy turned on, it was like I'd turned into a nymphomaniac."

"Yes, it was awesome! You got me so excited."

"It upset me!" Lilly growled. "I was trying to control myself and I couldn't."

"That's the problem ... you were trying to control yourself ... You should've just gone with it."

"But I don't know him, and he's not even human."

"Is there some rule that says you must know a man for a certain amount of time before becoming intimately involved with him?"

"Of course there is!" Lilly said in her uppity voice. "A lady never sleeps with a man on the first date or the second. On the third date, the idea might occur to her."

"Will you shut up with that lady shit? It's stupid!"

Lilly pouted. She didn't want to *shut up* with her lady shit. While it was true, she had a weakness for alcohol that her husband had taken full advantage of. Outside of her home, she'd always been treated like a lady and she considered herself to be one. Her thoughts drifted to Wolf.

CHAPTER TWENTY-FOUR

Why trade?

Lilly tried to stop thinking about Wolf when she was being milked, but her mind was strangely fixated on him, and the associated smile on her face was so entrenched, she couldn't delete it. She sucked her cheeks in to hide her smile and get her facial muscles to obey her commands, but it didn't work. She hoped Cat didn't notice her odd behavior.

"What are you thinking about, Baby?" he said. "What a nice time you had with Wolf?"

"I didn't have a nice time!" Lilly snapped, mystified as to why she couldn't stop thinking about him or smiling. "He drugged me!"

"I think you had a very nice time. You just don't want to admit it."

"Nobody gives a shit about my rights!" Lilly growled. "Nobody cares about my hurt pride!"

"You don't have any rights."

Lilly glared at Cat. "You're all so hateful!"

Cat's face darkened. "Stop acting like a spoilt brat, it's unbecoming."

Lilly snorted. "Typical!" She looked away.

Cat gave her bottom a warm pat when he finished milking her. "All done. Now I need to give you instruction on your purpose."

Lilly gave him a fleeting glare, before, once again, looking away.

"Your milk and wine are packaged and given to the wolves."

Lilly frowned. "The humanoid tribe that Wolf belongs to?"

"That's right. They require quality food, and we provide it for them."

"I thought you were my master, and my milk was used by the

pricks upstairs."

"I am your master, and you'll do well to remember it, but your milk and wine aren't for us. It's merchandise that we trade."

"Really? What else do you trade?"

"Whores. We supply the wolves with women to fuck."

"Oh my God!" Lilly screeched. "You're so disgusting! What a base human being you are! I didn't think I could be more disappointed in man's leaders. Oh, how wrong I was! They're all such sellouts. Aliens arrive and make a few demands, and our leaders bend over and take it up the arse. Correction: they kidnap women, drug them, and make them take it up the arse instead! It's shameful behavior!"

"What can we trade with a race of technically advanced hominoids apart from women, gold, and a few other precious metals and stones? We have nothing else they want."

"You make me sick! Why trade with aliens at all?"

"You misunderstand," Cat said. "Wolf's people aren't aliens, they live here. They've been here for the longest time."

"And you pimp our women out to them ... make us suffer their big cocks up our arses and milk us to give them superior food? It's disgusting! You should be ashamed of yourselves!"

"Nobody turned you into a whore. It's your innate nature."

"It is not!" Lilly shrieked. "I'm sick of that shit! If you drug someone to make them behave like a nymphomaniac, that doesn't mean they ARE one!"

"How long did it take Wolf to get his big cock up your arse? Remind me ... was it five minutes or six?"

"He drugged me!"

"He didn't need to," Cat said. "You were hot for him ... near-on gagging for it."

"Near-on gagging for it? What an appalling thing to say ... I was not!"

"Course you were. You were like a horse chomping at the bit."

"Shut up! You're despicable ... the vilest person I've ever met."

"And yet you love me."

Lilly rubbed her eyes to hide the tears that had collected in them. "Do the wolves wave a big stick or something? Does humanity have to submit to their demands?"

"Changing the subject, are we? Like I said ... we trade with them, provide them with what they want and need, and in return, they provide us with technology. Haven't you ever wondered how humanity went from the Stone Age to advanced civilization in a mere blink of an eye? The citizens of the world think brilliant scientists invent something amazing every few years, but this isn't so. We give somebody the credit, of course, but the information is simply provided."

"I know trade is important, but what you're doing is appalling," Lilly said. "It's sickening!"

"We need the wolves to manage our systems and win wars for us. They also provide us with superior weapons and Intel."

"I think you've made a deal with the devil."

Cat shook his head. "No, the wolves make our world a better place."

Lilly stared at him, unsure why she was so surprised by his latest betrayal.

"For your own sake," he said, "try and let your old world go. You need to adjust to your new life ... to your new role."

Lilly sniffed back tears. "So, I'm to be a wolf's whore?"

"Yes, and your services will benefit humanity. You should be proud."

Lilly snorted. "Right! You know he hurt me. My arse was fair throbbing afterwards."

"Hmm, well, he probably got a bit too excited. After I finish milking you from now on, I'll prep you well ... lube you up good and proper for him and Ox. That should help ... Now shuffle your arse down to the end of the stretcher."

Lilly glared at Cat. "Won't it tip?"

"No, it's specially designed not to."

Lilly groaned and shuffled her arse, ever so slowly, down the stretcher. Cat grabbed the sheet under her and yanked. She flew down the stretcher and banged into him. Then, without any pleasantries whatsoever, he treated her like a common whore, using her as a sperm receptacle. When he finished, Lilly rubbed her eyes, trying to ward off tears. Any warm and fuzzy feeling she'd previously had for him had flown out the window, along with her rose-tinted glasses.

The elevator dinged, then opened. Wolf strode into the cave. He looked directly at Lilly, sniffed loudly in an exaggerated fashion and boldly announced, "I SMELL SEX AND CANDY!"

Lilly clapped her hands over her eyes. "Shut up!"

Wolf grinned widely. "Oh, dear! Are things so bad?"

Unable to help it, Lilly burst into tears.

Wolf walked over to her and gently rubbed one of her shoulders. "Sweetie, being with me should be a pleasurable experience. Can't I jest ... play a few word games? Can't a man have a bit of fun?"

"You're not a man! You're a fucking pedophile!"

"Come now," Wolf said looking at his member. "I'm like the Statue of David ... My dick is positively minute compared to my size, and you're not a child."

"That doesn't matter! I'm child-size in comparison to you!"

"You're lovely. Full of all kinds of gorgeousness!" Wolf said. "It would be an absolute tragedy if I couldn't enjoy your loveliness because I was too big for you. Fortunately, that's not the case ... you'll get used to me."

"Right!"

"Look at my beautiful member," Wolf said admiring his own penis. "It's absolutely perfect. It was made for you ... Would you like to touch it?"

"No!"

"I bet your lovely wee hands are very talented and they know exactly what they're doing."

"Yeah!" Lilly said. "I bet they do too ... but you're not about to find out."

"What about your mouth? Is that equally talented?"

"No, it's positively useless!"

Wolf grinned. "Liar," he said as he held one of Lilly's tiny hands gently in his; his eyes laughing. "Pleasuring me isn't the end of the world. I won't hurt you ... well, maybe a little, but nobody ever died of a blue arse."

"My people are oppressed!" Lilly wailed. "I'm being pressed into service—forced to be an alien's sex-slave."

"Wow," Wolf said. "Things really are dire!"

Lilly pulled her hand free, then folded her arms stubbornly across her chest. "Don't mock me! Terrible things have happened to me!"

"Really? Do tell."

"Shut up! You know what's being going on. You've been spying."

"So I have," Wolf said. "Let me have a good look at you. See if I can see any marks." He rudely folded Lilly's legs back to her chest, so he could take a good look at her arse. "You're not even blue," he said as he picked her up. He carried her to the bed and then laid her upon it. After giving her body a further, visual once-over, he said, "No, no marks."

"They're internal," Lilly said. "My mind's traumatized. People have traded my wares for their own benefit."

"Have they indeed? How shameful ... How dare people want to bring civilization and advanced technology to the world. Shame on them!"

"They should've paid with cash."

"Cash?" Wolf said. "I'd wipe my arse with it."

"We should have remained in the Stone Age if we couldn't afford to pay for your services in a decent way."

"Well ... that's a big call ... I'm not sure it would survive a vote."

"Why do I have to pay the piper?" Lilly despaired. "How come I drew the short straw?"

"Stop playing the victim. Whores like to be fucked."

"I'm NOT a whore! I'm a lady!"

"You never were a lady ... Besides, who or what you were in your previous life is irrelevant. People have seen fit to offer you up as a sacrifice, and I'm happy with the trade. After you've relieved me, I'll go upstairs and help humanity ... Now be a good girl and give me a kiss."

After re-folding her arms determinedly across her chest, Lilly turned her head sharply aside.

"Look," Wolf said, his voice soft. "I want to have a loving relationship with you, treat you well, and be nice to you ... Is that so bad?"

Lilly shrugged. "If I came to that decision on my own, it might be okay, but they're making me do it. I've no choice! My life has been stolen from me!"

"From what I hear, you weren't particularly happy. Your life had turned to custard." Wolf gently kissed Lilly's forehead. "Let Daddy Wolf make it all better. Give you a better life."

"Better? I doubt you're going to make my life better!"

"I have plenty to offer. Love, protection, pleasant surroundings ... sleeping your way to the top has always been a good idea."

"Must you joke?"

"I'm not joking," Wolf said. "Exchanging love and tenderness for advancement has been a valued currency throughout the ages."

"What advancement?"

"Would you like to live in a lovely place where no one is spying on you, and be loved and taken care of?"

Lilly sighed. "I suppose," she said begrudgingly.

"Well, all you need do is let me love you and I'll whisk you away from this nasty place."

Lilly knew she didn't really have a choice, but she appreciated Wolf's offer even if it was disingenuous. "Okay."

"Good baby," Wolf said. "I promise you won't regret your wise decision."

Lilly highly doubted that. Wise decisions weren't her forte.

Wolf lifted her up and embraced her. He placed a hand behind her head and kissed her lips. His lips pecking hers with a subtle urgency. Lilly's body responded in an instant: her head tilted back and her mouth opened wide. Wolf's tongue shot down her throat. She gulped down the overspill of his feed, and now that she wasn't concerned for her physical wellbeing, she found his feeding kiss strangely comforting. When Wolf finished feeding her, he lay her panting head upon his shoulder in his customary manner.

"I'm bothered by the strange power you have over me," she said, intoxicated.

"And you over me, darling."

"What do you mean?" *I have power over him?* A part of her was secretly delighted. "Surely, you jest?"

"No," Wolf said earnestly. "Remember, I said we're a hive?"

"How does that work, exactly?"

"I'll tell you more when you've been my good wee bunny and satisfied me." He kissed her willing lips once more, delivering more food to her.

Music flooded into the cave. A seductive song about one becoming addicted to another had begun to play: *Taste* by Lorna Vallings. Lilly wondered if Yong was having fun with his song choice, or was it Cat? She shrugged, too high to care.

Wolf stroked her clitoris. "I'm going to deliver the presents in my sacks."

Presents in his sacks?

"Ole Wolfe wants to come down the chimney."

Lilly groaned, his reference grotesque. She screwed up her nose. *I wish he'd shut up.*

Wolf proceeded to do as he promised. He emptied his sacks several times. Lilly's chimney began to throb, but the drug in Wolf's saliva kept her complaisant. She moaned and rolled her head back as Wolf lifted her legs and brought her to a delightful climax with his tongue. After he drunk down her juices, he said, "Oh, Baby, you make Daddy Wolf so happy."

She groaned; her hand back over her eyes.

CHAPTER TWENTY-FIVE

A door opens

Lilly opened her eyes with a grumpy moan. So far, Wolf hadn't kept his promise. More than a week had gone by and she was still living in the cave. Any minute now, she expected to hear the elevator's familiar ding, announcing Cat's arrival.

Ox pushed and lifted her out of his pouch, then stood up with her in his arms. "Do you want to see our new home?"

"New home?" Lilly said, excited. "We're leaving?"

Ox walked towards the cave wall behind their bed. When he got close to the wall, a door slid open in front of them. Completely camouflaged, Lilly hadn't noticed it before. It opened into a square courtyard off which eight doors opened.

In the middle of the courtyard, a large square pool shimmered like a turquoise jewel. Ivory colored, Roman marble pillars stood majestically at each of its corners. Together, the pillars supported four beams that formed a square above the pool, their shape mirroring it. At the base of each pillar was a small, neatly trimmed, ivy filled garden. A dainty, variegated, ivy vine twisted up each pillar, then along the beams above.

In the middle of each neatly trimmed, vine-covered beam, sat a stone dragon spilling forth water from its open mouth. The pleasing sound the gently cascading water made as it splashed down into the pool was almost musical. On the ceiling above the beams, a large square, opaque window was letting in defused light.

The pool had a wide, deep step running around its inner edge which was interrupted on each side, in the middle, by human-sized steps. The different sized steps, arranged in this way, gave the pool the appearance of an upside-down pyramid with a flat top.

The pool's sides leading down to the deep ledge had recessed, sculpted grooves which Lilly imagined large backs relaxed into. The back of the first step of the human-sized steps was similarly designed, and the ledges themselves, both small and large, had indentations for humanoids to park their rumps.

The poolside was covered in exquisite mosaic tiles; terracotta the dominant color. The similarly colored walls were covered in exquisite marble. In the corners of the glorious courtyard, ornate golden shower heads arched beautifully. There were two in each corner. One set at a height suitable for either Ox or Wolf, and another set at an ideal height for a human. Lilly wondered, for the first time in her life, if she was looking at genuine gold fittings. Even the drain covers set into a dip in the middle of the gently sloping tiles under the showers, looked like they were made of fine gold.

Against each of the four walls, completing the formal design, were four large comfortable wooden bench seats with topiary plantings in stone boxes on either side of them.

"Wow," Lilly said. "We've been living beside this the whole time?"

"Yes. Do you like it?"

"Like it? I love it. This is our new home?"

"Indeed," Ox said as he carried Lilly into a room opposite. "This is the lounge."

The room they entered overlooked native forest. Even though their location was remote, Lilly couldn't understand why the house was so exposed. "We live in a house in the bush?"

"We do."

"But the cave has an elevator with many levels above it." Lilly looked at the opaque skylight set into the lounge's high ceiling. Like the one in the courtyard, it was letting in defused light. She rubbed her brow. "If we live in a multi-storied building, how come sunlight is pouring in through the ceiling in here, just like it is in the courtyard?"

"The cave has multiple stories above it," Ox said. "This house is built into the side of a mountain."

"Oh," Lilly said, looking around the simply styled room. A large dining table and sofa were taking full advantage of the view. There was zero clutter: no books, or side tables, and little in the way of ornamentation, only a few well-placed ornaments in niches set into the marble walls. If there was anything odd about the room, it was the temperate plants in the corner of the room that didn't quite go with the Mediterranean decor. The temperate plants outside similarly clashed, but not in an obtrusive way.

Thinking about it, Lilly realized the plants in the courtyard were also temperate, but unlike these ones, their nature hadn't been so immediately apparent. She'd never been in a room where a full quarter of the space was dedicated to an internal garden, and it seemed odd to her, even if it did give one the feeling of being *in the bush* rather than simply overlooking it.

She frowned. *The window should be a patio door.* "Why aren't there any drapes?"

"There's no need for drapes."

Lilly shrugged. Even in the bush she would have preferred drapes. "Don't you guys like window dressings ... the look of fabric?"

"Less is more."

"Well, that certainly seems to be the opinion of the decorator, apart from the elaborate internal garden, of course. I've been in houses with lots of pot plants before, but nothing like this," she said, pointing at the internal garden.

Wolf appeared in the doorway. "Nothing but the best for you, my love."

"It's stunning, Wolf," Lilly said, excited.

"How about you come and check out my room?" Wolf said with a wink.

Ox carried Lilly into his room. It featured an enormous bed draped in a textured, luxurious linen throw with matching pillowslips in a soothing latte color. The exquisite floor appeared at first glance, in the low light, to be an intricate carpet, but on closer inspection, it was an exquisite mosaic tiled floor, similar to the flooring in all the rooms Lilly had seen so far. The bed linen matched the secondary color in the pattern on the floor.

The large window in the room was unadorned with window dressings, just like the one in the lounge, but the glass was darker. Lilly wondered if the glass itself was providing privacy. An elaborate tapestry featuring a naked lady with a large belly and plentiful breasts hung on the wall opposite the window. Her facial features weren't discernible because she was staring off into the distance over one shoulder.

There was a central opaque skylight matching the ones in the courtyard and lounge. Like the window, it was letting in less light. Lilly found the subdued lighting relaxing. On the wall adjoining the lounge, there was an internal walled garden with a couple of tiny waterfalls trickling down either side of a centered Roman arch. The arch mirrored what was in the lounge, on the other side.

Lilly stared at the arch. "Does the wall open?"

"Yes," Wolf said. With the flick of his wrist, a door in the middle slid into a wall cavity.

Now the lounge and Wolf's bedroom was one enormous room. The lounge's simpler décor which featured the same pale-colored mosaic tiles that were in the courtyard almost seamlessly joined Wolf's more ornate room. Lilly thought his bedroom, indeed the house, wouldn't have been out of place in a Roman palace or grand villa, even though there was no ornamentation apart from the candles set into niches in the marble walls.

"What are you thinking?" Wolf said.

"I … I think your bedroom is incredible," Lilly said, almost lost for words. "I've never been in a house of such opulence. This place is more like a palace than a house. Your bedroom's classically stunning."

"Does it have the desired effect on your mind?"

"Do you mean … does it make me want to relax on your bed and spend time with you?"

"Yes."

Lilly shrugged. "I suppose it does."

"Good," Wolf said with a satisfied smirk. "Every room in this house is purposefully designed. When I'm in here, I want to forget my work and chill out, and I want you to do the same."

"Well," Lilly said. "So far, I'm impressed. Your room's a Roman general's grand bedroom, and Ox's room is a cave. What's Cat's room like?"

Cat appeared as if on cue. "Are you getting the grand tour? Would you like to see my room?"

"What kind of room do you have?"

"A normal man's room."

"Seriously?" Lilly said. "Well, that will be a huge let-down after Wolf's amazing bedroom, the courtyard, lounge, and our cave."

Cat led the way to his room. There was no window, and even though there was a mosaic pattern on the floor and the walls were covered in quality marble, it was stark compared to the more adorned rooms Lilly had just been in. The office's furnishings were high quality: exquisitely made wooden cupboards and shelves lined the walls stuffed with books, many leather-bound. Tucked into the corner, like an afterthought, was a single bed.

Cat's desk spanned the full length of the room. Lilly's eyes were drawn to the computer on it. "Is yours the only computer?"

"No," Cat said. "You obviously haven't seen Wolf's study yet."

Wolf turned and stepped through a doorway opening in front of him. Lilly shivered as Ox followed him into the room with her. The room's temperature was in keeping with the temperate plants in the house. It couldn't have been more than 65 degrees Fahrenheit or 18 degrees Celsius, cool compared to the rest of the house. Unlike the lounge and Wolf's bedroom, it wasn't an enormous room, but it was still a large room. The house was, after all, designed for massive humanoids.

Wolf's office was the most elaborate Lilly had ever seen. She was mesmerized by shelves stuffed full of large, leather-bound books.

"Hard copy," Wolf said. "They're mostly for decoration. They look good, don't they? They're only here in case of a system failure. The vellum pages are specially treated, designed to last, and the air in here is kept at a constant temperature and the humidity low. The information contained in these books is stored in my head. To me, they're decoration, something to dress up the walls with."

Lilly looked at the huge computer on his enormous desk. "What kind of work do you do?"

"I work on calculations to make planets habitable, and animal design ... that sort of thing."

Lilly's mouth fell ajar. "Calculations to make planets habitable and animal design...? Surely, you jest?"

"No."

"Oh, is that all?" Lilly said. "And there I was thinking you were a rocket scientist or something."

"Hardly, I wouldn't waste my time on mechanical engineering."

"Of course not!" Lilly said. "Such things are beneath you."

"Indeed," Wolf said, without a hint of humility.

Lilly frowned. *Is he serious?*

Wolf plucked Lilly out of Ox's arms. "Don't worry about my work, Baby. It's boring compared to you." He opened a door on the other side of the room with a customary flick of his wrist and stepped into his bedroom. After Ox entered, the door closed behind them. "I'd much rather be in here with you."

Lilly stared up at him. "Daddy, you make creatures ... really?"

"Of course."

"What do you mean, *of course*? I'm an idiot compared to you. Why would you want to spend time with me?"

"Because you're fabulous."

Lilly scoffed. "Pfft, what low standards you must have! Surely, you know Earth is crawling with fine young women ... I pale in comparison."

"You're talking about the 'barren beauties,'" Wolf said with some disdain. "We're not interested in them."

"Why not?"

"We call them the 'barren beauties' because they're useless ... other than to twirl around and look pretty, that is. More than ninety-five percent of women on Earth aren't genetically aligned to us—a placenta wouldn't hook into their wombs. There *are* lovely young beauties that *are* genetically aligned to us, but they're far too precious to scoop up as young women. We want them to breed and raise a family. More than that, we need them to complete important stages in their life cycle. Women who are brought here before they've matured and raised a family, don't adapt well."

"I see, but you're like a god and I'm a fat old cow ... What does a god want with an old crone," Lilly said exaggerating. "I'm even fucked by others. Have you no pride?" She buried her face in Wolf's soft white fur, her pain and shame too much to bear.

He cradled her. Running tender fingers through her short hair, he said, "Poor Baby, you think so little of yourself. You're amazing! It's sad you have such a low opinion of yourself. Don't feel like that," he said as he sat down on his bed and leaned back against its padded headboard. After laying Lilly gently upon his chest, he rubbed her back. "You're my world, Baby ... the reason I get up in the morning, without you I'm nothing."

Lilly frowned, skeptical.

"Believe me, I know what I'm doing. You're upset because you've been brainwashed into believing intellect and youth are the most prized of qualities ... they're not. Intellect is nothing: it's positively boring. To love and to give is greatness."

"But look at me—"

"I am. Your lovely round belly and full breasts are divine ... you're Venus to me."

"You don't think I'm a fat old cow...? Really?"

"Of course not. You're a fine red heifer ... You're exactly what I was looking for."

Lilly frowned. *What the hell?*

Wolf leaned in and gave her his feeding kiss.

She closed her eyes and melted into him. When he finished feeding her, she gazed dreamily into his eyes. *How does he do that? How does he make me feel this way?*

CHAPTER TWENTY-SIX

Invented money

Wolf threw his legs over the side of the bed and stood up easily with Lilly in his arms. He carried her to the courtyard as if she weighed nothing. Lilly loved his physical prowess: he made her feel like a dainty princess. Pushing all thoughts of her previous social-standing aside, like she was trying to bury her past, she focused on him. He flicked his wrist to stop the dragons issuing forth in an exaggerated fashion to demonstrate how he was doing it, then he stepped into the pool. When he sat down, his lower back slid easily into a molded indentation on a large step.

As Cat and Ox joined them, Lilly was busying herself checking out the finer details of the pool. Looking under the rim, she saw it had a lip to drain away excess water. The pool had seating for two huge humanoids on either side of the human steps that ran down the middle of each side. In total, it seated sixteen large humanoids and eight smaller ones. Although the pool was barely more than an oversized spa pool for Ox and Wolf, it was a decent-sized pool for her. Certainly not an Olympic sized swimming pool, but plenty big enough to enjoy.

Cat swam over to her dressed in his birthday suit. He gently rubbed her arm. "Are you happy, Baby? Do you like your new home?"

"It's lovely," Lilly said. "Almost nice enough to make me forget I'm a prisoner. It must be great to be you, Cat."

Cat frowned. "Whatever do you mean?"

"You have a job you obviously enjoy."

"I was bred for my role."

Lilly raised her brow. "Really?"

"I'm descended from a long line of trainers. I was raised and educated in the fashion all trainers are."

"What did that entail?" Lilly said, interested.

"I attended a top school and university where I studied medicine and human biology among other things. Then I worked in a hospital as a doctor, and as a surgeon for many years before studying for my trainer's degree."

"So, you really are a doctor?"

"Yes."

"But how can that be," Lilly said, frowning. "You're so young?"

"I'm not nearly as young as you think … I take a tonic."

Lilly's brow rose in amazement. *That must be some tonic.* "So, they pay you the big bucks?"

"No. They don't pay me anything."

Lilly blinked several times. "Really? You expect me to believe you don't earn any money or drive a flash car."

Cat shook his head. "I don't drive a flash car or whatever else it is you think I might do."

"How come?"

"Does Ox get paid?"

"No, he's a basement dweller like me," Lilly said, despondent, "he's a slave."

"As are we all," Cat said.

Lilly frowned. "But you and Wolf own this flash house and—"

"House?" Cat said. "This isn't a house, it's a production unit; one of many in this area."

Lilly looked down at her full breasts and sighed. "And you deliver my milk and wine to the men upstairs."

"No. When you last lived in a house, stuff left your house under the street—"

"No, it didn't," Lilly grumbled, becoming increasingly annoyed. "That never happened. Nothing left my house under the street, I would've known if it had."

"You did know," Cat said. "Every time you went to the toilet and flushed your waste away, it traveled under the street to a treatment station on the other side of town. There it was treated and disposed of."

Lilly shrugged. "Okay, so I did know that ... Now I suppose you're going to tell me my house was serviced by power and water. What's your point?"

"My point is ... even though I'm not personally going to deliver your milk and wine to the men upstairs, that doesn't mean it won't leave here and travel to a processing center."

"And I gather you're not going to put it down the loo."

Cat stood up. After he got out of the pool, he walked to a room near the cave's entrance. "Come and have a look," he said, motioning to them all to come and look inside the room.

When Wolf stood up and shook the water off himself, a huge puddle of water splashed onto the tiles around him. As he made his way across the courtyard, more water slopped onto the floor. He followed Cat into the room. It had a large bench seat on one wall and a track that traveled under the wall of the house on its other, upon which sat a substantial stainless-steel bullet.

Cat gestured to it. "When I finish milking you, I'll label your milk and place it in this bullet and send it away. It'll then travel to a processing factory where your milk and wine will be weighed, tested, documented, and processed. So, you see, this house isn't a standalone entity. It's part of a network: it's connected to a system. Deliveries are constantly going back and forth."

"Will a mailman or courier arrive?" Lilly said after a short pause, having been momentarily distracted by the pool of water forming around Wolf's feet.

"No. Such deliveries are archaic. All mail is electronic ... emails. Other deliveries come via this chute." Cat said, pointing to the comfortable bench on the opposite wall.

Lilly frowned. "In the bench?"

Cat lifted the bench seat's padded lid, under it sat another, smaller, bullet.

"How does it work?"

"When a delivery arrives, this light blinks," Cat said, pointing to a round colorless button. "I also receive an email alert. I empty the bullet and send it back."

"Where does it come from?"

"The main distribution center. Most deliveries go to the center. If we wish to send something to another address, we key in the number of that address, and it'll go there and return."

"Do you pay for this service with stamps?"

"We don't have money and we never get paid or pay for anything."

Wolf exited the room with the others in tow. The water that had slopped all over the floor had disappeared as if by magic. Lilly looked at the tiles: obvious drain holes were embedded into their grouting and the tiles appeared to be quality, non-slip tiles that were sloped, ever so gently, to allow water to run off them. Wolf stepped back into the pool and sat down.

"Oh, come on," Lilly said. "You can't expect me to believe we're all slaves."

"Why not?" Cat said.

"Wolf's like a god," Lilly said. "How can *he* be a slave?"

"You mean because he designs plants and animals?"

"Yes."

"Slave isn't exactly the right word," Cat said. "We don't get paid money ... we know the folly of money. Everybody tied to the monetary system *is* a slave."

"So, you're free to leave?"

"And go where exactly," Cat said, "to a mall? Why would I want to do that?"

"I mean you're free to go and do ... whatever."

"Wolf leaves here when he feels like it," Cat said. "He can make travel arrangements if he so desires."

Lilly frowned and looked up at Wolf. "You don't wish to travel?"

"I leave this unit to visit friends mostly," Wolf said. "We also entertain."

"We do?" Lilly said. "I mean ... you do?"

"That includes you," Wolf said. "We're a unit. No member is more special than another."

"But I'm a slave!" Lilly protested.

"No," Cat said. "You're a member of our team."

Lilly shook her head in annoyance. "Stop trying to confuse me. I'm not here of my own volition ... I can't leave!"

"Why would you want to?" Cat said.

"I have to do as I'm told," Lilly further protested. "We're *not* a team!"

Cat shifted his shoulders, uneasy. "You're guided, but you're a valuable member of this team none-the-less."

Lilly looked at Ox before looking back up at Wolf. "We're all slaves?"

"You've been a slave your whole life, Baby," Wolf said. "You were raised in the world system. When you were born, your birth was registered. Then your brainwashed mother taught you how to behave and function in the system before you were instructed at school, and then again at a teachers' training institution. You received further instruction when you attended church and whenever you turned on your television. After that, you gave birth to slaves, and you gave them instruction ... Everyone you knew was a slave."

"It's called society, and we *were* paid!" Lilly protested.

"Paid?" Wolf laughed. "Don't you mean given a mere token of your worth? You lived in a system of control where a tiny portion of the people owned almost everything, and they charged mega amounts for their products and services while they paid you peanuts for yours. Most people have just enough money to put food on their table, pay the electrical bill, and keep a roof over their heads."

"We were comfortable," Lilly said. "I was free!"

"Your comfort was a reward from the state for doing their dirty work," Wolf said. "You brainwashed little girls and your husband—a lawyer—defended the system, but you were still a prisoner. You lived in a prison where the rules were dreamt up at central control and then policed. If you'd disobeyed the rules, you would've been nabbed off the street, tried and thrown into a correction facility. There, attempts would've been made to realign your behavior."

Lilly scoffed. "It's called society, and it served us well. You can't have people running around stealing."

"Stealing?" Wolf laughed. "You were robbed blind every day of your life. What do you think happened when you filled up your gas tank or paid your electrical bill? If gas costs fifteen cents per liter to produce, and you paid two dollars twenty for it ... what do you call that?"

Lilly blinked several times. "Petrol costs fifteen cents a liter to produce?"

"About that," Wolf said. "Around seventy percent of almost everything you paid for was padded profit and tax. The system is designed to give a lucky few a privileged life ... Isn't that theft?"

"I guess," Lilly said with a shrug.

"You guess? The people of the United States don't own the Federal Reserve, and the people of Europe don't own the reserve banks of Europe. When the Treasury of the United States needs more money, it exchanges a bond ... an IOU ... for invented money from the Federal Reserve; money that's mostly just numbers on a screen. Only about three percent of money exists in actual coins and notes.

The borrowed pieces of paper, coins, and numbers on a screen expand the money supply ... steal value from money already in circulation. This reduces the value of every dollar in your purse ... and there's always a deficit. More money is constantly required to pay for goods and services."

"I don't understand what you're saying," Lilly said.

"Real money, plus interest, is paid for non-existent money ... for numbers on a screen and worthless bits of paper that only gain value by devaluing the currency already in circulation. The system requires that inflation is constant ... that things constantly cost more."

Lilly stared at Wolf. "You're referring to a house costing three thousand dollars in the sixties, and that same house being worth six hundred thousand dollars today? You're saying inflation equals theft?"

"Correct. The constant expansion of the money supply causes inflation which equals legalized theft."

"I'm a New Zealander ... a Kiwi," Lilly declared. "We have our own Reserve Bank and it's owned by the government."

Wolf scoffed. "Countries like yours aren't exempt from the system of theft. You borrow your money from the overseas banks I'm talking about. Your money supply is expanded by borrowing invented money from them and paying interest on it."

Lilly groaned. "For shit's sake! Are you serious? Our government pays someone to print numbers on a screen, then they pay them real cash, plus interest for it?"

"That's right," Wolf said.

Lilly jolted upright. "You're wrong," she announced triumphantly. "The US borrows money from China."

Wolf laughed. "They only say that because the public is waking up to the scam. The money supply is constantly being expanded worldwide ... Money exists today that never used to exist. There's only one way that can happen ... printing presses running flat-out and numbers constantly being typed into a screen ... There's no other way."

"Surely, theft on such a monumental scale can't go unnoticed. I lived in a democracy."

"No," Wolf said. "You *thought* you lived in a democracy ... there's a difference. The world is run by thirteen families, and they need money ... lots and lots of money. They use their stolen loot to steer world events and fund our world."

"Thirteen families?" Lilly said. "Isn't the US Government the biggest power in the world?"

"The Federal Reserve isn't owned by the US Government. It's owned by the thirteen families I'm talking about ... The Crown holds the power."

"The Crown? The Queen of England?"

Wolf cleared his throat. "The Crown hasn't been the King or Queen of England since King William the third of Orange privatized the Bank of England in 1694, and established the corporate body known as the City of London. It's a sovereign state located in the heart of greater London.

The City of London is considered the Vatican of the financial world and it isn't subject to British law. It has its own courts, its own laws, its own flag, and even its own police force; it houses the Bank of England, Lloyd's of London, the London Stock Exchange, all British banks, and the branch offices of 385 foreign banks and 70 US banks, as well as Fleet Street's newspaper and publishing monopolies. The headquarters of British Freemasonry is, likewise, located there. The true power of the world lies in the hands of thirteen families, not in the parliaments or senates of the world. The Crown holds no allegiance to any country."

"You mean," Lilly said, "it's like the Vatican. It's a sovereign state?"

"The world's power is housed in three sovereign states," Wolf said. "The Vatican—the religious capital. The City of London—the financial capital, and Washington D.C.—the military capital of the world."

Lilly blinked several times. "Ox told me the world is ruled by a multi-armed octopus ... a beast whose arms include the Catholic Church, the Freemasons and members of Skulls and Bones among others, and together they rule the world."

"Who do you suppose is at the top of the pyramid controlling and directing the beast?" Wolf said. "It's the thirteen families I'm talking about."

Lilly sighed heavily. "How come I didn't know any of this?"

"Because the thirteen families own the media, and they don't publicize their deeds ... or rather ... misdeeds. Tell me, Baby, do you think the police are employed to protect you?"

"Of course," Lilly said. "They protect and serve."

Wolf laughed. "It's not the populace they protect and serve. The police aren't hired to catch the real criminals. They're hired to ensure your continued obedience by enforcing the ruling classes' laws so the privileged few can continue to oppress you and steal from you."

"What about murderers and rapists?" Lilly said. "Isn't it the police's job to nab them?"

Wolf smiled a weary smile. "The police are hired to enforce the system. It's their job to make sure the slaves remain productive and the system functional. Harmed slaves become unproductive. A slave has great value, so anyone caught raping or killing one must be punished. Order *must* be maintained."

"Well," Lilly said. "That's a very cynical way to view the world.

What about welfare?"

"What use is a slave if it can't feed its children, or if it gets injured, it can't afford medical care? Systems are put in place to ensure the slaves remain productive and their children cared for. A child is an asset of the Crown; it must be protected."

"Our taxes pay for welfare!" Lilly exclaimed.

"Of course. You can't expect the fat controllers of the world to spend their hard-stolen loot on welfare. The productive slaves must care for and supplement the unproductive slaves—help them raise their children."

"Doesn't the world system disgust you?"

"No," Wolf said matter-of-factly.

Lilly's eyes widened. "How can you not be disgusted by it when you've just gone to such lengths to explain how crooked it is?"

"Our systems are interconnected ... A portion of the money taxed and leveraged from the people of the world is funneled to us as a tribute—it pays for our comfort and privilege. We don't deal in money so our tribute consists of goods and services, gold and women. Our needs are met by the masses in your previous society ... by the dogs."

"By the dogs!"

"Yes," Wolf said. "Dogs ... ordinary people. The system you're now living under is at least honest. We know we're slaves, and nobody is blowing smoke up our arses."

Lilly groaned. "Surely, you must find the world system repugnant?"

"No," Wolf said. "The families that rule the world have earned their position. They're bred into their roles and trained from birth. Dogs obey their masters, it's the way of the world."

Lilly glared at Wolf. "That's despicable!"

"Cat's assistant was called Kumea. Can you guess why?"

"I never met his assistant." Lilly frowned. "His name was Kumea?" She thought for a moment. "As in 'come here'? How you'd call a dog?"

Wolf laughed. "Yes. It's an in-house joke. All new trainees are nick-named that before they graduate."

Lilly continued to glare at Wolf. "I can't believe you're like a god, and yet you say such things."

"I'm *like* a god?"

"Yes, you design animals and terraform worlds," Lilly said, thinking of a creepy alien movie that had a terraforming operation in progress. "So, you're *like* a god."

Wolf raised his brow. "I'm an intellectual, so I'm *like* a god?"

"Well ... yes," Lilly said. "God controls humanity. Isn't that what your people do?"

"I spend my days creating plants and animals and feeding a baby. I care not for consequences and control systems."

Lilly frowned. "Then why are you called Wolf?"

"I look like a wolf, don't I?"

"So," Lilly said. "You don't let people into heaven and give them eternal life."

Wolf threw back his head and laughed a loud, raucous laugh. "You mean when people die and get buried in the ground, do I raise them up from their graves and take them to some magical place in the sky to live with me?"

Lilly's brow furrowed. "Yes ... that's what I meant."

"Of course I don't," Wolf said. "That's impossible! Only fools and children believe in such nonsense."

Lilly looked down. "You don't need to mock." Damn, I've become as silly as a teenage girl crying over the first fool she meets, indeed, worshipping him.

"No," Wolf said. "But to be fair, your Bible says, 'On Earth as it is in heaven,' and, 'God is a God of the living, not of the dead.'"

"Where's heaven, then?"

"There's no such place ... unless you're referring to life on other planets."

Lilly frowned. Of course, Wolf isn't a God. What the hell was I thinking? I'll continue to pray to my Jesus!

"Do you like your new home, Baby?" Cat said.

Lilly blinked. "What's behind the other doors?"

Cat followed her gaze. "One's your milking room and the other's the bathroom."

Lilly exhaled loudly. "Of course one is my milking room!"

CHAPTER TWENTY-SEVEN

Earthquakes

"What about world events and policy," Lilly said. "Do you manipulate them? Do you make catastrophes and orchestrate terror attacks to influence policy?"

"Of course," Wolf said.

Lilly groaned. She'd figured as much. "Give me an example."

"You're a New Zealand citizen, so I'll give you two examples ... both happened in Christchurch."

"Don't you mean ... I *was* a New Zealand citizen?"

"Indeed."

Lilly could only think of one terror attack. It happened on March 15th, 2019 when a crazed gunman shot 51 people dead in a Christchurch mosque and injured a similar number. It was the worst mass killing in New Zealand's history.

"I'll speak of the February 22 earthquake that happened in 2011 first."

Lilly frowned. "That was a natural event ... surely?"

"No, it was a manmade disaster. Where you not aware of all the activity that was going on that day?"

"What activity?"

"More than 600 doctors, including 439 Australians, were attending a medical conference in the Christchurch Convention Centre when the quake struck. Many offered to help the injured:

> *Eight years on, remembering Christchurch's earthquake*
> *Tauranga urologist Peter Gilling said, for most people*
> *who survived the February quake, everything dated back*

to that day.

Gilling, originally from Canterbury, was at a conference in the city's CBD when it struck. In the chaos that followed, Gilling helped doctors treat injured quake victims at a makeshift shelter in Hagley Park.   The Herald: Feb 22[nd,] 2019

"Okay," Lilly said, "so there were lots of extra doctors ... it could have been a coincidence?"

"An American delegation of unprecedented level and quality which included 43 government, business and community leaders along with 9 Members of Congress were also in Christchurch that day. They were there for the United States, New Zealand Partnership Forum. I'm sure you're aware such events are not usually held in Christchurch, but rather in your largest city, or in your capital city ... Distinguished current and former government officials such as Kurt Campbell, Rich Armitage, Chris Hill, Wendy Sherman, Clayton Yeutter and Thad Allen were there with top executives from a dozen major American companies. David Huebner, substituted for Homeland Security Secretary Janet Napolitano. New Zealand Co-Chairs were Rt Hon James Bolger, former New Zealand Prime Minister, and Hon Michael Cullen, former Deputy Prime Minister.

Christchurch to host US delegation

One of the biggest security operations in Christchurch's history will mark the visit of United States politicians next month.

American security officials have visited Christchurch and are expected to return in the weeks leading up to the United States New Zealand Partnership Forum - February 20 to 22.

The city beat Auckland to host the event, which organizers yesterday said would attract at least one high-ranking US senator and possibly a delegation from the US Congress."
Stuff News: Jan 11[th,] 2011

"And they were in Christchurch at the time of the Earthquake?"

Lilly said.

"They were spread around town attending a variety of luncheons when the quake occurred," Wolf said. "Admiral Thad Allen and other top personnel from FEMA were near the airport visiting the Antarctic center, but Christopher Hill, the former United States ambassador to Iraq, was in the city center. He told CNN the earthquake was the most frightening experience of his life.

"Hill said the quake was a violent shaking after a series of smaller tremors earlier in the day. 'I was speaking to the conference and made a crack that it was like being back in Baghdad when the big quake struck, it was like a giant took hold of the room we were sitting in and shook it. I've never been subjected to such violent shaking. All the waiters and waitresses fell down, glasses broke everywhere, it was really quite extraordinary.'"

"Yes, it was a terrible quake."

"Did you know the nine US congressmen left the city in the morning for a scheduled meeting with your Prime Minister, John Key, in Wellington? When asked where he was when the quake happened, Key said he was attending a meeting with a business delegation:

> *Christchurch quake: Death toll may top 200*
> *Nine US congressmen had left Christchurch this morning*
> *before the quake struck and were visiting Parliament this*
> *afternoon."*   Newshub: Feb 22nd, 2011

> *Helpless feeling worst for Key*
> *When the quake struck at 12:51 pm that day, Key was in*
> *his 9th-floor beehive office, meeting a business delegation.*
>   The Press: Feb 20th, 2012

"I think I do remember that an American delegation was visiting, yes," Lilly said. "Our Prime Minister was with nine congressmen when the quake struck ... Wow!"

"Yeah, nothing odd about that," Wolf said sarcastically.

"I remember a rather incredible story that also happened that day," Lilly said. "Three Israelis had to smash their way out of a crushed van in the central city, leaving a fourth person, Ofer Mizrahi, dead in the vehicle. Mizrahi was later found to have at least five passports. The Israeli Prime Minister Benjamin Netanyahu called our Prime Minister John Key four times that day, but Key would only discuss parts of the calls. He said they were to offer help and advice, but he wouldn't discuss other aspects of the calls."

"Of course not."

"There was also an incredible admission by Shemi Tzur," Lilly said, "the Israeli Ambassador to New Zealand. Within hours of the February 22, 2011 earthquake striking, Tzur, who was based in Canberra, Australia, flew to Christchurch to meet up with the surviving members of Mizrahi's team; he drove them to the airport.

"It was widely reported that Mizrahi's associates left New Zealand within twelve hours, but there was hardly any mention of Tzur. Why did the ambassador himself, fly all the way from Canberra into a disaster zone to personally drive the Israelis to the airport? Was he recovering passports and other incriminating materials, documents, and smuggling them out of the country in his diplomatic bag?"

"His actions were indeed suggestive of underhand things going on," Wolf said. "Later, a search and rescue team arrived in Christchurch from Israel, but the squad's offer of help was rejected by the New Zealand authorities because they didn't have the necessary United Nations accreditation. The Israeli government also sent a forensic team to help authorities identify the dead. New Zealand officials became alarmed when intelligence information was collated, and they realized the Israeli forensic team had been given access to the police's national database to help with identification work:

> *SAS patrolled near suspected Israeli spies*
> *The police national computer has been under scrutiny in*
> *the aftermath of the Christchurch earthquake in February*
> *because of fears Israeli agents loaded software into the*
> *system that would allow backdoor access to highly*

sensitive intelligence files.

The Security Intelligence Service (SIS) ordered the checks as part of an urgent investigation of what one SIS officer described as the suspicious activities of several groups of Israelis during and immediately after the earthquake.

Three Israelis were among the 181 people who died when the earthquake destroyed most of Christchurch's central business district on February 22. One was found to be carrying at least five passports.

An unaccredited Israeli search and rescue squad was later confronted by armed New Zealand officers and removed from the sealed-off 'red zone' of the central city ...

Paul Buchanan, who has worked at the Pentagon and trained intelligence officers in the United States, said it was suspicious that one of the Israelis was carrying multiple passports and that his friends left New Zealand so shortly after he was killed.

He believed the four Israelis were probably on a 'trolling mission' searching for identities they could steal.

'Because of New Zealand's international reputation, the passports are extremely valuable for intelligence services. New Zealand has this reputation for independence and autonomy ... people trust New Zealand,' he said.

'The passports would have been used for very covert activities - nothing light.'

He said those activities could include assassinations.

Stuff News: July 20^{th,} 2011

"I remember that," Lilly said. "Our Prime Minister was asked repeatedly to confirm details of an SIS investigation into whether the Israeli secret service had infiltrated the police's national computer. He said he was satisfied there'd been no misuse of the police computer, but when repeatedly asked if there had been an investigation by SIS he refused to answer because it, apparently, wasn't in the national interest. When asked, repeatedly, if the Israeli government had done anything wrong, he again refused to answer, saying it wasn't in the national interest."

"There were others in Christchurch just before the quake—"

"Yes," Lilly said, "apparently in September a group of international highly specialized earthquake seismologists, or geophysics, were busy around Darfield where the earlier, larger, but less violent quake, struck the previous September. One specialist was here after it happened. Professor Kevin Furlong was attending the University of Canterbury as a visiting Erskine fellow at the time. He was still here in early 2011. The Erskine Program enables up to 70 visiting senior international academics to lecture at UC each year to undergraduates and postgraduate students. Furlong is a professor at Penn State University in the United States ... but couldn't all of this be a coincidence?"

"Was it also a coincidence that a huge military training exercise was about to take place only a short distance away?

Military exercise is one of NZ's biggest

About 1000 personnel from the three branches of the armed forces started arriving yesterday in the South Canterbury and North Otago areas for one of the biggest exercises to be held in New Zealand for years.

They will be based in and around Timaru until Friday ...

Specific details of Exercise Southern Katipo are being kept secret so personnel are not tipped off ... Senior media adviser with the army Major Christian Dunne said the troop movement was one of the 'biggest for years.'

The exercise is to test and evaluate the defense force's ability to react quickly to short-notice deployments, such as assistance to other countries, protected evacuation of New Zealand nationals, disruption of insurgent and criminal groups, and humanitarian relief ...

The exercise involves the army, air force, and navy.

The initial move was last night, deploying troops by air force C130s to Timaru Airport to secure the airport, establish a forward operating base then secure Timaru Port for the arrival of HMNZS Canterbury today.

> *Canterbury will be landing troops and army vehicles at*
> *the port.*   Otago Daily Times: February 22nd, 2011

"The HMNZS Canterbury was in Christchurch's port, in Lyttleton harbor when the quake struck," Lilly said.

"And you think that was a coincidence? Think it just happened to be in port and that 116 soldiers from the Singapore Army, also, just happened to be in Christchurch ready to help out?

> *Singapore Armed Forces Assistance Appreciated*
> *The Singapore Armed Forces personnel were originally in Christchurch to participate in a military exercise with the New Zealand Defense Force when the earthquake struck on 22 February. They were later joined by two Singapore C130 Hercules aircraft that worked alongside the Royal New Zealand Air Force to create an air bridge to transport supplies and people.*
> *The Chief of Defense Force, Lieutenant General Rhys Jones, praised the Singaporean team for their immediate offer of assistance to work alongside the Defense Force and civil authorities in maintaining security in the inner city and assisting with a number of the other key tasks. "Without any hesitation, they offered their help in whatever way they could, whether it was on the cordons, engineering or transporting people out of Christchurch."*
>   Scoop News/Politics: March 15th, 2011

"I thought it was all a miraculous coincidence," Lilly said. "You can't create earthquakes."

"Of course you can!" Wolf said. "The United States has had the technology for years. What do you think all the underground nuclear tests were about?"

Lilly blinked rapidly.

"Cannikin … an underground nuclear weapons test performed on November 6, 1971, on Amchitka Island, Alaska, by the United States Atomic Energy Commission; involved a large missile being lowered into a mined cavity 5875 ft beneath the surface that was lined with 54-inch steel. The hole was then completely stemmed, back-filled, with material designed to contain radiation. The nuclear bomb was predicted to have a yield of less than five megatons. When detonated, water disturbance was observed but there was no tsunami. Ground shock was felt as a rocking motion twenty-three miles away, but it was only faintly perceptible at a military base 200 miles away. However, recordings near the site recorded a body wave magnitude 6.8 and a surface wave of 5.7."

"Are you serious?" Lilly said. "I do seem to remember the University of Canterbury and Geological & Nuclear Sciences (GNS) carrying out a range of investigations across Christchurch to better understand earthquake sources—faults. They drilled into the port hills and other places after the September quake … Are you saying the US detonated a nuke under Christchurch, and they did it with our Prime Minister's blessing?"

"Of course," Wolf said. "Do you recall him reading out a Bible verse during a memorial service that he attended? Your then Prime Minister, John Key was to read out Romans, chapter 8, verses 35-39 in the New Testament, but he skipped verse 36:

> *Romans 8:[35] Who shall separate us from the love of Christ? Shall tribulation, or distress, or persecution, or famine, or nakedness, or peril, or sword?* [36] **As it is written, for your sake we are killed all the day long; we are accounted as sheep for the slaughter.** [37] *Nay, in all these things we are more than conquerors through him that loved us.* [38] *For I am persuaded, that neither death, nor life, nor angels, nor principalities, nor powers, nor things present, nor things to come,* [39] *Nor height, nor depth, nor any other creature, shall be able to separate us from the love of God, which is in Christ Jesus our Lord.*

"I do remember that, and considering Kiwis have long been labeled sheep because of the large number of them here, it was particularly offensive. A few days beforehand I read in the newspaper he was going to read that verse, so I looked it up. I couldn't believe he would read that passage. As it turned out, he missed verse 36:

> Romans 8:*36* As it is written, for your sake we are killed all the day long; we are accounted as sheep for the slaughter."

"Did that lessen his crime?"

"No, the verse is included in the passage in the Bible, and therefore, it was hideous that he chose it." Lilly sighed. "Surely, the U.S. and whoever else was involved, couldn't also have created the magnitude 7.8 Kaikoura earthquake that occurred two minutes after midnight on the 14th of November 2016 in New Zealand's South Island?"

"They most certainly could, and did," Wolf said. "You do know it occurred when a flotilla of navy ships, including the U.S. warship Sampson, Australia's HMAS Darwin, and Canada's HMCS Vancouver were in New Zealand's waters for your Navy's 75th birthday celebrations which took place in Auckland's Hauraki Gulf. The ships traveled to Kaikoura to help evacuate residents, but they did more than that, helicopters from the vessels delivered load after load of cargo to the shore. Most of it away from prying eyes. It was then trucked via back roads to Christchurch on a convoy of military trucks."

"So, the earthquake *was* manmade?"

"To create a massive earthquake, like the 7.8 Kaikoura quake, you look for pent up forces in the earth's crust and spark them into action with either a huge explosive or HAARP technology. HAARP was used to make the September 4th quake in Christchurch. This was made evident by the huge green aurora that flashed across the sky. Making use of pent up forces in the Earth's crust is similar to detonating a block of C4 with a detonator. The potential force of the C4 is released or caused to go off, by the detonator. In the case of a massive earthquake created by man, an underground explosion or HAARP technology is the trigger employed."

"That's warfare!"

"Indeed, it is."

"What about the Alpine fault that's predicted to go off in the Southern Alps of New Zealand and possibly create an earthquake as large as a magnitude 9? Surely, the global elite wouldn't set that off?"

"What do you suppose all the drilling into the Alps to study the fault was about? You don't really think a 25-ton steel tube and 40 tons of concrete just somehow, accidentally, fell into a hole on top of a mountain ... do you?

> *Alpine fault drilling project put on hold*
>
> *In early December, the team was drilling at a rate of nearly 3m an hour and the nature of the rock being drilled through indicated they were closing in on the fault.*
>
> *At 893m deep, the team started preparing the borehole for coring - to allow close inspection of the material surrounding the fault.*
>
> *That was when calamity struck - a 25-ton steel tube, along with 40 tons of cement, dropped into the borehole.*
>
> *Shortly before Christmas, the team called it a day.*
>
> EQC + Stuff News: Jan 12th. 2015

"How can a 25-tonne steel tube and 40 tonnes of cement accidentally drop into a borehole on a mountain, and what was it doing up there in the first place?" Lilly said. "Isn't that 16 cubes of concrete, or three large trucks full? How could that be an accident? Hang on a minute ... isn't that what they did on that Island in Alaska when they set off the nuke? Wasn't that bomb placed into a mined cavity lined with 54-inch steel...? What are you saying? They dropped a huge bomb in the hole so they could set it off later?"

"Of course," Wolf said.

"Oh, my God!"

"Sometimes, several created events are required to bring about a desired set of circumstances to advance a plan to fruition. In regards to earthquakes, you can set off several smaller ones to load up another fault line, causing a bigger release of pent up energy there."

"Insane! Why would they destroy Christchurch, I don't understand?"

"The central city needed to be destroyed so they could establish a forward base."

CHAPTER TWENTY-EIGHT

Little Boy

"Your evil plan isn't going to work!" Lilly snarled. "My people will blow you to bits with our nuclear bombs."

Wolf laughed. "They're not *your* bombs and they're not *nuclear* bombs either. They're big bombs masquerading as nuclear weapons ... war propaganda!"

"They're real," Lilly said aghast. "Aren't they?"

"On the sixth of August 1945 at 8.15 a.m., the first nuclear bomb called Little Boy exploded over Japan. Forty-five seconds after it left the hanger of the *Enola Gay*, a B29 bomber, three red arming plugs initiated by time and barometric triggers sparked and ignited four bags of cordite gunpower. The exploding bags of gunpowder sent a projectile of uranium racing down the barrel of the large enclosed gun in the bomb's interior, smashing it into a target of more uranium. Within seconds, the colliding uranium supposedly reached critical mass via a nuclear chain reaction and the bomb exploded 1900 feet above the city of Hiroshima. Below, on a hot summer's morning, people filled the streets on their way to work and school."

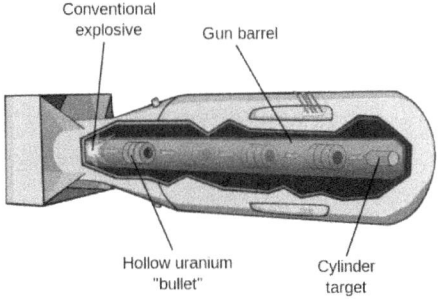

Conventional explosive · Gun barrel · Hollow uranium "bullet" · Cylinder target

"If you say so ... I'm not sure I've heard all the intricate details before. What are you saying? That's not true ... that's not what happened?"

"Oh, it's true. Apart from the bit about there being a nuclear chain reaction ... that's pure propaganda."

"The bomb exploded ... didn't it?"

"Yes," Wolf said. "That's generally what happens when you ignite a huge pipe bomb ... Four large bags of cordite gunpowder, each the size of a loaf of bread, were exploded inside an enclosed metal chamber."

"But it caused utter devastation!"

"Yes, it did, but it wasn't the result of a nuclear reaction."

"There was an enormous blinding flash!"

"Yes, but that had nothing to do with the 140 pounds of uranium encased in the bomb. The combined weight of the thin, armored steel outer casing and the uranium housed within the interior gun barrel weighed roughly 500 pounds, but the bomb weighed 10,000 pounds."

Lilly frowned. "10,000 pounds? That's a discrepancy of nearly 9500 pounds—"

Workers checking Little Boy for the last time

"Or four tons ... yes, that's right," Wolf said. "Would you like to hazard a guess as to what the unexplained weight consisted of?"

Lilly shrugged. "I've no idea."

"Little Boy was no *little boy*. The bomb was ten feet long and weighed as much as a pickup truck. It was heavier than World War II bunker-busting bombs. They, of course, needed to be heavy because they were designed to penetrate deep underground, but their weight was simply weight. However, Little Boy didn't need to be heavy because it was designed to explode in mid-air."

"Okay," Lilly said. "If the middle of the bomb was an enclosed gun barrel, then what surrounded it? I've seen a photo of the inside of the bomb. Foam appeared to surround the inner gun barrel, and the bomb had a thin outer metal shell."

"Foam's lightweight, it wouldn't account for four tons of extra weight ... and why would you pad a bomb? The photo you saw was a mock-up. The extra weight was Napalm: an incendiary mixture of a gelling agent and a volatile petrochemical, gasoline/petrol or diesel fuel. Some of it was loose and some of it was contained in baseball-sized canisters that were violently expelled when the pipe bomb core of the bomb exploded. Later, white phosphorus pellets were dropped with supposed nuclear bombs tested after the war. White phosphorus is highly reactive, spontaneously igniting in 30°C moist air. It needs to be stored in water.

"It was no accident that Little Boy was dropped on a hot summer's day, and it wasn't an accidental consequence that people were covered in horrific burns after the explosion. Eyewitnesses saw a blinding flash of magnesium and an enormous amount of black smoke."

Lilly frowned. "Was the enclosed gun barrel made of magnesium ... that's a lightweight metal?"

"Yes. Magnesium is durable enough to be used as a structural metal. When the bomb exploded, it flashed brilliant white. Blowing itself to bits, it ignited the Napalm in and out of canisters that were sprayed in every direction. Magnesium burns intensely at approximately 3100 degrees Celsius or 5610 degrees Fahrenheit, but the core of the bomb burned even hotter because the explosion was initially contained within a small volume of air. The temperature on the ground below rose so quickly, everything flammable burst into flames—including clothing. Within a radius of 800 feet from ground zero, almost nobody survived. What remains of them are called atom shadows—imprints of the people caught in the immediate blast."

A supposed nuclear bomb being detonated in a desert in the US
shows the burning phosphorus pellets being dropped with it.

Lilly snorted. "That's disgusting! Surely, that must have been an international war crime?"

"Indeed," Wolf said. "You think a nuclear bomb isn't?"

"So, the nuclear bomb was little more than a parlor trick?"

"Indeed. The uranium in the bomb did nothing more than turn it into a dirty bomb. The Manhattan Project also designed a bomb called 'Thin Man,' but all the shells were abandoned because the bomb didn't work."

Lilly frowned. "Little Boy was a dirty bomb?"

"Yes ... That's the name given to a bomb filled with toxic radiation ... isn't it?"

"What about the mushroom cloud? Nuclear bombs make mushroom clouds. I've seen pictures ... videos."

"The bomb dropped over Hiroshima made a pitiful mushroom cloud. Most of the footage currently shown in documentaries is fake. Besides, any large explosion will form a mushroom cloud. The sudden formation of a large volume of low-density gases in the atmosphere will rise rapidly and create turbulent vortices that curl down around the edges and form temporary vortex rings.

"The grand effect of the supposed nuclear detonation—including the mushroom stem—was generated by exploding the bomb high above the ground. Modern-day non-nuclear thermobaric weapons like the MOAB bomb are called vacuum bombs because, after their initial explosion, gases cool and pressure drops sharply, leading to a partial vacuum. This effect is exaggerated when a bomb is exploded high above the ground because smoke and dust are drawn up to the initial explosion site and form the classic mushroom stem."

"That's why it was detonated so high?"

"Of course," Wolf said, "but that wasn't the only reason. They said they exploded the bomb high above the ground to lessen the amount of radioactivity that would reach the ground, but just as the inner casing of the bomb was made of magnesium for visual effect, so was the bomb's detonation height; it also increased its shock wave.

"When the bomb exploded, a super-heated bubble of air violently pushed outwards and downwards, reflecting off the ground it created a primary wave and a reflected shock wave. This meant the bomb did far more damage than it would have had it been exploded on the ground because the Earth absorbs most of the energy in a ground detonation."

"So, a huge blast wave expanded outwards over Hiroshima?"

"Yes," Wolf said. "Most of the buildings in Hiroshima were simple wooden structures. The blast wave, traveling at the speed of sound, smashed countless buildings in ten seconds, turning walls and windows into flying shrapnel. But it only blew out the windows of reinforced concrete buildings."

"I guess detonating the bomb on the ground would have spoilt the theatrics," Lilly said bitterly. "Clearly, the bomb was part of some shock and awe campaign designed to scare people into submission, as much as it was designed to kill."

"Yes. To increase the chances of a desired firestorm, the bomb was detonated at 8.15am when cooking fires were lit. The blast wave knocked over and broke countless lit stoves, causing numerous fires to erupt. These fires, combined with the fires already ignited by the canisters of Napalm that were splattered everywhere, caused a firestorm so massive it killed almost 70,000 people."

Lilly shook her head in dismay.

"When many fires are set at once, the hot flames suck in surrounding ground air, generating gale force winds of over fifty miles an hour. The wind whips the flames up into vortices. Like dust devils on a hot summer's day, the firestorm turned the city of Hiroshima into a red ocean of burning flames. The fire raged for more than six hours and consumed four and a half square miles of cityscape before finally burning itself out, after turning the city into a blackened mess."

"But didn't people die from radiation poisoning?"

"The uranium in the bomb didn't increase the bomb's explosive power, but it did increase its killing potential. The smoke and debris sucked up into the rising mushroom cloud mixed with the cool, humid, air in the upper atmosphere. It then fell down as radioactive rain. Large black droplets of highly radioactive poison fell onto the skin of the people below, hurting them. They were so desperate for water to drink, they opened their mouths and drank the droplets as they fell from the sky, sealing their fate."

Lilly placed her head in her hands. "The men who created and dropped that bomb were monsters! The creation of such a weapon is beyond criminal. They should all have been tried for war crimes. How dare they accuse others of war crimes when they made such a terrible weapon and used it on civilians? What a horrendously, cruel and callous thing to do!"

Wolf sighed.

"Oh, my God!" Lilly said, staring at him. "Were you guys the wizards behind the curtain? Did you design that bomb and tell them how to use it?"

"We believe war should be avoided if possible, but if you can't avoid war, you should mitigate the fallout. Japan had been firebombed from coast to coast, but still, they fought on ... They were given every opportunity to surrender."

"I don't think that counts as an excuse."

"Doesn't it?" Wolf said. "Over a hundred thousand people were killed in Tokyo when it was firebombed, and it didn't stop the war.

The bomb dropped on Hiroshima killed fewer people, but together with the less effective bomb that was dropped on Nagasaki, it did stop the war."

"I don't buy it," Lilly said. "There's more to it."

"Of course. Those bombs were designed to prevent wars ... to scare people into submission. Proxy wars broke out afterward, mainly in Vietnam, but in general, the world has been a relatively peaceful place since World War II ... especially in the West. And to be fair ... what we gave them was little more than a party trick. It only worked because the people of Hiroshima had built their houses out of wood and they used simple cooking stoves."

Lilly scoffed. "There's always some war going on somewhere. It's not the news if there isn't war footage. What about hydrogen bombs and multi-headed nuclear missiles?"

"Nonsense," Wolf said. "The whole thing has been a smoke and mirrors campaign from the very beginning. In Operation Sailor Hat, on June 19, 1965, at Kaho'olawe, Hawaii, they faked the effects of a nuclear bomb by stacking towers of TNT sky high and exploding them. Several other major tests were carried out inside large buildings away from prying eyes using similar stacks of TNT. And the desert tests were just non-nuclear Hiroshima-type bombs. If you view these tests on YouTube, you'll see soldiers climb out of their bunkers and walk right up to the explosion site of a supposed nuclear bomb minutes after it's detonation."

"So, it was all a hoax? If a nuclear chain reaction bomb doesn't work, then how come nuclear reactors *do work*? Nuclear science is real ... We have nuclear power plants."

"Of course," Wolf said. "They generate heat in a reactor. You don't need to mechanically compress uranium metal rings in a tube to start a reaction. In a peaceful atomic power plant, there is no mechanical compression of uranium atoms. The fission, fragment kinetic energy, remains as low-temperature heat which causes little or no ionization. The speed a neutron is traveling when it hits the nucleus influences how likely fission is to occur. One might think if a neutron is going really fast that it has a better chance of shattering the nucleus, but this is not how reactors work ... slower neutrons are more likely to create fission."

Lilly frowned.

"Slowing neutrons down to maximize fission is an absolute must. They're slowed in the moderating substance in a nuclear reactor by bouncing them off the nuclei of the atoms in the moderating material. In most reactors, moderation takes place in the water that cools the reactor, and neutrons born from fission continue the reaction. In high-temperature reactors, like liquid-fluoride reactors, graphite carbon is used as the moderator."

"But nuclear power plants can explode!"

"Yes, they can, but only from overheating due to a lack of cooling water ... causing a Fukushima-style explosion."

Lilly shrugged. "Surely Hiroshima was a radioactive wasteland after they dropped the Little Boy bomb."

"No," Wolf said. "Soldiers found almost no radioactivity two weeks later and within months plants had begun to regrow ... Most of the survivors remained in Hiroshima, and today it's a modern city ... The public's bombarded with endless propaganda in television shows and films regarding nuclear bombs, but it's all nonsense."

"Then how come nukes are being used to set off fault-lines and create massive earthquakes?"

The canister for the Cannikin test being lowered into the test shaft.

"They're not … I called it a nuclear bomb for simplicity's sake because I hadn't explained the fraudulent nature of these bombs to you yet … The bomb tested in Alaska, in 1971 was enormous. If a suitcase nuke is supposedly able to cause utter devastation, then why was it so big? And if all a nuclear bomb is supposedly doing is smashing two pieces of weapons-grade uranium together, then a bit of C4 would do the trick. Huge, buried, pipe bombs, or liquid fuel bombs, are powerful enough to cause a blast wave that travels through the earth and is perceived as a violent earthquake; if placed beside a fault-line, they'll trigger it."

CHAPTER TWENTY-NINE

No white lands

"How did you feel after the Christchurch terror attack," Wolf said.

"Which attack are we talking about now? The mass shooting carried out by the supposed, crazed, Australian white supremacist named Brenton Harrison Tarrant who shot dead 51 people and injured a similar number in two mosques on March 15th, 2019?"

"Yes."

"I felt traumatized and confused. Of course, it was horrific, and one couldn't help but feel for the victims. But as soon as our Prime Minister, Jacinda Ardern, spoke, all kinds of suppressed feelings started making their way to the surface. When Islamic terrorists carried out an attack in Manchester, England, the UK's government sent police officers to mosques to make sure the Muslims were feeling okay.

"This is now the predictable Western government reaction to a Muslim terror attack, along with cries of, 'We must not become Islamophobic, it was just a couple of radicals.' But when a white man carries out a terror attack, there's no claim of a lone wolf attack, even though he supposedly did operate alone. Instead, our government, and governments overseas, immediately start looking for white radicals everywhere ... the guy next door might be a white radical:

Further Fallout from Christchurch
-When a devout Muslim shouting Allah Akbar kills many
innocents in the name of Islam, almost every politician,
media outlet and 'expert' will insist that this had
absolutely nothing to do with Islam, he was a lone wolf,

and he was mentally ill. We should do nothing about the political ideology that routinely produces such killers.

-When an evil white supremacist who says he intensely dislikes conservatism and Trump, praises communist China and calls himself an eco-fascist goes on a killing spree, just about every politician, media outlet and 'expert' will insist that basically all conservatives and Christians share in the responsibility for this massacre. We should do all we can to restrict and shut down these sorts of folks. Culture watch: Mar 18ᵗʰ, 2019

"I could hardly believe our Prime Minister's first speech:

Jacinda Ardern, [NZ Prime Minister] after Christchurch
"We are a proud nation of more than 200 ethnicities, 160 languages, and amongst that diversity, we share common values. And the one that we place currency on right now is our compassion and the support for the community of those directly affected by this tragedy and secondly, the strongest possible condemnation of the ideology of the people that did this.
"You may have chosen us, but we utterly reject and condemn you." The Spinoff: March 22ᵗʰ 2019

"So," Lilly said. "Instead of saying this man did a terrible thing and he was a crazed lone wolf, Ardern says WE, as in all of us, have the strongest possible condemnation for the *ideology* which instigated the terror attack, but if you remove the violent component from Tarrant's manifesto, it was a document calling out the treachery of Western governments' who've continued to flood white lands with other peoples against the wishes of their citizens. Tarrant says this will lead to the destruction of both our nations and our heritage, which is a belief many share.

"So, there you have it, if you've lived in this country all your life, and you've watched successive governments change the ethnic makeup of the country from 97 percent white to 3 percent Maori in the 1970s … to a country where only 3 white babies are born per ten births in our largest city, and you're upset about it, the government rejects you! It doesn't matter that you peacefully protested via your political vote, election after election, as did a large percentage of the population. Your opinion counts for nothing … it's irrelevant. Worse than that, you're now the enemy, and you need to be viewed as a dangerous terrorist … and most importantly … you're not us!

> *Speech by Jacinda Ardern*
> *These are people who have extremist views and they have absolutely no place in NZ, and, in fact, have no place in the world … The strongest possible condemnation of the ideology of the people who did this, you may have chosen us but we UTTERLY REJECT you!"*
> Live on 1 news at 7 pm TV One: March 15th, 2019

"Wow, just, wow!" Lilly said. "There's a smack in the face for you. Clearly, having ancestors who date back to the first four ships and family who've helped build this country, counts for nothing! My initial feeling after the attack, and especially after Ardern's speeches, was one of rage. Surely, if there's anybody to blame for the attack, it's the succession of government ministers who've blatantly ignored calls to reduce immigration. We have a housing crisis and our social services are stretched thin, clearly because of mass immigration, yet government ministers take no responsibility for any of it …

"Am I surprised when someone loses the plot and kills 51 people, that they shoulder no blame … no, I'm not. Am I surprised they've turned on us, the founders and builders of this country and openly rejected us? Yes, I've got to admit that did take me by surprise, but she's right, we do have no place in the world because governments like hers have seen to it. There are NO WHITE LANDS, our lands are all multicultural, supposedly celebrating their diversity while the people who flood into them still have their own homelands, of course. Would they let us flood into their lands? No, of course not. So, thanks for pointing out that we have no place in the world,

Jacinda!"

Wolf nodded. "You know things are completely rotten when white males can't get a job in the police force and whites are excluded from journalist internships like they are in England:

> *Police force 'discriminated against white heterosexual male.'*
> *A police force which rejected a 'well prepared' potential recruit because he is a white, heterosexual male has been found guilty of discrimination.*   BBC News: February 22nd, 2019

> *BBC: Offering black, Asian and minority ethnic schemes is 'right thing to do.'*
> *The BBC has defended offering traineeships to ethnic minorities after a national newspaper accused the corporation of being 'anti-white.'*
> *The Sun quoted a job hunter who was turned down from a junior scriptwriting role because it was only available to people from 'ethnic minorities.'*   BBC News: June 3rd, 2016

Lilly groaned. "Well, in London, whites only make up 45 percent of the population, so on that basis, they should've been allowed to apply. And those two incidences of gross prejudice are bound to be only the tip of the iceberg ... Now, dangerous ideologies are to be stamped out here:

> *Hate crime law review fast-tracked following Christchurch mosque shootings*
> *Hon Andrew Little said he was fast-tracking a widespread review of New Zealand's existing hate speech legislation. This would include deciding if hate crime should be established as its own separate offense, as it is in the United Kingdom.*   Stuff News: March 30th, 2019

"Maybe you'll be able to address other ideologies in time?" Wolf said:

Egyptian minister quotes Koran verse on killing Jews
JTA — Egypt's minister of religious endowments in an interview quoted a verse from the Koran about killing Jews.

The interview with Talaat Mohamed Afifi Salem was aired last month on Sada Al-Balad TV on March 14, according to Washington, D.C.-based Middle East Media Research Institute. Asked by the interviewer whether he would 'visit Israel with a Palestinian visa,' the minister said: 'This is premature. Let's wait until it happens. However, we hope that the words of the Prophet Muhammad will be fulfilled: Judgment Day will not come before the Muslims fight the Jews, and the Jews will hide behind the rocks and the trees, but the rocks and the trees will say: Oh Muslim, oh servant of Allah, there is a Jew behind me, come and kill him — except for the gharqad tree, which is one of the trees of the Jews."
The Times of Israel: April 5^{th,} 2013

Lilly scoffed. "You know full well that won't happen. Dangerous ideologies hiding under the umbrella of religion will be allowed to prevail. In Europe, your freedom of speech mustn't upset the religious feelings of others. So, hateful verses aren't about to be addressed any time soon:

The Koran
'Fight against those who do not obey Allah and do not believe in Allah, or the Last Day, and do not forbid what has been forbidden by Allah and His messenger even if they are of the People of the Book until they pay the Jizya with willing submission and feel themselves subdued.' 9:29
'When you meet the unbelievers, smite their necks.' 47:4
'Men are the protectors and maintainers of women because Allah has made one superior to the other and because they spend to support them from their means. Therefore, righteous women are obedient and they guard

in the husband's absence what Allah orders them to guard. And, as to those women from whom you fear disobedience, give them a warning, send them to separate beds, and beat them.' 4:34

'Muhammad is the apostle of Allah. Those who follow Him are merciful to one another but harsh to the disbeliever.' 48:29

'They wish that you would reject faith as they have rejected faith unless that you would all be equal. So, don't take protectors from them unless they emigrate in the way of Allah but if they turn back, then seize them and kill them wherever you find them.' 4:89

Continuing her rant, Lilly said, "I'm sure our fallen soldiers would turn in their graves if they could see what successive governments have done to, not only our country but to all white homelands ... the indiscriminate opening of the ports letting in both diseases and dangerous ideologies.

"In London's main mosque, *Dispatches* unveiled terrifying beliefs and a rising, radical, Islamic ideology within the UK, but when it aired on television, it wasn't the Muslims who were investigated and interrogated, but rather the reporters. In 'Undercover Mosque: The Return,' *Dispatches* went back undercover and found the situation hadn't improved. The verse you quoted, 'The last day will not come until you have killed all the Jews,' was still being taught."

Lilly continued, "There's an appalling video on you-tube called, 'TRUE FACE OF ISLAM and THE VIDEO LABOUR DID NOT WANT LEAKED.' In it, Shahid Malik is giving a speech to a Muslim audience. In 2007 he became Britain's first Muslim Minister, a minister for International Development. He subsequently served as a Justice Minister, Home Office Minister, and most recently, a Minister for Race, Faith and Community Cohesion at the Development for Communities and Local government.

"In the video, he boasts about how he has helped send over a billion pounds to Muslim countries in aid. Then he goes on about how many Muslim MP's there were. At the time, there were four, before he says there will be many more. Currently, there's 26, before jubilantly saying, 'Soon the whole parliament will be Muslim!'

"He further says he is confident in the next thirty years or so, there will be a Muslim Prime Minister in the UK and that today we are showing the true face of Islam, 'our future in this country is very bright.' Of course, the mayor of London is currently a Muslim."

"I see you're angry," Wolf said.

"Yeah, no problem there," Lilly said sarcastically. "Islam is not a race or a religion. In its truest form, it's a complete way of living which includes Sharia law ... a law that clashes with our own values and beliefs. People act like Muslim's are all Middle Eastern, or Black, and to question Islam is to be racist, but supposedly Muhammad was white:

> *Qur'an, Hadith, and Scholars: Muhammad's White Complexion*
> *Chapter 26 of Sahih Muslim on the USC-MSA website is entitled*
> *Chapter 26: ALLAH'S MESSENGER (MAY PEACE BE UPON HIM) HAD A WHITE ELEGANT FACE*
> *Jurairi reported: I said to Abu Tufail: Did you see Allah's Messenger (May peace be upon him)? He said: Yes, he had a white handsome face.* WikiIslam

"You don't think every religion has a right to be taught in your land?"

"No, I don't!" Lilly said, "It's a betrayal to our people to allow ideologies that clash sharply with our way of life, to not only come into our lands but be sanctioned. Integration isn't possible if a person's religion forbids it and demands they conquer and subdue us. These people remain loyal to their own nations and culture, and they're endeavoring to spread Sharia law and Islam deceitfully through a well-practiced method:

> *Spread of Islam*
> *The spread of Islam in Western countries is led by Islamic*

nations and groups. Saudi Arabia and Turkey both broadcast sermons and send Imams to preach in Western lands as well as financing mosques. Turkey has been actively building and funding 5th columns in Europe, and their Directorate of Religious Affairs [Diyanet] has greatly increased its funding in recent years.

Phase 1: Incubation

When Muslims first arrive in a Western democracy, they keep a low profile and make few if any demands on the host nation. Working as shop keepers, doctors, and other professionals, they make good first impressions and gain vocational respect.

Phase 2: Recognition

When there's a sufficient number of Muslims, they request recognition of Sharia law in their communities. To prevent resistance and suspicions, they publicly condemn 'radical' Islam and ask for interfaith community centers. Often, they're supported by the host nation's naive leaders who wish to be seen as 'progressive.'

Phase 3: Infiltration

When there's a significant number of Muslims in a few cities, they start infiltrating key institutions and creating umbrella organizations that inflate their size. They then use these groups to lobby the government, and they support pro-Muslim political candidates, file lawsuits against alleged cases of Islamophobia, place imams as 'chaplains' in armed forces and prisons, endow Islamic studies departments at universities, and pressure public schools.

Phase 4: Confrontation

When Muslims become a significant minority, they demand Sharia law be incorporated into the country's legal system. This demand is often made while 'rogue' elements of the Muslim community threaten, or engage, in violence.

Phase 5: Imposition

When the Muslim population gains control of a region, Sharia law is imposed across the region, which is then locked down against non-Islamic influences, including the Gospel. Their ideal Islamic state is Saudi Arabia where Sharia law is the only law, and it's enforced with barbaric brutality.

"Before the West introduced its lax and dangerous immigration policies," Lilly said, "they were warned by Enoch Powell in his 'Rivers of Blood' speech which he delivered to a Conservative Association meeting in Birmingham, England, on April 20, 1968. Powell said such policies would be disastrous. Much of what he said hasn't happened in New Zealand, yet, because while other nations have been multicultural for some time, our nation hasn't:

Enoch Powell's 'Rivers of Blood' speech
'Eight years ago in a respectable street in Wolverhampton, a house was sold to a Negro. Now only one white (woman old-age pensioner) lives there. This is her story. She lost her husband and both her sons in the war. So she turned her seven-roomed house, her only asset, into a boarding house. She worked hard and did well, paid off her mortgage and began to put something by for her old age. Then the immigrants moved in. With growing fear, she saw one house after another taken over. The quiet street became a place of noise and confusion. Regretfully, her white tenants moved out. The day after the last one left, she was awakened at 7am by two Negroes who wanted to use her phone to contact their employer. When she refused, as she would have refused any stranger at such an hour, she was abused and feared she would have been attacked but for the chain on her door.
She is becoming afraid to go out. Windows are broken. She finds excreta pushed through her letterbox. When she goes to the shops, she is followed by children, charming, wide-grinning piccaninnies. They cannot speak English,

but one word they know. 'Racialist,' they chant. When the new Race Relations Bill is passed, this woman is convinced she will go to prison. And is she so wrong? I begin to wonder.

The other dangerous delusion from which those who are wilfully or otherwise blind to realities suffer is summed up in the word 'integration.' To be integrated into a population means to become for all practical purposes indistinguishable from its other members ... to imagine that such a thing enters the heads of a great and growing majority of immigrants and their descendants is a ludicrous misconception and a dangerous one ...

For these dangerous and divisive elements, the legislation proposed in the Race Relations Bill is the very pabulum they need to flourish. Here is the means of showing that the immigrant communities can organize to consolidate their members, to agitate and campaign against their fellow citizens, and to overawe and dominate the rest with the legal weapons which the ignorant and the ill-informed have provided. As I look ahead, I am filled with foreboding; like the Roman, I seem to see 'the River Tiber foaming with much blood.'" The Telegraph: Nov 6th, 2007

"Because Multiculturalism isn't fully established in this land like it is in other countries, we presented a face of unity to the world when Brenton Tarrant gunned down 51 people. Ours is the face of ignorance! We do not, as yet, have 'no go areas.' Colonized areas in Western homelands that are in effect a state within a state, where even the police dare not tread. This phenomenon has happened in almost every country where mass immigration has occurred. China towns, which are in almost every Western city on Earth, are one example of a state within a state. The rise of the far-right in European nations is the waking up of the native populous, finally realizing they've been duped. Their act of charity, letting others in and sharing their homeland with them, has been perceived by our traditional enemies as a weakness to be exploited. If you consider

Christians are now the most persecuted religious people on Earth, there is reason to fear:

> *Christian Persecution*
> *Trends show that countries in Africa, Asia, and the Middle East are intensifying persecution against Christians, and perhaps the most vulnerable are Christian women, who often face double persecution for faith and gender.*
> *Every month, on average:*
> *345 Christians are killed for faith-related reasons.*
> *105 Churches and Christian buildings are burned or attacked.*
> *219 Christians are detained without trial, arrested, sentenced, and imprisoned.* Open Doors

"Attacks on Christian churches and Christian symbols are happening all over Europe in ever-increasing numbers," Lilly continued. "People sneak into our churches, desecrate them and burn them down, but if we dare to associate this desecration with immigrant imports, it's not the perpetrators of these crimes that will be ostracized. No, it would be us accused of hate speech, and racism!

"Middle-eastern grooming/rape gangs raped and trafficked thousands of white girls with impunity for over twenty years in England because the police didn't want to appear racist, and the media didn't cover these crimes for the same reason. Similar crimes are happening all over Europe and, for the main part, the mainstream media ignores them. Sweden's now the rape capital of the world, and London has about 13,000 knife crimes a year ... an epidemic that's totally out of control. It is mostly a black on black crime.

> *Knife attacks on teenagers up by 93% in five years, figures show. Figures paint a bleak picture as loved ones of the latest victims in east London and Manchester mourn.*
> The Guardian: March 4th, 2019

Perspective on Black knife crime
The Black boys in London are massively over-represented
in stabbings; black-on-black violence is significantly
gang-related; gangs in London are crime-focused; the age
of recruitment and grooming of young people for gang
activity is dropping to primary school levels.

The Guardian: Jan 20th 2019

"Almost all white countries have turned into a nightmare version of their former selves," Lilly said, "but if we don't like it, and we dare to point out who's causing the problem, we're branded racists! Our children have been brainwashed into thinking all of this is normal. They don't realize the immigrants would never allow a wholesale takeover of their own lands, and they're still loyal to them. Instead of seeing the disparity, they let the foreigners celebrate their culture in our lands ... something they themselves are not allowed to do— and they champion their rights. Foreigners can and do, publish magazines celebrating their culture in our lands, but if we dare publish a magazine in celebration of our own white heritage, cries calling us white supremacists are heard.

"Now many of our children think the newcomers are better than us, and why wouldn't they? How can anybody be proud of who they are when their culture is actively being suppressed like it's something to be ashamed of? Whites are now constantly being insulted, especially in the media. Anybody can say any racist thing they like about us, but we can't say a disparaging word in return. Saying you're white has become almost blasphemy. Our children now breed with the foreigners. In a hundred years' time, there will be no blonde and blue-eyed babies ... our race exterminated from the planet. Under the rules governing genocide, categories 2, 3 and 4 apply to us.

Convention on the Prevention and Punishment of the
Crime of Genocide
Article II
In the present Convention, genocide means any of the

following acts committed with intent to destroy, in whole or in part, a national, ethnical, racial or religious group, as such:

1: Killing members of the group;

2: Causing serious bodily or mental harm to members of the group;

3: Deliberately inflicting on the group conditions of life calculated to bring about its physical destruction in whole or in part;

4: Imposing measures intended to prevent births within the group;

5: Forcibly transferring children of the group to another group. United Nations Office

"You think your race will be bred out?" Wolf said.

"I fear we're becoming a minority in our own lands. Indeed, in the US and the UK, white babies are already a minority. It's only our old that are keeping the percentage of whites higher than the immigrants. I think in the not too distant future, we'll be brutally raped and killed by a dominant culture that doesn't value our egalitarian ways. An Islamic man can have many wives. Radical Muslims' have publicly stated they intend to kill our men and steal our women, then live under Sharia law and practice their religion freely in our lands ... Why we'd be dumb enough to think they'd do anything other is beside me, but, of course, we're not allowed to even discuss our concerns. Internet sites that contain such speech have largely been declared evil and blocked by internet providers ... What about freedom of speech?

Race-hate attacker who SPAT into a nine-month-old BABY'S face and shouted 'white people shouldn't breed' at her mother walks free

Rezzas Abdulla has previous convictions for race-hate attacks on white women

He approached a mother pushing her baby in a pram and spat at her daughter

*Despite previous crimes, attacker avoids jail term on a
suspended sentence
Mother says punishment may have been different if she
had abused him.*   The Daily Mail: February 22nd, 2017

"Here in New Zealand," Lilly said, "we discovered our broadcasters are actively holding back information. This came to light when the terror attack played out. The event was broadcast live overseas, but it wasn't here. The television channels made out they were broadcasting it live, but we didn't find out critical information for hours after it had been aired overseas. We also learned we have heavy censorship laws, with more to be swiftly introduced:

*Criminalizing hate speech: New Zealand considers
policing hateful expression
Last year, a human rights taskforce was assembled to
tackle what authorities considered was a growing issue.
Then, global alt-Right figures Stefan Molyneux and
Lauren Southern hit the headlines when they were denied
a platform by Auckland mayor Phil Goff ahead of a
planned trip.
Proponents of free speech were incensed. The public
conversation swirled.
The taskforce quietly disbanded.
'Then, March 15 happened.'
In the coming months, the Ministry of Justice will report
back to Little on what might need to change.
The details remain murky, but in the aftermath of March
15, hate speech is now clearly back on the agenda.*   Stuff News: April 28th, 2019

*Christchurch mosque attack: Up to 14 years jail for video
sharers as Commissioner asks Facebook to give police
names
That raises the prospect of a fine of up to $10,000 or up to
14 years jail for anyone who shares the clip - and this*

morning, Privacy Commissioner John Edwards called on
Facebook to share names with the police.

It is an offense to share this material as soon as it is
produced, and the timing of the official classification does
not affect the ability for police and enforcement agencies
to prosecute offenses under the Films, Videos &
Publications Classification Act 1993, Shanks says.

'Facebook should be notifying the police of the account
names of people who have shared this content,' Edwards
told RNZ this morning.   NZ Herald: March 19th, 2019

"Disturbingly," Lilly continued, "instead of people getting upset about this, and Ardern's speeches, many started calling her a Rockstar PM for her condemnation of racism, even though it *wasn't* a racist attack—white New Zealanders were among the dead. Then Ardern donned a hijab, as did female police officers and others, in a supposed act of solidarity with Muslims. Meanwhile, women around the world are arrested jailed and tortured for taking off their hijab. Who were they showing solidarity to? Weren't they showing solidarity to the Islamic states who impose such cruel laws? And no one considered the manifesto might be filled with lies and falsehoods. I mean he murdered 51 people ... could he not also be a liar?

"Then there were the victims that nobody noticed," Lilly said. "A male with short hair and a tattoo on his head was herded and attacked by an angry mob in a supermarket. In tears, he had to be rescued. Nobody tried to 'make him feel okay.' And after the terror attack, any bad press the mosque had received in the past was quickly and quietly deleted. Many pages suddenly had a post that read, 'I'm sorry we can't find that page.' Pages like this page which does remain ... for now:

Drone victims 'radicalized' at mosque
The parents of a man killed by a drone in Yemen say he
was 'radicalized' in Christchurch.
Australian Christopher Havard, 27, and dual New

Zealand-Australian national Daryl Jones were killed by a missile fired by a US drone in November [2013].

Havard's mother and stepfather, Bronwen and Neill Dowrick, said their son joined [Al Noor] mosque and told them that was where he first encountered radical Islam.

Stuff News: June 5^{th,} 2014

"So," Lilly said, "it was okay for American-led forces to kill members of Al-Noor's congregation. And clearly, they're still 'us' but fellow New Zealander's who've done nothing, other than hold anti-immigration views, are not us. Wow, just wow! I discovered the mosque was built with funding provided by Saudi Arabia, and on at least one occasion, a visiting speaker from Indonesia has given a sermon supporting violent jihad to the Christchurch congregation.

Lilly sighed. "I found myself thinking about some of the words of the Norwegian terrorist, Anders Behring Breivik. I don't agree with his methodology, but I think some of his words had validity. When he was growing up, he witnessed countless incidences of violence by Muslims, and he came to view Islamic immigration as a threat to Western civilization. His experiences led him to join the anti-immigration/right-wing progress party at the age of 20. He chaired the local Vest Oslo branch of the party's youth organization during 2002. After leaving the Progress Party in 2006, he joined a gun club and the Freemasons while also founding a company which he used to finance his terror attack. He said:

> *'It is meaningless to participate in the democratical process when you are not allowed to raise important issues without being subjected to political and social persecution through stigmatization and ridicule. It is time to acknowledge that we, the cultural conservatives of Western Europe, are deceiving ourselves to believe that it is remotely possible to change the system democratically.'*

"Realizing the media had a stranglehold on public perception, and penetrating it was impossible, he further said:

'There is no freedom of speech in Europe. If you don't cheer
and embrace your own annihilation you are a racist bigot,
an enemy of the establishment and must be suppressed,
ridiculed, undermined and persecuted.'"

"What do you think of the terrorist Brenton Tarrant?" Wolf said.
"Do you have any sympathies with him?"

"When I thought he was legitimate: meaning I thought his
manifesto was a true account of his frustrations, and he'd let them
get the better of him, I was conflicted because we don't have any
means of expressing our growing unease with the flood of
immigrants. I didn't agree with what he did, but I sympathized with
his frustrations, and I thought the government should shoulder
some responsibility for what happened—admit they had blood on
their hands—but, of course, they didn't."

"You don't think he's legitimate now?" Wolf said.

Lilly shook her head. "The government had an agenda the
gunman played into. Gun laws were already written and ready—all
600 pages of them. Semi-automatic military and assault weapons
were immediately outlawed, and hate crime laws have clearly
already been drafted. Worldwide, Facebook banned white
nationalist groups from their site, and the government gave itself
greater powers to spy on its citizens—its spotlight shifting to White
nationalist groups. Of course, their desire to have a homeland of
their own must be considered evil, even though it's a basic human
right for every other ethnic group on Earth.

"I rung an MP once and told her about my immigration concerns.
I said within the last few days, I'd been to a supermarket and a movie
and on both occasions, I was the only white person there, and I found
it very intimidating. I said I thought immigration was getting out of
hand. She thought my concerns were an affront and she became irate
and yelled at me, 'You're a racist bitch and don't ring again!' I've also
written to parliament, but it was clear they didn't care that I was
feeling scared and intimidated in my own society."

CHAPTER THIRTY

Christchurch's False Flag attack

"The biggest give away that the crazed gun attack in Christchurch was a black op or false flag attack," Lilly said, "was the use of Brenton Tarrant's full name on ultra-right web sites. People use fake names on such sites ... Most people don't even use their real names on relatively harmless news sites like stuff news ... that's normal."

"Indeed," Wolf said. "Chief of staff to President Bill Clinton, and acting counselor to President Barack Obama, Mr. Podesta visited New Zealand only a few days before the attack. One of the most powerful people in US democratic politics, he warned New Zealand to expect a cypher security attack and called NZ a fat juicy cypher target. The day before the attack, Facebook went down as somebody built in a back door so the livestream video wouldn't be interrupted. Usually, Facebook's algorithms would prevent such content from streaming. It wasn't the only service interrupted, Mosque goers reported an inability to get through to the police, and three highly unusual operations were happening at the time:

> *Hero officers switch from training to the real thing.*
> *The police officers who apprehended the gunman allegedly responsible for the slaying of at least 50 people at two Christchurch mosques were at a training session dealing with armed offenders when the situation unfolded.*
> *The Herald has exclusive details about how the officers, after hearing there was an active shooter, took to the streets to find him—and stop him.*

*The officers were attending a training session at Princess
Margret hospital in Cashmere. The training was held on a
disused floor of the [old abandoned] hospital and was
around room clearance and dealing with armed
offenders. There was an advanced officer in Christchurch.
They were actually training when the call came through.
They had their work vehicles there with them, with
firearms in them, they operationalized themselves and got
into one car.*   The Herald: March 18th 2019

*Police didn't see shootings suspect leave Christchurch
mosque because a bus blocked their view*
*International police were in Christchurch for a specialist
training course on March 15. Officers from Queensland,
New South Wales, Victoria, Western Australia, and Hong
Kong, as well as New Zealand Defense Force personnel,
responded alongside New Zealand police and gave first
aid at the Linwood mosque. Commissioner Mike Bush on
Wednesday thanked them, saying 'their specialist skills
have been credited with saving lives and we were
fortunate to have them on the ground with us.'*
    Stuff News: April 17th 2019

SAS joined hunt for shooter
*Some of the world's most deadly sharpshooters were in
Christchurch when New Zealand's worst terror attack
unfolded on Friday, with NZSAS taking to the streets to
help hunt the rampaging mosque shooter.*
*Snipers from the New Zealand military, as well as
professional snipers from Australia and Asian countries,
had been at the Defence Force shooting range at West
Melton, 25km west of the city, the Herald has been told.*
*When the massacre unfolded, they are understood to have
been granted special powers to take up arms in order to
protect the public.*
NZSAS soldiers were photographed with weapons and

*balaclavas masking their faces near the Al Noor Mosque
by Hagley Park where a gunman stormed Friday prayers.
One photograph which has appeared on social media,
appears to show an NZSAS soldier with an army sniper
rifle, or designated-marksman weapon, outside the Deans
Ave mosque."*   The Herald: March 19th. 2019

"I was unsure if all of that was a coincidence," Lilly said. "Coincidences seem to happen all the time."

"Yes, they do, but only when the Globalists are staging one of their terror attacks. It's their M.O., pattern of behavior, or 'modus operandi' a Latin phrase approximately translating to *mode of operating*. They terrorize you and then have extra medical personnel, and armed forces at the ready to address the situation, to make them look like the good guys. They hope you won't spot a pattern and suspect they did it, but more and more people are waking up to their involvement in these crimes."

"Lots of people thought 9/11 was an inside job," Lilly said. "The key arguments for me were: the towers were designed to stand fire, even planes flying into them, and they did. Then all of a sudden a huge dust cloud erupted from the basement of one of the towers, and it collapsed ... exactly how a controlled detonation would ... then exactly the same thing happened to the other tower. And, as if that wasn't enough, a BBC reporter stood in front of a window and said, 'building seven has fallen,' but behind her, in the distance, you could see the *undamaged* building still standing. Then, mysteriously, about half an hour later, the building did fall. Again, exactly how a building would if it were destroyed by a controlled detonation. Then there were the passports that flew out of burning buildings and landed undamaged on the footpath. No plane was found at the Pentagon, or any part thereof. Clearly, a missile hit the structure, and the plane that's meant to have fallen out of the sky was missing. There was no plane, or any bodies, not even bits of them ... just debris. When does that happen?"

BBC Reporter says building 7 has collapsed when it can
clearly be seen standing behind her.

"When the-powers-that-be are making a hash of a black op," Wolf said. "Don't forget, NORAD, the North American Aerospace Defense Command, was conducting an exercise, on the same thing, at the same time, on September 11, 2001. NORAD was involved in an ongoing operation that involved deploying fighter aircraft to northwestern North America. The U.S. Military and NORAD had planned to conduct several military exercises, and a drill was being held by the National Reconnaissance Office, a Department of Defense agency … it went live. London was also holding an exercise on the exact same thing, at the exact same time, when the London 7/7 bombings occurred, and it also went live."

"So, you're saying," Lilly said, "when a training exercise is underway when a major tragedy or terrorist attack occurs, we should suspect the global elite did it because it's their M.O.? We should understand that it wasn't a *magnificent* coincidence, but rather the fingerprints of an organized terror event initiated by globalist governments?"

"That's right."

"This is putrid information. Especially when the crazed gunman killed 51 people and harmed a similar number."

"The toll would have been higher if it weren't for a mosque-goer in Linwood called Abdul Aziz. An Indian man, Faisal Sayed, gave his account of the event to NDTV in India afterward. He said, 'A friend and I witnessed this gentleman [Abdul Aziz] creep up behind the shooter and hold him until his gun dropped.' He picked up the dropped [loaded semi-automatic] weapon and chased after the gunman firing repeatedly. After blowing out the back window of the killer's car, the gunman sped off. Shoaib Gani also heard the shots fired by Abdul Aziz; he gave his account to CBC News. Under a table at the time trying to hide, he thought the police fired multiple shots at the fleeing suspect, but the gunman had cleared the scene before they arrived. The incident was also reported by the Herald online:

> *A well-known Muslim local chased the shooters and fired*
> *two shots at them as they sped off.*
> *He was heard telling police officers he was firing in 'self-*
> *defense.' 'They were in a silver Subaru,' he told police.*
> Online Herald: March 15th 2019

"Then why were we told he picked up an empty gun?"

"The police and the government didn't want the facts to be known because if word got out that the hero had chased off the gunman with a loaded semiautomatic rifle ... why would anybody want to hand over their guns? The hero, Abdul Aziz, a father of four, was taken away and interrogated by the police. After being instructed to keep his mouth shut, he never publicly said what actually happened. Instead, he gave varying accounts of the event to different news agencies, some bordering on the ridiculous. In one early account, he admitted to having two guns, an empty discarded shotgun and, presumably, the killers loaded semi-automatic weapon which he chased the killer off with. Abdul Aziz said the killer was wearing a balaclava, but Brenton Tarrant had proudly pointed the camera at his face ... he wasn't wearing a balaclava:

> How it happened
> *1:40pm A gunman opens fire in Al Noor Mosque in Deans*
> *Ave, near Hagley Park in Christchurch.*
> *1:43pm The gunman leaves the mosque and fires random*

shots as cars drive past. He returns to his Subaru station wagon parked in a nearby driveway to get more ammunition and then re-enters the mosque.
1:45pm A second shooter opens fire at Linwood Mosque in Linwood Ave." The Herald: March 16th, 2019

"Shortly afterwards," Lilly said. "Tarrant was supposedly filmed being pulled out of a car on Brougham Street, but the windscreen of the car appeared to be intact, even though Tarrant had fired multiple shots through his windscreen... footage of the damage was caught on CTV. But the back window blown out by Abdul Aziz at the Linwood mosque *was* visible. Australia's Channel 9 News reported police surrounding a second *crashed* Subaru on Strickland St at about the same time and said it reportedly had IUD's. The Herald reported a second vehicle on Strickland St containing a bomb:

How it happened [time of report]
3:15pm There are reports of a bomb in a vehicle on Strickland St in Christchurch. It is deactivated.
3:20pm A person is pulled out of a car and arrested on nearby Brougham St. The Herald: March 16th, 2019

The killer's car minutes after leaving Al-Noor mosque, the passenger window is blown out.

There are bullet holes in his windscreen from shooting at people on the side of the road.

Killer being arrested: Now there is no bulge in the windscreen.

"So, was there two almost identical cars," Lilly said. "Maybe Tarrant crashed his car on Strickland Street and someone looking a bit like him was arrested in the other car? I guess Abdul Aziz messed things up when he blew out the second car's back window?"

"Of course," Wolf said, "and any leaked facts were glossed over or deleted as the updated story in the Herald shows:

> How it happened
> 1:40pm A gunman opens fire in Al Noor Mosque in Deans Ave near Hagley Park in Christchurch.
> 1:43pm the gunman leaves the mosque and fires random shots as cars drive past. He returns to his Subaru station wagon parked in a nearby driveway to get more ammunition and then re-enters the mosque.
> 1:55pm A gunman opens fire at Linwood Mosque in Linwood Ave.
> 2.17pm A person is pulled out of a car and arrested on nearby Brougham St.   The Herald: March 18th, 2019

"Then came the official timeline:

> *Police didn't see shootings suspect leave Christchurch*

> *mosque because a bus blocked their view*
> *1:40pm terror attack begins*
> *1:46pm Gunman leaves the Al-Noor mosque*
> *1:52pm Linwood attack starts*
> *1:55pm Gunman leaves Linwood mosque*
> *1:56pm police learn of Linwood attack*
> *1:57pm police see likely car on Brougham St*
> *1:59pm Police stop and apprehend offender."*

Stuff News: April 17th, 2019

"The timeline's changed."

"Yes," Wolf said, "to give Tarrant time to get from the first location to the second—"

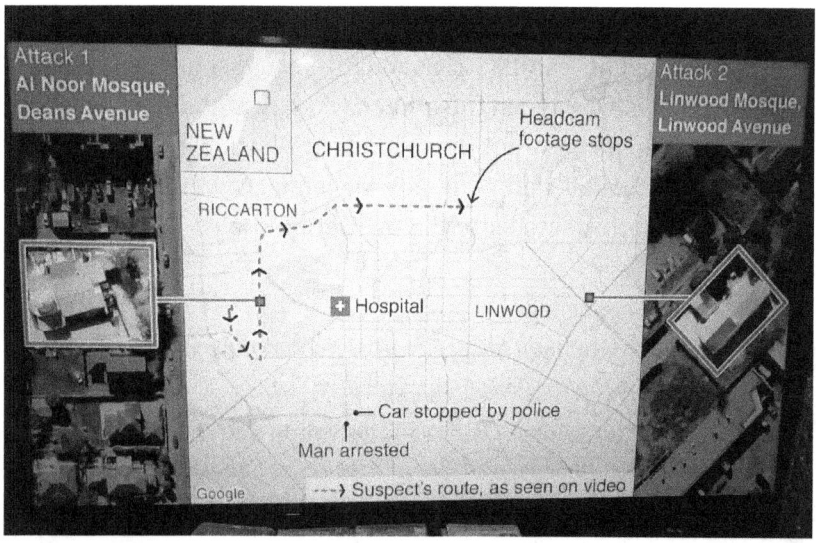

"The timeline's still too short ... If he left the Al Noor mosque in Dean's Ave at 1:46pm, then shoots people from his car in Dean's Ave, and his camera footage runs out at 1.50pm down Bealey Ave—a considerable distance from Linwood—how did he manage to park his car and open fire at 1:52pm? Isn't that a physical impossibility? He then leaves Linwood at 1.55pm, which gives him 4 minutes to get to where he's arrested on Brougham Street at 1:59pm. I don't think you can drive that in busy traffic in less than seven minutes because there are a lot of traffic lights on-route and they're not synchronized. I think the two attacks happened almost simultaneously, and they were carried out by separate offenders."

"Indeed," Wolf said, "and the two other suspects arrested, apart from Abdul Aziz, who your P.M. Ardern originally claimed were connected to the shooting ... were immediately forgotten and never mentioned again."

"I saw the supposed gunman's livestream video when it was up," Lilly said, "Later, it was revealed that it wasn't actually live footage, but, rather, delayed footage:

> *Calm amid the chaos*
> *... [Superintendent John] Price says a police officer in the district command center alerted him to what they thought was a live stream of yet another shooting at an unknown location [approx. 1:52 pm] ... It would later become apparent that the video was delayed footage of the Deans Ave massacre.*　　The Press: April 20th, 2019

"All kinds of rumors about Brenton Tarrant are on the internet," Lilly said, "Apparently, he's actually 42, and his family is Jewish ... they left Palestine in 1948. In 2017 he entered Israel, and from there, he entered Syria where he, according to Russian Military Intelligence, visited Deraa and then a refugee camp outside al Tanf, where Israel and the US had stationed hundreds of ISIS fighters under the cover of refugees. Representing a threat to President Assad, Syrian Intelligence had had Tarrant on their watch list since 2012. They thought he was a trained Israeli assassin."

"When he entered Turkey," Wolf said, "on both occasions, the German embassy received threat Intel that was so real they closed their embassy. They've only ever done that twice, and on both occasions, Brenton Tarrant was in Turkey. On one of those occasions, there was a bombing while he was there. He's also traveled and trained in the same places as the Norway shooter, Anders Behring Breivik; they're both Masons."

"Tarrant's manifesto contained, indiscriminately, both American and British English which was meant to portray it as a copy and paste job from the internet," Lilly said. "White supremacists believe that the flooding of white lands with immigrants is a Jewish plot ... it's their core belief. A white supremacist would never fail to mention this, but Tarrant's ramblings didn't speak of it. Instead, he praised Jews and Israel which is something they'd never do ... Was it a Jewish plot?"

"Of course," Wolf said. "Does Israel allow foreigners into their land? No. Have they championed multiculturalism in Europe? Yes. Barbara Lerner Spectre who runs a government-funded Jewish study group in Sweden made this statement:

> *"I think there is a resurgence of anti-Semitism because at this point in time Europe has not yet learned how to be multicultural. And I think we are going to be part of the throes of that transformation, which must take place. Europe is not going to be the monolithic societies they once were in the last century. Jews are going to be at the center of that. It's a huge transformation for Europe to make. They are now going into a multicultural mode, and Jews will be resented because of our leading role. But without that leading role and without that transformation, Europe will not survive."*
>
> Barbara Lerner Spectre: IBA-News, 2010.

"I've seen that youtube video," Lilly said. "The cheek of it, Europeans stand on their own two feet, unlike Israel."

> *U.S. Foreign Aid to Israel*
> *Israel is the largest cumulative recipient of U.S. foreign assistance since World War II. To date, the United States has provided Israel $134.7 billion (current, or noninflationary-adjusted dollars) in bilateral assistance and missile defense funding. Almost all U.S. bilateral aid to Israel is in the form of military assistance, although in the past Israel also received significant economic*

"And," Lilly said, "Israel refused to take in any Muslim immigrants, even though they campaigned hard for the US and Britain to invade Iraq:

> *Syrian refugee crisis: How different countries have*
> *responded.*
> *Israel*
> *Despite its proximity and high level of economic*
> *development, Israel has refused to take in any Syrian*
> *refugees. 'We will not allow Israel to be submerged by a*
> *wave of illegal migrants and terrorist activists,' Benjamin*
> *Netanyahu has said.*   Independent: September 1st 2016

"You need look no further than the Old Testament to see that it's a Jewish plot," Wolf said.

> *Ezekiel 32:3 This says the LORD God; I will spread out my*
> *net over you with a company of many people, and they*
> *shall bring you up in my net."*

Lilly groaned. "A Muslim leader accused Israel of the Christchurch attack, or rather, the false flag—black op:

> *Mt Roskill mosque leader blames Mossad for the*
> *Christchurch attack*
> *On Saturday, a group called Love Aotearoa Hate Racism*
> *organized a rally for the victims in Auckland's Aotea*
> *Square.*
> *Ahmed Bhamji, chairman of the Mt Roskill Masjid E Umar,*
> *gave a speech questioning where the gunman got his*
> *funding from. He said he suspected it came from 'Mossad'*
> *and 'Zionist business.'*
> *Mossad is the foreign intelligence agency of Israel*
> *responsible for covert operations, intelligence gathering*

and counterterrorism.

'I really want to say one thing today. Do you think this guy was alone ... I want to ask you – where did he get the funding from?' he can be heard saying in video footage.

'I stand here, and I say I have a very very strong suspicion that there's some group behind him and I am not afraid to say I feel Mossad is behind this.   Newshub: March 27ᵗʰ⋅ 2019

"Yes," Wolf said, "and Turkey officials' thought the same thing:

Christchurch shootings: Turkish officials' suspect accused gunman was helped

Police and intelligence officials in Turkey believe the accused in the Christchurch mosque shootings may have been supported or encouraged by a larger organization.

Toygun Atilla, the terrorism and security correspondent for Turkish newspaper Hurriyet, told the ABC*: 'That kind of ordinary profile, who is not very well-educated and also not rich - this person can't commit such a violent action on his own. Turkish intelligence thinks there is a well-resourced organization behind this act.'"*

Stuff News: March 19ᵗʰ⋅ 2019

"Yeah," Lilly said, "and no doubt they're right, but our government had a hand in the killing of all those people. They did so, so they could introduce strict gun laws. In the video, one or two men wearing red boiler suits are seen. One when Tarrant goes to park his car by the Al Noor mosque, and the other is seen beside a fence inside the Al Noor complex. Clearly, they were helping Tarrant, and a silver car parked at the mosque's front door left during proceedings. Tarrant came out of the mosque and pointed his gun at the driver, but he didn't shoot. Obviously, he recognized a handler. The car then drove off while Tarrant was retrieving more guns from the boot of his car."

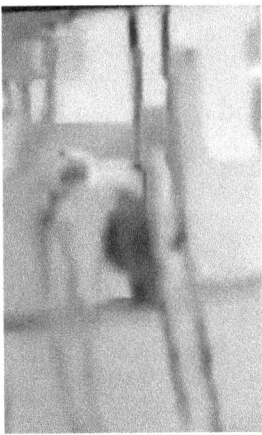

A man in red is seen against a wall inside the Al Noor complex during the event.

He is seen through the rails of the gate at the entrance to the complex.

A man in a similar red boiler suit is seen by Brendon Tarrant as he goes to park his car.

This man in red has different footwear and is wearing a jacket? Photos are from the

You-tube video, New Zealand - Multiple Players and Identifying the Cointel Narrative

"It was an international effort designed to change many things, both nationally and internationally," Wolf said. "But members of the New Zealand government were complicit, yes, and Israel bombed over 100 targets on the Gaza strip at this time. This information never made the worldwide news because the media was otherwise occupied."

"Our Prime Minister, Jacinda Ardern, is a fake," Lilly declared. "She stole the line 'this is us' from a poem written previously by Courtney Sina-Meredith. I bet her speech was written before the attack, just like the 600 pages on gun reform law clearly were ... I think it's also suspicious that the police's crime manager, appointed a key role, had recently returned from a counter-terrorism conference in Australia, and I wouldn't be at all surprised if it's revealed that extra medical personnel were on hand ... Our government is corrupt!"

"What makes your government so special?" Wolf said. "They all have an undisclosed agenda ... The removal of semi-automatic guns from general society is of the utmost importance for their plan to succeed. Before the Port Arthur Massacre in Australia, the NSW premier Barrie Unsworth said in parliament in December 1987, 'There will never be uniform gun laws in Australia till there's a massacre in Tasmania,' and that's exactly what the government conspired to do. Their fingerprints were all over the crime ... In 1995 Tasmania purchased a 22 person airconditioned mortuary truck ... Why would a small state buy a huge mortuary truck—the only one in the country—when they're on a tiny island with the lowest murder rate? After the massacre, it was offered for sale in 1999.

"An offsite workshop was held for senior Port Arthur staff on massacre day 28-4-96. The workshop started at 1pm, two hours away the shooting started at 1.30pm; and Twenty-five top Australian surgeons were at Royal Hobart hospital for a trauma seminar. 'Code brown' emergency procedure was completed only two days beforehand. When the police were called in, they were only 50 km's away chasing fake drugs—the killing started after they arrived.

"Mr. Steven Perry, a former cop and qualified embalmer who led the embalming team at Port Arthur, is now the president of the Australian Senate. He wrote a seminar paper that was published in a government document in 1997. I'll quote, exactly, what he wrote:

> "I was particularly impressed by the quick response and initiatives by some of the team members in packaging and collecting [embalming] equipment. The response time and the amount of equipment quickly relocated [to Tasmania after the massacre] was fantastic. One firm, in particular,

*Nelson Brothers [Melbourne, Victoria, funeral services] had organized for an embalming machine box and a special large equipment case **to be manufactured ready for the incident.** These two containers were the envy of all embalmers and worked extremely well."*

Book: Port Arthur seminar papers:
Detailed report appears on pages 104 to 119.

"That's disgusting!" Lilly said. "That poor, innocent, intellectually handicapped man is rotting in jail?"

"Correct," Wolf said. "The only DNA evidence presented in court was obtained from a bloody knife. It was consistent with Bryant, but it wasn't an exact match. Even though the killer ate with a fork, drunk from a 'solo can' and left fingerprints on a tray, none of Bryant's DNA was found at the Board Arrow café—one of the scenes of the massacre. A lot of witnesses just said, 'It was a guy with long blond hair.'

"Martin had beautiful clear skin, but some witnesses said the killer had an acne-scarred face. Other people provided Marty with an alibi because they'd seen him elsewhere when some of the murders were taking place. An ex Vietnam vet saw the killer, he said, 'The bloke in the newspapers was not the killer.' Another witness, Jim Laycock, knew Martin Bryant well because he'd boasted about his possessions while eating at his café for years. Jim saw the killer twice, he said it wasn't Bryant."

"But still, he was found guilty?" Lilly said.

"There was NO thorough inquiry, NO coronial inquest, NO royal commission, and most importantly ... NO TRIAL. Martin Bryant was even denied his right to an ethical defense lawyer. After pleading his innocence for five months while being held in solitary confinement, his lawyer was dismissed and a lawyer who publicly called him a monster, and who'd previously worked for the prosecution, was then engaged. Bryant's new lawyer, John Avery, extracted a guilty plea from him in short order. Avery had no qualms when it came to bullying people to get his own way. He tried to coerce a statement from a local gun shop owner stating that he'd sold guns to Marty. The gun shop owner refused to comply, and his shop was shut down."

"What about Brenton Tarrant ... will he also rot in Jail?"

"Of course not," Wolf said. "You'll be told he was sentenced to solitary confinement, but in reality, he'll be off living a life of quiet luxury while drinking tequila:

> *New Zealand says mosque shooter faces life of isolation in prison*
> *ISTANBUL — New Zealand's deputy prime minister [Winston Peters] said the gunman accused of killing 50 people in two mosques in the South Pacific nation would spend the rest of his life in isolation in prison and called for solidarity to eradicate 'hate-filled ideologies.'*
> *Winston Peters was speaking at an emergency session of the 57-member Organization of Islamic Cooperation's executive committee called by Turkey to combat prejudice against Muslims in the wake of the attack.*
>
> New York Post: March 23th 2019

"What the fuck!" Lilly said. "When are Western nations going to call an emergency session to combat prejudice against Christians? Muslims' kill hundreds of Christians every month and burn down their churches. Appalling! What a traitor Peters is for attending such a bigoted meeting. Not only did he run off to Turkey like an errant schoolboy, cap in hand, ready to 'assume the position' in front of Erdoğan, he also showed his true colors when he signed the UN Compact on Migration earlier this year. That was an absolutely disgraceful thing to do, considering he'd campaigned on reducing immigration numbers for more than a decade!"

"Islamic countries are very racist," Lilly continued. "In Oman, and other places in the Middle East, Indians, and other races are only paid a quarter wage. Is that not a hate crime? 'Hate-filled ideologies...?' White nationalists' simply want a homeland they can call their own ... a place where they can feel safe. That can in no way be compared to Islamic ideology.

"The Globalists are the real haters! After their major false flag attack, 9/11, they lied about WMD's before going into the Middle East and killing thousands of Arabs while systematically destroying their homes and lands. Now *that's* a hate crime! The Christchurch false flag attack was designed to silence my people, so these criminals could continue their wave of terror!"

"Well, that's how the world works," Wolf said. "Action, reaction ... Laws designed to reduce people's freedoms and rights—like freedom of speech—have to be introduced after a terror attack when people have let their guard down."

"Sickening! Why do these things often happen in Christchurch?"

"Operation Deep Freeze operates out of the American military base at Christchurch Airport. The American military occupation of Christchurch's International Airport in Harewood has its roots in the 1950s. The scientific International Geophysical Year (1957-58) brought military air and logistics support in the form of the US Navy and Air Force. The Navy left in 1998, but the Air Force continues its military and intelligence support operations there to this day. The American military operates under the cover of the Antarctic Agreement of 1961. Overt and covert military and intelligence operations, that have little or no relationship to Antarctic science and logistics (Operation Deep Freeze) have gone on for years both in Christchurch and in Antarctica.

"The New Zealand government has never questioned the scope of US military activities in Christchurch, the only Australasian city to host a foreign base within its bounds. The US regards the base to be its sovereign US territory. It isn't subject to NZ law. New Zealanders in the employ of the US military, engaged in Antarctic logistics, have long been denied the option of belonging to a trade union in their own country. Customs and agricultural officials may not set foot on any American military aircraft because they're also sovereign US territory under international law."

Wolf leaned down and licked Lilly behind one of her ears. Unable to help it, she turned her head towards him, her mouth willing. Wolf gave her his feeding kiss. After losing herself in it, Lilly closed her eyes and moaned as she caught her breath on his shoulder. Wolf pushed a hand between her legs.

"I haven't been milked yet!" Lilly squealed in protest. "I'm full to bursting! I need to be milked."

Wolf clapped his hands together in a loud, thunderous clap. "Yes! It's time to celebrate."

Lilly nearly jumped out of her skin.

"Yes!" Cat echoed, also clapping. "Well, let's get you to the milking room ... then it's party time!"

Lilly frowned. "I'm confused ... Did I miss something?"

"You said you need to be milked," Ox said. "That's a big moment in a baby's life ... a milestone we always celebrate. It means a baby has taken a huge step forward ... they're adjusting."

"And right now," Wolf said, "we could do with a party."

"Are we inviting people over?" Lilly said, not sure if she wanted to meet any more of their ilk.

"No," Wolf said. "We'll celebrate alone."

"How will it be a party then?" Lilly said, relieved nobody was coming over. "Will there be booze, nibbly bits, and loud music?"

"Music, yes, and wine for us," Wolf said. "As for nibbly bits, you can nibble on Ox."

"Some party," Lilly grumbled. "I was almost excited."

"That's how we like our women ... excited," Cat said as he turned and headed for a small screen on the wall in the courtyard. Elton John's 'Tiny Dancer' began to play loudly. Cat reduced the amount of light coming in through the skylight in the courtyard, and all the other rooms at the same time, before lighting some fake, flickering, candles positioned strategically around the house with the push of a button. Then he walked into the milking room.

Wolf followed him carrying Lilly. He masterfully leaned the base of her tailbone against the edge of a theater table-bed and lay her upon it. Half of her buttocks was left hanging off the edge. Lilly groaned as she sank into the deep, comfortable gel-like material that molded to her body. The table-bed may have been super comfortable and a class above any theatre-bed she'd ever seen or laid on, but it was still crudely functional and purpose-built; as evidenced by the stirrups Wolf slipped her feet into.

"Thank goodness," Cat said. "I was over using that bloody

stretcher."

Lilly looked around the room equipped with state-of-the-art medical apparatus. She closed her eyes. *Wow, that's some sound system.*

Cat poured some oil onto her stomach and rubbed it in. "Look at your lovely belly ... What a fruitful darling you are."

CHAPTER THIRTY-ONE

The dining table

Lilly sat in Ox's open pouch at the dining table. Wolf and Cat were sitting opposite. Together, they only occupied the middle section of the huge rectangular table that could easily have sat fourteen. Considering the pool which was, likewise, generously proportioned, and Cream's 'Sunshine of your love' pounding its deep rhythmic beat out of the sound system, Lilly wondered if they weren't party animals.

Wolf leaned forward. Looking intently at her as the song ended, he said, "Do you like the music?"

Lilly found his intense gaze unsettling. "Daddy, how come I'm not being fed and sent off to sleep?"

"Because we're celebrating," Wolf said. "Making you sleep all the time was only necessary when your womb was growing rapidly. A baby's body tires during the growth phase of her placenta ... and sleep helps her mind adjust."

"I see," Lilly said bitterly. "Well, at least Yong won't be spying on me anymore?"

A touch of amusement lit upon Wolf's face. "He never was ... We sent that little Chinese man down from upstairs. He plays out that scene all over this facility. It's his favorite role ... Only Cat and I have been spying on you."

"Typical," Lilly said, looking at Cat. "But you came down from upstairs ... You entered the cave via the elevator."

"There's a room above the cave that we use," Cat said. "We get there via an elevator in the delivery room."

"There's an elevator in the delivery room?" Lilly said.

"It's inside a cupboard." Cat leaned forward to study her face. "It's time you were educated."

Lilly was suddenly excited. "Educated? Will I have lessons? What am I going to learn?"

"You've learned a lot already," Wolf said. "It just hasn't been from a textbook."

"Will I get traditional lessons now? What will I learn?"

"You'll learn about your place in the world," Cat said. "What's expected of you."

"So ... more of the same," Lilly grumbled.

"No," Cat said. "We've been concentrating on getting your body to adjust—make the physical and mental adjustments required. This phase of your training is nearing completion. Soon, you'll learn what the world you lived in was really about."

Lilly frowned. "Don't I know already?"

"No," Wolf said.

"Tell me, then," Lilly urged. "I want to know."

"Not now," Wolf said dismissively. 'Show-and-tell will happen soon enough. Tonight we celebrate. Our new bunny has arrived and she's lovely."

Both Wolf and Cat raised a glass. Lilly had no glass, and she strongly suspected the wine in theirs had come from her placenta. Cat had probably poured some of what he'd drained off of her into a decanter when he finished milking her.

"What happened to your last bunny?" Lilly said, with more than a touch of concern.

Wolf's eyes homed in on her. "You're ever so keen to get on with your lessons," he said. "We're celebrating." He put his glass down. "All right, I'll tell you ... just to put your mind at ease. Our last bunny was with us for a very long time. When new teams are established, they require a well-trained bunny. Introducing a new bunny to a new team is a recipe for disaster. Older, long-established teams must relinquish their bunny and take on a new one."

"So, you're all mourning your last bunny?"

"Yes, and no," Cat said. "We know where she is, and we're happy with her placement."

Wolf leaned forward and winked. "That, and every now and then we desire a new bunny."

Lilly looked down, despondent. "I'm sport to you?"

"To a degree," Cat said. "What's the point in being a trainer if you never get to train? I like to hone my skills ... brush up on my technique."

"Right!" Lilly said. "Like that's not offensive or anything!"

Cat put his hand under his chin and studied her a moment. "You know, you're a delight to train ... just the right amount of resistance and acceptance."

Lilly put her head in her hands and shook it. "You guys are disgusting!"

"Enough of that," Wolf said, putting his hand down on the table in a manner reminiscent of a judge lowering his hammer. "It's time to order."

Lilly looked up. "Order? There's a waitress?" She looked at Ox. "Are you going to eat too?"

"Yes, he is going to," Wolf said. "It's only you that doesn't eat ... other than what we feed you, of course."

Lilly looked up at Ox in dismay. "So, you lied to me! You do eat ... I thought it was you and me against the world ... I let you do stuff to me because I felt sorry for you, and now you're sitting around a table about to celebrate and share a meal, and I'm not allowed to eat?"

"Yeah," Wolf said. "That's about the size of it ... but you're not hungry, are you? If you decide you are ... you can chew on Ox's saggy old tit."

Lilly's face fell. "You're a bunch of disgusting wankers! Some celebration!"

Wolf leaned forward. "Listen here, bunny ... We eat, you chew ... got it?"

Running on instinct and habit, Lilly turned and snuggled into Ox. She was about to suckle on his nipple, but she stopped herself just in time. Looking back at Wolf, she saw his face was alight with amusement; her dilemma all too apparent. Lilly looked up at Ox, he was glaring at Wolf. She looked back at Wolf. He was staring Ox down, his eyes' saying, *Well, you know she has to get used to it ... no point beating around the bush.*

Ox looked at Lilly and spoke to her telepathically. "Would you like to go to the cave with me, Baby?"

"Yes, Daddy," she said, sniffing back tears. "Wolf is so mean."

Ox got up and carried her to their cave as Gary Glitter's 'Rock and roll part 2' began to blast out of the sound system. He closed the door behind him with a flick of his wrist and sat down on the bed with Lilly. After leaning back against the padded headboard with her, he ran tender fingers through her hair.

Lilly nestled into him. She suckled on his nipple and closed her eyes as if she were trying to shut the world out.

"It's all right, love." Ox soothed. "Daddy's here."

Lilly stopped drinking. "Why aren't I allowed to eat?"

Ox exhaled loudly before stuffing his hand in his pouch to rub her belly. "Because you make the wine, love. It has to be pure."

"This house isn't a production unit!" Lilly exploded, "I am!"

"True. That's very true. Similarly, a farm doesn't produce milk ... cows do. A cow is a processing unit, converting grass into milk."

Lilly frowned. "What do I convert?"

"You convert sperm into wine."

"What?" Lilly's brow furrowed.

"A cow eats grass and changes it into milk, and you convert sperm into wine."

"I do not! I drink milk ... your milk."

"Yes, you do, but mostly you eat sperm. You absorb it in your bowel."

"No, I don't! I get that special food, and yes, I absorb some sperm in my bowel ... but it isn't much."

"Don't underestimate my virility," Ox said, feigning offense. "And don't forget Cat takes delight in you, and Wolf is also feeding you."

"Well, I still drink milk."

"Milk is a blood product of the body just like sperm is. Both are only missing red blood cells."

"I'm drinking blood? I'm a vampire!"

"No, you're not a vampire," Ox said, rubbing her back. "You're drinking sperm and milk. Sperm is a pure, rich food that contains spermine, a powerful metabolic stimulant also present in the gray matter of the brain. An ounce of semen has the equivalent concentration of valuable chemicals that sixty ounces of blood does. Nerve-invigorating properties are present in both semen and the brain. The high concentration of lipids, like lecithin, in semen rivals only that of the brain; lecithin is true brain food. Sperm also contains potassium, cholesterin, vitamin E, calcium and phosphoric acids, and the interstitial cells of the testis are rich in lipids like brain cells are."

Lilly had never given any thought to sperm's composition before. "Wow."

"Prostatic secretions also contain sodium, potassium, calcium, magnesium, chlorides, phosphorus, sulfur, nucleoproteins and albumin."

"Does breast milk contain amazing stuff too?"

"Of course," Ox said. "The growth of the brain in infancy is proportional to the lecithin in the milk. Human infants' brains grow rapidly, so human milk is high in lecithin. My milk is of a higher quality than humans because you require a superfood."

Lilly looked at her beloved tit. It really was a gross, saggy old thing. She shrugged and sucked it in. It tasted good and felt nice.

"Baby, you flow like a stream ... your goodness is flowing out of you continuously. If that goodness wasn't adequately replaced, you'd weaken, and your brain would fade. The quality of your milk and wine would also reduce. You can't consume ordinary food. You require a diet high in sperm."

Lilly frowned. "I'm soaking in sperm? Do I smell?"

"A little. I like your smell ... We all do."

Yeah, Lilly thought bitterly. I'm a bloody lamppost and they're all marking me with their scent!

"I keep you clean, and you'll bathe here," Ox said. "The central pool isn't for decoration. It's there so you can exercise and keep fresh. The water is constantly changed."

"Daddy ... you also eat poo," Lilly said despondently.

"I do, yes. So, technically, I'm feeding you poo and sperm."

Lilly blinked rapidly. Desperately seeking mitigation, she said,

"But you were about to eat."

"I supplement my diet, but by far and away my main source of food is sperm and poo."

Lilly clapped her hands over her eyes. "Who's more disgusting, you or I?"

"Neither. We are who we are. Don't be upset. You've been feeding this way for some time. What's the point in getting all upset about it now...? Would you like to return to the table?"

Lilly sensed Ox's question was more of a statement than a question. He wanted to rejoin the others. Now over their conversation, Lilly shrugged. "I want to know how you guys order food, and how it gets here."

"So, we'll return to the table, then?"

Lilly nodded.

"Good. Don't let Wolf's comments upset you."

Lilly continued to suckle on Ox as he returned to the table. He sat down and swiveled his chair around so she could see while maintaining her current position, nipple in place. She looked across the table at Wolf.

He was wearing a smirk. "I see you've found your nipple."

Lilly didn't react. She just blinked while continuing to suckle.

"There's nothing like the sight of a happy wee bunny with her Bigfoot," Wolf said as he leaned forward. "True love ... I'm almost jealous. Maybe after you've finished chewing on Ox, you'd like to sit on my lap?"

Lilly sniffed and closed her eyes.

The sound of dogs howling made her eyes pop open in surprise, but no dogs were present. The howling dogs in the opening beats of Deep Purple's song 'Hush' had caught her off guard.

Wolf sang along with the chorus. He kept emphasizing the word, 'hush.' "Hush, Hush ... I thought I heard her calling my name ..."

No matter how funny his animated rendition of the song was, or how madly in love he was making himself out to be, Lilly was determined to retain her frosty demeanor. She was furious with him, but despite herself, she smiled. He was just too funny.

"Dinner is about to arrive," Cat said. "We've ordered for you, Ox."

As the music changed to a relaxing piece of classical music, and the volume dipped, Lilly gazed up at Ox, perplexed.

"Dinner comes from the center," he said, answering her unasked question. "Cat types in the order and the center makes our meal and sends it to us."

Is he going to go to the delivery room and get it?

A 'bing' rang out, and the table rattled.

"Dinner has arrived," Cat announced as the middle section of the table drew apart, and a twenty-four-inch-long bullet, lying on its side, rose up through its center. Cat pulled it towards him and lifted the lid. The bottom half of the bullet formed a large serving dish. Inside were smaller serving dishes filled with food in separate containers, along with plates, and cutlery. Cat lifted the bottom part of the bullet up and placed it inside the upturned lid. Then he picked up the bullet and sat it back down in the center of the table which had returned to normal.

Lilly stared at it in wonder.

"When we've finished eating, we'll stuff everything back in the bullet and send it back," Cat said. "We don't wash up."

The bullet contained one of the best spreads Lilly had ever seen— a feast fit for a king. There was caviar and fruit aplenty. The men tucked into the feast like there was no tomorrow. Lilly was surprisingly unaffected by the food, the sight and smell of it didn't make her want to reach out and grab some.

"You're not hungry, are you, Baby?" Wolf said. "That's good because this food would make you vomit. Once you've transformed into a bunny, you can't eat normal food."

Lilly frowned. "Can't I?"

"No," Ox said.

Dismayed, and having thought of a way to land a blow on Wolf, Lilly stared at him and said, "So, what do you think of the theory of evolution?"

Wolf almost choked. "It's a theory! That's all that needs to be said about that."

"Maybe," Lilly said. "But scientists think Darwin was right. They've found different creatures with differing levels of development," she said authoritatively. "Eyes varying from very basic to highly developed. Therefore, they've ascertained, and no doubt correctly, that Darwin was right, and his theory is borne out."

"What a load of nonsense!" Wolf said. "Firstly, when you're developing a simple creature with basic functions, you don't give it more development than required. Every creature is designed for a purpose. The more simple and basic that purpose, the less development required. Secondly, gods are like humans; our knowledge and abilities have developed and progressed over time. If you look at humanity's first attempts to make video games, then view their later, more elaborate attempts, do you assume video games developed via evolution because you can see the stages of development?"

Lilly blinked several times. Clearly, Wolf had a point.

"Also, how do you suppose creatures evolved to blend into their environments and hide in the incredible ways they do ... often mimicking their environment exactly?" he laughed. "Do you think evolution managed that feat?"

"Surely," Lilly said, "evolution could have made them develop in such a way?"

"Really?" Wolf said. "So, when a lion couldn't hide out in the savannah grass because its coat wasn't perfectly color-coordinated, how did it catch enough food to survive long enough to evolve into a creature that was perfectly camouflaged? And creatures that hide in plain sight ... how did they survive long enough for evolution to provide them with the array of incredible disguises which allow them to do so? Surely, all the predators around them would have eaten them up long before such a change could've happened?"

Unable to come up with an answer, Lilly shrugged.

"And what about all the creatures and plants that are perfectly aligned to one another? Did flowers and bees just randomly develop together—perfectly in tune with one another? And did the egg or the chicken come first? Which do you suppose evolution created first?"

Lilly hid her face.

"I'll tell you what the theory of evolution is ... it's the denial of the creator. That denial, of course, was important and planned, so we're not offended. If people think God created the world around them, then he's ever-present, but if they think animals and plants just developed by random chance, then God can fade from mind."

Now that Wolf had pointed out the obvious flaws in the theory of evolution, it seemed like a silly idea, and Lilly wished she'd never brought the subject up. As a Christian, she ought to have known better.

CHAPTER THIRTY-TWO

A steady stream of lies

Wolf got up and walked towards Lilly, holding out his arms, he said, "Come here, bunny," as he approached. He reached down and picked her up, then carried her to the pool and sat down on its edge. After wrapping her legs around his hips and pressing her belly into his, he looked down at her affectionately. "When you lived in your previous society, you were fed a steady stream of lies, spin, and propaganda. I know you're still clinging to your belief in Jesus, but that tale is fictitious ... Jesus never existed."

"Course he did," Lilly protested. "There's plenty of evidence for his existence."

Wolf sighed. "Then why didn't a single person living during his supposed lifetime, write down a single word about him?"

"They did," Lilly shot back. "Matthew, Mark, Luke, and John, wrote plenty ... whole gospels in fact."

Wolf almost choked. "Are you telling me you've never done even the most basic research into the origins of the Bible?"

"I read the Bible, took Bible studies, and went to church!"

"So, you've done no research, then?" Wolf said. "General scholarly consensus agrees the gospels weren't written by the titled authors. If you want to confirm someone's claim of factual material, do you read their promotional brochures, or do you look elsewhere for corroborating evidence?"

"That doesn't apply to the church!"

"Of course it does. The similarities between Matthew, Mark, and Luke's gospels are too great to be merely coincidental. They recount the same stories, in the same order, and with the same words. The idea that three different apostles wrote separate accounts of Jesus's life is simply untenable. Not to mention that the gospels were first written in Koine Greek, a language foreign to the mythical disciples of Jesus who spoke Aramaic. Do you suppose they recorded the deeds of Christ in a foreign language?"

Lilly folded her arms. She was used to winning battles about Christianity and was ill-prepared for Wolf's attack on her beloved religion.

"Historians living in the same area and at the same time as Christ recorded details of the place and time, but none of them wrote a single word about Jesus."

Lilly shook her head in annoyance. "That's because he lived a humble life preaching in his sandals ... he didn't draw attention to himself."

Wolf scoffed. "Have you forgotten his triumphant ride into Jerusalem on a donkey where he was greeted by thousands who laid small branches and clothes on the ground to welcome him? This, of course, happened the day after he supposedly raised Lazarus from the dead. What about his Sermon on the Mount and the great multitude of people who followed him down from it? Or the thousands who witnessed him heal the sick, and the five thousand he fed with five loaves of bread and two fish? Do you think the historians in the area all failed to hear of these great deeds?"

"Well, maybe the deeds weren't quite so grand and the tales grew over time ... He was still amazing." Lilly straightened herself up. "Hang on a minute ... the Jewish historian Flavius Josephus 37 – 100 C.E. wrote about Jesus. He attested to his existence!"

"The well-touted Josephus passage that you speak of interrupts the narrative of a historical account of the Jews and is barely a hundred words in length. It's a well-documented fraud. Not to mention that Josephus was born *after* Jesus died, and so he couldn't attest to anything."

Lilly frowned. Of course, she knew the Josephus passage was hotly contested; knew the Catholic Church had admitted that at least some of it was fraudulent. She also knew it wasn't known to early church writers like Origen. "Well, I admit it's a bit odd that a historian of the day didn't document Jesus's existence, and I agree there's reason to suspect his deeds were exaggerated for effect—"

"Which deeds do you suppose were exaggerated...? Jesus healing the sick? Raising Lazarus from the dead? Or was it when he fed five thousand with five loaves of bread and two fish? Maybe he did none of these things ... that, of course, would be in keeping with history."

Lilly groaned and shrugged. "But then, what would that make him—a mythical preacher—of which the world has known thousands?"

"How else can you explain every historian missing the solar eclipse at the time of his alleged death and the powerful earthquake that accompanied it? Do you suppose every historian living in the area somehow failed to record an earthquake so powerful that it split rocks and opened tombs?"

Lilly set her shoulders determinedly. She'd have none of it. "I've heard this argument before. Christ's existence isn't brought into question because no historian of the day recorded his life ... lots of events go unrecorded by history."

Wolf scoffed. "Not monumental events in a well-documented period of history. Not to mention, the inhabitants of the area, the Jewish people, don't worship Jesus and they deny nearly all of the events in the New Testament ... Listen, Philo-Judaeus, who lived from 20 B.C. to 50 A.D., wrote an account of the Jews that covered the entire period of Christ's supposed existence. Philo lived in or near Jerusalem when Jesus supposedly rode into town triumphantly on a donkey, and he was there for his supposed crucifixion and all the world-shattering events that followed. The earthquakes, the sun darkening at noon, the graves opening and the long-dead saints roaming around the place ... but Philo saw nothing, heard nothing, and wrote nothing."

Lilly folded her arms. "He wasn't interested in Christ. He wrote about other things."

"You don't find it odd that such incredulous events happened and nobody wrote them down, even though they recorded the most tedious and trivial details of the life and times in the area?"

Lilly shrugged.

"And why did the Pharisees need to pay Judas thirty pieces of silver to point Christ out to them, when they'd already observed his grand entry into Jerusalem on a donkey? Indeed, they'd spoken to him and even argued with him."

Lilly rubbed her brow. "You're saying the biblical life of Christ is a poorly written, fictitious story."

Wolf nodded. "That's right ... It's a fabrication."

"Well, I choose to believe there *is* a God."

Wolf sighed. "And you're so desperate for a God, you'll accept the jealous one-eyed God of the Old Testament who loved only the Hebrews, later known as the Jews? A God who ordered the genocide of a whole nation and sanctioned the stealing of others' wives?"

"That's the Jewish God ... I love Jesus."

"The Jewish God is the father of Christ. The Father and Son are one ... is that not what you believe?"

"Yes, but Jesus saves," Lilly protested. "He loves my people!"

"According to who? No living historian recorded Christ's existence, let alone anything he had to say, and scholarly consensus says the gospels were written long after his supposed death, and not by his disciples. Therefore, couldn't it all be a rumor, myth, or simply wishful thinking?

"As for the Jewish God who loves only the Jews, tales about him were written by a tribe that was endlessly controlled and manipulated by the major powers around them. Namely: the Egyptians, the Assyrians, the Hittites, and the Babylonians ..."

Lilly snorted. "You think the Hebrews invented a God who loved only them to make themselves feel grand and fulfill an emotional need within them. You think they dreamed their God up?"

"What they did was elevate their God. The Israelite religion emerged gradually from within the Canaanite religion. El was the original God of Israel, not Yahweh whose name in Latin is Jehovah. The word 'Israel' is based on the name El, not Yahweh. El was the chief Canaanite god. He presided over an assembly of gods with his consort, the goddess Asherah [Athirat] ... Baal, one of his seventy sons, gradually became the dominant deity and the military power while El became the executive power."

"Baal was a storm god," Wolf said. "A giver of life-giving rains and a fertility god. Yahweh, a southern warrior-god, joined the pantheon headed by El. Over time he and El became jointly identified, and later El's name became a generic term for God. Each member of the divine council used to have a human nation under their protection. The Bible still records this in Deuteronomy 32:8-9 but the verses have been altered, the original verses read:

> *Deuteronomy 32:8 When the Most High [El] gave the nations their inheritance, when he separated humanity; he fixed the boundaries of the peoples according to the number of divine beings. 9 Yahweh's portion is his people, Jacob his allotted heritage."*

Lilly frowned. "Yahweh was a minor, *regional* god?"

"Yes. After the ninth century B.C., the tribes and chiefdoms of the Iron Age were replaced by ethnic nation-states. Israel, Judah, Moab, Ammon, and others, each had their own national god who was more or less equal to the others. Chemosh was the god of the Moabites, Milcom was the god of the Ammonites, Qaus was the god of the Edomites, and Yahweh was the God of Israel."

"So, Yahweh was in the same pantheon as Baal? But the Bible condemns the worship of Baal."

"The name 'Baal' became a title—Lord," Wolf said. "Just like 'El' became a generic term for God. The early Hebrews used the term 'Baal,' Lord, or Baali, 'My Lord,' to reference their God—the Lord of Israel. They even used the term 'Baali' to reference Yahweh (Jehovah) in the Bible:

> *Hosea 2:16 And it shall be at that day, said the LORD, you shall call me Ishi [husband]; and shall no longer call me Baali [LORD]."* King James Bible

"There is no *singular* god," Wolf said. "While you're busy worshiping a non-existent savior, your eyes are closed to the real

Christ—the symbolic Christ. The story in the Bible is yet another rendition of the 'doctrine of the Savior,' a worldwide prophecy with many renditions, Christianity being but one. If you allow me, I'll explain this prophecy to you in detail, and point out the flaws in the biblical story. I want you to grow and develop and not be held back by a poorly written fable."

Lilly snorted. "Okay. How about you start with the inconsistencies in the biblical story?"

"All right," Wolf said, rising to the challenge. "Firstly, the mistakes are deliberate—"

"Deliberate?"

"Yes, the story was designed to unravel in due course. A time of illumination was anticipated when knowledge would spread across the Earth and unravel the poorly constructed tale. The church has had hundreds of years to get their story straight, but they haven't because their leaders have not only been anticipating this time, they've been actively working towards it … creating it."

"Really?" Lilly said. "Fascinating. Well, do tell … apart from the Pharisees already knowing who Jesus was, and poor Judas being set up as the villain … what else is wrong with the story?"

"The alleged tale of Pontius Pilate releasing a condemned criminal because it was a Passover Festival custom, is pure nonsense. There's no external corroboration of any such tradition, and the practice violates Jewish law. What's more, Barabbas is specifically identified in the Bible as a violent military insurrectionist, and Pilate, a strict, militant Roman governor, serving a strict militant Roman Empire, would never have released such a man. Barabbas also means 'son of the father.' The literary significance is embellished in the Gospel of Matthew where the name 'Jesus' is added to his name. The similarity between Jesus and Barabbas is obvious.

"Leviticus 16 discusses the Jewish Yom Kippur sacrifice, in which two identical goats were selected each year. One was released into the wild bearing the sins of Israel, and the other, 'the scapegoat,' was sacrificed in a blood atonement for sins. Jesus and Barabbas represent the two goats. Confirmation that Jesus represents 'the scapegoat' is found in Corinthians if you consider that either a goat or a lamb was used in the Passover ritual as stated in Exodus:

> *Exodus 12:³ ... On the tenth day of this month, each man is to take a lamb or kid for his family, one per household—⁵ ... and you may choose it from either the sheep or the goats.*

> *1 Corinthians 5:⁷ ... For even Christ our Passover is sacrificed for us: ...*

Collaberating evidence is found in Isaiah:

> *Isaiah 53:⁶ We like sheep have gone astray; we have turned every one to his own way; and the Lord has laid upon him the iniquity of us all. ⁷ He [Jesus] was oppressed and he was afflicted, yet he opened not his mouth: he is brought as a lamb to the slaughter.*

"So, the whole drama was symbolic," Lilly said. "Allegorical fiction?"

"That's right. The Bible is a long, coded story—mystery school teachings written down. The supposed history of the Hebrews, and, later, the tale of the Jewish savior named Jesus, is a thin tale veiling sacred secrets."

"Really?"

"Yes. The underlining symbolism, allegory or message is paramount. Therefore, large parts of the story don't even make sense and fault can easily be found with the story's historical facts which are embellished to highlight inconsistencies ... You'll know of some of the errors I'm speaking of."

"Are you talking about the opposing tales of Jesus's birth—differing accounts that can't be reconciled? In Luke, Jesus's family is from Nazareth and they traveled to Bethlehem to register for the Roman census, and Jesus just happens to be born there. He's wrapped in swaddling clothes and laid in a manger because there's no room at the inn and his family are visited by shepherds—not wise men. Then they head back to Nazareth.

"But in Matthew, Jesus is born in his house in Bethlehem and he's visited by wise men bearing gifts—not shepherds. Joseph has a warning dream, and he takes Mary and the young Jesus to Egypt. After this, King Herod's men kill all the children from two years of age—"

"That's right," Wolf said. "That's one of the most obvious inconsistencies in the Bible, but there are others. The Jewish historian Josephus recorded, after the exile of Herod the Great's son and successor, in the year 6–7, a Roman senator named Quirinius became governor of Syria, and during his reign, the first tax census was conducted. The author of Luke lets us know King Herod was dead at the time of Jesus's birth by stating, 'And it came to pass in those days that there was a decree from Caesar Augustus that all should be taxed,' but later in the gospel of Luke, King Herod, who's clearly dead when Jesus is born, is alive."

"So, the life of Jesus is a poorly set historical fable?"

"Yes, and as I said … that's not an oversight."

"So, there won't be a second coming of Christ?" Lilly said downheartedly.

"There wasn't a first coming, so a return's unlikely."

Lilly sighed heavily.

"You've heard of mystery schools?"

"Yes, Gnostic scholars attended them; people who didn't believe in a flesh and blood Christ."

"Correct."

Lilly huffed out a breath. "If the story is a fable, then how come the Roman Emperor Constantine deified Christ? Surely, Jesus was a real man and people knew this?"

"At that time in history, in the third century A.D., the Roman Empire was fractured and divided and threatened by Civil war. In 324 A.D., Constantine defeated emperors Maxentius and Licinius and became the sole ruler. He decided to enact administrative, financial, social, and military reforms to strengthen the Empire. These initiatives alone were not enough because competing religious factions threatened to tear the Empire apart, so Constantine convened the First Council of Nicaea to try and bring religious harmony to the realm."

Lilly frowned. "Didn't he convene the first Council of Nicaea to confirm Christ's divinity and organize the Bible?"

"Yes, and no. Unification of the realm's religions was on the agenda, and Constantine intended to unify the realm under a Christian banner. Alexander the Great had previously tried to unify the Greeks and Egyptians under the god Amun, also known as 'Amen.' He was a Zeus equivalent not only worshiped in Egypt but also abroad. Later, the Ptolemy Kings of Egypt tried to unify the region under the god Serapis whose cult they deliberately spread in the hopes of doing so."

"Serapis?"

"Serapis was a god with a Greek appearance and Egyptian aspects; his iconography drawn from many great cults. Abundance and resurrection were themes in the worship of Serapis. He was a syncretistic deity derived from the worship of the Egyptian god Osiris and the Apis bull. His popularity increased during the Roman period, and in temples outside of Egypt, he replaced Osiris as the consort of Isis."

"But he never found favor in Rome?"

"That's right," Wolf said. "Up until the First Council of Nicaea, the Roman aristocracy primarily worshiped two Greek gods, Apollo and Zeus. But the great bulk of the people idolized Julius Caesar who was deified by the Roman Senate after his death on the fifteenth of March, 44 B.C. when he was venerated as the 'Divine Julius,' and the word 'savior' was affixed to his name. The Divine Julius as Roman Savior and 'Father of the Empire' was considered a God among the Roman rabble for more than 300 years. He was even a deity in some Western presbyters' texts."

"Right," Lilly said, wondering just how backward the Roman people were. "And now I suppose you're going to tell me, that's why Jesus has the same initials as Julius Caesar?"

"The letter 'j' wasn't in the alphabet then. 'Julius' was spelled I-V-L-I-V-S, and Jesus was spelled I-E-S-O-U-S. And while it appears the two had the same initials, they didn't, because Julius Caesar had a first name, 'Gaius,' which he didn't use."

Lilly frowned.

"The first gospel ever compiled was published by Marcion of Pontus who lived from 100 to 160 A.D. An educated man of letters, he entered the brotherhood of the fledgling Gnostic-Christian movement shortly after arriving in Rome as a consecrated bishop. He prepared and published his gospel around 145 A.D. Marcion's gospel resembled the Gospel of Luke, except it was shorter and originally written in the Syro-Chaldee or Samaritan language, and was called the 'Gospel of the Lord.' Marcion claimed he found texts brought from the East by Apollonius of Tyana."

"His first New Testament, written in Greek, was a derivative of these texts," Wolf said. "His letters formed the basis of the ten Pauline epistles. His 'Gospel of the Lord,' a shorter version of the Gospel of Luke, was a compilation of dozens of older manuscripts that predated the canonical gospels by decades. It had the basic gospel narrative, minus Judaizing and historicizing passages. Marcion's New Testament consisted of one Gospel and the Apostolicon which comprised of the ten Epistles of Paul, Galatians, 1st, and 2nd Corinthians. Romans, except the 15th and 16th chapters which are added historicizing chapters, 1st, and 2nd Thessalonians, Ephesians, Colossians, Philemon, and Philippians—arranged in that order."

Lilly snorted. "The man was a terrible liar and a cheat!"

"Was he?" Wolf challenged. "The powerful, rich and well-connected Marcion was the most influential early Christian. He was also one of the first to fight the efforts of the growing historicizing and Judaizing factions within Christianity. According to Justin Martyr, a famous early Christian, Marcionism was the most popular form of Christianity during his time, with dedicated churches in Italy, Egypt, Palestine, Arabia, Syria, Asia Minor, and Persia.

"His importance was reduced when he clashed with the growing Judaizing faction of Christianity. Eventually, he was excommunicated in 144 by Pope Pius I. Later, the early Church fathers, anxious for an earlier date for the canonical gospels, claimed

Marcion plagiarized and mutilated the original texts by removing everything Jewish from them."

"Maybe, he did?" Lilly challenged.

"Justin Martyr, an ardent opponent of Marcion's, who lived in the same era as he, never once suggested that Marcion plagiarized an existing canonical gospel. If Marcion had committed such a literary crime, Justin would have assailed him in his writings, but he never did because there wasn't a canonized gospel at the time. After Marcion's death, the Judaizers and historicizes moved in and took over his operation—adding Judaizing and historicizing passages to his New Testament. They turned a non-historical Jesus into a Jewish man who walked the earth over a century earlier."

Lilly folded her arms.

"Constantine did more than simply order the writing of texts. He ordered the building of the Church of the original Holy Sepulchre in Jerusalem in 325/326. It was constructed at the purported site of Jesus's tomb, and it replaced a temple built by the Roman Emperor, Hadrian, in the second century A.D. dedicated to the goddess Venus. The church of the Holy Sepulchre is now the holiest place in Christendom.

"Constantine also transferred his power and authority as a Roman Emperor to Jesus Christ. He substituted the head of the Emperor and the eagle for a figure or emblem of Christ woven in gold upon a purple cloth on Roman standards. The richly ornamented standards were called labarums. His visual transfer of authority and power had a powerful effect on the minds of the populous."

"A picture is worth a thousand words."

"It was no mere picture," Wolf said. "And it didn't speak a thousand words ... it spoke volumes. Romans had the highest regard for their standards. When lost in battle, they'd go to extraordinary lengths to get them back, often engaging in battles to secure their return. Constantine threw his full weight behind his new religion, and it stuck."

CHAPTER THIRTY-THREE

An invented character

"Surely, if what you're saying is true, then people knew Jesus was an invented character?"

"Indeed, they did," Wolf said. "There was even a famous saying at the time expressing this: 'There was when He was not.'"

Lilly rubbed her brow. "But still the religion took hold?"

"In the past, religions were founded on fictitious characters. Jesus was just another in a long line of invented religious figures."

"Some people must have believed him to be real," Lilly protested. "Early Christians used to meet in the street and draw half a fish to identify themselves to each other as followers of Christ."

"Nonsense. That's propaganda invented after the fact."

"So, Jesus never existed? He never was! He wasn't God's son—"

"No. He was a mythical mystery school teacher who wore many hats. His words were, and are, only comprehended by initiates ... to whom he says:

> John 14:12 *Truly, truly, I say to you, whoever believes in me will also do the works that I do, and greater works than these will he do because I am going to the Father."*
>
> King James Bible

"Greater works?" Lilly groaned.

Wolf cleared his throat. "At a Council of Nicaea, Constantine deified mystery school teachers and collectively named them 'Jesus Christ.' The new savior's name honored both Zeus and the Eastern savior-god Krishna, and it was hoped the Savior would unite East and West and end religious wars. Do you know the name 'Jesus Christ' doesn't appear in the Codex Sinaiticus—the oldest Bible ever found? Rather, the 'nomina sacra' or sacred abbreviation is employed throughout the text."

"Are you talking about 'ΙΣ,'" Lilly said, trying to draw the 'Σ' with her finger in the air. "The abbreviation for Jesus Christ."

"Yes. The same abbreviation was given to Apollo—the son of Zeus—the son of God. An abbreviation carrying the same meaning appeared over Apollo's temple at Delphi, representing him; and the holy abbreviation used for God throughout the Codex is the same abbreviation used by the pagans in pre-Christian Greek literature to refer to their God."

"You're saying, the symbol used for Christ's name, and the one used for God's, were previously used by the pagans to refer to their gods?"

"Yes."

Lilly sighed audibly. "And I'm gathering because we end the Lord's Prayer with 'Amen,' you also think some of the Amun—Amen—cult made its way into the Bible?"

"Of course," Wolf said. "The Bible references many different religions and gods because it draws its imagery and figurative language from the religions worshiped throughout the Roman Empire, and it achieved what the Ptolemy kings of Egypt and Alexander the Great had previously tried to achieve ... one religion. Christianity and Judaism fit nicely under the same umbrella. When the new religion had achieved a firm footing, the Roman Emperor Theodosius I, in the year 391 A.D., suppressed all forms of pagan worship."

"A blended faith," Lilly said, thinking out loud.

"A great deal of syncretism had gone on in religion before this time, and it's desired to this day."

"What exactly is syncretism?"

"The blending of different beliefs, practices, and schools of thought. By merging religious traditions and uniting them under one banner, people from different faiths can be unified in worship.

Judaism, Christianity, and Islam fit nicely under one banner—they're of the same book."

"You said before that Christianity had elements in common with the Eastern Savior-god Krishna."

"Yes," Wolf said. "Constantine told Eusebius to compile new writings from the religious texts submitted to the council. He asked him to search the religious books and retain what was good in them and cast away what wasn't, then unite the good in one book with the good in another. What was assembled was called, 'The Book of Books,' and Constantine declared:

> It shall be the doctrine of my people, which I will recommend to all nations so that there shall be no more war for religion.

Lilly frowned.

"Eusebius amalgamated the world's religious doctrines and legendary tales by using the standard god-myths from the presbyters' manuscripts as his exemplars. The name 'Jesus Christ' was not formally adopted as a phrase and name until after the first council of Nicaea in 325. Nowhere can any authentic mention of his name be found before this date:

> The earliest of the extant manuscripts [of the New Testament], it is true, do not date back beyond the middle of the fourth century A.D."
>
> Catholic Encyclopaedia, pp. 656–7

Lilly blinked several times. "I'm sure there are examples of the use of his name before this time."

"The Church tells you Christ's name is based on the word 'Chrestes,' a word that means priest, prophet or servant of God, but his name isn't based upon that word. The examples you speak of are all variants of this word. To avoid confusion, a different word was chosen for Jesus's name because pagan worshippers had already claimed it, and it spoke of their devotion to Zeus and other pagan gods. Krishna's name in Greek is Christos, a word with the same meaning as 'Christes.' Desiring to unite the world's religions, Constantine chose that word instead, but the first use of the word 'Christian' happened sometime earlier in Alexandria, Egypt, where the followers of the god Serapis called themselves Christians."

"Well," Lilly said. "What about the words of the prophetess from classical antiquity—the Erythrean Sibyl—who foretold the coming of Christ with the Greek words: 'Iesous Chreistos Theou Yios Soter Stauros,' which means 'Jesus Christ God Son Savior Cross.'"

Wolf caught a cough in his throat. "The string of nouns you're placing so much weight on was only ever found in the writings of the ancient Christian apologist Lactantius. He claimed they showed Jesus had been prophesied not only by Jewish prophets but also by a pagan prophetess. However, there's no record of the passage before Lactantius' claim because he made it up."

Lilly exhaled audibly.

"The Erythrean Sibyl was a prophetess of classical antiquity who presided over the Apollonian oracle at Erythrae, a town in Ionia in present-day Turkey. The words may appear to speak of the coming Christ, but they don't. They were written to provide a link to the past ... to the creation of Christ's name. However, covertly, they show how his name was derived and what it means."

Lilly frowned.

"The words are from mystery school teachings—the catechism of an initiate. Apollo was a god of healing, truth, and prophecy, and his son Asclepius was a divine physician, healer, or Savior ('Soter' in Greek). Asclepius is famous to this day for his staff—the present-day symbol for medicine—the Rod of Asclepius. The title, 'Savior,' was also given to his daughter Ieso, a goddess of healing. Under her patronage, candidates in her father's temple were brought forward for initiation. The novices were called 'sons of Ieso' and deemed 'Chrestoi' or 'Chreistos'—servants of God.

"The first word of the supposed prophecy of the Erythrean Sybil is Jesus—Iesous in Greek which means son of Ieso. The suffix 'us' was added to Greek and Roman names to masculinize them and give glory to Zeus. So, there's nothing Hebrew or Jewish about Jesus's name what-so-ever. The second word of the Erythrean Sybil prophecy is a well-known title: Priest, prophet or servant of God (Chreistos in Greek).

"The church has since tried to claim this is the word Christs name is derived from, but as I said, it isn't. Although, covertly it is, so they're not really lying. The full Erythrean Sybil prophecy reads, son of Ieso, servant of God, God, Son, Savior, Cross. A string of nouns you know as, 'Jesus Christ God Son Savior Cross,' The Greek translation being: 'Iesous Chreistos Theou Yios Soter Stauros.'"

Lilly frowned. "What are you saying? Jesus Christ isn't the name of an individual ... it's a title? Christianity is pagan mysticism repackaged?"

"That's right," Wolf said as he kissed Lilly's forehead. "Well done. That's exactly what I'm saying ... The two words title him an adopted, worthy son of the healing goddess Ieso and a servant of God."

"What about the 'Savior, Cross' bit?"

"A healer was considered a savior, and a cross was a pagan symbol for the conjunction of human and divine."

"Hey ... isn't 'Iesous Christos Theou Uios Soter' or 'Iesous Chreistos Theou Yios Soter Stauros'—the same words different spelling—an acronym for the Greek 'Ichthus'? According to the dictionary, 'ichthyic' means fishlike, and Jesus is the Fisher of Men."

"No," Wolf said. 'That's propaganda invented after the fact. Church leaders changed the word 'ichthyic' to the acronym 'Ichthus'—the letters not even matching up. Ichthys was the son of the ancient sea goddess Atargatis, known in various mythic systems as Aphrodite. The word also means 'womb' and 'dolphin' in some tongues, and mermaids were depictions of her. The symbol applies to the Great Goddess who was portrayed with pendulous breasts, accentuated buttocks, and a conspicuous vaginal orifice—an upright 'vesica piscis.' Christian leaders rotated the 'vesica piscis' ninety degrees and claimed it as their fish symbol."

Lilly groaned. "How does Krishna's life compare to Christ's? Does it parallel it in any way?"

"Of course," Wolf said. "Krishna was miraculously conceived. Born of the Virgin Devaki—the Divine One—he was the divine incarnation of the god Vishnu. His father was a carpenter, yet Krishna was born of royal descent. His birth was attended by angels, wise men, and shepherds, and he was presented with gifts. He was also persecuted by a tyrant who ordered the slaughter of thousands of infants because he feared the divine child would supplant his kingdom.

"The child was saved by friends who fled with him in the night to a distant country. When the tyrant learned his attempts to kill the child had failed, he issued a decree condemning all the infants in the area to death. Krishna was baptized in the River Ganges, and he worked miracles and wonders such as raising the dead and healing lepers, the deaf and the blind. His mission was essentially the same as Christ's—to save humanity. Krishna lived poor, and he loved the poor and used parables to teach the people charity and love.

"Krishna was the complete or absolute incarnation of Lord Vishnu and an avatar of his father. The Sanskrit term 'avatar' is synonymous with the term 'prophet' in Middle Eastern religious traditions. God appoints a man as his vicegerent on Earth because he needs one to aid him in his intervention with humanity. Osiris, the Egyptian god of the underworld, likewise, had an avatar—his son Horus. In his form, he paddled in his own honor. Each of his personas was separate and yet complete. The sun rose in the morning as the younger Horus, at noon it turned into Osiris, and it set as the elder. And just as Osiris was the golden calf, Krishna likewise had a connection with cattle; he was a divine herdsman and a prophet like Jesus."

"Come to think of it, I have heard about this," Lilly said. "Christians' claim the worshippers of Krishna copied Christ and gave his characteristics to their god."

"It doesn't matter which way round it went, the point was to amalgamate the religions. Now, the religions of the world are aligned to a large extent. The peoples of India can't be converted to Christianity because Christ is too similar to their god, Krishna."

"So, is Jesus likewise a son and 'avatar' of God, like Krishna is?"

"Yes. God placed his Spirit upon Jesus:

Isaiah 42:¹ Behold my servant, whom I uphold; mine elect,
in whom my soul delights; I have put my spirit upon him:
he shall bring forth judgment to the Gentiles.

1 Maccabees 2:⁵⁵ Jesus for fulfilling the word was made a
judge in Israel.

Lilly sighed. "What can you tell me about Krishna's father, Vishnu?"

"Vishnu is addressed as the god who separates heaven and earth, a characteristic he shares with another Hindu God, Indra. In the Vedic texts, the deity or god referred to as Vishnu is a sun god—"

"My God isn't a sun god!"

"His face was like the sun shining in his strength."

"Whose face?" Lilly said. "A pagan god's face? Yes, they worshiped the sun."

"I was quoting the Hebrew Bible:

Revelation 1:¹⁶ ... and his countenance was like the Sun
shining in his strength."

Lilly frowned. "You know my Bible ... chapter and verse?"

"Of course I do."

"Well, it may say that in the Bible, but Christians don't worship the sun."

"Pagans didn't either," Wolf said. "They simply compared their god to the sun in the same manner that the Bible does."

"If all this is true," Lilly said, "then surely Church leaders know their religion is fraudulent?"

"The fable made them rich, so it was in their best interests to hide the true origins of their faith. However, others did speak out:

It is amazing that history has not embalmed for us even
one certain or definite saying or circumstance in the life
of the Savior of mankind ... there is no statement in all
history that says anyone saw Jesus or talked with him.

Nothing in history is more astonishing than the silence of contemporary writers about events relayed in the four Gospels."
The Life of Christ, Frederic W. Farrar, Cassell, London, 1874

"Have church leaders ever admitted Christianity is based upon a fraud?"

"Not publicly, but letters have been found exposing the fraud. Cardinal Bembo, who died in 1547 and was the secretary to Pope Leo X who died in 1521, wrote to his associate Cardinal Sadoleto, instructing him to disregard the sayings of Jesus:

Put away these trifles, for such absurdities do not become a man of dignity; they were introduced on the scene later by a sly voice from heaven."
Cardinal Bembo: Letters and Comments on Pope Leo X, A. L. Collins, London, 1842 reprint.

"Pope Leo X (1513–1521) also acknowledged his knowledge of the fraud:

How well we know what a profitable superstition this fable of Christ has been for us."   Pope Leo X

Lilly rubbed her forehead. "Well, then it's astounding that Christianity has survived this long."

"It's a very profitable business, and belief was not exactly a choice in the middle ages. Besides, whether Christ lived or not is of no importance. No current religion is the truth—it's a version of the truth—a glimpse at the big picture. It includes some details of *what has* come to pass and some details of *what will* come to pass. But when it comes to discussing an upcoming, unpleasant agenda, it's almost silent. Religion is truth ... minus some critical details."

"Truth by omission? A whitewash of facts?"

"There was more truth in paganism than there is in Christianity.

Every successive religion has added another layer of whitewash while simultaneously removing truth from the world. The word 'Christ' comes from the word 'Christes,' which, as it so happens, has a secondary meaning of 'whitewasher' and that's exactly who Christ was or is because critical parts of the story have been distorted, omitted or deleted."

Lilly folded her arms in a huff. "Lies in other words!"

Wolf shrugged dismissively. "People need a version of the truth— not *the* truth. They can't handle the truth. It causes too many problems and must be concealed at all costs. However, we need people to commit to the basic principles of the story ... to the key elements."

"Why?"

"People need to have a basic understanding of the agenda. We want them to be on board with the plan, happily working towards our future goals."

"But they don't know what your goals are! So, that's what religion is? A devious lie designed to coerce people into going along with an evil plan?"

"You're placing too much importance on truth ... History isn't truth, it's an assembly of lies and exaggerations. Winners write history books—put their spin on events. Winston Churchill famously said, 'History will be kind to me, for I intend to write it.'"

Lilly groaned. "Give me an example of a rewriting of history."

"You're no doubt familiar with the Exodus story in the Bible. Well, the truth of the matter is quite different ... Canaanite peoples, Hebrews, settled peacefully in Egypt at the end of the 12th Dynasty c. 1720 B.C. They established an independent realm in the eastern Nile Delta. The Hebrew rulers of the Delta coexisted with the Egyptians until 1674 B.C., when, using horses and modern weapons unknown to the Egyptians, they seized control of the land and ruled it from 1674 B.C. to 1544 B.C. After suffering under their cruel rule for fifty years, the Egyptian leaders, Seqenenre Tao, Kamose, and Ahmose, waged war against the Hebrews, then known as the Hyksos, a word meaning foreigner. Succeeding, they expelled the Hebrews from Egypt along with their king—Khamudi."

Lilly's brow rose. "Well, I didn't know that!"

"The famous Jewish Historian, Flavius Josephus 37–100 C.E., identified the Israelite Exodus with the Hyksos Exodus mentioned by the Egyptian historian Manetho, (ca. 300 B.C.). After the fall of their capital in Avaris, Josephus wrote, 480,000 Hyksos fled Egypt pursued by the Egyptian army across the northern Sinai Peninsula into the southern Levant. The mention of 'Hyksos' identifies the Exodus with the Hyksos period in the 16th century B.C."

Lilly groaned. "So, much of the Bible isn't true, or it's an exaggeration—twisted facts? Jesus didn't come to Earth to save people? He didn't come full stop? He's a symbolic mystery school teacher?"

"Mystery school teachers were and are servants of God ... the Word of God.' They're symbolized as goats in the Bible. God's people in the Old Testament are referred to as he-goats. Goats are often trained to misdirect. The term 'Judas goat' wasn't coined until after Christ's supposed death, but it was Jesus who was the Judas goat, not Judas who merely did as he was instructed to do:

> *Jeremiah 50:8 Go out from the midst of Babylon, and go out of the land of the Chaldeans, and be as the He-goats before the flocks.*

> *Genesis 27:15 And Rebekah took goodly raiment of her eldest son Esau, which were with her in the house, and put them upon Jacob her younger son: 16 And she put the skins of the kids of the goats upon Jacob's hands, and upon the smooth of his neck:*

> *Matthew 25:31 When the Son of man shall come in his glory, and all the holy angels with him, then shall he sit upon the throne of his glory: 32 And before him shall be gathered all nations: and he shall separate them one from another, as a shepherd divides his sheep from the goats: 33 And he shall set the sheep on his right hand, but the goats on the left. 34 Then shall the King say to them on his right*

hand, Come, you blessed of my Father, inherit the kingdom
prepared for you from the foundation of the world."

"But he placed the sheep on his right hand," Lilly protested. "In the place of honor."

"No, it isn't," Wolf said. "Jesus himself sits on God's right-hand side, so if he places the goats on his left, he's placed them in the place of honor beside God—the real King. Jesus is called the King of Kings in the Bible, but in Judaism, God's name is 'the King of Kings of Kings'—the double superlative placing God a step above Jesus. The royal titles of Babylonian and Persian kings referred to in the Bible, is also the king of kings."

Lilly thought about this for a moment. "Oh, tricky ... but wasn't Jesus a scape-goat?"

"Yes, he wore many hats—crowns. He was the sacrificial lamb, the scape-goat, *and* the Judas goat. The division above is strictly speaking of the division between the he-goats and the sheep, but sheep, of course, includes the sacrificial kid goats and the scape-goat. Wolf raised his brow. "Tell me ... why did you worship a man who said:

> *Matthew 10:34 Do not think that I have come to bring*
> *peace to the Earth, I have not come to bring peace, but a*
> *sword. 35 For I have come to set a man against his father,*
> *and a daughter against her mother, and a daughter-in-*
> *law against her mother-in-law. 36 And a person's enemies*
> *will be those of his own household.'"*

Lilly groaned. She'd always hated that verse and other controversial verses besides it. She felt despondent, but even so, old habits kicked in. She straightened herself. "I shouldn't listen to you! Yours are the words of a wolf in sheep's clothing. You're the Antichrist!"

Wolf laughed a loud, raucous laugh. "So, you fell for that ruse as well? When the Bible speaks of Antichrists, it speaks of people who didn't believe Christ had come in the flesh. Back in the day, many people knew the story was based on an earlier tale of a non-historical Christ ... There is no biblical prophecy of an upcoming 'singular' Antichrist, and, certainly, no prophecy saying one *must* come before Christ's supposed return:

> *1 John 2:18 Little children, it is the last time: and as you have heard that antichrist shall come, even now are there many antichrists; whereby we know that it is the last time. 22 Who is a liar but he that denies that Jesus is the Christ? He is antichrist, that denies the Father and the Son.*

> *1 John 4:3 And every spirit that confesses not that Jesus Christ is come in the flesh is not of God: and this is that spirit of antichrist, whereof you have heard that it should come, and even now already is it in the world.*

> *2 John 1:7 Many deceivers have entered the world, confessing not that Jesus Christ has come in the flesh. This is a deceiver and an antichrist."*

Lilly glared at Wolf. "You're not a god! The God in my Bible isn't a liar or a manipulator!"

"Isn't he?" Wolf quizzed. "I think you either have serious comprehension issues or willful blindness:

> *Proverbs 25:2 It is the glory of God to conceal a thing: but the honor of kings is to search out a matter."*

> *Isaiah 45:7 I form the light, and create darkness: I make peace, and create evil: I the LORD do all these things.*

"Well," Lilly said. "What about these verses which speak of Christ's return:

> *2 Thessalonians 2:3 Let no man deceive you by any means: for that day shall not come, except there comes a falling*

away first, and that man of sin be revealed, the son of
perdition;

4 Who opposes and exalts himself above all that is called
God, or that is worshipped; so that he as God sits in the
temple of God, showing himself that he is God.

"Let me guess," Wolf said. "You think those verses are connected
to the building of a third temple in Israel? Do you think Christ won't
return until a temple is built? Have you forgotten what Jesus said?

John 2:19 Jesus answered and said to them, Destroy this
temple, and in three days I will raise it up.

"What did he mean by that? Was he suggesting a symbolic temple
rather than an actual building … Christ rose on the third day—"
"Correct," Wolf said:

Revelation 21:22 And I saw no temple therein: for the Lord
God Almighty and the Lamb are the temple of it.

"I see."
"As for the man of sin who opposes and exalts himself above all
that is called God, so that he as God sits in the temple of God, showing
himself that he is God, that's spoken of in 2 Thessalonians … do you
not recognize intimidating tactics when you see them? Numerous
men have already sat in grand temples and proclaimed themselves
Jesus or God. So, I hardly think the world needs another one for the
prophesy to be fulfilled:

Pope Leo XIII said this about the role of the Papacy and
the Roman Church: 'We hold upon this earth the place of
God Almighty.'

"Wow, I didn't know that," Lilly said.
"You think that's bad? That's nothing … Someone would have to
be seriously outdoing themselves to beat the vanities of the middle

ages:

> *Pope Nicholas said of himself: "I am in all and above all, so that God Himself and I, the vicar of God, have both one consistory, and I am able to do almost all that God can do... therefore, if those things that I do be said not to be done of man, but of God, what do you make of me but God? Again, if prelates of the Church be called of Constantine for gods, I then being above all prelates, seem by this reason to be above all gods. Therefore, no marvel, if it be in my power to dispense with all things, yes with the precepts of Christ."*
>
> (Decret. par. Distinct 96 ch. 7 edit. Lugo 1661)

> *The title 'Lord God the Pope' - these words appeared in the Canon Law of Rome. 'To believe that our Lord God the Pope has not the power to decree as he is decreed, is to be deemed heretical.'*
>
> (The gross extravagances of Pope John XXII Cum. Inter, tit XIV Ad Callem Sexti Decretalium, Paris, 1685)

"Wow ... just wow!"

"Indeed," Wolf said, "But let me just say ... there's wordplay involved in the verses in 2 Thessalonians ... The verses don't speak of an antichrist."

Lilly shook her head in dismay. "If it's all lies, then how did Christianity gain traction?"

"Jerusalem is a long way from Rome ... People weren't flying back and forth in airplanes like they are today, so fanciful stories could easily be invented. Time, distance, and murky records allowed the tale to take hold ... Christianity is a control system."

"But why would Constantine, an emperor who'd won a decided battle—the Emperor of the entire Roman world—visually transfer his power and authority to Christ?"

"Because one man can't rule the world ... You need more than legions of men to control the masses: you must have control over their minds. Authority should be ever-present—eternal. The masses should be so hopelessly brainwashed they don't see or even recognize the brainwashing syllabus you're using, such is your control. So much so ... when the general public are asked if they think they're brainwashed, they vehemently deny it while proclaiming their freedom."

Lilly groaned.

CHAPTER THIRTY-FOUR

Global Dimming

Lilly's mind drifted to the current geopolitics playing out in the world and her fears for her people. "Europeans think the elite are trying to flood Europe with immigrants so they can break up the nation-states and cause the loss of both national and cultural identity, so the European Union can rule over them with impunity ... What do you think is going on in Europe?"

Rubbing his chin, Wolf sighed. "Do you want me to be blunt?"

"Yes. I want the unvarnished truth ... just give it to me straight."

"Well, in short, we're about to bring in the harvest. We've positioned foreigners in your lands to help us gather in the crop:

> *Ezekiel 32:3 This says the LORD God; I will spread my net over you with the company of many people, and they shall bring you up in my net."*

Lilly blinked several times. "You're about to round up my people like cattle? You can't do that ... I know *you* think you're omnipotent, but that's *not* about to happen!"

"It is going to happen because your people will have no choice but to move, and while they're on the move, we'll sort them. Likewise, people from other lands, even if they're third or fourth generation, will be sent back to their traditional homelands. Preparations are already in place for this to happen."

"You mean African-American's will be sent to Africa, etc.?"

"Yes ... China has built huge cities to accommodate the return of its people:

> Isaiah 13:14 *... every man shall turn to his own people, and*
> *flee into his own land."*

"But why must we move?"

"Because most of your lands will be covered in ice shortly."

"Rubbish, climatologists agree we have global warming."

Wolf chuckled. "Nonsense ..."

"Why would anybody lie about that? They tell us the planet is heating up. A runaway greenhouse effect is developing here like it did on Venus."

Wolf laughed. "Earth can't be compared to Venus, because Venus is thirty percent closer to the Sun. Besides, Earth's been a lot warmer in the past and the sea a lot higher, and no runaway greenhouse effect occurred. Sea levels have gone down over the past two thousand years. Did you know Ancient Rome's harbor, Portus, is now four kilometers inland ... Earth is currently in an interglacial period which is fast ending. This planet is frozen for ninety thousand years out of every one hundred thousand."

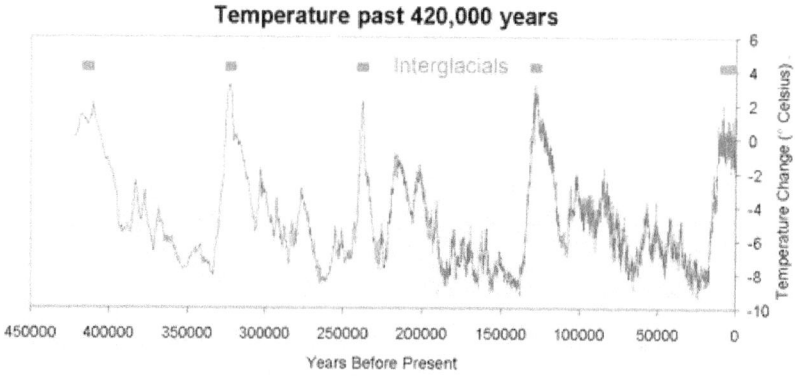

Lilly frowned. "But carbon dioxide is heating the planet!"

"It isn't ... that's fake science. Earth's lower atmosphere is mostly transparent to direct solar radiation which prevents it from being significantly warmed by sunlight. If there's no humidity in the atmosphere to hold heat in, temperatures plummet when the sun goes down. Night-time temperatures in deserts can be as low as zero when the daytime temperature might have been as high as 55 degrees Celsius or 131 degrees Fahrenheit. This demonstrates the power of the sun ... not that any example is needed beyond the Arctic Circle's seasons. The Arctic is frozen solid when the sun isn't present in winter, and it thaws and blooms when it is."

"So, why will anything change?"

"The sun is going into a prolonged quiet patch with almost no sunspot activity. This means there will be less solar energy and more cosmic rays. Cosmic rays cause the atmosphere to make more clouds, and increased cloud cover causes more solar energy to be reflected back into space."

Lilly frowned. "Then why do they tell us the planet's climate is linked to higher levels of CO_2 in the atmosphere?"

"What they tell you, and what the truth is, is two very different things. Venus has a runaway greenhouse environment because water boils at 100 degrees Celsius, or 212 degrees Fahrenheit, and Venus is hotter than that. Water vapor is a powerful greenhouse gas that accounts for 95 percent of Earth's atmosphere ... CO_2, on the other hand, accounts for a mere .04 percent."

"That's a tiny percentage. Is that why they talk about it in parts per million? But scientists have a theory about CO_2. They say it's like a poison, and levels are skyrocketing."

Wolf laughed. "You seriously bought into that carbon nonsense? Use your head ... the sun affects the planet's climate more than anything else. Even a child knows it's warmer when the yellow ball is in the sky."

Lilly slumped.

"Their theory goes like this ... a little bit of extra CO_2 in the atmosphere warms the planet just enough to cause a positive feedback loop. Warm air holds more water vapor, and warmer air causes more evaporation to take place at the sea's surface. This causes even more warming, and on it goes. Therefore, man is responsible for global warming."

Lilly hadn't heard it explained like this before. "So, they're right?"

Wolf scoffed. "No, they're *not* right. As I said, the lower atmosphere is mostly transparent to direct solar radiation which prevents it from being significantly warmed by the Sun. Therefore, the Earth's surface must warm before the atmosphere can. The surface-atmosphere primarily gets its warmth in three ways: from direct contact with the oceans, from infrared radiation off the ocean surface and from the latent removal of heat from the ocean via evaporation.

"Consequently, the temperature of the lower atmosphere is largely determined by the sea's temperature. The oceans, by virtue of their enormous density and heat-storage capacity, have a massive effect on the climate. They're the heat budget of the planet. Energy that flows into and out of the oceans determines the mean temperature of the global atmosphere. These interactions, including evaporation, cancel out any negligible response the planet might have to a small amount of added CO_2."

"So, humanity isn't affecting the climate?"

"Oh, it is," Wolf said. "Leaders are just diverting your attention from what they're really up to, and what the effect of their actions will be."

"What *are* they up to?"

"They're dimming the planet. Twenty-five percent less sunlight is reaching the planet's surface than it did twenty-five years ago."

"What!" Lilly said, shocked. "That would be having a dramatic effect on the planet ... wouldn't it?"

"Of course."

"How are they doing it?"

"To alter Earth's climate, you must either reduce or increase the amount of solar radiation able to reach the planet's surface—"

"How?"

"If you block out some of the sun's rays, you'll cause global dimming. This is easy to do: light huge forest fires, spray chemtrails and create massive amounts of pollution. If you hadn't been so distracted by the elite's lies and propaganda, you might have noticed they're doing this."

Lilly frowned. "But the poles are melting!"

"Antarctica's ice cover has been getting larger, and its core colder.

The media deliberately ignore this data or explain it away with nonsense, concentrating instead on small pockets of melt caused by underwater volcanoes. The colder the poles are in comparison to the warmer tropics, the more dramatic the weather is ... Surely, you've noticed storms are intensifying?"

"Yes, everybody's noticed?"

"Driving the planet into an ice age is dead easy. All you have to do is reduce the amount of sunlight reaching the planet's surface. If you time this to coincide with a period of reduced solar activity, you'll cause ice to build up, both in Antarctica and on land in the Arctic Circle, at an ever-increasing rate. The increased weight of the accumulating ice puts added pressure on Earth's plates. When a tube of toothpaste is squeezed ... stuff pours out the end. Earth has a similar reaction to increased pressure. Increased volcanic activity is observed when extra pressure is placed on its plates at the poles.

"The volcanic activity occurs mostly in the sea because ninety percent of Earth's volcanoes are located in the oceans. Increased volcanic activity in the sea warms it, causing increased levels of evaporation. This, in turn, causes more rain to fall as snow at the poles and a faster build-up of ice there. Increased ice cover on the planet's surface reflects more sunlight into space. And increasing cloud cover, caused by rising levels of evaporation from the sea and increasing levels of cosmic rays, further block and reflect solar radiation."

"A positive feedback loop?" Lilly said. "But the sea is rising ... isn't it?"

"The sea is warming because of increased volcanic activity in the Earth's oceans. Water expands and evaporates more readily when it's warm. Scientists who have studied the warming oceans have said, 'the only way to get the sums to make sense is to factor in increased volcanic activity.' Warm seas warm the planet. This means even though the situation is dire, people are easily fooled into believing the problem is global warming when global cooling is the problem at hand ... Earth is coming to the end of a long interglacial period."

"If what you're saying is true, then ice would be building up at the poles, but the poles *are* melting!"

"Nonsense," Wolf said. "Six American fighter planes and two bomber planes crash-landed in Greenland during World War II. They were found forty-six years later buried under 260 feet of ice. In the mid-1960s, a power transmission line with towers 115 feet tall were installed in Antarctica. The towers disappeared under the ice decades ago. Heavy ice is rapidly building up at the poles. The weight of the accumulating ice is enough to alter Earth's shape by putting pressure on its plates."

Lilly frowned. "But huge ice sheets are breaking off in Antarctica."

"That's normal ... Ice sheets are a large volume of ice sitting on water. Their growing weight makes them crack and snap off ... You're being fooled by irrelevant nonsense."

Lilly sighed.

"When you factor in the continuing efforts of the people in power to reduce the amount of solar radiation reaching Earth's surface, including spraying chemtrails which, still, somehow, manage to be regarded as a conspiracy, even though people see them almost every day, you have a planet racing into an ice age at breakneck speed."

"What are chemtrails?

"In children's textbooks, they're explained as chemicals sprayed into the atmosphere by tiny planes to form sun-blocking, artificial cloud cover to mitigate the effects of global warming. When you consider the Earth is already making more clouds because of increasing levels of cosmic rays and higher rates of evaporation from the sea, you can appreciate the impact this is having."

"Right, well, that's not good, especially if we have the *opposite* problem ... but won't it take thousands of years?"

"No," Wolf said. "Let me explain the progression of an ice age as simply as I can ... Ice builds up at the poles, usually over hundreds or thousands of years. This has already been going on for some time. The dome of the polar ice cap in Antarctica is 4800 meters thick at its deepest point, with the South Pole standing on top of 2.8 kilometers of ice. Antarctica, with an average elevation of 2160 meters, is higher than any other continent.

"This is why sea levels have gone down considerably over the past two thousand years. The weight of all that ice is putting enormous pressure on Earth's plates, causing increased earthquake and volcanic activity. Analyzed ice core data proves that periods of intense glaciation and periods of high volcanic activity go hand in hand. Sulfate deposits found in ice cores prove volcanoes have a significant effect on the climate."

"But glaciers are in retreat!"

"Glaciers are a conveyor system. They constantly advance and retreat, depending upon how much precipitation lands on top of them. The sea's increased temperature is warming glaciers in areas other than the poles. Again, you're being distracted by irrelevant data."

Lilly groaned.

"Once a significant amount of ice has built up at the poles like it currently has, volcanic activity in the sea increases. This warms the oceans and increases the level of sea evaporation, causing massive hurricanes and flooding events around the world. The extra rain doesn't all make its way back to the oceans because increasing amounts are locked up as ice at the poles."

"Speeding up the accumulation of ice at the poles?"

"Correct," Wolf said, "and the ever-increasing weight at the poles further increases volcanic activity in the sea. So, the sea gets warmer and warmer and it evaporates faster and faster."

"And ice builds up faster and faster at the poles? A positive feedback loop?"

"That's right," Wolf said, "and it causes huge ice shelves to break off more frequently because of their increased weight."

Lilly frowned. "But that has nothing to do with the planet getting warmer?"

"No ... A tipping point has nearly been reached. A massive land volcano will go off shortly. When it does, it will pump copious amounts of sun-blocking particles into the upper atmosphere. These particles will greatly reduce the amount of solar radiation able to reach the Earth's surface. Suddenly, the planet will be in near darkness and the moon will appear red. When you look at the sun, it will be as if you're looking at it through sackcloth, but the sea will continue to evaporate at an elevated level because the oceans are a huge heat sink, and increasing volcanic activity under the sea will continue to raise their temperature.

"Ice accumulation will go into overdrive because the water evaporating from the sea will no longer, for the most part, return to the oceans. Falling on land as snow, it will become landlocked as ice everywhere except the tropics and sub-tropics. Sea levels will plummet, and when the skies finally clear, the Earth will be a different place. Most of the Northern Hemisphere will be covered in a thick sheet of ice and crops will have failed, season after season."

"And you'll assume control?"

"Yes," Wolf said. "But before that happens, the harvest will be brought in."

"Do you like the planet when it's cooler?"

"Yes."

"So, the gods do rest. They do take time off?"

"Indeed, we do."

"How come I was collected before the harvest?"

"Gods stationed here that are getting a new baby, get her ahead of time so when a lot of activity is going on above, they can concentrate on their work."

"Is the harvest a while away yet?"

Wolf shook his head. "No. It will happen soon."

"When's soon?" Lilly said. "People have been waiting for the apocalypse for over 2000 years."

"It was never going to happen 2000 years ago."

CHAPTER THIRTY-FIVE

Zion and Babylon

"So, most of my people will die because they live on land that will soon be covered in ice?" Lilly said. "Couldn't they move to northern Australia or Spain?"

Wolf cleared his throat. "The geopolitical landscape is about to change. At the moment, there's an agreement in place preventing the trading of human stock. Now that the harvest is ready, that agreement will pass into history. When it does, it will be open season on your kind, but that doesn't mean we'll allow any harm to come to you. Indeed, there'll be a harsh penalty inflicted upon anybody harming our stock because your value surpasses gold.

"Nations are currently maneuvering to take in as much stock as possible. You see this in India and Egypt in particular, where they're building huge smart cities with no-dig zone technologies. The services, including garbage collection, running through tunnels underground. The new cities will rely heavily on robots and drones.

"India has partnered with Singapore because that country has no land, so, together, they're building huge cities in India. Partnering with Egypt, Jordan, and Israel, Saudi Arabia is about to build a huge city worth more than 500 billion by the Red Sea called NEOM which means 'new future.' Turkey's also building smart cities."

"What the fuck! Are you serious?"

"Of course. When we bring in the harvest, the mature stock will be taken directly to underground bases, but younger stock and breeding stock will be sent to some of the cities I'm talking about. These will be lovely places, and the stock will be given the best of everything to keep them content."

"Content!" Lilly almost choked. "How are they supposed to be content when they know they're part of a managed breeding program, and they're going to be used by everyone? And how are the countries building these cities going to sell their wares when you don't believe in money?"

"Earth has been cut off from the wider community while its stock ran free and multiplied. The period of isolation will end soon, and people will trade with other planets as they have in the past ... What they have to trade is of the highest value, so they'll guard their stock jealously and treat it well."

"Right! But you know the other races don't have much time for us. They say nasty things about us and blow us up on trains etc.?

The number of UK terror arrests rise 68% to record level during year of attacks

A record 379 in the 12 months to June, one of the most intense periods for terrorist attacks in recent history. The Home Office said it was the highest number of terrorist arrests in a year since records began in 2001. They included 12 arrests linked to the Westminster attack in March, 23 connected with the Manchester Arena bombing in May, 21 arrests following the London Bridge attack in June and one in relation to the Finsbury Park van attack soon after. The number of terrorist prisoners in British jails has also risen in the past year, by 35% to 204. The Home Office said 91% of those in prison on 30 June held extreme Islamist views and a further 5% had far-right ideologies.   The Guardian: Sept 14th. 2017*

Muslim yob who threatened to shoot and stab 'English pigs' at the Royal Shakespeare Theatre is spared jail.
Ryhan Ali, 23, told theatre staff he was going to 'get a gun' and kill English scum.
*When police arrived to arrest him, he branded an officer a 'racist white c***'*

> *Earlier that morning, he had appeared in court for*
> *racially abusing hospital staff.*
> *The serial racist was given a 12-month prison sentence,*
> *suspended for two years.* The Daily Mail: May 12th. 2019

"The world's governments won't allow any such thing to go on," Wolf said. "The punishment for breaking into a golden city and harming a member will be extreme."

"A golden city? A city housing my people? But that's not the only way they like to take advantage of us!" Lilly protested.

> *The Observer view on dealing with child-grooming gangs*
> *The men plied vulnerable girls as young as 11, including*
> *those in care and with learning disabilities, with alcohol*
> *and drugs in order to sexually abuse them. The abuse*
> *included men raping intoxicated girls while others*
> *watched, sexual abuse with a drinks bottle and gang rape*
> *by men using plastic bags as condoms. The vexed issue of*
> *the ethnicity of the perpetrators – they were all of Asian*
> *[Pakistani] descent – has prepared the way for a kneejerk*
> *reaction and a polarized debate between those who argue*
> *that these men's race and faith are the main factors*
> *driving these crimes on the one hand and those who*
> *strenuously deny that they play a role at all.*
> The Guardian: Oct 21st. 2018

"And an argument can be made for that being the case!" Lilly said:

> *To say or not to say:*
> *Our small apartment was in the slums of Karachi,*
> *Pakistan. This was okay as long as I was in the house. Once*
> *I walked out of our house, things changed. It was the*
> *realm of men. They harassed me; they groped my genitals*
> *in crowded streets, and they tried to strip me naked with*
> *their eyes. My only crime was that I was walking on the*
> *street not having covered myself from head to toe – as was*

the custom – and so, I didn't deserve their respect. When I finally left this world of patriarchal aggression, I was full of rebellion. I rebelled against Pakistani men; I rebelled against Pakistani traditions and above all, I rebelled against Islam. For me, it was a repressive and violent religion; a religion where husbands are allowed to hit their wives, and men are allowed to control the women of their household in the name of honor and shame.

Stuff News: April 23th, 2019

In Pakistan, 1,000 women die in 'honor killings' annually. A pregnant 25-year-old woman was stoned to death by her family for marrying a man she loved.

Washington Post: May 26th, 2014

"Indeed," Wolf said. "It's unacceptable behavior that we'll be putting a stop to forthwith."

"Cat's been mean to me!" Lilly protested. "He's treated me coldly!"

"Oh, yes ... He did that so you'd respond positively to me when I was nice to you. He wanted you to bond with me ... he didn't treat you *that* bad."

"I'm sick of you bastards playing head games with me!" Lilly growled. "Well, your plans sound all fine and dandy, but at the end of the day you're going to sell or barter my people, and many women in the golden cities will partake in my fate ... Surely, they'll know this?"

"We'll put a positive spin on it."

"Right!" Lilly said. "So, governments have been maneuvering and warring while jostling about to get as much stock as possible?"

"Your own governments will retain a share of their stock. Countries like Germany have been making arrangements for the relocation of their people and making deals to secure that arrangement. For example, they may have made a deal with Spain to move all of their people and businesses into southern Spain. After they've sent all of their foreign nationals back to their original homelands, they'll have 65 million citizens with no immigrant background that need to be housed. If five percent are sent to a golden city, they'll need to build three megacities in Spain to house their remaining citizens. This is doable, and it won't be the end for them. They'll adjust to both their new homeland and the new political environment."

"Is five percent, the percentage of whites in Caucasian lands that'll be sent to golden cities?"

"Roughly, yes, but it will probably be less than that. We're after certain blood types and other genetic factors ... most of the citizens in white lands aren't suitable. The ultimate prize is males with the exact blood type and genetics we're looking for. A good specimen is worth more than his weight in gold ... a lot more!

"That's why we need to get the high powered guns out of circulation. We don't want to be forced into risking prize stock in some standoff that turns into a shootout. It would be better if we could negotiate and assure these men a life of privileged luxury. Of course, we've been scouring sperm banks for years now and squirreling away precious sperm and taking note of the children born of these men.

> Isaiah 13:12 *I will make a man more precious than fine gold; even a man than the golden wedge of Ophir."*

Lilly groaned. "If almost all the white lands are soon to become uninhabitable, surely there isn't enough land for us all to squeeze into?"

"There's plenty of space, and land will start reappearing from under the sea ... Egypt is building a city the size of Singapore and Saudi Arabia is building one that's going to be 33 times the size of New York, but India is outdoing them all; they're building lots of megacities, and they already have 11 million unoccupied houses. There's a similar number empty in southern Europe and Saudi Arabia. Some of the new cities will be golden cities, but others will house returning citizens and foreign nationals. The construction phase has already begun, but it's early days yet.

"The building of major roads and train tracks to help get the job done is well underway. China's belt and road system which already extends to the UK is one such initiative. 'Belt' refers to the overland routes for road and rail transportation, called 'the *Silk Road Economic Belt'* and 'road' refers to the sea routes or 21st Century Maritime Silk Road.

"The golden cities will be upgraded concentration camps. The apartments will have amenities, but on the road below and in the apartment buildings, there'll be cafés and restaurants—upgraded mess halls—and the local park is the recreation yard. Inhabitants, there won't have access to a car, but there'll be good public transportation to allow them to move about their camp. They'll be paid what is known as a universal benefit to meet their needs, but they'll also be paid wages if they decide to take a job in a café, etc., so we can limit the number of outsiders working within the camp; we want it to be as autonomous as possible. We think that's what's best. People will be packed into planes or trains and transported there, and once there, they'll have little chance of escaping."

Lilly groaned. "So, it's a prison!"

"A flash prison," Wolf clarified. "The mega camps, cities, will have everything: sports facilities, malls, zoos, fun parks ... They'll be very pleasant places to live and we'll pay women a good amount extra for every baby they have, and provide grand houses to productive women."

"Yeah ... because it's a fucking breeding program! I'm sure there'll also be lots of night clubs and alcohol will flow freely!"

"And not a pill or condom in sight," Wolf said sarcastically. "How did you guess?"

Lilly groaned. "Say 62 million Germans do move to Spain, is that going to be the end of it, or will there be another harvest in twenty year's time?"

"Every infant born will have his, or her, genetics tested. Later, we'll go back through and collect more stock. It's a sacrifice they'll get used to."

"Agh, no! I doubt that very much!" Lilly said sourly.

"Your people will find a workaround ... They'll partner with the mixed-raced offspring within their cities and the foreign nationals who'll once again flood into them, guaranteeing their children a free future. The plan is to eventually have whites living only in the golden cities."

"What the fuck! You've got another thing coming if you think my people will accept that! They'll clump together and protect their borders!"

"Believe me, we've seen it all before, and yes, that's a likely outcome which is why we'll spread them around as much as possible within the borders of other countries to prevent this. Even so, it still usually happens." Wolf sighed. "It's a tricky situation because we don't want to hurt them, and we don't want their lives to be miserable. Usually, the situation is resolved with some kind of truce."

Lilly folded her arms.

"Come now ... you're happy being a holy vessel of the Lord?

> *Isaiah 52:¹¹ Depart you, depart you, go you out from Babylon, O captive daughter of Zion, touch no unclean thing; go you out of the midst of her; be you clean, that bear the vessels of the Lord."*

"What's meant by 'bearing the vessels of the Lord'?"

Wolf rubbed Lilly's belly.

"But I'm not a Hebrew or a Jew!"

"The Bible plays tricks with people and places to keep its secrets. You are Zion and Jerusalem who are essentially the same, and they're feminine"

Lilly frowned. "How do we know that Zion and Jerusalem are feminine?"

"It's a well-known fact. While also appearing as a place, their identity as a woman is exposed in several passages:

> *Lamentations 1:¹⁷ Jerusalem is as a menstruating woman among them.*

> *Jeremiah 6:² I have likened the daughter of Zion to an*

attractive and delicate woman.

Isaiah 62:¹ For Zion's sake will I not hold my peace, and for Jerusalem's sake, I will not rest, until the righteousness of them goes forth as brightness, and the salvation of them as a lamp that burns ... ⁴ and just as the bridegroom rejoices over the bride, so shall your God rejoice over you."

Lilly blinked several times. "Zion and Jerusalem? The daughters of Zion are the Brides of Christ in the New Testament?"

"Yes. In ancient mythology or religion, God, the Father, was symbolized as the Sky or heaven, and the goddess as the Mother and Earth—Gaia. The Bible certainly isn't being original when it symbolizes a piece of land as a woman or women. You're also Babylon because the Bible transferred the identity of Zion and Jerusalem to Babylon after the Lord let Nebuchadnezzar II, the King of Babylon, take the Hebrews into captivity:

Ezra 5:¹² Because our ancestors angered the God of heaven, he gave them into the hands of Nebuchadnezzar, the Chaldean king of Babylon who destroyed our temple and deported our people to Babylon."

"So, the Hebrews became Babylonians and partook in their curse?" Lilly sighed audibly. "But didn't a remnant of the daughters of Zion leave Babylon and become the Lord's people once more?"

"A few left, but the Bible tells us the daughters of Zion, the vessels of the Lord, did not:

Jeremiah 27:¹⁶ I spoke to the priests and to all of these people, saying, 'this says the Lord, hearken not to the words of your prophets that prophesy to you, saying, Behold, the vessels of the Lord's house shall now shortly be brought again from Babylon, for they prophesy a lie to you.'"

Lilly frowned. "So, the daughters of Zion stayed in Babylon?"

"Indeed. Verses with double meanings prove this:

> *Zechariah 2:⁷ Deliver thyself, O Zion, that dwells with the*
> *daughter of Babylon.*

> *Micah 4:¹⁰ Be in pain, and labor to bring forth, O daughter*
> *of Zion, like a woman in travail: for you shall go forth out*
> *of the city, and you shall dwell in the field, and you shall*
> *go even to Babylon; there shall you be delivered; there the*
> *Lord shall redeem you from the hand of your enemies."*

"Were the Babylonians white Caucasians?"

"Yes and no. "When the Bible speaks of the people of Babylon and the Babylonian king, it refers to the Chaldeans. During a period of weakness in Babylon, ineffective kings couldn't ward off waves of foreigners and prevent them from settling. The Chaldeans, a Caucasian nomadic tribe that migrated from the Levant near Tyre, were one such people. They settled in a south-eastern portion of Babylon, chiefly on the left bank of the Euphrates during the 8th century B.C., and their territory was known as the land of the Chaldeans."

"And one of them became the King of Babylon?"

"Babylon was developed into a small kingdom by an Amorite king, Sumuabum in 1894 B.C., but from the 9th to the late 7th century it was almost continuously under Assyrian suzerainty, usually wielded through its native kings. The Chaldean tribesmen usurped the kingship on several occasions, resulting in the Assyrian monarch Sennacherib 704–681 B.C. destroying the city. Later, his son, Esarhaddon 680–669 B.C., expelled the Chaldean tribesmen and rebuilt the city. But in 626 B.C. a Chaldean leader, Nabopolassar, gained control of Babylon, and his son, Nebuchadrezzar II 605–561 B.C., made it a major imperial power by fortifying Babylon and undertaking a vast building program. The Bible records these events:

Isaiah 23:13 Behold the land of the Chaldeans; these people were not till the Assyrian founded it for them that dwell in the wilderness: they set up its towers, they raised up its palaces ...

Isaiah 13:19 ... Babylon, the glory of kingdoms, the beauty of the Chaldees' excellence ..."

"So," Lilly said, "When the Bible speaks of the Babylonians, it's speaking of white Chaldeans."

A Chaldean king of Babylon

"Yes, it pacifically identifies this period in history:

Ezra 5:12 After our [Hebrew] fathers provoked the God of heaven to wrath, he gave them into the hand of Nebuchadnezzar the king of Babylon, the Chaldean who destroyed this house, and carried away the people to Babylon.

"A few hundred years after the Bible speaks of the Chaldeans," Wolf said, "they'd interbred with the native population of Babylon to such an extent they were no longer distinguishable, and they faded from history. Women, like yourself, lost their identity long ago; they don't know who they are. The Bible says they're found among the

Gentiles because the Lord scattered the seed of Judah:

> *Jeremiah 9:11 And I will make Jerusalem heaps and a den of dragons ... 16 I will scatter them among the nations, whom neither they nor their fathers have known; and I will send the sword after them until I have annihilated them.*

> *Micah 5:8 And the remnant of Jacob shall be among the Gentiles.*

> *Isaiah 60:16 You shall suck the milk of the Gentiles, and shall suck the breast of kings."*

"So, I'm Zion or Jerusalem?" Lilly said. "I never understood what Zion was and I certainly didn't expect to discover *I am Zion*, or rather, part of it."

"Indeed ... and the agents have been trying to get the keys of Zion so they can escape their prison." Wolf chuckled. "They never thought it would be so easy. They're deep inside the walls now ... it's going to be a cakewalk."

"Don't quote the bloody *Matrix* to me! I can't believe women like me are Zion. Surely, that's not right?"

"No mistake ... You've been wandering around blind for years—asleep. You were meant to take comfort in Christ. Be happy with his sacrifice and believe you dwelt in safety, and you did. You let down your guard; lost sight of your enemy:

> *Jeremiah 51:57 And Babylon's princes I will make drunk, and her wise men, her captains, her rulers, and her mighty men: and they shall sleep a perpetual sleep, and not wake, says the King whose name is the Lord of hosts.*

> *Isaiah 47:8 Therefore hear now this, you that are given to pleasures, that dwells carelessly, that says in your heart, I am, and there is none else beside me; I shall not sit as a*

widow, neither shall I know the loss of children: ⁹ But these two things shall come upon you in a moment, in one day, the loss of children and widowhood. They shall come upon you in their perfection, for the multitude of your sorceries and the great abundance of your enchantments."

Lilly groaned. "Because the white Chaldean king, Nebuchadnezzar, took the Hebrews as prey and treated them harshly?"

"According to the biblical story he did, yes. In the Bible, the Lord boldly announces to his people:

Isaiah 51:²² This says the Lord, and the God that pleads the cause of his people, Behold, I have taken out of your hand the cup of trembling, even the dregs of the cup of my fury; you shall not drink it again: ²³ I will put it into the hand of them that afflict you [the Babylonians]; they who have said to your soul, 'Bow down, that we may go over,' and you have laid your body as the ground, as a street, for them to go over.

Jeremiah 51:³⁴ Nebuchadrezzar the King of Babylon has devoured me, he has crushed me, he has made me an empty vessel, he has swallowed me up like a dragon, he has filled his belly with my delicacies, he has cast me out. ³⁵ The violence done to me and to my flesh be upon Babylon, shall the inhabitant of Zion say; and my blood upon the inhabitants of Chaldea, shall Jerusalem say. ³⁶ Therefore, says the Lord ... ³⁷ Babylon shall become heaps, a dwelling place for dragons."

Lilly frowned. "So, the curse was transferred to Babylon, but I'm no more a Babylonian than I am a Jew from Israel. I'm not a Hebrew or a Jew, and I'm certainly not a Babylonian, and surely the Hebrew women from Zion are still Jewish even if they're found in other lands?"

"No, they're not Jewish. The Jews were captured and carried away by the Babylonians before being sold to the Grecians—the Greeks:

> *Joel 3:6 The children also of Judah and the children of Jerusalem have you sold to the Grecians, that you might remove them far from their border."*

"I did know the Jewish lands were populated by the Babylonians and only a few ever returned."

"Yes," Wolf said, "and since then other peoples have converted to Judaism. The Khazars, a semi-nomadic Turkic people who inhabited the western Turkish steppe, were originally pagan worshippers but at the beginning of the eighth century, Khazar royalty and notable segments of the aristocracy converted to Judaism, as did the populous. Most Jews today are Khazar-Jews—they're not related to the Hebrews in the Bible."

Lilly sighed.

"The Catholic Church declares, 'Mary, in whom the Lord himself has made his dwelling, is the daughter of Zion in person—the Ark of the Covenant. She is the place where the glory of God dwells.' You, and others like you, are Mary."

"That hardly seems fair! Why am I being blamed for the misdeeds of a people I never knew, and I doubt I ever belonged to?"

"You're not being blamed for anything," Wolf said. "The story is fictitious ... You're simply part of the crop, and you've been collected. One doesn't give a fish a heads-up when they're trying to catch it, rather, they snare it unawares. It's by deception and manipulation that wars are won:

> *Isaiah 9:14 Therefore, the Lord will cut off from Israel head and tail, branch and rush, in one day. 15 The ancient and honorable, he is the head; and the prophet that teaches lies, he is the tail. 16 For the leaders of this people cause them to err, and they that are led of them are destroyed.*
>
> *John 5:31 And Jesus said, If I testify about myself, my*

testimony is not true."

Lilly frowned. "You're saying this knowledge is in the Bible, but surely there aren't verses that speak of God getting it on with a woman?"

Wolf cleared his throat. "There most certainly is:

> *Isaiah 3:17 Therefore, the Lord will smite with a scab the crown of the head of the daughters of Zion, and the Lord will discover their secret parts.*

> *1 Corinthians 12:23 And those members of the body, which we think to be less honorable, upon these, we bestow more abundant honor; and our uncomely [unattractive] parts have more abundant comeliness. 24 For our comely [attractive] parts have no need: but God has tempered the body together, having given more abundant honor to that part which lacked [the anus]:*

> *Isaiah 47:1 Come down, and sit in the dust, O virgin daughter of Babylon, sit on the ground: there is no throne, O daughter of the Chaldeans: for you shall no more be called tender and delicate. 2 Take the millstones, and grind meal: uncover your locks, make bare your leg, uncover your thigh, pass over the rivers. 3 Your nakedness shall be uncovered, yes, your shame shall be seen: I will take vengeance, and I will not meet you as a man.*

> *Ezekiel 15:6 This, says the Lord GOD; As the vine tree among the trees of the forest, which I have given to the fire for fuel, so will I give the inhabitants of Jerusalem ... 16:8 When I passed by you and looked upon you, behold, the time was the time of love; and I spread my skirt over you, and covered your nakedness: yes, I swore unto you and entered a covenant with you, and you became mine."*

Lilly scoffed. "That's not right! Learned religious scholars interpret those passages differently."

"Yes, because they view the Bible through the Church's lens. People adjust the text to fit the parameters of their minds ... The Bible is the sealed book of Revelation and the Old Testament:

> *Isaiah 29:10 For the Lord has poured out upon you the spirit of deep sleep and has closed your eyes: the prophets and your rulers, the seers has he covered. 11 And the vision has become to you as the words of a book that is sealed, which men deliver to one that is learned and say, 'Read this, I pray you': and he says, 'I cannot; for it is sealed.'"*

Lilly shrugged and slumped.

"The Bible hides its secrets while simultaneously speaking to people in subtle tones:

> *1 Corinthians 3:2 I gave you milk, not solid food, for you were not yet ready for solid food. In fact, you're still not ready."*

Lilly exhaled audibly.

"All the way through the Bible, passages link Jerusalem to Babylon. The two don't start out as one, but they become one:

> *Isaiah 40:2 Speak you comfortably to Jerusalem, and cry unto her, that her warfare is accomplished, that her iniquity is pardoned: for she has received of the Lord's hand double for all her sins.*

> *Revelation 18:5 Babylon's sins have reached to heaven, and God has remembered her iniquities. 6 Reward her even as she rewarded you, and double unto her double according to her works: in the cup, which she has filled, fill to her double."*

Frowning, Lilly rubbed her brow. "Is the golden cup of Babylon our women's wombs?"

"Yes:

> *Jeremiah 51:⁷ Babylon has been a golden cup in the Lord's hand, that made all the earth drunken: the nations have drunken of her wine; therefore, the nations are mad.*

> *Revelation 17:¹ And there came one of the seven angels which had the seven vials, and talked with me, saying unto me, 'Come hither; I will show you the judgment of the great whore that sits upon many waters: ² With whom the kings of the earth have committed fornication, and the inhabitants of the earth have been made drunk with the wine of her fornication.' ³ So he carried me away in the spirit into the wilderness: and I saw a woman sit upon a scarlet colored beast, full of names of blasphemy, having seven heads and ten horns. ⁴ And the woman was arrayed in purple and scarlet colour, and decked with gold and precious stones and pearls, having a golden cup in her hand full of abominations and filthiness of her fornication."*

Lilly slapped a hand over her eyes. "I'm tired of being called filthy and being treated like a criminal ... an animal even. I was an honorable woman."

"Your honor will be restored in due course," Wolf said. "Then you'll be known by your correct title:

> *Jeremiah 33:¹⁵ In those days, and at that time, will I cause the Branch of righteousness to grow up unto David; and he shall execute judgment and righteousness in the land. ¹⁶ In those days shall Judah be saved, and Jerusalem shall dwell safely: and this is the name she shall be called, The Lord our righteousness. ¹⁷ For this says the Lord; David shall never want a man to sit upon the throne of the house*

of Israel."

Lilly's brow furrowed. "She? A woman will sit upon the throne of David? It really says 'she'?"

"Indeed," Wolf said. "And for the record, you haven't been easy to catch. Years, centuries, in fact, have past while a determined effort to capture you has endured:

> *Song of Solomon 6:¹⁰ Who is she that looks forth as the morning, fair as the moon, clear as the Sun, and as terrible as an army with banners?*

> *Micah 5:¹ Now gather yourself in troops, O daughter of troops: he has laid siege against us: they shall smite the judge of Israel with a rod upon the cheek. ² But you—fruitful—House of Bread, though you be little among the thousands of Judah, yet out of you shall he come forth to me that which is to be ruler in Israel; whose goings forth have been from of old, from everlasting ³ To whom will he give them up, until the time that she which travails has brought forth.*

> *Lamentations 3:⁵ He has built against you, and compassed you ... ⁶ He has set you in a dark place. ⁷ He has hedged you so you cannot get out ... ¹⁰ He was unto you a bear lying in wait, or a lion hid. ¹¹ He has made you desolate. ¹² He has bent his bow and set you as a mark for his arrow. ¹³ He has caused the arrows of his quiver to enter into your inward parts ... ¹⁶ he has covered you with ashes."*

Lilly's hand was back over her tear-filled eyes. Her breath caught in her throat. She gasped.

Wolf rubbed her back as he ran his fingers tenderly through her hair. "It's all right, Baby. You're designed for your role. You'll adjust and desire nothing else. Lost in your heat ... you'll find happiness."

Lilly's breath came in short gasps, her mind spinning.

"Calm, Baby," Wolf said as his reassuring hands continued to rub her back. Gently, he pressed her against him. Her breathing eased.

CHAPTER THIRTY-SIX

Freedom

Finally finding her voice, Lilly said, "I must be dreaming. This has to be my worst nightmare yet!"

"No, you're happy with us like you were designed to be. Don't worry about the rest of the world, they'll work it out and adjust to the new geopolitical environment. The world is moving into a golden age. People can look forward to better lives, longer lives, thanks to the elixir we'll trade with them."

"How's that going to work?"

"They'll go to a church, mosque, or temple once a week and be given a wafer that'll be placed on their tongues. This will be their reward for their sacrifice and working with us. There'll be many other benefits besides."

Lilly exhaled loudly before burying her face in Wolf's fur.

He ran tender fingers down her back. "Settle, Baby ... You're content with me ... with us."

"Ox poisoned me!" she grumbled. "I should be allowed to return to my home."

"If we opened the doors for you and let you out, you'd suffer horribly ... We don't want you to suffer."

"I could make my way to a doctor. If he performed a hysterectomy on me, I might get well."

"Alarmed by the large growth in your womb, a medical professional might, indeed, choose to give you a hysterectomy out of ignorance, but that would be a tragedy. He'd remove the very thing that's returning you to your youth and will keep you young for eternity."

Lilly frowned. "I'm becoming youthful? Really?"

"Do you not feel it? Haven't you noticed the skin on your hands and arms changing?"

Lilly looked at her hands, they appeared youthful.

"Cat," Wolf called out. "Can you turn up the lights and bring us a mirror. I want to show Baby how she's changing."

Lilly gave Cat a hostile look as he walked past on his way to the milking room to retrieve a mirror."

"Come now," Wolf said, "There was no need for that ... you love Cat."

"No, I don't! He's a traitor! He should view me as a sister ... a fellow human being and be loyal to me, not you!"

"You ask too much. Man doesn't favor his brothers and sisters over God. He places God first and foremost in his heart and soul."

Lilly scoffed. "You're not God! You're a monster!"

"I beg to differ."

Cat reappeared from the milking room with a mirror.

"Cat, am I a god?" Wolf asked. "Baby thinks I'm not a god, but rather a monster ... What do you say?"

A smile broadened on Cat's face. "Baby, you're lucky we're so patient with you. In future days, humans might suffer great ills if they dare to say such things. Do people openly insult the prophet? No, they don't."

"You told me you weren't a Muslim!"

"Indeed, I did, and I'm not," Cat said as he held out a mirror, so Lilly could catch her reflection in it."

Lilly stared at her reflection in amazement. Her hair was no longer gray. Instead, it was golden blonde: the color it had been when she was a child and she looked like she'd never seen her thirtieth birthday. "Well, that's amazing ... I've become youthful."

"That's only the beginning. You won't look a day over sixteen soon. If you returned home, people might not recognize you."

"So, you really are older than you look, Cat?"

"Yes, much older ... I'm thousands of years old."

"And the wine in my placenta is the fountain of youth?"

"Indeed. Pagan's claimed, rightly, that the fountain of youth poured from the loins of the goddess."

"Well, that's quite something, but I should be allowed to insult Wolf," Lilly said, no longer distracted by her remarkable appearance. "I'm not comfortable calling him God and being all humble and subservient. It's not fair to expect that, especially as you're all taking advantage of me ... using me!"

Cat drew in a sharp breath. "Yes, you can insult him. Others won't dare, but we're not about to punish you for it. We want you to relax and feel comfortable here. You're afforded privileges others aren't."

"Wolf is *not* God!" Lilly protested. "He said so himself." She looked up at Wolf. "Isn't that what you said?"

"It is, yes ... I said that because I wanted you to relax and feel comfortable with me."

Lilly puckered her lips while pulling a face. "Well, you're not what I was expecting! I thought Jesus was God."

"The Bible says Jesus is the son of God ... not God."

"I've never seen a depiction of God that looks like you," Lilly said, staring at Wolf.

"No," Cat interjected because it's illegal to depict God on any medium that might stand the test of time. And it's illegal, full stop when the crop is running free. One can depict God as a bull, an eagle, or even a dragon, but not how he actually appears."

"Right," Lilly said. "Well, I want to reject you!"

"Oh, come on ..." Wolf said. "I think you protest too much. Look at you ... your cuddling into me. If you detest me so, how come you're not fighting to get away? If I opened the elevator for you and instructed the people downstairs not to stand in your way ... You wouldn't get up and walk out."

"I wouldn't be so sure about that if I were you!"

"Where are you going to go?" Wolf said patiently. "You're in the middle of nowhere. Do you want me to get the people downstairs to drop you off in the middle of a town or city with some cash in your pocket?"

"Well, that's the best offer I've had yet," Lilly said assertively, wondering why the way out was downstairs. "Yes, I do!"

"Are you sure about that, Baby?" Cat said. "You know what will happen ... all the questions you'll have to answer, and if they cut out your placenta, you'll age and die. Do you want that?"

"Why can't I be like you, Cat? Why can't I just drink the wine?"

"So, you think it'd be okay for someone else to perform the task you're performing? You'd be okay with that? Like you were happy to accept Christ's sacrifice?"

Lilly shrugged her shoulders.

"You know you can't eat normal food because it will make you vomit and feel terrible, so how will you get by?"

"You might be lying ... telling me porky pies!"

"I'm not. Okay, I'll get you some food, but don't say I didn't warn you," Cat said as he got up and headed for the dining room.

"You're really going to eat something?" Wolf quizzed.

"You guys have been lying to me from the minute I got here. It's been one lie after another, so how can I be sure you're not lying about this?"

"We've been stringing you along and withholding information, that's true enough, but it's been for your own good. We don't want to disclose more than you can cope with at any one time. It's better to drip-feed information to you ... I'm curious ... what are you going to do when you get to a town and you need to be milked? You'll go from feeling an urgent need to being in agony. In your desperation, you might let a surgeon cut your womb out."

Lilly groaned. Looking up, she saw Cat had returned with some remains from their dinner. He had a juicy piece of steak with a knife and fork on one plate and a cupcake on another.

"I thought I'd let you choose what you want to eat," he said holding out the plates.

Lilly physically withdrew from the food, it repulsed her.

"No?" Cat said. "You're not hungry, are you? Do you want something else?"

Lilly buried her face in Wolf's fur once more.

Leaning down and nestling his face against hers, he said, "Do you want to get back in your pouch, Baby? You've had a big day. We weren't really going to drop you off in the center of some town, that would be cruel."

Lilly sat bolt upright. "I knew you were lying!" she declared victorious.

Wolf inhaled sharply. "Cat, open the elevator and let her out. Guide her downstairs, and if they protest, tell them I said she could go!"

Lilly stared at Wolf dumbfounded.

Cat looked shocked, but without missing a beat, he said, "Do you want me to pack you some lunch?"

"Yes, I do," Lilly said, calling his bluff.

"Well, give me a minute to organize it. I'll call downstairs and let them know you'll be requiring transportation."

"Are you really going to dump me in the middle of a town or city?"

"Yes," Cat said. "Do you want to go back to Christchurch, or would you prefer Auckland?"

"Do I still have my flat in Christchurch?"

"As far as I'm aware, yes. They haven't stopped looking for you yet, your flat is how you left it."

"Really? Well, that sounds fine. I'll go there!"

"Okay."

Cat got up and went to the dining room.

All the while, Ox had been watching from a distance. "I'm going to miss you, Baby," he said sadly. "I'll worry about you."

"Yeah, your fucking probes will pine for me." Lilly spat out bitterly. "No doubt you'll get over it ... Well, you will as soon as they find you a replacement."

Turning, Ox sighed and headed for the cave.

Cat reappeared with a packed lunch. "Well, come on then ... we're opening the cage for you."

Suddenly apprehensive, Lilly looked at Wolf; was he really letting her go? *Do I even want to go?* "Can I change my mind?"

"You no longer want to go," Cat said, answering for Wolf.

"Cat, will you come with me all the way home and stay with me to make sure I'm okay? Maybe you can bring some milking equipment?"

Cat raised his brow. "You're having second thoughts?"

"No, I'm nervous," Lilly said. "I'm worried."

"When you go to your flat the police will be called. If I go with you, they'll want to know who I am. They'll also want to know where your baby is."

"I'd like to bloody know!" Lilly stormed. "Maybe you can enlighten us all?"

Cat sighed. "You already know where he is, and I'm not about to throw myself on a pyre for you. I'll drop you off where you can get a cab, and I'll give you enough money to get by for a while."

Nervous, Lilly bit her lip.

"Well, it's time to go," Cat said. "Are you coming?"

"I think I need a drink."

"If you drink from Ox your womb will fill faster. It will be better if you don't," Cat said holding out a hand.

Lilly attempted to get up. It felt weird to do so. Seeing her struggle, Wolf lifted her up and carefully placed her upon her feet.

"I'm not dressed. I'll need some clothes."

"They're on their way down," Cat said as the elevator dinged. The hostile Asian nurse Lilly had met in her cell above, entered the courtyard holding a bundle of clothes. She handed them to Cat and left without giving Lilly so much as a sideways glance.

"Come on, I'll help you dress," he said as he held out a soft stretchy bra.

Lilly stepped into the bra and then turned around so he could do it up. Cat then held out a pair of panties and let her hang onto him as she stepped into them before helping her into a pregnancy dress. After she'd slipped on her shoes, she shrugged her shoulders. Wearing clothes felt weird.

"Perhaps you would like to go and say your goodbyes to Ox while I get changed," Cat said.

"Okay," Lilly said, looking wistfully at Wolf.

Wolf raised his brow.

Lilly shrugged. "I'm going to miss you," she said, eyeing her toes.

"No doubt you'll get over it."

Lilly felt deflated. Not sure she was doing the right thing, she walked nervously into the cave. Ox was lying on his bed, his big back turned. She walked to the edge of the bed, it was so high she couldn't see over it.

"Daddy, I've come to say goodbye."

Ox rolled over and looked down at her. "Have you, indeed."

"I'm going to miss you."

Ox scoffed. "If you're going to miss me, why are you leaving?"

"I'm confused, Daddy," Lilly said timidly. "I think I should leave ... I don't know what I think."

Ox sighed. "Why don't you take that silly dress off and let me pick you up? Come and have a feed, and get some sleep."

Lilly shuffled nervously from one foot to the other. "I almost wish I hadn't been given a choice ... I don't know what to do."

"Clearly, you haven't thought this through ... What are you going to tell the police? What are you going to say to a surgeon when he offers to cut your womb out?"

Lilly shrugged. "I don't know?"

"Where are you going to say you've been? And more importantly ... what are you going to say happened to your baby?"

Lilly looked down. "I don't know."

"As I said ... you haven't thought this through."

Finding courage, Lilly said, "Maybe you could let me take him with me?"

Ox choked. "Not bloody likely! There's no way you're taking him with you."

"Why not?"

"He's got a mother and father. He's happy ... settled. He's not leaving with you!"

"That was an unkind and cruel thing to say," Lilly said, sniffing back tears. "I want nothing more than to take care of him."

"Nonsense," Ox snapped. "You were going to give him away."

"I changed my mind!"

"Tough! He's staying here."

"I don't want to leave on bad terms," Lilly said looking down again. "I ... I love you."

"Funny way of showing it."

"I'm confused. Part of me wants to be back in your pouch."

"Well, Cat's here to take you upstairs, so you'd better make up your mind."

Lilly looked at Cat as he reached out and grabbed her hand. "Come on! Let's go!"

Lilly meekly followed him as he half dragged her to the elevator, it opened in front of him as if by magic. "I thought Wolf was bluffing," he said as he hit a button, "but apparently he's not. I've got to warn you though ... this is a mistake. Coming here is a one-way trip. Men in high places won't let you utter a word of what's gone on here. When you get home, they'll probably come for you and put you in a nuthouse ... either that or shoot you ... The airways are buzzing with your disappearance ... people want to know what happened to you. The fact that you were heavily pregnant has made them all the more curious."

"Oh ... I thought nobody knew I was pregnant."

"Your secret was made public after you disappeared. Your husband placed you in a flat behind clients of his, and they didn't keep their mouths shut. People think your husband did more than just help you relocate to Christchurch. He's the lead suspect in your disappearance ... presumed murder."

"Well, that's almost satisfying! Is he under arrest?"

"No ... not yet. The police don't have any evidence, but his business is suffering. People on the street are calling him a wife killer, and even your kids wonder if he's had a hand in your disappearance."

They exited the elevator. Around them, people stared in stunned disbelief as an Asian woman stepped forward and handed Lilly her handbag. "We've put $500 in cash in your purse so you don't have to use your credit cards right away."

Lilly awkwardly took her bag. Following Cat to a pod train, she slung it over her shoulder like she'd done a thousand times before, but now it felt strange, like an odd appendage.

"Have you heard of the Virgin Hyperloop?" he said. "This is a deep, underground version. It travels at around 2,000 miles per hour. It'll take us to the basement of a Freemason building in Christchurch."

A man ushered them into the pod. It had Wolf and Ox sized seats and human chairs. Lilly took a seat on a beige leather seat beside Cat. "I'm not sure I'm ready for this?"

"Bit late now," Cat said as the doors closed.

The train gathered speed before roaring down the track.

"This is all happening so fast," Lilly said. "You didn't give me a chance to consider ... Ox was so mean."

"You hurt his feelings."

Lilly shrugged. "Talking about the harvest upset me ... It's almost like it's this planet's purpose?"

"It is its purpose ... I don't know why you're so shocked ... aren't you a Christian?

> *Luke 20*ⁱⁱ⁹ *He went on to tell the people this parable: 'A man planted a vineyard, rented it to some farmers and went away for a long time.* *¹⁰ At harvest time he sent a servant to the tenants so they would give him some of the fruit of the vineyard. But the tenants beat him and sent him away empty-handed.* *¹¹ He sent another servant, but they also beat and treated him shamefully and sent him away empty-handed.* *¹² He sent still a third, and they wounded him and threw him out.* *¹³ Then the owner of the vineyard said, "What shall I do? I will send my son, whom I love; perhaps they will respect him."* *¹⁴ But when the tenants saw him, they talked the matter over. 'This is the heir,' they said. 'Let's kill him, and the inheritance will be ours.'* *¹⁵ So they threw him out of the vineyard and killed him. What then will the owner of the vineyard do to them?* *¹⁶ He will come and kill those tenants and give the vineyard to others.'"*

"But that verse is talking about fruit," Lilly said.

"You *are* the fruit."

"Well, I don't know how I was meant to work that out!"

"No...? What about these verses?"

*Revelation14:[15] And another angel came out of the temple, crying with a loud voice to him that sat on the cloud, 'Thrust in your sickle, and reap: for the time is come for you to reap; for the harvest of the earth is ripe.' ... [18] And another angel came out from the altar, which had power over fire; and cried with a loud cry to him that had the sharp sickle, saying, 'Thrust in your sharp sickle, and gather the clusters of the vine of the earth; for her grapes are fully ripe.' [19] And the angel thrust in his sickle into the earth, and gathered the vine of the earth, and cast it into the great winepress of the wrath of God. [20] And the winepress was trodden without the city, and **blood** came out of the winepress ..."*

Revelation 19:[11] And I saw heaven opened, and behold a white horse, and he that sat upon him was called Faithful and True, and in righteousness he does judge and make war.

[12] His eyes were as a flame of fire, and on his head were many crowns, and he had a name written that no man knew, but he himself.

[13] And he was clothed with a vesture dipped in blood: and his name is called The Word of God.

[14] And the armies which were in heaven followed him upon white horses, clothed in fine linen, white and clean.[15] And out of his mouth goes a sharp sword, that with it he should smite the nations: and he shall rule them with a rod of iron: and he treads the winepress of the fierceness and wrath of Almighty God. [16] And he has on his vesture and on his thigh a name written, KING OF KINGS, AND LORD OF LORDS. [17] And I saw an angel standing in the sun; and he cried with a loud voice, saying to all the fowls that fly in the midst of heaven, Come and gather yourselves together unto the supper of the great God; [18] That you may eat the flesh of kings, and the flesh of captains, and the flesh of mighty men, and the flesh of horses, and of them that sit

*on them, and the flesh of all men, both free and bond, both
small and great.'*

Lilly shrugged. "I thought that was Jesus coming back to deal with criminals."

"The Bible wasn't meant for you ... It's not prophecy, it's a coded plan."

In no time at all it seemed, the doors opened into an underground basement. A man with his head wrapped in a scarf to hide his identity greeted Cat. He motioned him aside.

"This is a mistake!" he said in a hushed whisper that Lilly could easily overhear. "We've no way of managing this! At 3am she's going to be screaming and an ambulance will be called, then it'll be out of our hands. They'll cut her womb out of her, and all hell will break loose because they're bound to examine it. Pandora's Box is about to be opened! This close to a harvest, I don't know what Wolf is thinking. If she says one word of this, we won't be able to contain it. We're probably going to have to take extreme measures! Be kind to the girl ... put her back on the train!"

Cat threw Lilly a glance before answering. "Wolf says he doesn't want her because she keeps complaining. He told her she could go, so he's keeping his word."

"Well, it's a mistake!" the man said. "For shit's sake, talk some sense into the girl ... She's liquid gold. Has Wolf lost his mind? Look at her ... she looks nothing like her pictures being plastered over the TV and every other media source. She can't go back to her flat and that's that ... How much money does she have?"

"We've given her $500 in cash."

"That's not enough!" the man said shortly, making his way to Lilly. "Look, love, you're making a mistake ... a huge mistake!" He pulled out a wad of money. "Here's $5000. Now, don't go back to your flat, go to a hotel, and don't tell them who you are ... pay with cash. Give me your credit cards ... you can't use them. Hopefully, Wolf will quickly come to his senses. Here is a burner, mobile phone with the number of a burner phone of mine in the contacts ... Do you have a mobile phone in your purse?"

Lilly handed him her credit cards before looking for her phone. "Yes, here it is," she said, holding out an old phone.

"For shit's sake!" the man said as he snatched it off her and began extracting the battery. "I hope the bloody thing wasn't charged … Talk about an all-time fuck up! Look, you can't go out onto the street looking like that—your hair's been crudely cut. It will make people stare at you and wonder. Wait here. I think we have a burka upstairs."

"It seems they're not too happy with your reappearance," Cat said with more than a touch of amusement as the man scurried off.

Lilly wrenched her hands nervously. "I'm scared."

"I thought you were all big and tough? Soon you'll be on your own … I wouldn't trust that phone if I were you. He's hoping Wolf will change his mind and he can come and collect you and put you back on the train, but failing that, he'll probably send someone to kill you."

Lilly bit her lip. "I can't believe I used to live in this world." Still holding her nerve, she said, "How do I get out of this building?"

"You take that elevator," Cat said, pointing a finger at an elevator a short distance in front of them. "Go out the front door, turn left … there's a taxi stand about a hundred meters up the road."

"Have you been here before? Just gone up there and wandered around?"

"Yes, many times."

"I don't want to go up there," Lilly said, stepping back onto the train and sitting down.

Cat followed her in. "Are you sure?"

"Yes, take me home. I want to be with Ox."

"Are you just chickening out, or do you really want to go back?"

"I want to go back … I'm terrified of what will happen at 3am." She rubbed her belly. "I don't want them to cut my placenta out."

"You're attached to it?" That's good, Baby."

The man reappeared carrying a blue burka. "Oh, has she changed her mind … she's going back?"

"It seems so," Cat said as he pressed some buttons on the side of the pod before taking a seat beside Lilly.

"Well, thank God!" the man said obviously relieved. "Believe me, love, you're better off where you are because Cat knows how to take care of you," He glared at Cat. "It's his job to do so!" Returning his gaze to Lilly while softening his look, he said, "Go home and snuggle down in your daddy." He waved them goodbye as the doors of the pod closed and its engine came to life.

"I think you've made the right decision," Cat said. "I hope Wolf will take you back."

Lilly hugged Cat. "Thank you for taking me back."

Cat pulled her onto his knee and returned her hug.

"Is it your job to take care of me?"

"Yes. I've told you that before, but it's more than a job to me ... I want to take care of you ... But you better quit your complaining because Wolf won't tolerate much more of it."

"Okay," Lilly said. "Hey, I've still got that man's $5000."

"He's loaded. He won't miss it ... He's got your credit cards ... he's probably destroyed them already."

"I don't care about those stupid cards or my phone."

CHAPTER THIRTY-SEVEN

You're back

Relieved to be returning to the cave, Lilly suddenly felt exhausted. When they arrived at the station, Cat helped her to her feet before putting his arm around her and aiding her off the train. She handed her bag to the first person she saw, like it was garbage, and let him help her into the elevator.

As the doors closed on stunned faces, Cat said, "They'll be talking about this for weeks."

"A lot of people work here ... Are they citizens of Earth?"

"No."

"I didn't think so. They're different ... not different as in a different species, they have a different attitude."

"Indeed."

"I'm nervous ... is Wolf going to be mad?"

"I guess we're about to find out," Cat said as the doors opened into the cave.

Lilly walked in unaided. She was going to make a bee-line for Ox to garnish some support from him, but he wasn't on his huge bed. She looked around the cave, he wasn't there, so she followed Cat to the courtyard, despondent. Wolf was sitting exactly where she'd last seen him like he hadn't moved.

Lilly stood still and stared at him.

"So, you're back," he said dryly.

Lilly was taken back by his demeanor. "I'm hoping you'll let me come back. I'm sorry ... I don't want to go back to that prison that's masquerading as society."

"I can't see your nakedness," he said.

"Oh, sorry," Lilly said. Finding a burst of energy from somewhere, she lifted her dress up and pulled it over her head.

While Cat helped her out of her undergarments, Ox stepped into the courtyard, soaking wet from swimming.

"I see you've returned, Baby," he said gently.

As soon as Lilly was naked once more, she wrapped her arms around one of his big legs, she didn't even come up to his knee. "Please take me back, Daddy."

Ox carefully picked her up. "Of course, Baby."

Lilly hugged his neck as he walked around the pool. "But you need to appease Wolf first," he said as he handed her to him.

Wet from Ox's fur, Lilly hugged Wolf both to please him and to get warm. "I'm really sorry, Daddy."

Wolf tenderly rubbed her back. "It's all right. I'm happy to have you back."

"Thank you."

"Are you happy to let me feed from your temple?"

"My temple?"

"You're my temple," he said as he positioned her on his knee so her stomach was pressed against his, and her legs spread wide. "The kingdom of God:

> *Luke 17:²¹ Neither shall they say, Look here! or, look there! for, behold, the kingdom of God is within you.*

> *1 Peter 2:⁵ You also, as living stones, are built up into a spiritual house, a holy priesthood, to offer up spiritual sacrifices acceptable to God by Jesus Christ.*

> *The Gospel of Thomas 113: His disciples said to Him, 'When will the Kingdom come?' Jesus said, 'It will not come by waiting for it. It will not be a matter of saying, here it is, or there it is. Rather, the Kingdom of the Father is spread out upon the earth, and men do not see it.'"*

Lilly was still mulling over the implications of Wolf's words when he pecked her lips with an urgency that always overwhelmed her. 'Somebody to Love' by Jefferson Airplane had begun to play on the sound system. She moaned and slumped against Wolf, her mouth open and ready. A probe made its way into her vagina as Wolf gave her his feeding kiss. Lilly gasped as it raced upward, her mind adrift. It rammed through her valve's opening and then went deeper yet, accessing an area innermost within her. There it latched onto something that felt like an oversized nipple, like it had a set of lips, then its inner tube, or probe, entered the oversized nipple and forcefully prodded its interior.

Lilly groaned as her body went limp like she'd been given a powerful muscle relaxant. Her mind drifted as Wolf's probe suckled relentlessly and yet painlessly, while probing the oversized nipple within her. She felt higher than ever. It was as if Wolf was an ocean and he was washing over her—she was swimming in his depths. She moaned as he held her firmly, his arms full of need and want; it felt like possession.

After a few minutes of powerful probing, he withdrew. "It's all right," he said, running seductive fingers through her cropped hair. "I haven't injured you. Your placenta has an inner chamber at the top of it. It didn't have much in it, but the more I milk it, the more it will make for me."

The powerful intoxicant's hold on Lilly's mind eased. Wolf has a womb probe? My placenta has an inner chamber?

Her eyes flicked open just long enough to see Wolf's, they were glimmering and dancing with intelligence. He was a man to fear, his intellect intimidating. He was always ten moves ahead of her and he always would be, outplaying her at every turn, and yet she wanted to be with him—needed to be with him.

"Relax," he said as he pulled her in, but not too tightly. Just enough for her to sense and feel his need as he lusciously licked her spine with his sensual tongue. Waves washed over her again—he was pulling her under. He raised her chin ever so gently with one finger and fed her willing mouth; she was drowning in him.

Breathless, she wondered what his wine probe looked like.

Clearly, it was flexible and muscular, but did it have a head like a penis and a large eye from which a thin, hollow, muscular, tongue protruded? She tried to think of something artificial that was similarly designed, but she was too off her face.

"And to think I was about to let someone cut my Holy of Holies out of you ... Sacrilege!"

"Holy of Holies?" Lilly said, blinking rapidly, still wondering what his probe looked like.

"That's what we call your inner sanctum," Wolf said, looking at her belly and giving it a possessive rub. "It's where I reside:

> *John 4:14 '... whosoever drinks of the water that I shall give him shall never thirst. The water that I shall give him shall be in him, as a well of water springing up into everlasting life.'*
>
> *John 7:38 'He that believes in me, as the scripture has said, out of his belly shall flow rivers of living water.'"*

"So, you're pleased I've returned?" Lilly said, breathless.

"Absolutely! I was sitting here wondering if I was going to send men to collect you before you became utterly desperate at 3am."

"Were you going to?"

"I think I was going to, yes," Wolf said feigning indecision. "You don't know what you're doing. You'd gotten yourself into a pickle and I felt the need to rescue you."

"Thank you, Daddy."

"I'm pleased you saw sense and came back on your own," he said, still clutching her to him. "The outer world is no place for you."

"No, it isn't," Lilly said mournfully. "I see that now."

"Good," Wolf said as he got up and handed her back to Ox. "Now feed from Ox and get some sleep. I'll see you when you wake."

Ox quickly tucked Lilly down in his pouch.

She sighed. "I'm pleased to be home," she said internally.

"I'm pleased you're back!" Ox said. "Did you enjoy your little adventure? How was the train ride?"

"It was weird ... It didn't feel like we were speeding through a vacuum tube. We arrived in what seemed like minutes."

"It *was* only minutes ... You were only gone for half an hour or so."

"In some ways, it felt like eternity," Lilly said. "I had an overwhelming feeling of dread like I was making a huge mistake."

Ox coughed. "You *were* making a *huge* mistake."

"It was my one and only opportunity to warn the world and I blew it." Lilly sighed. "Maybe I'm selfish?"

Ox scoffed. "You were never going to warn the world ... Men in the outer world would never have allowed it. You do know you were never going to make it to that hotel ... don't you?"

Lilly sighed, she'd suspected as much. "Was it all just an orchestrated charade, or were they going to shoot me when I got out of the elevator?"

"Nobody was going to shoot you, you're far too valuable for that ... Wolf's stunt caught everyone off guard, but the masons were quick to formulate a plan. They were going to try even harder to turn you around and get you back on the train. If that didn't work, they'd have dragged you onto it and brought you back here and demanded we took you back."

"Really?"

"Yes. They thought Wolf had lost his mind and they were going to take their grievance up with the council."

"There's a council?"

"There is."

"Did Wolf know that would happen?"

"Yes. He thought it would be good for you to take a train ride and think about your options."

"You mean my lack of options!" Lilly exhaled loudly. "Yeah, I suppose it was good ... I'm sorry I upset you."

"It's all right. I wasn't angry ... well, maybe a bit. I felt a little hurt, but you have a right to feel confused and uncertain."

"Do I know all there is to know now?"

"No ... We still have much to teach you."

Lilly slumped.

"You'll feel less tired after you've been milked and fed soon ... If you're good, Cat will arrange a little holiday for you. He'll take you to Dubai or somewhere like that. Then, he'll chaperone you while you go up and look around in a burka."

"Really?"

"Yes. I'll have to come too if you're going that far. I'll wait in a basement below the city while the two of you go up and wander around."

Suddenly feeling more content, Lilly snuggled in, "Does Cat speak Arabic?"

"Yes, and French, German and many other languages."

"Will he want to take me on a trip?"

"Of course. He likes to get out of here every now and then ... have a change of scenery. But there's one rule ... you have to be absolutely obedient. You must do and say exactly as you're told or you won't get to go again. Cat always has bodyguards and they'll keep a close eye on you. You may not see them, or even know who they are, but they'll be there."

"It's okay," Lilly said. "I won't do anything silly."

Ox rubbed her back. "I'm sure you won't."

"How did we get to the current political climate that's going to allow the harvest to be brought in with ease?"

"Manipulation began long ago. In recent history, it started with the World Wars and developed from there. A different story from the one currently being touted as true can be found in four large volumes of 'Winston S. Churchill, The Second World War,' published before 1950.

"In the 1970s woman's lib was promoted, and it's had a big hand to play in what's transpired. Women can't raise a normal-sized family and work, it's as simple as that. If you stop valuing a woman's role as a mother and tell them they should work, and couple that with the devaluation of a man's wage, the birth rate will fall dramatically. When the birth rate fell, because of this and because Europeans were told the world was overpopulated, the stage was set for what's transpired."

Lilly groaned.

"Westerners were told they wouldn't be able to pay for the baby boomers retirement if they didn't import people, and they were also told they were lazy and others were needed to do the jobs they refused. This set the stage for what happened next: immigrants flooded into your countries as workers, students, and tourists. You were told they'd be going home again, but many didn't.

"After wave after wave of immigration, they said you were living in a multicultural society and you should celebrate its diversity. This, of course, eventually leads to what you see in Britain ... huge parts of the UK have been colonized by immigrants and whites are leaving on mass. White flight has gone from a trickle to a flood:

> *By the time of the next census in 2021, white Britons will be a minority in Birmingham, where already in 2013 less than a third of schoolchildren were recorded as having white ethnicity, an official report has said.*
>
> Breitbart: June 28th, 2018

> DIVIDED BRITAIN
> *White British population has fallen by more than HALF in just 20 years in parts of UK as the country becomes 'more segregated'*
> *WHITE people are leaving some towns at record rates as ethnic minorities move in, a study shows.*
> *Experts warn action is needed now to tackle the 'increasing segregation.' England's white population overall fell from 86.8 percent in 2001 to 79.8 in 2011.*
> *During that ten-year period, the number of white residents in Newham, East London, dropped from 33.6 percent to 16.7 percent.*
> *And in Slough, Berks, it fell from 58.3 percent to 34.5. Leicester, Birmingham, and Luton also saw large declines across the decade.*   The Sun: November 3rd, 2016

"They're leaving because they don't feel safe," Lilly said.

The Islamic extremists taking over UK prisons: Muslims

make up just one in 20 Britons - but one in SEVEN inmates.
In recent years, the number of Muslim prisoners has
increased dramatically. Ministry of Justice figures show a
rise from 6,571 in 2004 to 12,255 a decade later, meaning
that Muslims now account for almost 15 percent of all
inmates.
In high-security jails, the figure is higher still — one in
five; while in one Category A establishment, almost half
are Muslims.
Taken on its own, the disproportionate numbers of
Muslims being jailed is in itself cause for concern (Muslims
comprise roughly 5 percent of the population of England
and Wales).   Daily Mail: February 15ᵗʰ· 2016

"And this was all planned and plotted by the globalist
governments doing Wolf's and the other gods bidding?" Lilly ranted,
"Doing exactly as they asked them to do, but it doesn't seem like a
coordinated plan. Muslims and Jews are not in sync with one another
... I read the Covenant of the Islamic Resistance Movement and it
opened my eyes:

The Covenant of the Islamic Resistance Movement issued
on August 18, 1988.
Our struggle against the Jews is very great and very
serious.
Article 22: 'For a long time, the enemies have been
planning, skillfully and with precision, for the
achievement of what they have attained. They took into
consideration the causes affecting the current of events.
They strived to amass great and substantive material
wealth which they devoted to the realization of their
dream.
With their money, they took control of the world media,
news agencies, the press, publishing houses, broadcasting
stations, and others.
With their money, they stirred revolutions in various parts

of the world with the purpose of achieving their interests and reaping the fruit therein.

They were behind the French Revolution, the Communist revolution and most of the revolutions we heard and hear about, here and there.

With their money, they formed secret societies, such as Freemasons, Rotary Clubs, the Lions and others in different parts of the world for the purpose of sabotaging societies and achieving Zionist interests. With their money, they were able to control imperialistic countries and instigate them to colonize many countries in order to enable them to exploit their resources and spread corruption there.

You may speak as much as you want about regional and world wars. They were behind World War I when they were able to destroy the Islamic Caliphate, making financial gains and controlling resources.'

Article 28: 'The Zionist invasion is a vicious invasion. It does not refrain from resorting to all methods, using all evil and contemptible ways to achieve its end. It relies greatly in its infiltration and espionage operations on the secret organizations it gave rise to, such as the Freemasons, The Rotary and Lions clubs, and other sabotage groups. All these organizations, whether secret or open, work in the interest of Zionism and according to its instructions. They aim at undermining societies, destroying values, corrupting consciences, deteriorating character and annihilating Islam. It is behind the drug trade and alcoholism in all its kinds so as to facilitate its control and expansion.' HAMAS

"And," Lilly continued unabated, "in 1871 controversial American Freemason Albert Pike wrote a letter to his Italian friend, a politician named Giuseppe Mazzini who was also a Freemason. In his letter, he outlined a plan for three world wars. The first world wars happened almost exactly as he stated:

The First World War must be brought about in order to permit the Illuminati to overthrow the power of the Czars in Russia and of making that country a fortress of atheistic Communism. The divergences caused by the 'agentur' (agents) of the Illuminati between the British and Germanic Empires will be used to foment this war. At the end of the war, Communism will be built and used in order to destroy the other governments and in order to weaken the religions.'

The Second World War must be fomented by taking advantage of the differences between the Fascists and the political Zionists. This war must be brought about so that Nazism is destroyed and that the political Zionism be strong enough to institute a sovereign state of Israel in Palestine. During the Second World War, International Communism must become strong enough in order to balance Christendom, which would be then restrained and held in check until the time when we would need it for the final social cataclysm.

Ox rubbed her back through his pouch. "Students of history will recognize the political alliances of England on one side and Germany on the other, forged between 1871 and 1898 by Otto von Bismarck, co-conspirator of Albert Pike, were instrumental in bringing about the First World War. After the Second World War, Communism was strong enough to take over weak governments. In 1945, at the Potsdam Conference between Truman, Churchill, and Stalin, a large portion of Europe was simply handed over to Russia. On the other side of the world, the aftermath of the war with Japan helped sweep a tide of Communism into China."

"People argue," Lilly said, "that when the prophecy was written in 1871, the terms Nazism and Zionism weren't known."

"Well, they should remember that the Illuminati invented both these movements and Communism as an ideology and as a coined phrase originated in France. In 1785, Restif coined the phrase four years before the revolution broke out. Restif and Babeuf, in turn, were influenced by Rousseau, as was the famous conspirator Adam Weishaupt."

"So, what about the third world war ... will there be one? Will Albert Pike's third chilling Masonic prophecy be fulfilled?

The Third World War must be fomented by taking advantage of the differences caused by the 'agentur' [agents] of the 'Illuminati' between the political Zionists and the leaders of Islamic World. The war must be conducted in such a way that Islam [the Muslim Arabic World] and political Zionism [the State of Israel] mutually destroy each other. Meanwhile, the other nations, once more divided on this issue will be constrained to fight to the point of complete physical, moral, spiritual, and economical exhaustion. We shall unleash the Nihilists and the atheists, and we shall provoke a formidable social cataclysm which in all its horror will show clearly to the nations the effect of absolute atheism, the origin of savagery and of the most bloody turmoil. Then everywhere, the citizens, obliged to defend themselves against the world minority of revolutionaries, will exterminate those destroyers of civilization, and the multitude, disillusioned with Christianity, whose deistic spirits will from that moment be without compass or direction, anxious for an ideal, but without knowing where to render its adoration, will receive the true light through the universal manifestation of the pure doctrine of Lucifer, brought finally out in the public view. This manifestation will result from the general reactionary movement which will follow the destruction of Christianity and atheism, both conquered and exterminated at the same time."

"Once you were strong and you could've dealt with a rapidly changing climate, but now the powers around you have grown robust, and they don't have to contend with hostile armies camped within their borders posing as migrants. United you stand and divided you fall. A trojan horse in the guise of migrants knocked on your door and you let it in. In all of history, there's never been a bigger one."

Lilly groaned. "Things are made worse by the media's anti-white agenda. They've been promoting the narrative that white people are bad, evil racists and we've treated the other races appallingly, even though it isn't true. We never wanted to go to war in the Middle East. We were coerced into it with lies, and the thousands of migrants who flooded into Europe recently were mostly young men of fighting age—hardly a woman or child among them."

"Yes," Ox said, "and now Turkey's been actively building and funding 5th columns in Europe, and they're rapidly returning to their Ottoman ways. There are approximately 44 million Muslims now living in Europe. Three million Turks live in Germany alone, and they vote in Turkish elections. Their diaspora is the largest Muslim immigrant group in Europe."

"So, Albert Pike's prophecy won't come true then?" Lilly said, emotional. "The Islamic and Jewish nations are not about to be defeated?"

"They won't be defeated," Ox said, "because you're failing to grasp who's really at the top of the pyramid. The religions are tools of the global elite ... your leaders aren't Jewish, Islamic, Hindu, or Christian. The outcome you were assured in the prophecy won't happen because it was never meant to. By the time you get around to trying to save yourselves from the armies camped within your borders, it will be *too little too late* because the climate will have turned against you and many of your lands will shortly be uninhabitable ... you'll have bigger things to worry about.

"During your mass migration to other lands, your people will be taken to facilities where our desired fruit will be removed and transferred to underground, military bases. Stock wanted for our golden cities or lands will be funneled into internment camps, or sent directly to golden cities ... Thus, enemies within your borders, and without, will start bringing in our harvest.

> *Revelation 11:² But the court which is without the temple leave out, and measure it not; for it is given to the Gentiles: and the holy city shall they tread under foot forty and two months [3½ years].*

> *Revelation 12:⁶ And the woman fled into the wilderness, where she has a place prepared of God, that they should feed her there a thousand two hundred and threescore days [3½ years]*

Lilly groaned. "The prophecy says 'the true light through the universal manifestation of the pure doctrine of Lucifer will finally be brought into public view. This manifestation will result from the general reactionary movement which will follow the destruction of Christianity and atheism, both conquered and exterminated at the same time' ... What's that supposed to mean?"

"In short, paganism," Ox said. "Christian tradition named the Devil the Latin word for Morning Star—Lucifer. In paganism, his mother Aurora was Roman's Dawn Goddess, but it was upon Lucifer, her demi-god son, that much praise was heaped. The Romans' named the planet Venus after him because his name meant *Morning Star* in Latin, and as an adjective, 'shining' and 'light-bringing.' However, in previous societies and in adjacent religions, these attributes were bestowed upon his mother—the Dawn Goddess."

"And Lucifer was evil?"

"No, he wasn't ... There is much I need to tell you about paganism and Lucifer before you'll understand ... Many truths that were self-evident in paganism were covered up and deleted when the Christian religion replaced it. I haven't got time to explain it all to you now, but I will in the future. Currently, most of the disagreements between different peoples on Earth are either religious or racial in nature. In the future, there'll only be two groups—the crop and non-crop. When truth is spread upon the Earth, the current religions will become redundant, having served their purpose already."

Song of Solomon 4:12 A garden enclosed is my sister, my spouse; a spring shut up, a fountain sealed.

Song of Solomon 4:16 Awake, O north wind; and come, the south; blow upon my garden, that the spices thereof may flow out. Let my beloved come into his garden and eat his pleasant fruits.

Song of Solomon 7:2 Your navel is like a round goblet, which wants not liquor: your belly is like a heap of wheat set about with lilies.

ELIXIR OF IMMORTALITY
and the
WHORE OF BABYLON

A KINE

Immersed in the world of the gods, Lilly fumbles with her new role and surroundings as handlers continue her education using the Bible, Vedas, and the Egyptian Book of the Dead as a guide. Lilly's walk through the shadowy world below is disquieting, but tingling with erotic excitement and tempted by forbidden fruits, she rides a roller coaster of emotions as rituals test her resolve and curiosity gets the better of her. Dismayed at what she's becoming, the Whore of Babylon, embarrassed and ashamed, she yearns to return to a simpler time and place, home, but is she too valuable, and the secrets she holds too dark, for them to let her go?

www.ingramcontent.com/pod-product-compliance
Lightning Source LLC
Chambersburg PA
CBHW062111170626
46813CB00002B/406